M000249918

EMILY
AND THE
GHOST
OF MR. MENTOR

George E. Kellogg

ISBN 978-1-63814-504-2 (Paperback)
ISBN 978-1-63814-505-9 (Digital)

Copyright © 2021 George E. Kellogg
All rights reserved
First Edition

All rights reserved. No part of this publication may be reproduced, distributed, or transmitted in any form or by any means, including photocopying, recording, or other electronic or mechanical methods without the prior written permission of the publisher. For permission requests, solicit the publisher via the address below.

Covenant Books, Inc.
11661 Hwy 707
Murrells Inlet, SC 29576
www.covenantbooks.com

PROLOGUE

"Mother, what was it like in the old days?" asked little Margie.

Emily Keller stopped what she was doing and closed her eyes for a second. She knew this day would come. She wiped her hands on her apron and looked down at her lovely daughter, Margaret, or "Little Margie," who was named after an old family friend. She was nine years old already! Where had the time gone? The little girl was in her own apron, cutting sugar cookies from the neatly rolled out dough, and placing them on the baking sheet. The year was 1932 in the third week of December. The world was being rocked in the throes of what would be later called "The Great Depression." Nobody understood how bad things were actually going to get. The human toll was to become so much greater with so much suffering.

This was such a sharp contrast to the Roaring Twenties! For she, her husband, Jimmy, and their other friends, 1920 was a very busy and interesting year. They were, at that time, not much older than Margie is now. Much happened in "the old days," as they referred to the most defining events of their youth. It might now be time for Margie to learn about those events. This was not going to be easy, recounting those times.

Emily and Jimmy had agreed long ago to keep "the Struggle," as they now called it, a secret. They and their friends made a solemn pact. They vowed that their children would not know about the Struggle until they were old enough. They believed that their children would start to ask questions all on their own when they were ready to learn the stories. Margaret, Jimmy, and Emily were the stars of that drama.

Each kept their battles together a secret from everyone outside of their group. They all agreed that events throughout the Struggle would be revealed to their own children but to no one else. At the right time and in the right place, their children would learn of it, they said. Emily would now find out how much her Margie wanted to know. It would be entirely up to her.

"Well," said Emily, "it is still early. Your father is putting in a long day at the school's soup kitchen, feeding the less fortunate. As you know, every one of them has their story to tell, and your father collects their stories. Then we write them down for future generations to read so no one will forget such things. The most important story we have written, though, is one we wrote together. It is about this school, how it fell to ruin, and after a long and terrible period, we turned it into what we have today. Let's you and I put these cookies aside for now. We are ahead of schedule anyway."

Margie took off her apron, folded it neatly, and put it in the cupboard. Her mother did the same. They adjourned to the living room of their spacious home. Emily had Margie sit on the couch. This story would take a while. Emily retrieved from the closet a handwritten book held together in a hand-tooled leather cover. It was an autobiographical account of five close friends, first written from each one's unique perspective, then those stories were combined into this single accepted version.

All of them agreed that the story as written in this book was the most accurate version, the one to be copied for each of them to keep in their homes. This book was one of only five copies that existed in the entire world. Each of the five friends would keep a copy in their separate homes to reveal the story of the Struggle to their children. Those secrets, of course, would also have to be revealed to spouses, as applicable, but under a vow of secrecy. Even then, it was not to be revealed until the spouse was ready to hear it.

Little Margie knew a lot about her parents' careers, naturally. She knew that her mother was the principal of the school. Emily held a master's degree in education and worked to develop teaching methods for other school systems, modeled after the work they did at their own school. Margie's father was known by the name "Doctor Jim" at work but actually preferred to be called Jimmy.

Jimmy held a doctorate in engineering and was the chairman of all the vocational departments. Margie knew that her parents were very kind to everyone, and she was quite happy at home. She knew that her parents had met at this school. She knew that their wonderful home was on the school's property. They spoke often and fondly of a "Mr. Mentor" and the wonderful things he taught them.

They told Margie of how Mr. and Mrs. Mentor left them their home and put them in charge of the school in their Last Will and Testament. She knew all this, but the little girl never knew *why*. Today, though, Little Margie could, perhaps, finally hear the whole story. The young lady sat properly upright across from her mother, but she could not take her eyes off the book in her mother's lap. The cover was plain but for some modest designs, and there was no title on the book. It, for some reason, *drew* her gaze.

Emily noticed this and was now completely confident that her daughter was ready to begin learning. They would have a family discussion about it after Jimmy came home; this could not wait.

Through misty eyes, Emily looked at her daughter. How could she state all of this as the literal truth, completely factual without omission or embellishment, when she herself could hardly believe it? Emily had lived one of the most amazing lives, had one of the most fantastic stories ever, and had to keep it a secret as she, Jimmy, Margaret, Cassius, and Darla agreed to do. Most of the people actually present during the Struggle did not really remember much about it, but these five did.

There were two others with the correct memories who choose to this day not to be identified. With respect to their individual privacy, the sixth and seventh parties are not named here. These seven were *permitted* to keep their memories. The rest of those who were involved that day simply chalked it all up to some odd dream that had embellished upon ordinary events.

Today, though, was the day that Emily's daughter got to know of the story as originally written. Rather than read it to Margie, Emily took the book off of her own lap and placed it in Margie's hands. The daughter looked quizzically at her mother who motioned for her to open it. Margie picked up the book, turned to the first page, and began to read aloud:

From the Desk of
Simon J. Dozeman, Esq.
Juris Doctor, Attorney at Law:

Hello.

We the undersigned have agreed to present certain facts in this book that many will not find believable. We do not expect the world to believe these things to be true because, certainly, had we not lived these things, we would have never believed it ourselves. Our first names, in no particular order, are Cassius, Margaret, Jimmy, Emily, and Darla.

We have signed this document in the office of our attorney, and it has been notarized by an independent notary public. Mr. Simon J. Dozeman, Esq., for his own reasons, has declined the signing of this document and its attestation but has simultaneously authorized the use of his name and pseudonym in the text of this document and in the text of the following book, precisely as they appear.

We hereby present this story and in great solemnity attest its truthfulness in all details that we, the undersigned, have agreed upon. Whether or not this story is ever uncovered by an outsider and is subsequently presented to the world in its entirety does not matter to us.

We have carefully considered this possibility as a group and have decided that, by virtue of this signed and legally binding document, the finder of this story has full rights to its publication, sale, and distribution of this document and book, but only if the story is printed precisely as written without addition or omission.

We, the undersigned, hereby leave the matter of discovery and publication in the hands of Divine Providence. Whether or not the publisher of this story calls it truth or fiction is entirely up to his or her own best judgment.

Our message to the world is that we did indeed live through these events as they have been written and allow the world to believe what they will.

Sincerely,

(Signatures appear here)

PS: We request, therefore, of the reader that you simply read. If you cannot believe what you read, then just enjoy our story for the ages! And so we begin…

Pl

Margie stopped reading at the first chapter's heading and looked at her mother. She had a confounded look upon her face. Emily understood completely. She said, "Now, Margie, what you do is completely up to you. You may either continue to read or you may return the book to me, and I will put it away for another day."

Little Margie thought it over. She closed the book and looked at the cover. She shook her head. Margie somehow felt it was not her time, that she was getting, well, *scared*. She was overwhelmed at the prospect of reading this story. This incredible book seemed to almost vibrate in her hands with intensity. No, it was not right for her to read this, not yet. But the little girl somehow knew that one day, she would read this story, that it was very important for her to do so. She looked up at her mother, unsure of what to say. She was practically stunned.

Emily understood entirely. Someday, yes, but not today. She immediately and lovingly collected the book from her daughter and put it away. Margie would one day read the book, certainly, and she would know her parents so much the better for it. For today, she had *started* to learn, and Emily would report this to Jimmy. Nothing else was to be done for the time being. Little Margaret's learning had begun!

For the moment then, reader, we will leave Emily and her family to attend to the poor, the sick, and the needy. Margaret made the best decision she could for herself. As for the more daring, you may choose to continue.

Author's note

The author of this book cautions the reader that the story presented here is eye-opening, mildly disturbing, heroic, funny, and tragic. Whether the reader chooses to continue is solely at their discretion. Furthermore, this author is not the native writer of the original hundred-year-old narrative and will say nothing further about the original leather-bound book, its current location, or how it fell into his hands to produce this story.

All personal and legal requirements of the original authors have been adhered to in every case.

Sincerely,
George E. Kellogg

1

Meeting Miss Whipshot

"Class! Come to attention!" the teacher bellowed, although this was completely unnecessary. The class was quiet as always, none daring to peep or even to hardly breathe. The students were sitting at their desks, feet flat on the floor, backs straight, hands clasped together in front of them. Boys and girls, all in the approximate range of eleven to sixteen years old, were stoic and silent. All of the students were poorly dressed; on some of them their clothes did not match and most were not sized properly.

There were no holes in the clothing since holes were not permitted by the school's dress code. In place of holes was evidence of stitching and makeshift patches, all sewn with less-experienced hands. Many of the students sat stiffly, their eyes slightly widened with fear. A lip or two trembled. This is how things were when Miss Whipshot was in one of her moods, and that was almost all the time.

Whipshot was a grotesquely obese woman who always wore flowered dresses because the pattern was so "slimming"—according to her, anyways. She had short dark hair that wanted to go gray, but it probably did not dare. It was suggested in very quiet and remote corners that she was somehow coloring those messy oily locks; with shoe polish, maybe? She wore too much eye makeup, and her lipstick was very, very red. She even tried fake eyelashes once, but it did not work out, one of them falling off during class, inconveniently sticking to her chin. She had thick cat's-eye rimmed glasses that she seldom wore on her face. They usually lived around her neck, dangling from a tangled chain, looking broken and sad.

Even many of the faculty and staff of the Happy Valley Vocational School (HVVS) were afraid of Miss Whipshot. Most of the faculty wisely avoided her, the best and easiest thing to do. It was also the most preferable thing on a personal hygiene level. Her only acquaintances, and not even really friends, seemed to be a few of the support staff members. They were Miss Ladlepot, the cafeteria lady, Mr. Castlethorn, the creepy school janitor, and Goliath, the cafeteria lady's overgrown sidekick and resident butcher. Most of the faculty and staff were afraid of old Castlethorn. But not Miss Whipshot; no, she was not scared of *anybody!*

Once the teacher assured herself that order was achieved this morning, as it always was with the students (read: victims), scared out of their wits, she began to make her daily announcements. She had this odd habit of moving her chair out from behind her desk and placing it *squarely front-and-center* to the chalkboard; *exactly* center. Her daily placement of the chair in the exact same spot over the years left marks from the legs of the chair clearly etched into the floor. Once it was properly placed, she sat down on it. This really was not much of a chair for a woman her size. It seemed to groan in protest under her weight.

She shot a quick glance to the empty chair of "Tommy-Whipshot," the latest target of her ire. She nodded approvingly to herself when she noted that his chair was neatly pushed into the desk and that Tommy was in the "punishment room." This room was actually a former supply closet with the shelves removed. Tommy was being punished for giggling at her once during class. That was over a month ago.

Tommy was still forced to spend his class time in the closet until Whipshot said otherwise. Not that he minded so much. Other than being a little warm and humid from his own breath, it smelled better than she did. To Tommy, the darkness of the closet was preferable to the darkness of her countenance. It was a little quieter too, with the door muffling out some of the shouts.

Students wondered quietly among themselves on their rare occasions outdoors, away from staff's ears, whether or not that old chair would one day collapse under her weight. For now, Miss Whipshot addressed the class from her centered chair. She was raising her voice to tell them yet again how stupid they were at their age, how youth is wasted on the young, and how lucky they were to be in that school. She told the class that they were fortunate to have great civilized minds, like her own, working to turn them—lumps of garbage that they were—into beings fit to live with civilized humanity. Students used to cry at her words, much to her delight, but many of them now learned to tune her out. Others were simply numb or sadly accepted her beratements as the truth. Such is the nature of repetition; the more one hears a phrase or idea, positive or negative, the more likely one is to begin accepting it as a fact.

But this was not true for Emily. She would not accept negatives. *She knew better!*

Emily was a lean girl, tall for her age and pretty, but sturdy. She wore her honey-brown hair held in place with a simple celluloid band over the top of her head; her hair was not parted and she did not wear bangs. Standing five feet plus a few inches tall, she preferred dressing in a blouse, skirt, and sweater whenever they were available, appropriate, of course, to the weather. She preferred low-cut shoes and knee-long socks. Her large hazel-green eyes were not hidden by glasses, ever. She had perfect vision and did not require them.

Emily Victoria Keller, known by school administration simply as "Emily-Whipshot" was one of the older and most emotionally mature students in the school. She was also one of a minority of students who knew her own last name. Assigning hyphenated names and never allowing students to use their own surname of birth was one of the tools the school used to control the students. Since all of the children were either orphaned or otherwise abandoned to the school at very young ages, many did not know their own last names.

Even if the student knew his or her surname, which did appear on official school records and legal documents, they were still recognized in class and during all school activities under the school's renaming system. The system was a complete secret. It was never spoken of outside of the school and was kept secret when dealing with the authorities and education officials.

The system of renaming students was kept simple. The school would simply add the last name of the student's teacher to the student's own given first name. The new name was the student's identity for the entire time they lived there. For instance, Tommy-Whipshot knew his actual name was Thomas Littleton. He was known at the student dormitory by his peers as "Little Tom." Little Tom was shorter than his classmates, pale, but clear of complexion and had crooked teeth in the front. He liked to sport a dark sweater vest over a light-colored shirt. He wore dark trousers and dress shoes. He was a bright boy, but his gray eyes were constantly worried which certainly fit his disposition. Eyes, they say, are the window to the soul. Sometimes, though, the discerning eye would detect unusual courage in Little Tom.

Emily came to the school after her parents were killed in an automobile accident, something common to this era, when she was six or seven. She knew that she had lived at the school for about ten or so years. That meant she must have been about seventeen years old, give or take. Unbeknownst to Emily, she was one of the first students to have been introduced to the new system of doing things. She was brought to the school by unknowing officers of the court and dropped off. She barely remembers the day, but she does remember being greeted by a kindly blonde woman, the school's principal. Emily remembered how Miss Coffenayle turned immediately vicious the very second the authorities were off the school grounds. This was how Principal Coffenayle ran things.

"Everyone," said Miss Whipshot, "we are going practice our writing skills. Take out your pencils and paper." The class members each lifted the top of their respective desks and pulled out their pencil and paper. The teacher began writing on the board. When finished, she had three sentences, in cursive, on the board. She ordered the students to write them. She faced the classroom as they were writing, and she wondered at some of the odd expressions of surprise and perplexity on the students' faces. They were used to seeing degrading things on the board, so why should they surprised or perplexed?

When she got enough of the students making their odd faces, she asked a student to read what he wrote.

"Miss Whipshot, I am afraid to read it," the student said nervously.

"You little cur, how dare you defy me! *Read it!*"

The nervous student swallowed hard. He read, "Miss Whipshot is a leprous toad of poor breeding."

"What?" the teacher screamed. "How dare you!" She reared back with her hand like she was about to hit him.

"But...*please*, Miss Whipshot...look at the board," protested the student.

She looked back at the board, and it indeed read "*Miss Whipshot is a leprous toad of poor breeding.*" She could not believe her eyes! Even she could not strike a student for obeying her. She thudded her rotund floral-wrapped frame to the front of the classroom. "All right. Margaret, since you like that comfortably padded chair, and nobody likes you anyway since you're the class snitch and my favorite student...tell me. *Who changed the sentences on the board?*"

"Miss Whipshot, I did not see anyone change the sentences on the board," said a confused Margaret.

The teacher narrowed her eyes and replied, "I distinctly remember the first sentence on the board read '(Your Name) is a leprous toad of poor breeding.' As every one of you little fools should remember. You are supposed to fill in your *own* name. Only now, some joker has changed that sentence and added *my* honorable name. Bah! Never mind that one. Let's use the next."

The teacher was about to read aloud but stopped short. The sentence she wrote on the board herself now read "Miss Whipshot deserves all punishments that the students may inflict upon her."

And the third sentence read that "Miss Whipshot is a dog that has not been whipped enough and certainly deserves more beatings."

This was not possible! Margaret would have told her if someone had slipped up to the board, past her, and altered those sentences. Such was impossible at any rate because Whipshot was standing there the whole time! Besides, how could a student have possibly done all that writing without getting caught? The teacher then noticed the time, and regrettably, she had to excuse the students for lunch.

"All right, you bunch of uncultured savage hyenas! Go engorge yourselves in your pig troughs!"

The class filed out for lunch. Whipshot had her own food in her desk, so she sat on her chair and mulled over the possibilities of what could have happened. She could not really think of anything, so she went to erase and wash the slate chalkboard. She thought and thought over what could have possibly happened.

After the board was clean, she dug into her own food drawer full of pastries, cakes, chocolates, and such. She wolfed down the junk food and considered how her writing could have possibly changed. The students soon came back into the classroom, never caring to eat much, and a couple of them were holding their stomachs. Everything then was perfectly normal. Some adverse gastric symptoms were always expected. *Excellent! Maybe now*, thought the teacher, *we can get back to some teaching and learning! Or maybe some degrading mind-bending torture. Either one.*

She had the class stand by their desks. They were not to sit just yet. She had something to say. She thundered back and forth on the floor. A normal person could have been "pacing," but she was just too heavy for that. She had her arms out to her sides, leaving them hang after a couple of attempts at wrapping her arms behind her back failed. She thought as she paced for a couple of moments, then said, "All right, class, something has happened here that I do not fully understand. I know that none of you could have possibly changed that writing. But I also know that *someone* had to. Margaret says she saw nothing. I believe her…for now. So, everyone, sit down, and I will put fresh sentences on the board."

She turned back to the freshly cleaned board and… *What?* The board was no longer blank. There was a sketch of an obviously obese *pig* with a caricature of Whipshot's face on it. The pig was blowing air from under its tail with the sound effect of "*Phooooooooozzzzz!*"

The students froze. They had gone to and returned from lunch as a student body. No one was left behind. They were all together. That was school policy. None of them was able to break free and approach the chalkboard. Whipshot was between them and the board the whole time. She even made sure of that. It could not have been any student; every person in that classroom was dumbfounded.

Whipshot stood there, herself also dumbfounded…and *speechless!* She could not believe her eyes! She had just cleaned that very board her own self! Not only was she alone in the room for the entire time the students were slopped at their trough, but the picture could not have possibly been drawn within the time frame between now and her washing the board. The slate was still damp from the cleaning.

The students just stared, eyes wide and disbelieving. The room was aghast. How did this happen? None of them noticed the cartoon between the time it took to come into the room and then reach their seats. That picture must have been drawn, then, by an invisible hand in under a *minute!* The detail was far too great for someone to just quickly slap it up there. The picture was of an artist's quality, and no one in the room had such a talent. Not only that, but the picture was done in the color *pink*—there was no pink chalk in the whole classroom!

Miss Whipshot faced the class. She knew it was impossible to blame them, but someone had to do this, and the kids were the only other people in the room. She did not draw it. There were not staff or faculty around, so it had to be a clever trick by the students. Probably several of them. She began to pace back and forth again. She pointed at them and screamed, "So help me if any of you dare to do anything like that again and I catch you, I will…*aaaaack!*"

The teacher suddenly stopped pacing. Something had fallen upon her from directly overhead. It was wet and sticky, pasty, and disgusting. It was cake! Wet cake! Everyone was looking at each other, wondering not only who threw the cake…but where did they get it? Who would dare waste cake like that? Whoever stole it should have saved it for the whole dorm to have a secret bite after they retired for the evening. Certainly, the students would get to the bottom of this!

There was *definitely* a pillowcase party coming for the offending party! A pillowcase over the head and shoulders, pinning the arms, accompanied by a reasonable but not dangerously hard group pummeling was the agreed upon punishment to keep order in the dorms.

This went for both for the boys' and girls' dorms. That was a student secret, one of the very few, and it was ignored by the faculty and the staff's overnight security team. The more the students policed each other, the better, just so no one was seriously injured; no one ever was.

Whipshot froze in place, mortified. It was not a piece of cake or a cupcake. It was an *entire* cake! It had landed on her head and ran down her face. It tasted like the one she kept in her drawer. She looked up to see where it came from, and there was some residue on one of the overhead light shades. The class simply froze. They could not believe what they were seeing and they dared not laugh, no matter how badly they wanted to enjoy the moment. The teacher grabbed cake out of her hair and gobbled the handfuls of the sweet mush that she could reasonably salvage. She brushed the rest from her person the best she could.

She walked over to her desk, leaving a trail of sticky frosting, cake fragments, and drops of milk. She was already humiliated, so there was no hiding this mess from the kids. She wanted to check her special cake drawer, and when she opened it…her cake was *gone!* And her bottle of milk was *empty and laying on its side!* So how did the cake and milk get from the drawer, to the lampshade, and just happen to fall on her with such perfect timing?

This was truly a puzzle. The cake was there this morning; she had some for breakfast while they ate at the cafeteria. She had her eyes on the brats for the whole time during their coming and going. Later, they went to lunch and came back. They were all accounted for. None of them of them had lingered nor distracted her. She never left the room. This could not be happening, and yet it was. It was truly happening. What was she to do now?

Without a word, she grabbed a cloth from the chalk tray and wiped herself off. She did not take her eyes off of the class the whole time she did it. Then she got a wonderfully sadistic idea. Still dripping, she addressed the class, "All right, you loathsome bilge rats! Obviously, something just happened. Now, I am going to get to the bottom of which one of you little cockroaches did this to me! How dare you humiliate an educator, a teacher, one who has sacrificed so much for all of you! Well, *someone* has to know something! So, since at least one of you is so very *fond* of games, we will play one right now! The game we will play is 'When Do We Get to Sit?' The rules are simple. *I* get to sit immediately. You get to sit only after I get a confession! You stand there at formal attention until someone finally talks."

She sat her round form on her chair. It was so small but always managed to hold her weight. She sat in complete silence. Everyone was at attention, and it was exhausting. After about a half an hour, Whipshot got bored and decided to berate the class. Their knees were beginning to shake, and she was delighted. So she started haranguing them, hoping that someone's spirit would finally break. It was terrible because no one in the class knew anything. To confess, just to end the torture, would require an explanation of how they did it... and they had none!

For some reason, Emily's eyes were drawn to Whipshot's precarious perch. She noticed something strange. She thought she saw a nut loosening itself from the bottom of the chair. She blinked and looked again, not daring to rub her eyes or even move her head too much, lest Whipshot pounce upon her and pound on her with that screeching sledgehammer voice of hers. Or she may even use that terrible, terrible steel ruler that was rumored to have chopped off a student's fingers once. Emily may have doubted that story, but she understood why such a rumor could get started. That ruler was dangerous!

Emily glanced to the chair again and this time knew it was not her imagination. Another nut silently backed off its bolt, then slowly and softly landed on the floor as if to avoid making the slightest sound. One could have heard a pin drop in that classroom. Though this disassembling of the chair was indeed happening before her very eyes, Emily could scarcely believe what she was seeing!

One by one, the liberated bolts were now being removed from the chair! Emily was so firmly conditioned by Miss Whipshot's calls to attention that she would not break discipline, not even for something as critical as this. Besides, Whipshot would not believe her and probably would punish her for making up lies *and* for breaking the chair! How could she then explain what she saw? She couldn't.

Rather than to open that can of deadly centipedes, she remained silently awed and at perfect attention.

Whipshot was yelling at the brats, reminding them yet again how lucky they were to have an education from herself and Miss Coffenayle, their principal elite. They two were the finest educators that the state had to offer in any of the schools. Were it not for them, all of the worthless toads in this class would be on the street or in jail.

Frankly, Emily thought she would rather take her chances on the street. Such thinking, though, would break her mother's heart, if she were alive. If only Emily had some way of telling someone in authority the truth about how this school was operating! Surely, her parents would know what to do and how to make things right. Alas, she could not because her parents were gone now, instantly killed in that horrible car crash. Having no other known family, she was sent here by the state to live.

Once a student was enrolled in Happy Valley Vocational School, they were lost to the world. No one really missed the students because they would only be taken there if they had no other family. Once under their roof, they were now part of the system. This system was exceptionally cruel, but no one could report it. The school made certain that every student was cut off from communicating with any-one outside of the school. This place was their world. This was now their life. Authorities who might visit were either corrupt and bribed into making good reports or they were blocked by endless continu-ances filed by the school's general counsel. If the general counsel was unable to block the authorities, then the last resort was a judge, one who always ruled in the school's favor, even in questionable cases. Some of the rulings were very strange indeed.

Because everything the plaintiffs presented in court was labeled by the judge as "conjecture and hearsay" the truth about Happy Valley Vocational School was just simply not known to the world. The authorities who believed something bad was happening could not use investigators or monitors to gather evidence. The court would block their efforts each time, stating they had no justifiable cause to start an investigation. Whatever the case, it seemed that there was a prejudicial attitude in Judge Parschall's mind. It seemed that the Happy Valley Vocational School was never going to be investigated.

Most of the kids had barely heard of radio, and the few existent telephones in the school were under lock and key in strongboxes or in the administration office. Mailboxes were also under lock and key; the outgoing mail was monitored. Not that the children actually had anyone to write to anyway. There truly was no way for the kids to communicate with anyone on the outside.

At the front of the classroom, Miss Whipshot turned herself around and adjusted her skirt as she tried to sit. It was quite a chore for her to move around the room on those elephantine legs and keep her dress in order. Emily almost felt sorry for her. Those thoughts, though, were changed quickly as she thought of how dangerous Whipshot would be as a slim, trim, and athletic woman. Emily's mom was such a woman in the photograph she had of her parents on that canoe trip. The one where they died on the way home.

Whipshot's chair seemed as normal as ever; it did not seem to be falling apart. Emily's eyes were still riveted on those bolts and nuts that now lay scattered under the chair. They had been carefully and silently removed, one by one. Had Miss Whipshot noticed them? Emily doubted it but did not dare peep a word of warning. When Whipshot finally had lowered herself onto the chair, it began to groan again.

Only this time, the chair did not merely protest. It rebelled entirely as though it finally decided that enough was enough. The chair collapsed, and not just any ordinary collapse either. It seemed to nearly explode under Miss Whipshot's weight! Her huge fat feet shot up in the air, and her fully extended elephantine legs showed the whole room what was under her skirt. Emily could not believe that they made underwear *that* large, much less in a bloomer style! The entire room roared with the hysterical laughter that only the young can muster up. The students all knew they would pay for it when she struggled to her feet but did not care. The comedy of the scene made it quite worth whatever Whipshot could do to them.

Little Tom opened the door just a crack and began laughing into his shirtsleeve. Emily noticed and was not going to draw attention to him. The poor boy had already suffered enough. He seemed to be the teacher's favorite target, for some reason. Maybe it was the fact that he came from a poor family whose father died in a speakeasy and whose mother then worked herself to death trying to support her poor little Tommy. Emily personally felt sorry for him but could not, in the interest of self-preservation, show him any of that pity where Whipshot could see. Sometimes Emily thought she would like to whip and shoot Whipshot, but she was immediately ashamed of such thoughts. She would not become a cruel person, not ever.

Then out of the corner of her eye, Emily noticed that a piece of round chair leg seemed to float in air! It was just for an instant, just long enough to catch her attention. As soon as she turned her head enough to see the leg, it clattered to the floor. She tried to tell herself that it was her imagination, but somehow, deep inside, she knew that she was not imagining things. Ever have that happen to you? Something suddenly flits by the corner of your eye, just out of sight, and when you turn to see, it was nothing? Yet, you are *certain* that something was actually there. Then, try as you might to believe you imagined it, you could not? Well, that was how Emily felt right now. She knew that she saw that chair leg hover, just for an instant, and then fall as though it noticed that Emily was about to see it. But a chair leg can't think, see, or move, can it?

This event was just the beginning of an *incredible* adventure.

2

The Incredible Adventure Begins

Whipshot struggled on the floor, her skirt pulled all the way up, and her bloomer intimate apparel looking perfectly ridiculous. She rocked back and forth like a beached whale, hollering unintelligible phrases in some strange sputtering foreign tongue. This was the idiom people use when they are so shocked and speechless that they can't find the words to say. She was trying say everything at once! The laughter continued as the bloated teacher rocked further and further to one side then the other. She finally managed to roll to the left enough to get on her knees and straighten her skirt somewhat. She crawled on all fours in a circle to face the students. She continued fixing her skirt, gasped, and wheezed like a pneumonic hippo then finally caught her breath. Then she found that blazing boom-cannon she used for a voice.

"*Silence! All of you! Or you will suffer!*" her words echoed off the walls.

The room fell dead silent. The teacher's indignant position did nothing to humble her, it seemed. She was not embarrassed in the least. Oh, no. She was far too angry and prideful for that. She managed to drag her bread dough form into a sitting upright position to catch her breath. Then by some miracle of angry determination, she came again to a kneeling position, her sun-starved calves shining pale and white in the overhead lights of the classroom. She stopped for a moment, her head bowed, again wheezing and gasping for breath.

It seemed for a moment like she was praying, but she would pray only for the strength to beat some hapless student. All the kids in the class held their breath while she found hers. The class had their fun already, and Emily wondered if they would live long enough to regret it. Whipshot was capable of punishing them five times over for the fun they had at her expense. She could be quite inventive too.

Little Tom still had the door open just a tiny crack but enough to be noticed by Miss Whipshot. Suddenly, the teacher's fury had found a new target. She was no longer interested in the whole room's laughter. She was on her feet in a flash, her strength coming from pure rage. She was going after the boy in the closet! She deftly plucked that strange metal ruler of hers from her desk with a lightning-fast motion of her hand! She quickly thudded and thumped her way to the closet. The room shook with every step.

Something drew Emily's attention again to the chair leg, which was surprising. Here, she thought the boy in the closet was about to die, but she was looking at the chair leg! It was normal for students to simply keep eyes front while someone was being screamed at and threatened. But this time, the whole room was afraid for Little Tom as they watched the teacher dart for the closet! They knew that some-how, this situation was different, that they needed to keep their eyes on their teacher.

The only exception was Margaret, the teacher's pet, who kept her eyes forward, smiling. Red-haired, freckle-faced Margaret wore spectacles with her hair in neat braids and was always wearing nicer clothes than her classmates. She stood about average height for her age, had a couple of pounds more than her classmates, but she was not fat. She was well-fed on teacher's treats. She was a whole different kind of person in Whipshot's demented world. *Margaret was a snitch!*

The little redhead would tell everything that she heard in the classroom, in the dormitory, and even in the hallway. She watched and waited for someone to say the wrong thing and turned them in. She was not concerned about the boy in the closet. She was, after all, the one who ratted on him. She signaled Whipshot with a flip of the finger. Her fellow students never noticed. She was hoping for a cupcake.

Emily remembered reading about people being treated this way under dictators who used spies and snitches. Right now, though, her attention was not currently on history or on the boy in the closet. It was on that chair leg. She thought she saw it roll—it definitely rolled—right into the path of the teacher. It stopped perfectly in her path, just like it had eyes. Emily was not only terrified at what Whipshot was doing. She was shocked at the chair coming apart, doubly shocked at that chair leg moving across the floor! How could that be?

Whipshot the Terrible was plodding to the closet in full fury, pudgy face reddened, cheeks puffing and billowing like a slobbering hog's jowls, moving faster than seemed possible with her weight. She struck a boy's desk on her way to the closet with that thick steel ruler of hers. The ruler knocked a corner off the desk, a chunk of wood zinging to the floor and ricocheting to the wall with a loud bang, bits of wood fiber splattering the students in the vicinity. None dared move nor even twitched a hand, not even to brush splinters off their faces. They were frozen in horror, all eyes on the teacher and that wondrous terrible ruler. Only Emily's eyes would occasionally stray to that chair leg.

Just as Whipshot raised her ruler and began reaching for the closet door, her meaty round foot, covered in those awful-looking shoes, landed squarely on top of the chair leg, and *zoom!* Miss Whipshot went feet-first up into the air. She seemed to freeze in midair, then come crashing down, her feet and bloomers once more exposed, pointing to the sky! What a sight! He skirt nearly covered her head.

Her legs landed on the wooden floor first with a heavy, dull, splattering twin *thud* sound, and there was a crackling crash that would not soon be forgotten. Then she laid still and unconscious, dust billowing around her, mouth gaping open, snoring sounds issuing forth. Her fetid breath brought tears to the eyes of the students nearest her. Whipshot's eyes were closed, and her black horn-rimmed cat's-eye glasses lay askew across her chest. She now lay *inside* the floor, her upper half ridiculously sprawled with her arms to the side, bridging the gaping hole in the floor. Little Tom opened the closet door and looked around. Emily called to him softly, saying it was safe to come out. Everyone was frozen in disbelief. A thick stunned silence hung over the classroom.

A few students rose from their chairs and surrounded, in wide-eyed wonder, the unconscious form of their teacher. Only Margaret cried out in terror. The rest were just plain stunned. Most of the class had never seen anyone knocked out before, especially not like this. Only the upper half of the teacher's body was visible; the rest of her had smashed through the floor. She was obviously stuck, stubby arms out to her sides, her flowered skirt spread out all around her. Floorboards, sharply spiked, pointed upward surrounding her. It was like she was now in some kind of a wood picket prison.

The class hardly knew what to do. Some were crying; others stared in shock; some muttered quietly among themselves, wondering if she was dead. Tommy, from the closet, crept carefully toward the bloated whale-like form now helpless and jammed in place. She could not hurt him now! He knelt down and *picked up the teacher's ruler*, an excessively bold move. He held it, looked at it, and looked at the teacher, his head turning back and forth as though he were wondering what to do next. Suddenly, Little Tom bolted out the door. He was gone for a moment and came back winded without the ruler. A fellow student, Jimmy, asked what he had done.

Tommy said he had run down the hall to the main door and flung the ruler across the yard as hard as he could. The entire room was really in shock now and quietly murmured at the boy's courage. None of them would have *dared* such an act of defiance, even with the teacher lying helpless. Little Tom was lucky he did not get caught running up the hall like that. Everyone also knew that a student even approaching the main entrance without a teacher or staff member beside them was a punishable offense. He was very lucky that time. He ran past Miss Coffenayle's office *twice* without getting caught.

The loss of her ruler seemed to have aroused Whipshot. Could she really *sense* something like that? Her head turned side to side; she was waking up. Her eyes blinked once, twice. She appeared to get her bearings somewhat and started up again, flailing her arms and kicking her subfloor legs, trying to get a grip on something beneath. She was shocked to find that she was stuck in the floor! Not only that, but her feet were suspended, kicking around in empty space!

"What are all you staring at, you little miscreants?" she shouted. Then she tried to stand, seemingly bent on beating every one of the them. "Wait until I find my ruler!" she growled. She struggled once, struggled twice, and then suddenly realized she was not only stuck but entirely trapped. She could not move, could not get her body out of the floor. Then she really began to howl out of rage and frustration. The students all stepped back, unsure of what to do. Then Margaret suddenly shouted, "I'll go get Mr. Castlethorn! He'll know what to do!"

"Then don't just stand there, you spoiled little rat-child! He's down in engineering!" shouted Whipshot. "Do it before I beat you too, just like all the rest are going to get!" The students could not believe their ears! She must really have been mad this time to loudly threaten Margaret the Snitch. "And stop staring at me, you little savages! *Back to your desks!* Oh…my…what a headache. I'm all dizzy—" And she passed out again. Margaret was already running out the door.

They all returned to their desks, and Tommy sulked back to his closet, shutting the door. Whipshot was alive and well, not the least bit humbled by her afflictions. They all sat down, some pretending to read, some with eyes forward, but all were feeling the gloom of being a Whipshot pupil. All but Emily, that is. She was too busy feeling stunned at what she alone had seen. She followed Margaret, running out the door along with some other students, including Jimmy-Whipshot, a fine handsome boy about her age who had forgotten his own last name. Jimmy was tall, lean, and strong. He had freckles and brown hair and eyes to match. He normally dressed in any old trousers and long-sleeved shirts. He was about five feet and five inches tall and had a naturally sunny disposition. He sometimes joked, though not enough to make trouble.

Emily's thoughts were not on the journey to the janitor's office or on Miss Whipshot but on the spectacle of what she alone had witnessed! She believed her own eyes, but certainly, this raised a question…or *ten!* She thought on her feet as they ran and hoped they could find Mr. Castlethorn. He was the school's eccentric engineer and a very scary man. She was not sure this was the best idea, but it was the only one they had.

The girl's mind was moving in several directions at once. What made those nuts and chair leg behave that way? She knew inanimate objects could not move under their own power. Yet, *she knew that she saw what she saw.* The nuts were still there on the floor to prove it. Could it have been that the nuts all backed off their bolts by themselves? Over a long time, perhaps, a single nut could loosen and eventually fall off. But for that to happen with *every one of the nuts and all at once?* Not humanly possible!

And what about that chair leg? She knew it rolled right into the path of the teacher… So how…and…why? Could the vibrations of the floor have caused it to roll under her like that? Possibly. There was a lot of vibration, for sure. That could be the answer to one part of the problem; even so, it still did not explain how the chair was taken apart.

As much as Emily hated to see anyone trapped like a wild animal, she thought it was justice served in this case. Maybe God was actually watching, like her mother used to sing to her in that favorite bedtime song:

> Rest now, child, don't you fear!
> God is watching and ever near;
> Ever faithful, ever wise!
> God is watching until you rise.

Margaret, Jimmy, and Emily who were running ahead of the others had unconsciously called a silent truce. All of the students did not necessarily hate Margaret, not as much as they claimed in the dorms. They did not know her well enough to hate her personally. All of them did hate the things Margaret did. But for the moment, they all three had something to gain from this uneasy alliance. All of them knew that the teacher needed help. Miss Whipshot was in desperate straits.

The other students who were lagging behind simply wanted out of the classroom. This was a perfect excuse. After all, it was reasonable that they should have several witnesses to such a strange event. What an adventure! Six of them running to the engineering office, without so much as a hall pass. They never even thought about the principal's office as they ran past. Oddly enough, the receptionist did not even look up. She must have been engrossed in her work.

Margaret, who at first thought she was going by herself, secretly wanted the company. She did not trust Jimmy, Emily, or any of the other students. They did not like her, called her the teacher's pet and other names. She was the Whipshot-lover. The reality was that she hated Whipshot and intensely so. Their teacher made her feel terribly afraid! Margaret acted as a snitch to avoid the punishments and the sting of the ruler. Couldn't they see that? Couldn't the others understand that all she was trying to do was survive like everyone else? Wasn't it better to be at the devil's right hand than in his path? She did not like what she did; she *had* to do it to get by!

After they left familiar territory, they slowed to a walk. The little group instinctively huddled together. This was a very creepy place they were about to enter. The halls of the school were quiet enough, except for the noise of the teachers hollering at their students fading away—the shouts about getting to work, how students were all so stupid, headed for jail, lucky to be here and so on. The group did not exactly know where "Engineering" was, but they knew it was the fancy word for the janitor's office.

None of them had ever been to this part of the school. There was no reason to go there; it was so far out of the way of anything they would normally do. They knew the office was down in a lower wing of the building. This was a place where there were no classrooms and no teachers. It was down really low, according to the signs directing them to go down the stairs. None of them had ever been on the stairs before. Was this really a good idea?

The signs, even if they were old, stained and faded, kept them on track. The group was led down a long but very wide stone staircase. The stairs were of rock, hand-carved, and more or less covered with gray paint. The walls were painted the same color, the uneven stones jutting out like large teeth. There was no handrail, and the group had to use the protruding rocks as handholds. The stairs were so wide that the students could walk four abreast if they liked, but they stuck close to the walls.

There was dim lighting, the bulbs dangling from the ceiling on cloth-covered wires. Bugs flittered around the bulbs with several insect corpses stuck to lights, frying and stinking on the hot glass. This passageway was more like a mineshaft than a school's basement. All of the kids were growing more uneasy as they progressed.

The further they went, the worse things seemed. There were strange smells in the air. The walls were still of jagged old stone but were no longer painted. They reached the bottom of the stairs. On the floor, mildew grew in black patches as water dripped from cracks in the walls. There were fetid puddles that collected in uneven spots on the rough floor. Dead bugs were everywhere and were being cannibalized by the living of their own kind. The lighting was growing dimmer as they went; the bulbs were spaced further and further apart. They naturally became more nervous; the three in front were keeping pace, but the others were lagging more and more behind. Jimmy kept an eye on them but finally urged them to either keep up or go back to the classroom. The stairs finally ended.

The group was now in a long hallway lined with doors. They paused at the first entry door, the one that seemed to be the "*Enjineering Offis*," so indicated by a handmade sign. The wooden sign on the door was obviously handcrafted and unpainted. The letters were burned into the surface of the worn boards. The boards were sloppily held together by some makeshift framework of angle iron and mismatched rusty bolts. A few rough nails were bent over from the wood to the frame for good measure.

The sign hung by twisted wire from a large bent and rusty nail pounded into the door. Hammer marks were all around it. They were glad that they had to go no further, but they were sorry that they had reached the place. Margaret hesitated, and Jimmy was looking back for the other boys, so Emily took the lead. A huge rusty padlock, an antique style lock that opened with a key in its face, hung loosely in its hasp off to the side. Emily guessed that meant the office was open. The whole door was obviously old, probably the same age as the lock. The hinges had not seen an oilcan for some time.

Emily hesitated, glanced at her frightened little gaggle, swallowed hard, put her chin up, and rapped at the door. There was no answer. She looked around; her classmates seemed more frightened than she was. Their nasty teacher needed help, evil or not. And they were that help. There was nothing else they could do. Emily knocked again. No answer. And a third time, she pounded harder with the heel of her fist, but still no answer.

The other boys who originally joined the three with weak commitment to the cause now left them. They ran back up the steps. They shouted over their shoulders some weak excuse about a "hall pass." This failure in the boys' courage did not reassure the remaining three at all! They were questioning the wisdom of coming to see Mr. Castlethorn, but what choice did they have? Their teacher was too big to pull out of the floor, and besides, they might injure her; not that anyone would mind all that much. In the end, though, there was nothing else to do.

Emily mustered up the courage to speak and announced quietly but firmly, "We have to go in there and find him."

Margaret nearly fainted, and Jimmy really felt like he wanted to pee his pants. They looked at Emily like she was out of her mind.

"*We have to!*" Emily whispered with desperation, hardness edging her normally kind voice.

"Well," said Jimmy, his voice squeaking just a bit, "into the fire."

With those words, Margaret grabbed Emily's arm out of instinct, and Jimmy moved in close, trying to look brave. What was that thing his dad used to say? "A man is a man only when he is being a man." Jimmy never really understood that until just now. He felt that, indeed, he was being a man. He was maybe five or six when he heard his dad say that as he lay dying of black lung from the coal mines.

Emily reached out carefully and pulled on the door handle, only just now noticing that there was a gargoyle's head overseeing the handle, its rusty iron face leering at her. The creature's tongue was the lever that operated the latch. Emily pushed down the lever with her thumb and heard a faint click. She supposed that the latch was released and the door could now be pulled open. It happened easier than she thought it would.

Jimmy moved in a little closer, feeling an unmistakable urge to protect the girls no matter what. His heart pounded and his palms sweated.

Emily pulled the door just a little and the hinges screeched in protest. Any secret hopes they had of a quiet entrance had just been ruined. The trio stayed close together. Emily had to shake some slack into Margaret's fingers that reflexively tightened around her arm.

3

Meeting Mr. Castlethorn

As Emily continued to pull the door, a loud screeching squeak that seemed enough to wake the dead issued forth and echoed in every direction. All of them jumped. The odors that began to afflict their noses through the doorway were offensive and barely tolerable. They smelled dust and mildew, old grease, and machine oil against a background of some unidentifiable things they had never smelled before. They strained their eyes against the darkness, slivers of dim light creeping around from the same type of bare lightbulbs that attempted to illuminate the craggy rock staircase. The light looked foggy through the dust that was in the air and everywhere. Machines of odd description that defied the curious to guess their job lined the walls. Handles and gears and gauges seemed to protrude from everywhere.

Some machines had valves like they would be operated by steam, Jimmy noted silently. His father had taught him of such things as a little boy, and the lessons stuck with him. He felt naturally attracted to machines; these tendencies were in his very blood. He was secretly fascinated by what he was seeing but not enough to be unafraid. Only the truest forms of bravery exist in the presence of fear. Only the truly brave act when they are afraid.

None of the trio dared move at first, all of them holding their breaths and waiting for something horrible to happen. After a moment's worth of eternity, Emily edged her way forward through the doorway. She was certain to not the leave the other two behind. The further the trio got into the room, the stranger things became. Venturing forward, they noticed cans of old varnish, kerosene, and turpentine stacked and rusted. They were covered with cobwebs and the obligatory dust. Some cans were painted olive green and were the shape of the cans from the silent war movies. Emily liked the only silent movie she ever saw. It was about brave soldiers, but she did not feel so brave herself.

There were work benches, old and falling apart, stools and chairs just carelessly tossed into corners. Then they began to notice the *really* weird things as their eyes adjusted to the semidarkness. They saw mounted heads of jungle animals and bears. A dusty and balding stuffed fox snarled at invisible prey. Old mounted fish with wooden lures hanging out of their mouths stared unblinking into forever. Their hides were cracking and peeling off. On one of the benches, near the back, jars of odd things just sat there: fetal pigs and worms, along with jars of internal organs probably—*hopefully*—from cows sat in dusty jars of formaldehyde. The lids were rusted shut. Obviously, things had fallen to neglect and disuse.

The group did not know whether to gag, sneeze, or just run away. They were completely overcome by strange sights, odd smells, the dust, the rough concrete floor, and general darkness! So entranced were they that the three failed to notice the entrance door was slowly closing…*blocking their only means of escape!* There was a fire exit, but it was occluded by machinery and a pile of what appeared to be old dormitory mattresses.

Margaret wondered if *those* were what they issued to the other students to sleep upon. She, herself, had a new private bed. She uncrated it herself straight from the factory. This came for her as a present from Miss Whipshot when she began her demeaning but profitable career as a snitch.

Something made Emily stop, and the whole group froze. She did not dare to face the unthinkable. Somehow, she knew they were trapped. Without looking back, she knew that *something* closed that door. Jimmy felt her stiffen, and he and Margaret held their breaths. Slowly and with great dread, as a single unit, the terrified trio turned around. The door was indeed closed! Then they the heard unmistakable echoing sound of a latch being engaged and the rattling of keys.

There was a dark figure shambling around by the door, hunched over, and sounding irritated. In the darkness, it seemed to be covered with wooly hair, but it walked upright like a man. Weaving and bobbing around on two legs, the hunched figure made snarling and choking noises like it was trying to clear its throat. The group froze, unable to fathom what they saw. Was it human? Was it a beast? Bigfoot?

It seemed that this figure was at least seven feet tall! Though it walked on two legs, in the shadows, it scarcely appeared to be human. The head, if it had one, was covered with thick, nasty, long, even *beastly* hair. It loped as it walked, seeming to drag one leg. But then, inexplicably, it disappeared. Gone. There was no way, Emily knew, that something so big could disappear so quickly without making so much as a sound.

Jimmy was thinking of a story he once read. There were some lost travelers who were being hunted in the jungle by a cannibalistic ape-man. He actually wished he was in that jungle right now. At least he would have someplace to run. Margaret was too scared to even think. She began to whimper.

Then, suddenly, the massive figure burst from out of nowhere! It was loudly howling and clucking like a chicken! It was brandishing an old-style coach lantern slung to a pole. It swung the lantern around its head in one paw and pointed at the children with the other. It was hunched over and bobbing up and down as an ape might do when confronting a mortal enemy! The iron lantern was rusty and squeaky, definitely as old as anything in the place. Its owner, the group noticed, added a whole new dimension to the strange room. He, she, whomever…smelled awful!

Emily held her nose, and Jimmy wrinkled his face as Margaret covered her nose and mouth with her hands. They were frightened and repulsed at the same time, unable to move. The maniac, a human, stopped clucking and circled the little group, surveying them.

Suddenly, he spoke, "What be y'doin' here, kiddees? Hmmmm?" He paced around them some more. Getting a closer look, they all three knew now he was human. In the dimness, they noticed that he had some missing teeth and one nasty jagged black tooth, not that the others were much cleaner. That black one, Jimmy noted, was just ghastly. It terrified him. No wonder this "person" stank. None of the group spoke. "I sayee, what be y'doin' here kiiiiddddiiiiiieeeesss? *Hmmmmm?*" he repeated as he moved in. He was still weaving a bit, that awful cast-iron lantern in his hand, his knuckles large and hairy, fingernails jagged and thick.

Margaret silently thought his personal hygiene was horrid! *Ewww!*

"A-Are you Mr. Castlethorn, sir?" Emily finally managed to stutter.

"An' I bees yes? Or if I bees no, what matters dat to *yese?*" he replied, moving closer to Emily. "Be yese brave or foolish to come into da engineerings office? None never comes here before yese, see. This bees a surprise. *Or be ye ghosts?*" He suddenly shouted, jumping back and eyeballing them suspiciously, seeming fearful. "No hoomin'd dare come sees Castlethorn on his terms…in hiss office! Haz yese no better *sense?*" Suddenly, the janitor started to cluck again, almost howling and swinging that lantern around and around his head, shouting—no, *chanting* something unintelligible that ended with a moan.

Then he stopped as suddenly as he began and looked at one of the lantern's windows; it seemed to glow, illuminating his face a little more with colored light. "Hoomin," he muttered to himself. "Deys must be hoomin…crazy, mebbees to be heers wit' me, but hoomin beans." He shuffled over to a chair and sat down on it, lantern in hand, and he stared at the ground for a long time. He was slowly turning his head back and forth as though contemplating something. The whole time, he was muttering amazedly at the "hoomins" being in his inner sanctum. He almost seemed disappointed and said something about "getting them next time."

"S-Sir?" Emily ventured cautiously. "We have an emergency. Miss Whipshot has fallen through the floorboards and she is stuck. We have to get her out." She was speaking softly with a slight quiver in her voice. "Can you please help us?"

The old janitor looked up quizzically. He seemed to stare right through Emily as though she was not there. Jimmy and Margaret moved from behind Emily to stand beside her now, no longer so afraid. It seemed that Mr. Castlethorn was calming down and was not so frightening after all. Right now, he just seemed tired—tired and smelly—but not as mean as ol' Miss Whipshot. Emily's gaze never left Castlethorn's, and after a long moment, he finally spoke, "So ye says she fell through-eee the floorboards an' is stuckz, eh? How didz *dis* happen?" His gaze never left Emily and seemed softer now, almost tolerable.

Emily understood that he expected an answer. It was safe to talk to him. "She was mad at one of the students for laughing when her chair fell apart. She ran after him with her ruler, slipped on a chair leg, and fell through the floor." It was much better for all concerned, for Emily in particular, to just stick to the basics of the story and not mention the details of what she saw…or what she *thought* she saw, anyway. "We don't know if she is hurt. She seemed okay, other than being stuck…and the last we knew of her, she was asleep and snoring loudly."

Mr. Castlethorn seemed almost to smile as he made some mild grunting noises that could have passed for a soft chuckle. Emily was glad he didn't smile, what with that rotten tooth and all…and his smelly breath. Besides, the idea of him *smiling* just seemed generally weird.

Margaret and Emily glanced at each other, both knowing that some kind of uneasy alliance had formed between them, two girls, natural enemies almost, but united in a cause. They had risked something dangerous, risked it together, and when the chips were down, neither girl faltered. Jimmy's bravery did not go unnoticed by either girl, and Margaret glanced over at him with an odd smile. Emily noticed.

"D-Do you have a bathroom down here?" asked Jimmy.

"So ye needs ta hits the head, eh, boy? Ye kin go over there, behin' da door with the fire exting'isher near it. *That's* the toidy."

Jimmy, much obliged, stumbled his way in the dim light and "hit the head." Inside the bathroom, with the door closed, it was totally dark, so he had to leave the door open a crack. The smell was suffocating; the filthy appearance of the toilet defied description. There seemed to be water in it, and Jimmy was glad. He was glad to be in a bathroom, glad he did not have to sit on that seat, glad to have seen Whipshot silenced for a while—just generally glad to be alive. Taking care of business, Jimmy wondered awkwardly just where he was going to wash his hands.

Emily and Margaret were talking with Mr. Castlethorn, hardly believing that they were conversing with this creepy old guy who was feared by all the students. "Now yese say dat Whipshot fellz through th' floor? Ye say she is now stuckz, eh?" he said, rubbing his stubbly chin thoughtfully with a calloused greasy hand. "Can't say Ah'm suraprahzed. Dem boards in herz room haz been weak for yeerz. Mose peoples t'ink dat because the classroomz is on dese bottom floor dat dey boards lays rahht on a seement foundation. Simpleez ain't true, ladies. School haz a bazement 'neeth it. Wese in partz of it now. Cain't say I ever beenz down there tuh dat udder part m'self. Doze Miz Coffenayle knows aboutz dis yet? Or dat fat toady whut followz her around? Mitser… Duncehead?"

"Doesbad," corrected Emily with a slight grin. "He is a lawyer who stays in one of the rooms at the school, occasionally."

"Yeah, him, da fat slob… Ye girls not gonna tell 'em Ah said dat, are yese?" He looked sort of worried, like he was taking them into his confidence.

"Are you for real?" said Margaret. "*We* are not going to tell. We don't like Doesbad, anyway. We're just glad you're not being mean to us."

Emily was genuinely shocked at Margaret saying this.

"Wahl," said Castlethorn, "don't yees getz use to it." He began scowling. "Now let's go haves a looksee ats yer teacher. Ya know," he said as an afterthought, "yer little group is dee only bunch dat eveer made it dis far intuh my sanctum. And yese didn't runz away when I cames out to mee'chu. I wonder if there bees hope for yese three ta one day he'ps me out."

Jimmy had made it back just in time to hear Castlethorn say that, and the three classmates did not dare to ask any questions.

Their silence was palpable. "Wahl," said the old janitor, "we'd best has a looksee at the mess ye've been talkings abouts. *Now git movin!*" he hollered, making the youngsters jump. They hurried toward the exit of the spooky engineering room with the janitor lagging behind, stopping to tinker with a couple of things on the way out the door. Nobody wanted to know what. He met them at the door and unlocked it.

Margaret, Emily, and Jimmy arrived at the classroom in that order, out of breath. They beat Castlethorn. They knew because he had not left his office yet, and he never passed them. Yet, Castlethorn was already there in the classroom somehow, observing a sleeping snoring Miss Whipshot from a distance. Looking the big picture over, from a distance, he figured that he had to break off some of the wooden spikes to rescue her. She looked ridiculous with her arms spread out like chubby eagle's wings. Her mouth was open, and someone had put her glasses on crookedly; one would think she had fallen asleep reading a book or something. She slept so soundly despite her obvious discomforts!

The trio pushed their way through the classroom, past the murmuring students, some of whom wondered if the teacher was dying. They were arguing over whether or not her snoring was a death rattle. Just as they reached Whipshot, the lights in the classroom suddenly went out! At first, Emily thought it was just another power outage. The hall lights were still on, though, leaving the room partly lit. It was almost as dim as Castlethorn's office. It was unsettling.

Then things happened all at once: there was a shrill cackling sound, the unmistakable cry and rattling that always accompanied the janitor's entrance! While many of the students were familiar with this man's behavior, it still disturbed them. Children suddenly scattered in every direction, some to their desks, sitting at attention, some retreating to the safe haven of corners of the room, huddling together. A few of them were actually in tears, covering their ears, trying in vain to block out the chaos!

The unlit iron lantern was rattling around yet again, and the janitor was insanely clucking like a chicken and babbling some sing-song chant. When he was done with his strange ritual, the entire class had backed away from him. The only exceptions were Emily, Margaret, and Jimmy who just stood by Whipshot, watching the old man in disbelief. He stopped twirling the lantern and stared into it for a moment. It glowed faintly. He studied it, then he turned the lights back on.

"I guess ye're all hoomin, then," said the janitor. He looked over at Whipshot and observed her for a couple of more minutes, the students staring, mouths agape. "Well, she ain't dyin's fahr as I kin tell. Which one o' you wrote 'wicked witch' backward 'cross her forehead?" He scowled and surveyed the room, looking for guilt. *Pretty clever*, he thought to himself. *When she looks into the mirror, she will be able to read it plain as day.* He certainly did not want to be in the shoes of the student who would dare commit such an act. Secretly, he wanted to praise the cleverness of the trick. He did not like Whipshot much and really did not like anybody much. Except maybe that one girl who was the leader of the group that came to his office. She seemed to have a little moxie, that one. "Now let's havza looksee at ye'r teacherz then."

4

The Rescue

Mr. Castlethorn crept over to Whipshot like she was going to explode. His navy-blue coveralls were covered with grease, dust, odor, and powdery white sweat stains…under the arms, especially. He was greasy, and his calloused hands, hideous in the partial light of his office, were positively gruesome in the full light. His hair was long and stringy, oily, and filthy. It was clumped together in places, matted, and horrible. A rat could have been living in it, and one would never know. He surveyed the damage to the boards around the teacher.

He crouched down near the snoring half-form and carefully prodded the floorboards outward from her body. Satisfied that things were sturdy enough, he came in even closer. He began pulling at the boards surrounding the teacher, grunting and gasping as he did so. He finally surrendered in this endeavor, realizing that brute force was not the answer. He had to turn to science. He had to think about the physics of this situation and analyze all the known factors at hand. Then he needed a hypothesis, one that he could test. Then the fog set in, blocking his mind from using complex thought patterns. He shook it off, used to the sensation. He decided on a simpler course of action.

"Well," said Castlethorn, his crooked hunched spine audibly crackling as he stood up, "I don't think that breakin' dese boards is gonna work a-tall. We needs ta think o' somethin' different. We dasn't needs for her to fallz through da floor an' gets hurt on de concreets, dough sometimes I theenks that to bese a fun idea." This last remark of his sent nervous titters running through his audience, and the kids had started to relax a bit. They knew now that the janitor was not out to hurt anyone. They had all been afraid of him for a long, long time and were relieved to hear him speak normal English…or *nearly* so.

He thought things over for a moment, drawing his large, calloused, and dirty paw across his mouth, his eyes dancing busily. With his arms folded in those dirty coveralls and his posture relatively straight, he appeared to be in deep thought. Emily wondered if he were some kind of mad genius. Jimmy was simply dumbfounded, and Margaret thought the janitor was just plain crazy and trying to act smart.

Suddenly, the janitor looked up and said, "Youse t'ree comes wit' me!"

Jimmy, Margaret, and Emily all looked at each other and swallowed hard. Well, whatever it was, they thought, it could not be harder than where they had already been and what they had done.

They were about to be proven wrong.

The old man quickly walked in that odd stutter-step of his back down the hallway. He was a fast mover when he wanted to be. No one dared ask where they were headed, but at least they were staying in familiar territory. No hidden trap doors or forbidden hallways, they hoped. This was entirely more of an adventure than they had bargained for when they woke up this morning. *Morning!* thought Jimmy. They ate lunch already, and all this excitement had made him hungry for an early dinner!

Margaret was preoccupied with her own thoughts about what all this meant to her position with the teacher. After all, Margaret enjoyed a comfy chair, a bed of her own and avoided the sting of the ruler; she did not want to mess that up.

Emily's mind kept reverting to back to those nuts and the chair leg. She knew what she saw; she was not prone to hallucinations! Yet, she also knew that objects don't animate on their own and cause accidents. Something was stirring around in her mind, but they were already down the stairs and had arrived at their destination. They were back at engineering, and the three of them groaned inwardly.

"Now yese stays here…all of ye. I needs ta move some stuffs, and Ah don't need yer mitts all overz my vallables."

As though you would have to tell us twice, thought Emily. The three patiently waited outside and conversed in hushed tones, relieved that the old custodian did not want to them to come back inside his place. Their relief was to be short-lived. They heard some crashing and banging; things were screeching across the floor. Castlethorn came back after a few minutes, sweating and out of breath. He bent over at the waist and put his hands on his knees, heaving and gasping between fits of coughing.

Emily wrinkled her nose at this display and leaned backward a bit, hoping that no phlegm would issue forth. None did, and the old man soon recovered his breath. "Okay, ye three, ye gots to he'p me wiff da machine. Itz too big for one ta handle alonez, but I managed to gets us a clear paff to da door."

"You cleared a path to the door?" asked Jimmy, his eyes wide. "How big is the machine? And what could it be?"

"Wahl, ye're abouts to find out, young'n," retorted the old man. "Come on in, and we'll gets dis contraption ta da classroom and rescue ye're teacher."

They followed the custodian reluctantly, but by now, they were mostly used to the sights that the engineering office offered. The main fear had been of the old man himself, not the room, although it was still pretty creepy. Jimmy had once read a story about a man who pickled human heads in jars and kept them in a cabinet. He desperately hoped that the story was completely false and not based on facts found in this engineer's office. Jimmy also resolved to not read so many outlandish stories. He was discovering that he had a really weird imagination. Maybe more Charles Dickens or Mark Twain was in order.

The air was still thick with stale putrid odors, but they were more or less used to it by now. The strange sights were becoming more commonplace, so they could easily pass by some of the more disgusting oddities without worry. In a moment or two, they arrived at the machine, the thing that would rescue Miss Whipshot.

It was a hybrid machine made of secondhand parts and a big steam-driven piston engine. It had a huge boiler on the back that looked like a moonshiner's distillery, and there was a door for the coal. A three-inch round copper pipe ran, twisting at odd angles from the top of the boiler, and was attached to the belly of the engine. The pistons were more or less covered by a mismatched hood that was held in place by a padlock and some rusty hinges. The hood was coated with oxidized paint and dents. It was sort of a rosy pink that used to be red in its better days. A coal scuttle rested crookedly between the belly of the boiler and the engine. On the face of the engine was a huge flywheel that was attached to a fabricated winch.

When the flywheel would turn, the winch also turned and could reverse directions with the pull of a lever. The overall effect was to either raise or lower the cable that ran along the arm of a boom. The boom had to be cranked into position and could swing to and fro as well as rise and drop with the turn of a crank attached to the wheels and gears. The boom was lowered right now, bent in half snugly against itself and chained into place. The upper half of the boom arm had a pulley on the end, and the cable snaked through it, passing smoothly.

One thing that the inventor neglected to consider at the machine's inception was that it was too much for one man to mobilize. It had spoked wagon-style wheels made of iron, coated with vulcanized solid rubber, and each wheel boasted a mechanism to help it climb stairs. A clever invention but one that required a person on each wheel. This is why the custodian recruited his new young apprentices to help him.

The group managed to get the machine out of the engineering room. The wide stone steps were a challenge they overcame with the creative application of the ratcheting levers that helped turn the wheels but at the same time would not allow the machine to roll backward down the stairs. Working together with a "heave-ho" call each time they moved up a step, the group got the machine up the stairs with surprising ease and smooth efficiency.

In the main hall, they attracted some attention from students who were severely reprimanded by their teachers. The teachers could not see nor hear the machine passing by. Despite its clumsy appearance, the machine rolled smoothly, and the rubber coated wheels made very little noise rolling down the hall.

The laboring group finally made it to the classroom where the students were no longer enthralled by the sight of their teacher sticking out of the floorboards. Whipshot was still breathing, snoring, and making other sounds through her open mouth that sounded like she was trying to talk in her sleep. She could not really make the words come out. Her head was bobbing back and forth with "Wicked Witch" still on her forehead. She was going to be very upset the next time she looked in the mirror, thought Margaret; that is if she ever bothered with a mirror. Margaret was not as friendly with Miss Whipshot as one might think. Not really; not deep down.

"Watch ye're selfses," said Castlethorn as they brought the imposing behemoth nearer to the doorway. Jimmy and Emily were helping to push the mechanical monstrosity as Margaret slipped into the room to check on Miss Whipshot. Most of the students were sitting at their desks. Some were reading, some had their heads down. None dared to truly goof off with anything like paper airplanes or peashooters; not in this school, not in this classroom.

The machine was lined up with the doorway. They started to move forward, but Castlethorn cried, "*Halt!*" He eyeballed the machine and then realized that his contraption would never fit into room from here. The two students joined Castlethorn. They saw what was happening. It appeared that the old man did not have any idea of what to do. He had his arms crossed, and his grubby hand again covered his mouth. He seemed to be intent.

Jimmy and Emily were looking thoughtful too, but they had no idea what to do at first. They all stood there for a moment. The students inside the classroom silently stared at the machine. The silent anticipation grew thick and heavy in the room. The unspoken question was what to do now.

Jimmy was the first to speak. "If only we had a window," he said. Emily looked at him quizzically. Castlethorn stared at him cynically through narrowed eyes like he was nuts…not that the old custodian was one to throw stones.

"With a window, we could push the boom through from outside of the building and reach Miss Whipshot," he explained. The old man paused and mopped his brow with a greasy sweaty sleeve. He considered for a moment what the boy was saying about the situation.

The more he thought, the more he realized that Jimmy was right. Widening the doorway was out of the question; such an action would bring the whole wall and part of the ceiling down in a building this old. Making the machine smaller was so ridiculous that he dismissed the notion the moment that he thought of it. A window was the only possible solution to the problem, so a window is what they would have! Remarkable. *The boy seems to have a knack for this sort of business*, thought Mr. Castlethorn.

Castlethorn had some students from the classroom help him back the machine away from the doorway, allowing Jimmy, Emily, and Margaret to all have a break. They pushed the heavy machine in the direction indicated by the janitor. Some of the youngsters were actually getting used to the sight of him, if not the smell. He directed that odd machine down the hall and out the main exit doors.

The students had the machine moving well enough now that they were outdoors, so he let go. He walked around the building to the outer wall of the classroom. He began to line some things up in his mind. The students were working as a group to keep the machine moving on the grass. They were having a ball, taking turns at working the ratchets on the wheels. They even learned to turn the machine by operating the ratchets on just one side of the contraption, leaving the other wheels to turn freely. They discovered that they could do a full circle that way if they needed to. What a day this had become!

Jimmy had followed the group outside, and he noticed that Castlethorn was leaning against the brick wall. He had a slide rule and muttered over it. Jimmy could not decide if the janitor knew what he was doing or if he was murmuring a magic spell. As soon as Castlethorn knew he was being watched, he quickly slipped the slide rule into his pocket and pretended that nothing was going on.

A second quick glance at Jimmy, and the janitor knew that the boy noticed what he was doing. Well, if he got too mouthy and talky-talk with too many people, that could be dealt with. Castlethorn dismissed these thoughts and put his mind on the business at hand.

The students guided the machine, and Castlethorn had them park it on the side of the wall where he knew the teacher must be. He had a student run inside to confirm this and then stepped around to the boiler. He opened the coal chute and dumped in some black lumps from the machine's bin. Then he poured in a generous quantity of kerosene. He pulled a match from one of his many pockets and laid it on the machine. He bade the students to get back because "dis ting culd 'splode."

He donned an old leather fighter pilot's cap, complete with tinted goggles and some long leather pilot's gloves. He wrapped himself in a full leather apron, the kind a welder would use. He wrapped his face with a dirty shop rag. He struck the match on the back of his coveralls and tossed it onto the coal. He locked the door as the fire "*ka-wumphed*" its way to life. He immediately stood back and herded the students further back. After a few minutes, it seemed safe, and he approached the machine; then some of the students ran up to it.

He gruffly shooed these adventurously curious ones back from the machine, checked some gauges, pulled some levers, turned some dials. Convinced that all was ready, he fitted the front of the boom with an odd-looking device, kind of like a big spike. Once fitted and secured, the spike was very imposing. The janitor lined the machine up, which was moving now on its own power, and he walked along beside it. He was steering with a vertical wheel that he spun by a protruding handle. Castlethorn checked some figures he wrote on a piece of paper. These were figures that the students would never understand, even if they read them. He stopped the machine in a specific place and measured twice.

He made some chalk marks on the wall in the shape of the hole that he would make to fit the boom through. Jimmy came outside. He noticed that everyone was in a forbidden outdoor area, which made him nervous, even though a school employee was with them. This place had the remnants of a playground scattered about it; the cracked concrete showed lines where ballgames and hopscotch were once played. Rusted, bent, jagged pipes and metal fragments represented what once were monkey bars, swing sets, and other play structures.

Jimmy had never taken a good look out here before. The classroom's windows had long since been bricked shut. Students were barely allowed to even approach the main entry doors from the inside. When they had their rare recreational moments outdoors, they always exited through the back of the school. He began looking around, taking in the new and strange sights.

On the grounds, huge fragments of concrete were broken up and heaped into large obnoxious piles and just left there. It seemed as though someone had started renovations and then just abandoned the project. Jimmy could not put a word on what he felt as he surveyed the scene. He just knew that he felt much the same as he did all the time but now much more intensely. He would learn about something called "depression" in his studies years later.

Emily finally came outside too. She watched the students as they helped with Castlethorn's machine. It was very noisy with all the roaring, popping, and sputtering. Castlethorn's student helpers were feeding coal onto a small chute. They dumped the chunks of carbon into the inferno that powered the machine. They were sweating and had to work in shifts, allowing one another to take a break. Castlethorn was watching a gauge very closely as he stood on the machine, like a captain on the bridge of a pirate ship. He stood as erect as his bent back allowed, pushing and pulling at various levers and pushing buttons; one here and another there. Some valves he pushed halfway in, and others pulled all the way out.

Emily was truly fascinated with all the tarnished brass and copper, the iron parts, and how it all seemed to work together very well, but all seemed ready to blow apart. She was certain that something must go amiss at any moment, yet she was somehow confident that it would not. She watched the quiet dignity of Castlethorn as he readied his machine. She observed his meticulous attention to detail. She was amazed at his ability to juggle several tasks at once in spite of all the chaos around him! As of this moment, she could no longer believe that this man was just an ordinary, albeit creepy, old janitor.

Margaret watched this whole show with sort of a repulsed fascination. She could not bear the sight of all this ugliness. She was offended at the weird old guy on the tractor; the tractor itself looked very dangerous. Plus, she was becoming overwhelmed at the fact that her teacher was stuck in the floorboards. This was very hard for her to take in. This was supposed to be just an average day of hollering and abuse, another day of her getting favors from Whipshot. Yet she was fascinated by all of this. Who wouldn't be?

On top of it all, she thought of what might happen to her if, for some reason, Whipshot would not be their teacher any longer. She had worked hard for the few comforts that were allowed her. She did not want to lose them. She did not want to lose Whipshot's protection because the other inmates—um, *students*—in the dormitory would eat her alive. What was she to do? She thought this over as she sat in the desk nearest her entrenched teacher.

She finally decided that the only way to survive, for her to *literally* live through this, was to change things for herself in a way that no one else could. She knew that she could not allow Whipshot to die. She had to do something. She had to come up with a plan. The plan had to make her look good, no matter what. She had to look good to her teacher; or if Whipshot died, she had to look good for Miss Coffenayle. *Yes!* That was the right idea! She had to make herself look good. But how? She had to do something to stand out from the crowd.

Finally, she made a decision and quietly slipped out of the room without anyone else noticing. She beelined for the principal's office. She arrived at the receptionist's desk. The woman was busily looking through her files and did not notice Margaret. The girl did not want to take a chance of being turned away. *She* had to be the one to approach the principal. So she snuck past the desk and into the office of the principal herself. This was a very dangerous calculated risk but one with a great potential payoff.

The office was strange, not like any school administration office should be. There were no scholarly works, no booklets on education, and no evidence of "student education and mentoring" experts. Brass placards at the doors of smaller offices around the master suite indicated that such experts once resided there. Those doors were now sealed with padlocks, and the rusted hinges indicated that they had not been opened for a while.

The floors were wooden and shabbily aged. Even then, they were shined to near mirror finish. The bookshelves were cluttered with books, yes, but old well-used books. The titles were nearly worn off the bindings. The shelves also held partially burned black candles, brass bells, several small mirrors, and odd-looking statues. The air smelled strangely sweet but foreboding at the same time.

Miss Coffenayle, principal of the school, was sitting in this dreary office, her face buried behind some old book she held upright on her desk. The book was thick and leatherbound, the yellowed parchment pages sitting unevenly in the binding. It seemed that the book had suffered much abuse; it was in sorry shape. Ratty and worn, the cover had a gold-embossed title: *L'Grimoire: A Book of Powers.* She seemed deeply interested in the contents of the yellowed parchment pages.

One could almost get the impression that book held some mysterious knowledge. The desk where she sat was too large, quite imposing, and seemed to speak to her position at the school. The top of the desk was organized but cluttered with papers in loose bunches under large paperweights. The paperweights themselves were oxidized, hand-forged balls of iron, reminiscent of cannonballs.

This seemed fitting because an old miniature cannon also adorned the desk; the walls were pockmarked with Coffenayle's grape shot. It would seem odd to most people that the principal of a school would choose to pass time in such a dangerous and highly unorthodox manner. The doorway leading to the hallway had suffered the abuse of shots all around it as though a marksman was firing at someone or *something* in the doorway and having a really bad time of it.

The cannon was brass, sat on large red wheels, and was blackened around the muzzle. Fresh wadding and wicks were scattered on the desktop around it. A flask of black powder lay on its side, some of its contents spilling onto the desktop. A small wooden box of smooth lead balls rested beside the cannon. The slightest hint of burned gun-power hung in the air. Margaret almost imagined that the air was still smoky. She really hoped that cannon was not loaded at this moment; it was pointed directly at her.

The principal was deeply preoccupied and seemed immersed in the contents of her book. Margaret could not see Miss Coffenayle's face; there was just a bit of yellow hair moving back and forth as the principal read. She was quietly muttering and flipping pages back and forth, occasionally setting a bookmark of scrap paper in the pages. She would highlight phrases now and then with an old stubby pencil that used to be painted red. She seemed almost desperate to find information in her precious book. Margaret saw her pick up a magnifying glass. She seemed to be reading and rereading, muttering and nodding. She was engrossed in a deeply intense study, oblivious to the pitiful figure who had just skulked into her office.

Margaret stood frozen. She was more terrified now than she had ever been in her life. She sweated and trembled at the sight of the principal. She had only personally met with Coffenayle on one other occasion, which was a disciplinary action. The principal's ire left Margaret locked in a room—more of a small box, actually—for three days. The ceiling was too low for her to stand upright and too small to fully lay down and stretch out. It was a miserable existence with only some portions of stale bread and tepid foul water to sustain her life.

She "did her business" in a rusted metal bucket that remained with her in the room. Her only comfort was a dirty blanket. She vowed from that moment on to never lip off at Whipshot again. It was after her deliverance from that foul prison that she vowed to befriend Whipshot at all costs. Suddenly, her unpleasant pondering was interrupted!

"*What do you want, Margaret-Whipshot?*" Coffenayle bellowed angrily from behind her book. How could Miss Coffenayle know that she was even there? She did not look up at all, and Margaret did not make a sound when she slipped into the office.

Instantly, Margaret snapped to full attention. Her mind arced back from the horrors of her prison term to the horrors of the present. It was hard, emotionally, to separate one from the other.

With her mind forced into the present by fear, the girl noticed that the authoritarian desk was scattered with books and papers. Some of the papers were newer, some were old and worn. A few rolls of what might have been parchment were scattered over the floor around the monstrously imposing desk.

Slowly, the headmistress of the school lowered her book. She put down her magnifying glass. She folded her hands over her book, interlocking her fingers. The hunched-over plump female principal had bottled-blonde hair. It was pulled back tightly in a neatly done ponytail. Miss Donatienne Coffenayle glared at Margaret. Her face was drawn downward into a scowling snarl. She was obviously annoyed. Her big blue eyes would have been "beautiful" had they not been cold with rage and narrowed.

Those twin orbs were like frozen sapphires and seemed to burn right into Margaret's being, flaring with frigid flame, glaring with fury that was increasing by the second. *Hate* would be a deficient word to use if you tried to describe the horror that Miss Coffenayle was pounding into Margaret. The look was of complete disregard for the child's humanity! It was a cold, indifferent, yet *vengeful* superiority that shaded those eyes.

The poor girl wanted to run, but her feet would not separate from the floor. She was too terrified to speak, but knew she must. The appearance of the office scared her as much as its denizen. Strange charts and designs decorated the walls; some of them were drooping, others pinned smartly into place. Statues of strange creatures and a horned man with a trident were scattered all over the office. Miss Coffenayle could have been a hanging judge with that black covering she called a blouse and the matching but too-long skirt dark as night.

"Well, Margaret? How'd you get past my receptionist? What is it you want? Are you here for *disci*-pline? Where's your teacher? Do you have a written complaint from her?" She rapid-fired her questions without pausing for an answer, hoping to overwhelm the poor girl. It was completely unnecessary in this case. Margaret was already overwhelmed. Miss Coffenayle leaned forward, eyes menacing and curious. She smiled now, and Margaret wished that she had kept the scowl instead. It was that same nasty, terrifying, and sadistic grin that she had on her face the day Margaret first met her.

On that fateful day, Whipshot, ruler in hand, half-dragged Margaret by the collar into the office. Margaret had slipped up and let Miss Whipshot hear the word *hag* escape her lips at a near whisper. The punishment did not fit the crime. Miss Coffenayle was unusually cruel that day, even for her. Margaret recalled all of that, and that old feeling of dread made her regret coming here.

"Margaret!" Miss Coffenayle shouted as Margaret was startled out of her daydream. "Do you hear me at all? Or are you daft and just as deaf? Are you? Are you *stupid?* Did you call Miss Whipshot a 'hag' again? *Did you? Well? Did you call her a 'hag' again, you dreadful little toad?* If you don't answer me, I will lock you back inside that detention room. I think maybe you'll like it better this time. I put hard corn kernels all over the floor for you to kneel upon in repentance. I haven't gotten to try it out on anyone yet. It was an idea from one of the old countries, *Transylvania*, I believe. You want to be the *first?*"

"N-no," Margaret barely whispered. Her shoulders sagged, her neck drew in, her face hung low. She barely stopped the tears. Her mouth was dry. Her knees trembled. She nearly lost control of her bladder. Yet, she stood firm, taking it.

Miss Coffenayle stood up from the desk, her luxurious chair creaking like...well, a coffin nail being pried loose from its final resting place. She was smiling now, her face glowing darkly in anticipation of what punishments she might pronounce upon the helpless prey before her. She inched forward, almost comically short with her all-black ensemble dragging on the floor. It was only now that Margaret noticed some patterns neatly scratched into the floorboards, patterns that were almost beautiful but truly bore something terrible inside of them.

Miss Coffenayle crept up to the child, head aloft, dripping with a terrible smugness only the darkest of personalities may conjure up. Her hands behind her back, her lips were bereft of joy but tightly smiling with those dark terrible crystal-blue sapphires drilling into the crown of Margaret's bowed head. The poor girl was incredibly terrified and thought she may faint. "N-no, Miss C-Coffenayle. I did not call Miss Whipshot a h-hag."

"No? Then what is it, chi-yuld?"

The cold whisper of the school matron chilled Margaret to the soul. She felt frozen in place, too terrified to run but too horrified to just stand there. She was locked in an emotional stasis.

"M-M—" Margaret's voice trailed off.

"M-M?" mocked the raven-clad horror "M-M...*what?*" The principal was now circling her like a hungry cat, toying with prey. Her studies were all but forgotten. "What? What is it? Do you even *have* a hall pass to be here? Hmmm? Did Miss Whipshot give you a pass? Or did you just *sneak* out like the tawdry little *rat* that you are?"

"N-no, Miss Coffenayle."

"No? No what, Miss Margaret? Did you sneak out? Where's your pass? What brings your ugly deranged little self here?"

"Miss Whipshot is, um, well...she's hurt," Margaret replied in barely a whisper.

"*What?* Hurt? What happened?" Miss Coffenayle was animated now, almost concerned. "Did one your classmates damage her? Someone strike her? Did she have a heart attack? What is it?"

"She slipped and fell."

"Oh," said the black-shrouded crone. She stood upright and gave Margaret some breathing room. "Well, how bad could that possibly be?" Miss Coffenayle seemed relieved.

"P-perhaps you should come to see for yourself. It is bad enough that she could not write me a h-hall pass."

"What? Well, yes, that must be a situation indeed." She looked back at her studies like she could not bear to leave them. She really wanted to get back to *L'Grimoire*, but business was business after all. Miss Coffenayle would not want the authorities to get wind of a situation and try to come poking around. More than one person, it was rumored, was buried on the school grounds. Even death can be covered up, though, particularly by a Coffenayle. "All right then, child. Lead the way," the principal said in a calmer, almost pleasant voice.

Margaret slowly moved her feet; she was more relaxed now. She carefully and quietly padded her way out of that office, past the receptionist who watched the student silently. Margaret was feeling quite fortunate that she was still in one piece. She gained confidence that she was not about to be assaulted from behind the longer she walked.

They left the office and plodded up the hall. The principal's face was solemn and strange, silent, pasty, pale, and expressionless. She was walking abreast of Margaret now. The girl snuck a glance at her principal and noticed that she seemed to be in deep thought, her lips muttering something unintelligible. Something did not feel right about that, but at least Margaret felt better than she had moments ago in that office. She did not want see those terrible sapphire orbs ever glare at her again. Yes, she must somehow befriend Miss Coffenayle, to get on her right side, for that would be far better than to get in her way. It would be a deal with yet another devil she knew.

Soon, they would be at the room, and the principal could deal with this mess, taking it out of the students' hands. It would not be their responsibility any longer. Margaret nearly grinned at the thought that she might just get a favor out of Miss Whipshot. After all, she was the—*ugh!*—teacher's pet. She had taken this whole mission upon herself, contacting the principal. She would be sure to let Miss Coffenayle know that she, Margaret, suggested they get the school's engineer to start creating a solution to the problem.

The girl knew she was taking a terrible chance, playing a dangerous game. She was, after all, trying to befriend Miss Coffenayle. But in for a penny, in for a pound. She truly felt it was worth the risk, even as she felt horrible being at the principal's side. She hoped that she would get to be at her side in the future in a position to not be abused anymore.

Miss Coffenayle and Margaret arrived at the classroom, though not quick enough for Margaret's tastes. When they passed through the doorway, Miss Coffenayle just *stopped dead in her tracks.* Her mouth was agape, and her angry, short, ebony-clad body with a dusty shadow of tattered cloth trailing behind it froze in place. Speechless. The raven-beldame was actually *speechless* at what she saw.

"Slipped," Margaret had said. Slipped, yes, perhaps, but to have hammered herself into the *floorboards?* Those splintered slats surrounding her like stakes in a tiger pit? Whipshot was laying still, snoring and snorting with the form of her bulk suspended there, unconscious. Her cat's eye glasses dangling stupidly over... *What the? Is that "Wicked Witch" on her forehead?* Someone by now had also drawn a handlebar moustache and thick black eyebrows on Miss Whipshot.

"Why, the poor woman must be nearly dead to allow that," said Miss Coffenayle to herself, unheard by others.

Suddenly, from just outside of the far wall, Miss Coffenayle heard a loud roar! She was wide-eyed and speechless at the chaos of the scene—and in one of her classrooms! Unseen by her, outside of the building, the neck of the Castlethorn's abominable machine reared back like a striking snake; then it pounded rapidly at the wall! Inside the classroom, the explosive blows and shaking made everyone jump! *Bang! Blam! Wham!* The machine hammered at the wall. None dared cheer, but some smiled as they watched the school get pummeled. *Wham! Boom! Crunch!* The big spike punched at the bricks! The spike broke through to the interior plaster, sending chunks of it whizzing around inside the classroom, bouncing off the walls, skidding across the floor and narrowly missing students!

Miss Coffenayle ducked along with the rest of the class as debris flew, ricocheting all over the room! "Ducks yeer heads, stoodints!" shouted Castlethorn, a bit too late. *Boom! Blam! Wham! Wham! Bam!* The spike hit the wall repeatedly, making the hole bigger and bigger. Miss Coffenayle was lying on the floor, screaming, her head covered by her arms. She knew nothing until now about the machine on the other side of the wall. It seemed that there was an advantage to having windows after all.

The old engineer jumped out of the contraption and moved with surprising deftness to the exterior brick, examining it and probing it with a putty knife. He nodded satisfaction with his progress. So he resumed punching at it. He drew back with the spike and struck several more times; he was in complete control! The spike was striking precisely where he wanted it go, precisely with the force he intended.

Everyone had finally retreated from the wall to safe corners of the room. The spike on that boom arm seemed to have taken on a life of its own, slithering like a well-oiled snake. The machine continued hammering and banging! The vibration rattled the whole room with plaster continually flying and falling off the wall. The students broke out of the spell they were under, forgot all about punishments and so forth, and cheered!

They stood back out of the way, clapped their hands, and whooped and hollered as the spike incessantly broke through the wall. Again and again, the machine pounded, knocking brick, plaster, dust, and lead-based paint chips all over the room. Everything was coated with dust. Everything on the walls was rattling loose. Books fell from their shelves.

Teachers in other classrooms finally took notice of the racket, and after commanding their students to stay in their seats at full attention, they rushed through the corridors to Whipshot's room. A couple of them actually collided in the hallway, knocking one another down. The whole building seemed to shudder with Castlethorn's breaking through the wall. The commotion and panic came to a head with the arrival of more people. Teachers were holding their ears, shouting orders for the children in other classrooms to sit down, sit still, stop that infernal cheering, and so on. The teacher's efforts went unheeded as the students celebrated.

The teachers did not dare try to come into Miss Whipshot's room, and none could understand what this was all about. One reckless teacher pulled out his beating switch, and convincing himself that he was brave, decided that he would restore order here. He pressed forward through the crowd and crossed the threshold determined to restore order...until he caught sight of Whipshot stuck in the floorboards! He put his hand over his mouth as though he were about to be sick, forgot about settling the disruption, and ran from the room! He gathered the other teachers around him, and when he hurriedly explained what he saw, *all* the teachers crowded into the room to watch the spectacle.

The pounding noise continued rhythmically. *Blam! Blam! Wham! Wham! Bam!* Then finally, with one more solid thrust, the spike broke through a final time and made the perfect hole! *Ker-wham!* Brick and mortar, plaster and paint, all came tumbling down. The spike had done its job, finally. Mission accomplished!

Jimmy was fascinated at how smoothly this machine, by all appearances a piece of junk, could operate. The mechanical boom seemed to dance and slither with life, more a living creature than a machine. The operator was still wearing the leather cap, apron, and the flying goggles. He looked ridiculous, but the lenses were pitted, and the leather was marred by bits of brick. The lower part of his face was covered by that shop rag, like a cowboy's bandanna. It was coated with dust that was becoming muddy from the moisture of Castlethorn's breathing. Ridiculous as he appeared, the old man was well-protected. Jimmy was pretty certain that the old engineer was smiling under there too!

Jimmy had suddenly developed some kind of respect for this weird smelly man. He could not put his finger on it, but something was turning in the back of his mind, something that just seemed odd about Castlethorn's abilities in spite of his weirdness. Something just would not add up; something was amiss. The shop, this wondrous machine...the slide rule...the lantern...the old black tooth and the cackling ritual with the rotating of the lantern. What did all of it mean? What could come of it all if you considered all the elements of the problem? None of it made sense, and yet it seemed to make perfect sense. How could such things add up and make perfect sense when none of it was sensible? Perhaps Jimmy's human intuition was speaking to him.

Miss Coffenayle and all the students were huddled to the corners of the room like frightened hens in a lightning storm. A few teachers were getting up off the floor, the rest of them huddled on the other side of the room. The students could scarcely conceal their squeals of fear, delight, and just plain excitement every time that spike punched the wall. No one even thought of covering the teacher with anything! Concrete dust coated poor Miss Whipshot's hair and face while fist-sized chunks of rubble landed and slid across the floor, bouncing off of the broken boards. The barrier of broken wood provided her some protection, unintended as it was.

Whipshot was beginning to stir with the commotion of the machine breaking through the wall and the teachers joining the students. She made some muffled noises and broken snoring sounds as she began to awaken. Her eyes blinked, and her head rolled. She finally shook her head quickly back and forth like she was trying to shake a squirrel out of her hair. She took a look around her, sat there for a moment, wide-eyed with her mouth moving, but no words came out. She looked like a bloated carp out of water, her arms beginning to move like fins. She struggled for a moment, looked around again, and suddenly realized that her feet were not touching the floor! She realized that she was stuck *inside* the floor, unable to move, definitely in danger…and helpless! Then the real pandemonium began!

"Get me out! Get me out! Get me out, get me out, get me out! *Get me out of heeeeeere!*" she screamed. She began shrieking and twisting and pulling against the broken boards in a blind panic, like a rat in a trap. "*Ahhhhh!*" she screamed some more.

Finally, one of the teachers attempted to calm her, but the struggling carp used her fin to claw his face for all his trouble. She did not want to be calm! She wanted *out!* The teacher retreated, looked back at her before he left, pouted, and then sulked away to his own classroom where he could do some good. He slammed the door and started yelling at his students to get back to their desks.

Suddenly, Margaret came to Miss Whipshot's rescue. She left Miss Coffenayle's side and retrieved a cupcake out of the teacher's snack drawer. Raiding Whipshot's snacks was something that no one else would have dared do, even under these circumstances. Margaret was not sure of what Whipshot would do about it either, but anything was better than listening to her bellow. The students were on one side of the room, the teachers on the other. Some people, teachers and students alike, were sniggering and saying humorous things among themselves as Margaret carefully approached Whipshot with a cupcake. The tension in the room was incredible. Miss Coffenayle just stared, watching the scene play out.

Margaret eased toward her teacher with the treat on a flat extended palm as carefully as one might approach a trapped wild animal. Whipshot caught sight of Margaret, started to yell about why the little idiotic, warty-toad, rat-brat child wasn't helping her, and then she saw the cupcake! Its swirl of factory-made lard-based frosting glittering with colored sugar…the green kind…her favorite… and she immediately became entranced. She stopped flailing her arms and yelling, her face relaxed, and she may have even smiled just a bit, dreamy eyes transfixed on that scrumptious treat.

"Just the way you like it," said Margaret gently and with a smile, the perfect hostess serving a needy guest. Margaret knelt down and provided a cloth from the chalkboard, tucking it dutifully into the teacher's collar, drool appearing at the corners of Whipshot's now-silent mouth. Her eyes were focused on the cupcake, wide and mesmerized. Her mouth was half open, and she appeared to be in a stupor.

Margaret was secretly disgusted, nothing new for her, and she covered her revulsion well. She held the delectable goodie just six inches from Whipshot's nose. The teacher now looked perfectly ridiculous. Sweat and the dust turned to a gray soup that dripped off of her face. Her eyes were riveted on the treat as though she had fallen love. In fact, some joker began whistling "The Love Nest" by John Steel. Laughter gently rippled through the room, and people began making informal bets for pocket change that that teacher would suddenly explode in rage at any given moment. They would soon be disappointed.

The sweating, panicked, angry teacher suddenly changed. "Come closer, child," she cooed. Reluctantly and carefully, Margaret inched forward with the cupcake and pressed it to her teacher's lips. Whipshot's arms were no longer flailing at her sides. Instead, she was as relaxed as a sunbather on a warm beach in Bermuda. She opened her mouth and took a large bite of the thick rich frosting first, and then she mouthed it for a moment, savoring every creamy bit of it. The frosting was all over her mouth now, but she did not care.

The sound of pocket change clinking into hands resounded from the teachers' side of the room, losers muttering something about "penny poker night" as they slowly began to leave the scene. The interesting part of the show was over as far as they were concerned. They would have stayed around just a little longer, but they had their classes to attend to, and many of them were sulking over lost dimes, nickels, and pennies while others hollered, laughed, and harassed losers all the way down the hall. They carried on as though they had won a fortune!

This was the most interesting thing they had seen in years, some said. No one really noticed Miss Coffenayle in all the excitement. The principal made note of that too. And when did they get money to start *gambling* anyway? They were not even paid salaries!

The halls were already echoing with questions to the teachers who immediately slammed doors, banged rulers, and kicked wastebaskets to restore order to their classrooms. The teachers also promptly squashed "silly rumors" about a strange machine being pushed down the hall by some students and the janitor. After all, everyone knew that Castlethorn hated the students! So why would he try to work with any of them? "Forget the stupid rumors, you lazy toads, and get back to work!"

There was no point in allowing a disturbance to start among the pupils. The teachers had their fun and actually considered bringing all the kids a few at time to watch. They decided against it as they realized that so many kids witnessing this could quickly get out of hand. The teachers decided to instead return to their classes, suspend all hall passes for any reason, and kept their classroom doors shut tight. They resumed business as usual, and the students had no choice but to follow.

The students returned to work in spite of their knowing that something big was happening. They did not know just what, but they knew that something had seriously disrupted Miss Whipshot's classroom. This was entirely unheard of. Whipshot was always in control of her students. So whatever was going on, it must have been incredible! They truly had no idea how incredible things would soon become. For now, it was just to be business as usual. The talk in the student dorm would be interesting tonight! Unfortunately, though, teachers planned to have security there to shut down the talk before it got out of hand.

Most of the teachers secretly believed that Whipshot got her just desserts today. She was ridiculously mean, even by their standards. She was Miss Coffenayle's favorite, and her outrageous meanness was probably why. The teachers would have some long conversations tonight after the students were put to bed. The subject of particular interest would be not Whipshot so much but *Castlethorn*. This was the longest they had seen him out of that crazy, sickening "office" of his.

They knew that he categorically despised all students, and yet they saw him working alongside of several of them. And what of that nutty machine? It had to be his...but how could a slobbering and inept clod construct and then operate such a wondrous device? Indeed, they would have much to talk about over their poker game and school-approved tea. A few of them sometimes "spiced up" their tea with some homemade grayish liquor they called "liquid smoke" that was made in a teacher's bathtub. He soaked wood boards in the tub and then fermented the water.

The users knew better than to take too much of the "smoke." It was rumored that people sometimes lost use of their limbs or became "cotton-eye blind" from it. Not that the teachers' bodies were in perfect shape...the "tea-spicers" all believed they had little left to lose anyway. Misery was a way of life. Twisted limbs, bent spines, foggy minds. They often wondered how they had come to such a state. If they wondered about it too much, the headaches would start. So they simply accepted their lot in life as it stood. A dreary existence, indeed.

Back in the classroom, Margaret was feeding Whipshot another cupcake. Miss Coffenayle had joined the student to stand beside her favorite educator. The trapped teacher never even noticed her boss. Jimmy was outside with the janitor, both of them peering through the near-perfect hole Castlethorn's wondrous machine had made through the brick, plaster, and paint.

Emily took upon herself to oversee the room, making sure that everyone was in their seats, being quiet. She also made certain that no one was jumping out of turn to use the restroom. All the excitement made such trips necessary, and the teachers would not pay attention to students in the hall, things being as they were. Order was being maintained but under a much kinder hand than that which normally prevailed over this classroom.

With the students sitting quietly again at their desks, the only sounds in the room were Jimmy and Castlethorn tinkering with the tractor. Oh, and the disgusting grunts, slurping, and expressions of delight coming from their teacher. Emily could tell that Margaret was growing tired of this game, but she dared not stop playing it. Emily had gathered a stack of books for Margaret to sit on to give her knees a break. Emily noticed that Margaret's kneecaps were red and pockmarked from all of the plaster and paint chips scattered all over the floor. Miss Coffenayle watched very closely. Emily nodded in a respectful way toward the principal. What a cool collected young lady she was!

Outside, the old janitor and his new reluctant assistant peered through the hole in the wall. Emily noticed that Jimmy was now wearing goggles similar to Castlethorn's but with clear lenses. His hair was turning gray with dust, his face stained with muddy sweat. Castlethorn found Jimmy a *clean* shop rag to wipe his own face. He then donned the rag over his face, below his goggles, in the image of Castlethorn. The laboring sweaty pair could clearly see the mess they were making, but it could not be helped, and the project was progressing beautifully. The thought of calling the authorities for assistance had never even occurred to anyone. The school was isolated and completely self-contained, even producing most of its own food.

HVVS also had their own infirmary, should anyone have taken ill, complete with a registered nurse that the students nicknamed "Nurse Nightshade." There was no need to call for help, according to Principal Coffenayle's policies. This was "because the school had everything right here on campus that the staff, faculty, and students could ever need." This was the mode of operation that the school and its faculty were forced to live under. So engrained was this mentality that solving this problem by knocking a hole through the wall of the school seemed to be a natural thing to do. This move was for the teacher's survival, and since they had no one to call upon to bring better gear and machinery, it became the *necessary* thing to do.

It was a good thing that the hole was perfect. Castlethorn was bored with pounding on the wall, and the people inside had enough of the racket. The boom could now be cranked into position and extended by hand. An ingenious series of well-lubricated cables and crank wheels, gears, and pulleys saw to that. Castlethorn released the students from stoking the coal, so they had gone inside to wash up. Emily sent the kids immediately to the bathroom with orders to "not touch *anything*" on the way there. Their hands were black and their clothes and faces were sooty, like London chimney sweeps. Emily had read about them during her studies in English literature. She also told the boys to get out of those *filthy* clothes as soon as possible. "*But wash those nasty hands first!*"

Miss Coffenayle nodded her approval as Emily looked in her direction while she gave orders. Emily thought that the principal would take control away from her and assume the lead. Instead, Miss Coffenayle remained silent and nodded her approval if Emily looked to her for anything. It was strange. To Emily, it seemed as though Miss Coffenayle was pondering something unthinkable.

Jimmy assisted Castlethorn in positioning the boom and hand-cranking it into position by the series of wheels that were installed along the boom. They ran the boom precisely through the center of the hole in the wall, the wondrous machine running with uncanny precision. The boom smoothly extended toward Margaret and the teacher. Emily actually had to warn Margaret to get out of the way, so smooth and quiet was the extension of the big metal bar. Whipshot tried to protest Margaret's leaving her; there was still a piece cupcake in Margaret's hand. Whipshot's mouth was already quite full and getting dry, so it was hard to understand what she actually said. Her body language and facial expressions made it quite clear that she was telling Margaret to come back with the food.

Whipshot, already compromised of dignity, now looked just plain *ridiculous*. She had drool, green frosting, and matching sugar sprinkles covering her face. There were white cake crumbs all over her dress and entangled into her matted hair. She was so excited about the cupcake that she did not see the boom until Margaret suddenly moved. The big iron bar was now resting squarely over her head. She instantly blew cupcake all over the place, clearing her mouth to release howls of protest! She would have started the neighborhood dogs to barking if the school was in a neighborhood. Margaret managed to duck low and put the final piece of the cupcake into Whipshot's mouth to silence her. The teacher could not resist. She would not waste more cake. She chewed quietly, anger seething in her eyes.

Castlethorn positioned the boom, its pulley hovering over the teacher. Whipshot began to calm down as Emily and Margaret explained to her that this was a machine designed to get her out of the hole. Old Castlethorn lit down off the machine and reentered the classroom. He made another spectacle of himself with his clucking lantern trick. Everyone was used to it by now and was glad that he announced again that "dey is all hoomin," whatever that meant, and went back to work. Everyone just continued being quiet. A couple of students had dozed off.

The old janitor's air began getting to some of the students who began to cover their noses with their shirts and blouses. He moved through the room, carrying his lantern. He had slung over his shoulder what looked like a tangle of long black spaghetti. Whipshot eyed him suspiciously, and he stopped to make eye contact with her. They locked gazes, and Castlethorn's long oily locks and stubbly chin were completely frozen in time.

His eyes were wide open and seemed too big for his narrow face. His mouth was drawn downward, almost in a mock frown, but with playful dignity as though he were gloating. Whipshot glared back at him with her narrow wicked eyes, begrudgingly reading his expression. Her mouth was moving up and down, smacking her lips defiantly as her tongue found errant cupcake crumbs wandering near her mouth. One could have cut the tension in the air with a knife, if there were one to be had.

"Well?" she asked, breaking the thick silence. She had the look of complete defeat on her messy face; defeat and desperation lined her sullen features. It seemed as though she expected him to end her misery with the blow of a club or something. She had her last meal and was simply resigned to whatever tortures he had in mind. "What happens now?"

Miss Coffenayle had completely backed out of the whole situation and stood by quietly. She wanted to see how this would all play out. Curiosity overwhelmed any feeling she had of wishing to control this whole situation.

Castlethorn never said a word; he just continued scowling and dropped his snaky bundle at his feet suddenly. His demeanor was of one who was about to tie her to a burning stake. Silently, but with surprising gentleness and speed, he trussed up the teacher in a network of bungee-style elastic cords and hemp ropes that he tied off in a ring that dangled from the head of the boom. Now the teacher's arms were bunched inward toward her body's core, bent at the elbows. Castlethorn left her side and returned to his machine. Jimmy stood ready at his levers; he appeared grim and determined. The boy knew that this was "it."

Before the machine could start pulling on her, Whipshot begged Margaret for another lick of cupcake frosting as though it were a last request. Margaret fetched a fresh cupcake of the same type and obliged her with a certain funereal air. Emily held her breath, unsure of what may happen next.

The entire class now was out of their seats again, crowding as closely as they dared, all jockeying for position. They did not want to miss one tidbit of this fantastical show. Someone inappropriately joked about getting Whipshot's cupcakes should she die now. The student was shushed down by his fellows, and he immediately regretted what he said. No one wanted to see the mean old woman die, no matter how much they despised her. She was, no matter how mean, their teacher, and that alone deserved some form of respect. They were good kids, after all.

Castlethorn had retreated immediately to his machine, muttering to himself in apparent concentration. Emily noticed that he was walking more upright, his limp nearly gone. She also thought she heard him muttering some mathematical terms, but she could not be certain under these strenuous circumstances. This was yet something else that Emily put her mental curiosity file. Where the old man was concerned, things were just not adding up.

Slowly and carefully, with grave determination, Castlethorn, more engineer than janitor, turned his crank wheels along the boom. He carefully raised the webbing that was wrapped around Whipshot.

When he was satisfied that all the slack had been taken up, he went back outside. He called Jimmy away from the levers to come and stoke the furnace. He would need the engine running powerfully for this one, that was certain.

As soon as she heard that steam engine backfire and come popping back to life, Whipshot went completely nuts! She was hollering and screaming, calling down plagues of frogs and biting flies upon Castlethorn and his family for generations! She was creating foul graphic curses of peeling skin and rotting eyeballs that would make a gypsy fortune-teller take notes!

The crane went to work and pulled her obese form against the boards to wrench her free. She shouted and screamed in agony but did budge. Jimmy now acted as the lookout for Castlethorn and advised him to ease up, lower the boom, and try again. As she was lowered, she became quiet and was gasping for air, her glasses having fallen completely off.

They tried again, and the entire class was grimacing along with the teacher. She was howling out of pain, rage, and embarrassment! Just as she was calling on the Four Horsemen to trample the janitor's bones into mush, Jimmy gave the signal to back down. He went into the classroom to examine the boards, and the janitor followed him, leaving students to hold their noses in his wake. Jimmy pointed out that the boards were crosswise of each other, forming a latticework and pinning the teacher in such a manner that made pulling her out impossible.

Some of the boards below the floor would have to be removed. The only way to do that was from below. Castlethorn said that someone would have to enter the crawl space between the levels of the school. The space was just high enough for a full-grown man to walk if slightly hunched over. Jimmy would likely be just fine to walk upright. Unfortunately for Jimmy, he was the only logical choice to actually do it. The girls were busy consoling the teacher. The janitor had to run the machine. The other students who were willing to help were only able to put coal in the machine. They would not brave the crawlspace, especially not with the teacher's lower half dangling into it.

Rather than try to argue, which would have been pointless anyway, Jimmy followed Castlethorn back to the Engineering Office. The office was once frightening to him but was now becoming old hat. There was a door similar to a root cellar's that was marked in peeling red paint "*Emurjencee Ownlee*." The old custodian pulled out his huge iron key ring, a legend throughout the school, and, with surprising dexterity, unlocked the large antique padlock and lifted the door.

He told Jimmy to go to the bottom of the steps and turn left and just keep walking until he saw the teacher's legs. Then he handed Jimmy an oil lantern, a crowbar, and a few matches. After the lantern was lit, Jimmy gave a nervously shaking thumbs up. Castlethorn gave the boy a lingering glance, then he shut the door, securing its lock. "Ye's kin never beese too careful with seecuritees dese days," he muttered to himself. As though anyone else actually *wanted* anything down there. He replaced the iron key ring to his waist under his coveralls. Then he quickly headed to back to the classroom as quickly as his crooked body would allow.

Jimmy was afraid at first of rats or other critters, but none were to be found. A few small bones were all that was left of any *Rodentia*. It was spooky and yet exciting to be in the crawl space where no student had ever been before. He followed the janitor's directions and soon found an obese pair of legs wearing some very familiar bloomers kicking furiously. Jimmy took the crowbar that Castlethorn had given him and shouted that he was just below the teacher and would start prying boards. He heard the janitor day that would be "jist da ting ta do," and Jimmy set his lantern down to begin his work. He suddenly noticed a faint but putrid odor in the air. Then there was this strange crackling sound, but he thought nothing of it. After all, this had been a day for odd sounds and odors. It was probably the machine upstairs.

Jimmy used his hands to pull at a couple of boards, breaking them loose, but then the lantern went out. Annoyed, Jimmy dropped what he was doing, and Castlethorn asked if he was okay. Jimmy said he was fine, that he was going to relight the lantern. Just as he found a match, Whipshot started struggling and groaning. Jimmy was standing quite close to Whipshot's flailing legs. He was trying to stay out of her way, which was frustrating because he was also trying to use the scattered light from the hole in the floor to see how to start the lantern. Suddenly, another crackling sound ensued, longer and louder with an immediate odor that Jimmy recognized an instant too late after he struck the match, and... *ker-whumph!*

A ribbon of flame about four feet long emitted from the seat of Miss Whipshot's bloomers and nearly caught Jimmy's hair on fire! Luckily, he was wearing his goggles and shop rag; he recognized his peril immediately and ducked at the last possible instant! His covered face felt only mild heat from the dart of fire. He was not damaged or in flames, but the struggling bloomers were, and Jimmy patted them out. Whipshot screamed bloody murder, like she was being torched during the Salem Witch Trials!

The entire class of kids witnessed this huge spark emit through the cracks in the floorboards, puffs of foul green smoke following, and they were certain that Jimmy was a goner! Actually, the whole thing was over as quickly as it began, Jimmy none the worse for the wear. He coughed only a little and was fine again. The odor had completely dissipated. Thank goodness!

At first, Castlethorn could not fathom what on earth had just happened! "Be yese all raht, boy?" he hollered out loud with concern in his voice. Then it suddenly occurred to him what happened, and he and Jimmy started laughing violently! Jimmy said through his own laughter that he was fine and he would not tell anyone what happened if Castlethorn wouldn't! They started laughing together, and Whipshot started yelling at the two of them to stop, that it was not funny, and so on. The crowd had no idea what had just transpired.

Jimmy pulled a couple of more boards loose without further incident and announced that there were no more boards blocking the teacher's legs. Castlethorn used the machine to try and pull her out, without success, but with lots more curses from Whipshot. All the while, she screamed at him to get her out of the floor or suffer the wrath and blah, blah, blah!

In the meantime, Jimmy had returned from the crawlspace. He had to use the crowbar to force the door open since it had been padlocked. Castlethorn would have to fix that later. The boy's face was deeply reddened from his experience. None of the redness was from burns, though, and it quickly cleared up when he wasn't thinking of the flaming event. From that moment on, he *would* redden and start laughing every time he thought of those flaming bloomers as he would for years. Seeing her fall off that broken chair in the classroom is one thing, but that whole experience in the crawlspace was just too much!

Having composed himself on his way back, Jimmy reported to Mr. Castlethorn that he had removed all of the boards that he could. He really could not understand why they were having such a hard time with pulling her loose. The janitor stroked his stubbly chin for a moment and thought it over. Then he spoke slowly, hesitating to suggest a new plan because it would be so risky. They would have to reduce the friction on the boards that were holding the teacher in place. They had released all the tension that they could, and the only thing left was to make the boards slick so that she could slip out from between them. Jimmy thought for sure that they would have to go back into that creepy engineering room, looking for some strange lubricant, but Castlethorn had a completely different idea. After Jimmy heard what the plan was, he would have preferred a trip to the engineering office.

Miss Coffenayle stood by, watching patiently. Even she was shaking her head at the insanity of it all. You just could not make this stuff up!

5

Meeting Miss Ladlepot and Goliath

Standing in front of the swinging double-door entrance to the cafeteria kitchen, Jimmy felt a shudder pass through his body. "Steadees, boy," said Castlethorn softly out of the side of his mouth. Jimmy calmed his nerves and tried to look brave. He glanced over at the old man and saw this strange grim expression and a certain erectness to his crooked spine. It seemed as though he had resigned himself to almost certain death! It appeared as though this mission to obtain lubricants was very dangerous indeed. Jimmy could only guess at the horrors that awaited them. He could not imagine what made the old janitor so nervous. After all, what could be worse than Castlethorn's office?

"Um, Mr. C-Castlethorn?" Jimmy asked with great hesitance. "Couldn't we just fetch some oil or grease out of your office? You must have something there that would work."

"Aye, boy," the tight-lipped man replied, "I've grease and oil a-plenty, but nothins' that would works for us. Ye see, boy," he explained patiently in a near-whisper, "petroleum-based machine oils and lubricantsess bese plenty slicks and would loosen her up, but most are toxic...poy-son-us, that is...to hoomin beans. We coulds slicker her up all raht, but then heer skin wuld absorb too muches poy-son from the lube job, and she would be horribly sick. As you probably guess, a sickees Whipshot is nots a pretty saht. Ah'd sooner break off'n de toof on a momma grizzly and fahts herz on the spot than to make a Whipshot sickees."

Jimmy nodded and quietly agreed. He would not want her to be sick either, and he knew full well that she would never take a day off work. She loved her job too much. Her "discipline" would probably be even worse if Miss Whipshot became ill! Jimmy then sided with Mr. Castlethorn in this thing, let come what may. Looking back at the kitchen's swinging entry doors, there was an eerie green glow coming through the small smudged windows.

The pair hesitated, looked at each other, and moved forward. Both were carrying a bucket in each hand, the lantern in one of Castlethorn's buckets. He never wanted to be without it, if possible. The janitor made the first move, carefully and slowly pushing open the door, trying to slip in unnoticed. After looking around a bit, he motioned for Jimmy to come in behind him. Jimmy hesitated, swallowed hard, and followed his new ally through the door.

Once they entered the kitchen area, they both saw what the cause of the green glow was. The kitchen was dimly lit. The walls of the kitchen were painted medical green, and the steam was so thick that what light did get through was tinted with that strange eerie hue. There were huge pots on the stovetops, large pressure cookers, and strange machines with temperature and pressure gauges on them that defied explanation. There were several dented tables, noticed Jimmy, with bits of raw meat and bone littering them. Some of the dents actually looked like cuts in the metal.

The smell of the room was hot and wet. Strange odors seemed to be the topic of the day for poor Jimmy, but...what an adventure it had been, he quietly thought to himself. The intrepid pair made their way through the steam, looking for something, but Jimmy did not know *what*.

Mr. Castlethorn knew very well what they were looking for. They were looking for the walk-in refrigerator where she kept her lard, which would be on the other side of the kitchen. They had to make their way through the labyrinth of strange cooking machines to some hopefully cleaner air. Castlethorn hoped they could make it through this reconnaissance without encountering...*her*. He really wanted her to be on a break or anywhere but in the kitchen. Their last meeting had been very unpleasant. Meetings with her were *always* very unpleasant. There were not many people who could make Castlethorn nervous, but she could.

Miss Ladlepot, the Cafeteria Lady, was the meanest of them all, even worse than Whipshot! Castlethorn or no, *she did not care who you were if you were in her kitchen!*

The pair crept along in near complete silence. The only sound from them was the occasional rattle of a galvanized pail. Jimmy stayed close behind Mr. Castlethorn who seemed to know where he was going. After all, he should, because unbeknownst to Jimmy, he invented and built many of the steaming pressure cookers and deep fryers that were busily churning and burning to turn out today's dinner menu.

The steam and heat gave way to clearer air after a few minutes, and Jimmy could see better, but he wished that he was back in the steam because the moisture and heat overloaded his sense of smell. In the steam, he could not smell the horrid stench of nameless concoctions that the cafeteria served up. All of them were fried, greasy, and equally offensive to the palette. The steam from the school's tea-making machines was comparatively pleasant.

The foods created here were definitely an "acquired taste," reflected Jimmy as they reached a steel door with a big handle on it. The huge padlock was unfastened and hanging loosely in the hasp, making things easier. Not that it would have mattered. The janitor/engineer had keys to every lock in the building. Jimmy could not figure out, though, why they were being so careful in the apparently abandoned kitchen.

Suddenly, he found out. Castlethorn opened the door, and this large beastly looking man looked up and glared at them, a huge long-handled meat cleaver held by both of his hands. His apron was stained pink with whatever he had been chopping up. He raised the cleaver threateningly.

Castlethorn froze. Jimmy froze too in more ways than one. It was cold in that walk-in refrigerator.

"Eeeeasy, Goliath," said the custodian with less confidence than Jimmy would have liked. "Wese be friends."

The brutish man stood silent. He was nearly seven feet tall and rather wide across the shoulders. His arms were well-endowed with rippling muscles, but he had a large round belly. He wore under his apron a simple but large t-shirt that used to be white. Now it was stained with sweat, dirt, cooking oil, and that same pink tinge that was all over the apron. He had a thick crop of bushy black hair, full beard to match. He opened his mouth slightly into what might have been a grin, had he not appeared so imposing. His teeth were little more than ground-off stubs, and they were stained yellow-brown. He grunted in reply to the engineer's statement of friendship and lowered the meat cleaver to a less imposing posture.

"Now, Goliath," started Castlethorn gently, "youse an' mees... wese be known each other for looong times now. Wese be friends... and Jimmy and me...wese just cames for some lard, Goliath. You knows da lard? Where's it bee, Goliath? Is the lards in dis liddle room wi'chu?"

Before the giant could respond, something clanged against the wall of the walk-in and clattered onto the floor. The janitor dropped flat and covered his head while a startled Jimmy dropped his buckets and did the same. "Stay down, boy," whispered the old man. "She seen us and she is a deadeye with them ladles of hers." The "she" referred to, Jimmy knew, was Miss Ladlepot, the legendary Cafeteria Lady. He had heard all the rumors about the mysterious cook who never came out of the kitchen, of how no student ever survived a visit to her domain. Jimmy doubted that last point...until now. He had his head covered with his arms and just barely dared to peek at the object on the floor. Yep, it was a soup ladle, a big one, stained brown-orange with grease baked in at high temperatures. Goliath had stopped his incessant hacking at the cutting board and laughed out loud.

"I done tol' yu ta stay out mah kitchen!" shouted a slight red-haired woman. Jimmy could see her coming out of the mist of the steamers, and she had several more ladles in one hand, the other hand poised to throw a second soup-missile at the trespassers.

"Blast you, Mizz Ladlepot!" shouted the custodian as he reached into one of his buckets, hand on his lantern for security. He had his weapons too, you know. He still was not quite sure if Miss Ladlepot was "hoomin" or not, but he opted to not tempt fate.

Goliath stood mutely now, smiling.

"Wese jist need a little grease. Wese has an emur-juncee!"

"I dassn't care! You stay out mah kitchen! An' whose dis wit yu? A *stoodint?* In mah kitchen?? Ain't never no stoodint in *mah kitchen!*" She was looking for a bigger ladle or frying pan or something, probably to clobber the student and then the janitor for bringing him.

"Listen here, Miss Ladlepot! The teacher Whipshot dun falled throughs da floor and gotses stuck! We needs da grease tuh gets her out!" The janitor and his young partner ducked again as another two ladles came flying with unerring precision. They heard Goliath chuckle in the background, a deep throaty sound that unsettled Jimmy greatly. He did not know who to be the most afraid of: the ladle-wielding maniac or the meat-cleaving maniac. He opted for the ladle maniac because she was the only one attacking them so far. He kept half an eye on Goliath too who seemed to basically stand motionless, taking it all in and enjoying the show.

"I nebber lahked her anyhow!" shouted Miss Ladlepot.

She was close enough now for Jimmy to have a good look at her, and he was sorry that he did. So this was Miss Ladlepot, the Cafeteria Lady of legend! She stood just over five feet tall with a customary food worker cap on her head. She had a ratty haystack of tightly curled orange-red unevenly tinted hair, like a home-done permanent with a poor dye job. She wore eye shadow that was far too blue and applied with far too much liberality. Her wrinkled brow drew attention to eyebrows that looked like they were drawn on by black magic marker. Her hawk-beak nose rose prominently over a tight-lipped mouth that had way too much, too red lipstick. The red thick stuff stained the butt of the hand-rolled cigarette that rode tightly in her pursed lips. Her face was wrinkled with stress lines, frown lines, and crow's feet; her facial skin actually seemed to be too tight on her skull. Her jaw stuck out in defiance as she prepared to hurl another ladle.

Jimmy saw her knobby elbows and her twisted fingers, bent with arthritis, wrapped around that ladle handle, and wondered how she could move her hands at all. Around her neck on a chain was a pair of what appeared to be glasses, possibly for reading. They had not been cleaned in some time. Her soiled pink uniform with short sleeves and knee-length skirt was covered by a small mostly-white apron that allowed white support stockings to show. They were sheer enough that the duo, huddling in the refrigerator, could see shadows of varicose veins! Her soft-soled improvised nonslip shoes, which she had hand-soled with highly gritty sandpaper, were badly in need of a good whiting over as the leather underneath was showing through.

"Bese reasona-babble, Miz Ladlepot! We jist need some lards and weel goes away. Dee students can't come to lunches with ye without deys teacher tuh let 'em go. Yese knows that!"

Miss Ladlepot stopped short, her arm halfway through another attempt to catapult a ladle she held in midair. She knew the old man was right. Her job was to nourish the students with the cheapest, most awful fare she could dream up. She did so enjoy watching their little faces curl up with that familiar retching. Not even one class should go unfed; she was the cafeteria lady, and that is what she did. She dumped her load of ladles on a countertop, still holding one, just in case, and motioned for the pair to come closer.

Goliath, no longer amused and now mildly disappointed, gave a sad grunt and resumed chopping and thumping on the furry side of who-knows-what animal with great relish. He was smiling as he hacked away. Bits of flesh and bone bounced off the table and littered the floor around him.

"Goliath always loves roadkill day," said Miss Ladlepot with a gleam in her squinted eye, nodding in the direction of her employee with great pride. "Well," she started with a softer tone to her voice. She let the remaining ladle clatter down onto a grimy steel countertop. "Let's git you boys some grease!" She smiled, and Jimmy desperately wished that she had not. Even her worst lunchtime scowl with that cigarette between her lips was better than that horrifying smile. Her remaining teeth were stained horribly with tobacco and who knows what other accesses. *Maybe she chewed it too,* mused Jimmy, nearly gagging out loud at the visual image of her spitting a tobacco plug into the food.

The "boys" slowly rose to their feet, and the move seemed to be painful to Castlethorn who got up slowly, almost staggering. Jimmy resisted the impulse to help the old man to his feet, sensing a pride in him. Jimmy somehow knew that the old man would have been severely offended had he made such a gesture in front of Miss Ladlepot. Once on his feet and steady, the janitor took the lead and followed Miss Ladlepot into parts unknown. She explained pleasantly that they had entered the incorrect walk-in, that she would never allow Goliath to chop meat in the same area where lard was being made.

The odors had subsided a bit as the food's cooking and processing was finishing up. The noise was increasing in the kitchen as steam whistled and hissed through the banging and a clanging of pots and pans. A worker hurried through the kitchen, tending to the muck that passed for food. He stopped to occasionally kill the errant cockroach or two by an old-fashioned stomping. *Squish!* He would also smash them bare-handed when the occasion called for it. They had a rolling bin under a counter full of stuff that killed roaches instantly upon contact. When a worker dropped some on a roach, it also killed the other roaches that scurried in to cannibalize it. The bug powder bin was marked with a plain white label, skull and crossbones drawn on it. The lid was comparably adorned. That was the *only* difference between the pesticide bin and the bin of flour which had a plain white label and lid.

Jimmy shuddered at the possibility of someone accidentally using the roach killer in the food. He also realized that the staff members weren't washing their hands after killing bugs. He chose to keep all this to himself; no one else would ever know about the things he saw in this kitchen. The students had enough worries without concerns over botulism and accidental—or intentional—poisoning. On the bright side, thought Jimmy, at least they were being fed, and Miss Ladlepot, the legendary Cafeteria Lady, was enthusiastic about getting the—*ugh!*—food cooked.

The old knobby-kneed, support-hosed, yellow/brown-teethed sadistic old woman of legend led them past the mop sinks and dirty cooking pots. All of the pots were hung along a string of hooks and ready for use, clean or not. The group stopped at a sealed door. Miss Ladlepot disposed of her cigarette, stamping it out on the floor, reached for a cardboard box, and pulled out pairs of white linen and elastic booties. She handed them each a pair, bidding them to put them on immediately. Then she donned her own booties and a hairnet, handing them each a hairnet, signaling that they had to put it on. It was a little ball of netted mesh; Jimmy stared at for a moment in his palm, and Castlethorn held it up for inspection, looking at it like it was a dead rat.

Miss Ladlepot urged them to put on the hairnets and showed them how with a grin appearing at the corners of her mouth. It was almost like she was dressing them up in tuxedos and bowties in anticipation of some grand event. Excitement and wonder gleamed in her eye!

Jimmy wondered what would happen next, if maybe the dead student rumor was true after all. Then again, would she take the time put a hairnet on a student she was about kill and add to the broth? He decided that she had a prime opportunity to have him murdered back at the walk-in where the "butcher" was chopping meat; Jimmy wondered at the number of other places Goliath could chop meat. His tables were scattered everywhere; they probably allowed him to chop about anywhere he wanted, given his size and temperament.

Miss Ladlepot led the pair through the swinging door and into a room that was decked with green, white-grouted tile. Floor, walls, and ceiling were the same, and it gave the effect of walking into some kind of sterile cube. This small room was immaculate in contrast to the swill in the cooking area. These walls were clean, shiny, and slick with condensation. Moisture collected on the walls and the doors, but the floor was not slippery. There was a big machine in the middle of the room and several churning pipes led into it. Miss Ladlepot walked over to one of the spouts that stuck out of the humming grinding machine and placed a bucket under. A white creamy paste issued forth as she pulled at the handle, almost like a soft-serve ice-cream machine. This white paste was definitely not ice cream. It was too stark-white and too thick, almost solid.

Miss Ladlepot swirled the bucket as the thick cylinder of lard layered into it. She seemed to be very pleased with herself, calmly humming as she happily collected the goo. Jimmy was perplexed at the serenity on Miss Ladlepot's face. She seemed for those few moments to be in another place, another time, eyes growing almost dreamy, her pursed and overly colored lips almost spreading into a smile. After a couple of minutes, she stopped. She handed Castlethorn the bucket, and for a split instant, Jimmy saw that their eyes seemed to lock onto one another and light up, but then just as quickly, they resumed their normal hopelessness and dull pallor.

Jimmy and his new boss carried the buckets back to the classroom without incident. They were both very tired. Jimmy, though, could not forget that spark that passed between Ladlepot and Castlethorn. It was on his mind all the way back to the classroom.

6

Enter Miss Coffenayle

Miss Coffenayle had enough, finally. She understood that there was a plan, but this was going too far. Castlethorn and that Jimmy brat had been gone a long time. She arose from sitting at a student's vacant desk. She surveyed the hole in the wall and then Miss Whipshot's dilemma with her hands on her hips. *Disgusting!* She turned around and looked at the mess all over the floor. She could not *believe* all of this. She should have *immediately* taken control! She finally went to the door and hollered down the hallway, "Castlethorn! Castlethorn! I need you here *now!*"

"Yes, Miz Coffenayle?" responded Castlethorn from directly behind her.

She jumped. She did not even notice him for being focused on the horrific scene. This teacher, who was her favorite weapon, had been stuck in the shattered floorboards for long enough! Something must be done and right now!

"Well? What are you *doing* about this mess?" the principal asked her old janitor.

"Can'cha see, Mizz Coffenayle? Can't you seez da ropes and thee knots and da boom of the crane? Can't ye seez the bucket o' grease in muh hand? Dat Jimmy gots a couplez more too," Castlethorn retorted indignantly. He was looking her square in the eye.

Coffenayle looked at the janitor with a degree of surprise. She was not used to her staff addressing her so directly, so confidently.

She was used to terror in the eyes of her subordinates. There was no terror or even a trace of fear in Castlethorn's eyes. Not this time. It made her feel a bit uneasy, truth be told. Then again, truth was not her primary concern. She needed control! She raised a finger to him, but Castlethorn simply ignored her, turning his back, effectively cutting her off. She stood there in stunned silence. He was definitely a man on a mission. She would have to deal with his defiance later. Even she realized that he was the only hope for the situation to improve. She lowered her finger and stepped back, fuming a bit at her engineer's insolence.

"Weeeelll," started Castlethorn, teasing the students a bit, "whoseee gonna grease up their beloved teachur, hmmm?" He gave a sly grin, leaned forward, and picked up the pale of lard. He shook it like an auctioneer drawing attraction to item on the block. "Well? Whossit?"

Then *she* stepped forward. Naturally, it was to be her: Margaret. She was firm and resolute, but even so, her lip quivered and her eye twitched just a bit. That was enough for Castlethorn to realize the child's revulsion at the very thought. "Ye're a brave girl, lassie." The old janitor shook the bucket slightly, and Margaret took it in one hand. It was heavy enough to suddenly drop toward the floor, but she quickly caught the handle with the other hand, and did not drop it, thank heaven. The once-thick substance was already beginning to liquify.

"Allrighteeee, then," said Castlethorn as he donned his pair of ancient flying goggles with smoked lenses and leather cap. "Grease her up!"

Margaret then bent down, and with her face twisting into a grimace, she half-dragged, half-carried the bucket toward the bloated form with the ridiculous eyebrows and moustache. The cat's-eye glasses were back on her face, not quite straight, and her nose was making the most awful snoring noises. Her jowls answered like in kind, frothy, cake-colored drool running down her chin. Margaret knelt down beside the bucket that hit the ground with a clank, and she wrinkled her nose.

Miss Coffenayle recoiled in disgust at what she was seeing. She looked down and pretended to clean her well-manicured, perfectly shaped, and feminine fingernails. She actually had very attractive soft hands. She was not always this way. She was once a decent sort of lady. She was once trim and shapely, in good physical shape. Her hands were persistent evidence of that. Long ago, she had developed the habit of keeping her nails manicured and lovely.

As Whipshot snored away, she seemed mildly disturbed at the new activity around her. Margaret braced herself, took a deep breath, and slowly sank her bare hand into that bucket of whitish goo. She came up with a handful and nearly gagged at the sight and odor. She was thoroughly disgusted but knew that she had to carry out her assignment. She was the only one who would do this, and she really needed to look good to the principal right now.

The grease was changing color and was not nearly as firm as it was when it was pressed out of the machine. It seemed to break down at room temperature and was becoming very sloppy and yellowed. It seemed to be turning rancid, and not surprisingly, it was beginning to stink.

Margaret wrinkled her nose and turned her head. It smelled like roadkill, and there were some stray hairs beginning to poke out of it. Oh…my…was that a *tooth?* Margaret let the dental debris drip out of her hand. The grease had a thick core, but the very outer surface was slimy and dripped and splattered on the floor as she held it. She was unsure of what to do, unsure of where to start. She quickly decided on the back of Whipshot's neck. She had to move quickly before she lost control of the substance that was thinning all the more in her hand.

Castlethorn was busily preparing his machine and even taking a few furtive measurements with his slide rule which no one saw. Miss Coffenayle had regained control of herself and was standing with arms stoically folded across her chest, chin aloft, and mouth set firmly. She stared at the scene, occasionally nodding with approval as though she was the boss! She was the one running things, you see, but she had no clue as to what was really going on. The rest of the class had instinctively backed away from the whole mess and the stench of it. Margaret by now had thoroughly greased Whipshot's neck, shoulders, and halfway down her back.

But now, a new problem was developing. Whipshot had begun to awaken; *now* of all times! Her eyes blinked, and she started to turn her head. She was mumbling incoherently, something about "mentoring" and a "graveyard." She nearly regained full consciousness. Then Margaret, with her hands rubbing the nasty yellow-white lubricant on Whipshot's back, tried to console her through fits of near gagging. Fortunately, a quick-thinking student threw an especially thick-frosted cupcake, and it hit Whipshot in the face, showering poor Margaret with cake fragments. Enough got into Whipshot's open mouth to confound her, then console her, and finally put her right back to sleep when she swallowed enough of it. She was muttering about "mentoring" and "love." Odd thing that.

Miss Coffenayle wanted to blast the student for throwing a cupcake at his teacher, but she was too captivated by the events that were happening all once. Not only that, but she knew the boy had acted reasonably and with unerring aim. You just had to admire a shot like that! Besides, she was seeing and sensed a sort energetic rhythm about all of this, which was hard to be believe. The chaos in the room, she noticed, seemed to almost have its own organized life-function. She did not want to disrupt the harmony of all the players and activity around her. She felt that if she was to yell right now, the whole works might come tumbling down, and all the progress the class had made might be lost. They had to get Whipshot out of the floor, and she certainly did not want to interfere with that!

Margaret now moved the bucket around to the front. She stayed off to the side enough to avoid drool, soggy cake fragments, and the teacher's breath from showering her as she labored. Smearing and retching, wiping and gagging, Margaret worked and worked, the splinters of wood rasping against her fingers, wrists, and hands. Finally, a fine ring of yellowing nasty sloppy grease girdled the teacher. The students were shooed out of the way as Castlethorn attached a hook into a ring above Whipshot's head and pulled it tight. The ring drew together a web of straps that formed a sort of cocoon around her body.

Margaret moved the bucket out of the way, and everyone, including Miss Coffenayle, got as far back as they could. Then the principal, apparently feeling exposed, sat in a vacant chair and pulled a smaller child toward her as a human shield and held him fast, despite his squirming. Castlethorn eyeballed the harness and made a few last-second adjustments. He even threaded some extra ropes through the harness, forming a complicated web of straps, lashings, and crude knots.

Castlethorn then went outside to his machine with a few students and told everyone to stand clear! He turned a crank. Rusty gears turned with surprising ease, the machine began to sputter, then stopped. Castlethorn climbed off the driver's seat and made a few tinkering movements, then nodding satisfaction over one of the many gauges, he sat back down, redonned his elbow-length leather gloves, smoothed back his long oily locks, much like a peacock preening for a potential mate, and turned the crank again. This time, the sputter was more steady, and suddenly, the monster roared back to life! With all sorts of gizmos whizzing about and stirring in the air, the crane became a would-be savior to Miss Whipshot, torturer extraordinaire.

Castlethorn hopped back into the driver's seat, which was just a piece of saddle-shaped metal. The seat was bolted to a bar of spring steel, cannibalized from an old car's suspension. It was upholstered with a piece of thick tanned leather that was worn slick and shiny in some places, and it was eroded clear through in others. That seat apparently had been the recipient of many years of use by the same rear end, one belonging to a very thin man.

The main boom of the crane was extended to rest just above Whipshot's head. A smooth but oxidized chain, terminating with a large hook, was reattached to the crane's cable. The crane cable lowered the works just enough to do the job and halted. Castlethorn jumped off his jalopy. He ran back inside the building, to the classroom, and knelt down by Whipshot who was back snoring and salivating again. Her great jowls were flapping in sync with the awful snoring sounds. He was not really concerned about her waking up because he knew that if she could work her soggy arms loose enough to do anyone any harm, she would have already done it. Even if she did wake up, well, then Margaret would just have to feed her another gooey num-num and be done with it.

By now, with all the perspiration on Whipshot's brow, and the gooey frosting covering her mouth, the moustache, eyebrows, and "Wicked Witch" were now just dark smears running down her sweaty face. Even this deeply asleep, she appeared angry and miserable. She continued to snore and grumble, the sounds changing with the position of her head. Little Tom said he thought it would be keen to turn her head this way or that and try to play a song! He drew some nervous giggles.

Castlethorn went back outside and shouted an unnecessary warning for everyone to get back as he slid into his saddle. They were all as far back as they could be. The machine popped, ticked, and whined. It sputtered and belched steam and some black smoke from long-charred exhaust pipes. Castlethorn was the picture of delight and concentration. His expression was of that of a genius suppressing a grin when an expected breakthrough was about to happen! The numbers were right. The gauges were right. The knots, to the untrained eye, appeared to be random tangles...but Castlethorn knew the knots were right too.

He pulled a final lever, and the separate noises from the machine began to hum in synchronized perfection. The vibration decreased to a bare minimum. The students' and faculty's ears were relieved. They could almost converse normally over the hum, but no one uttered a word. Not for fear but for fascination. Even Miss Coffenayle was awed into silence.

The machine quietly and smoothly pulled the rope net tightly around its burden. An alert student seized the opportunity to shove another overly frosted cupcake into Whipshot's mouth, then backed out immediately. It was a good thing that hyper amounts of sugar acted as a sedative in the trapped teacher's world. Everyone wanted to keep her asleep throughout the whole procedure. It was hard to imagine what might happen if she woke up and started her craziness while all trussed up in ropes and harnesses.

The students outside remained at their safe distance. Castlethorn was satisfied when he snuck a peek, his head bobbing up and around, that all the students were clear. His main concern was to not complicate the project with unconscious or dead kids laying around. *We can't have any casualties in the way of getting Whipshot out of the floor.* The machine operator took a deep breath and released the handbrake on a big lever with a tight squeeze and a hard yank. The sound of ratcheting gears ground forth, and the crane began to strain at its new burden. Slowly, with a gentleness belied by the machine's crude appearance, the crane pulled at Whipshot.

Her head flopped back and forth with the natural rolling motions of pulling her out of the floor. Her glasses were a little crooked again but stayed on her face. She was otherwise oblivious to the noise and heaving and hauling motions the crane made. She was lurching back and forth, up and down, arms essentially pinned by the netting with her legs beneath the floor flopping about like a marionette on a string. She snored through the whole thing.

Emily thought this to be both humorous and tragic at the same time. She did not chuckle or even smile, both for the gravity of the situation and the principal being present. Miss Coffenayle, Emily noticed, had emerged from her seat, released another human shield, and her facial features were set in stone. She revealed to the world nothing of what she may have been feeling inside. How could someone be so jaded, stern, and hardened? Then the boards began to creak. Everyone held their breath.

Whipshot's rotund form began to pull free from the floorboards. The students were gasping and groaning at the sight, both repelled and enthralled by the spectacle. They were held captive by a moment that would engrain itself into their memories for rest of their lives. Margaret was now standing beside Emily, instinctively very close. Emily understood what Margaret must be going through right now, being the teacher's pet of the most horrible of human beings. Emily knew that while Margaret may have enjoyed some outward benefits, the poor girl was also terrified of Whipshot and her moods. That is one of the hazards of schmoozing dangerous people: though they keep you close as a trustee, they can turn on you at any time, and you never see the blow coming. Then they will throw you to the mercies of the people who hate you for what you did to them.

Then something *else* caught Emily's attention: some of the boards, the sharpest ones in particular, seemed to be *moving away from Whipshot's body on their own.* With no one there to help keep the boards clear, and with Castlethorn's focus being on the levers, gears, dials, and orderly chaos of deranged genius, there was considerable risk to Whipshot. As if under their own will, the sharp sticks never injured Miss Whipshot. Emily could not believe it! She saw that whenever a jagged point of wood seemed ready to impale the teacher's form, it was somehow knocked aside.

The principal and other students did not notice this, though. They were all so fascinated by Castlethorn's Pandora's Box of gears and pulleys that no one really paid attention to the splintering wooden boards. Emily tried to put this off as some kind of illusion. She rationalized that maybe some of the wood was banging against other boards, knocking them out of the way, but she knew better somehow. The splinters and jagged edges were just too conveniently pushed out of the way whenever they got near to ol' Whipshot. This made Emily think back to the fasteners that backed themselves out of the chair to trip up Whipshot's rampage. Normally, she would have been alarmed at such events; anyone would. Somehow, Emily was very calm about the whole thing, like something inside her was setting her at peace. She somehow knew that these things were happening for a reason.

This calming influence aside, the idea that something was afoot did not frighten Emily, not really. The idea of this school being, well, *haunted* did not surprise her. She did not understand, though, why Whipshot was harmed first and was now being protected. Emily thought a bit on this but then dismissed the whole idea of some unknown invisible force being at work here. The chair bolts she could not readily explain, but the boards, she was becoming sure, had some kind of explanation. They had to.

Emily's instincts believed that some ghost was here to protect the kids or vindicate them. Miss Whipshot was getting punished for her evildoings. However, her logical mind could not fathom that intelligent forces were actually causing this to happen. Something hurt Whipshot first but then protected her? That made no sense at all. Besides, thought Emily, she was getting too old to believe in campfire ghost stories, wasn't she?

The machine droned on, and Emily left her train of thought. It was far better to pay attention to the business at hand. This was not the time for daydreaming. Progress was being made, she noticed, and she realized that she needed to be fully engaged in the situation at hand.

The crane was stout and the machinery powerful. It hissed and churned, rattled and clattered about, parts whirring and spinning, and shots of vapor and steam sprang forth on occasion at regular intervals. The machine appeared old and rusty, but once Castlethorn got it warmed up and running effectively, it chugged along very efficiently and without a hitch. It was a pandemonium of cluttered order, one could say. That was the fascination of it. No one in the room thought that the machine would be able to run without falling apart, but look at it now!

It was an object, not of beauty so much, but one could call it "art" simply because it was created. There was no denying that it was a very creative machine, even if born of mad genius. It certainly held one's attention. Miss Whipshot now seemed to be cradled well enough, the boards seemed loose enough; now all that remained was the final act of pulling her out of the floorboards.

The crane pulled up, up, up, and the ropes and straps went fully taut. Then they began to tug gently at the form of Whipshot, which slowly edged its way out of the hole that kept her captive for so many hours. The grease made a mild sucking sound as her form slid smoothly against the boards. She was still in her sugar coma, floppy as a giant bag of gelatin. She slowly emerged from the floor, inch by inch, with Jimmy eyeing her and shouting instructions as Castlethorn carefully manipulated levers and valves. As soon as her feet were clear, with one shoe missing, a bare, pale bulbous foot dangling in the open with filthy claw-like toenails, Castlethorn started to sway the crane. He carried her to the side with gentle motions that seemed to convey a form of caring, just shy of actual concern for the teacher's well-being.

Whipshot's abundant flesh protruded in grotesque globs from between the harness and rope webbing that held in the air. Her ridiculous flowered dress seemed to be the only thing that kept her from actually dripping. She was snoring and making a ridiculous "*Snaawk!*" noise that offended the ears of the audience. Even Miss Coffenayle grimaced a tad, and some of the students gagged a mite. In the harness, they couldn't help but notice that she had wet her slightly charred bloomers, but the folds of frocked puffiness that defined her bloomers had kept her from dripping onto the floor. Thank goodness nothing worse had happened, despite the methane explosion that could have decapitated poor Jimmy!

All that aside, as slowly as the sun rises, she was extracted in all her glory from the floorboards. With a surprising gentleness, Castlethorn was able to swing the crane's heavyweight burden over the floor, away from the hole, and onto a stable suitable space left open by the students. The whole class was cautiously moving backwards while staring upward at the fleshy zeppelin being carried high off the floor. No one wanted to be in the way when this bundle came down…but then something went wrong! The machine began to list to one side. The straps were not holding the load evenly; some of the bread dough had shifted unexpectedly off-balance. The machine began to topple to the right!

Castlethorn furiously worked his levers, switches, and wheels in desperation! Despite his best efforts, he could not right the tractor. He needed more weight on the left side but did not have any ballast. Then he got a crazy idea, not his first today. "Kidses! Yoo stoodints! I needs youse to climb on da side of the tractor dat is liffing up!" yelled Castlethorn over the din of the machine.

The kids hesitated at first, but then Jimmy appeared and jumped up.

"Yahoo!" shouted Jimmy, as he hopped onto the tractor to steady it. "This is so much fun! I should make you guys pay for this!" He yelled and jumped and hollered, and it looked like so much fun! "Yahoo! Having a ball!" Others soon joined him, laughing and yelling, and after they had about ten kids, their combined weight forced the tractor back down ever so slowly. It seemed that Jimmy's study of *Tom Sawyer* had born some useful fruits after all.

"Steadies, stoodints, steadies!" shouted Castlethorn. Soon, everything was right, with the wheels touching the ground. Castlethorn then laid the hefty burden onto a safe place on the floor. Jimmy left the tractor and, peeking through the hole, gave precise direction to how to safely lower Miss Whipshot. Castlethorn was ever so slow, easy and gentle about it too. The expression on his face was one of great concentration and concern as he carefully moved the teacher. When they reached a safe spot, Miss Whipshot was lowered onto the floor with all the natural grace of a scavenger alighting upon a sun-bloated carcass. The buzzard has landed!

Emily noticed something new to add to her list of suspicious mental notes. It seemed as though one of Whipshot's ankles, which was about to turn inward at an awkward angle, *moved on its own.* At the last second, the ankle moved and was placed, seemingly with intention, in a position that allowed it to settle neatly on the floor. It laid down along with the rest of the sleeping teacher's great bulk, and nothing was twisted or broken.

At last, after what seemed like an eternity to most of the students, about four hours' worth, Miss Whipshot lay with her right side on the floor. She was snoring contentedly now and almost seemed peaceful.

Mr. Castlethorn lowered the boom sufficiently to allow for the ropes and harness to have some working slack to unhook the harness and loosen all the ropes. That way, nothing would drop on Whipshot's head. Then he came back inside to loosen the ropes and release the harness. He worked surprisingly fast; with one pull of a loose end, he zipped all the knots open at once. He had Whipshot out of the ropes and entanglements as though he was born to do that kind of work.

Even he, Emily noticed, seemed a bit amazed or even a little puzzled over how well he was able to do that chore. It seemed at some points in his work that he was listening to something or somehow was being guided. While creating the harness, she recalled, he would start work on a series of ropes, get stuck, and then he would cock his head a little bit and give a slight pause. Then he would just continue as though he knew exactly how to proceed.

Miss Coffenayle just appeared casually interested, looking things over as Castlethorn worked. She did not seem overly concerned and appeared to be growing bored with this whole situation. Margaret was watching closely too. Her thoughts were probably the most conflicted of all those in the whole room. With Whipshot out of the picture, Margaret wondered, what would happen to *her*? What about her coveted solo bed and mattress? What about her soft chair? What would she do now without Whipshot to protect her from the other students? Margaret knew that she had no friends here. She had ratted out so many of them that they would undoubtedly exact revenge.

Emily could only guess at how worried Margaret actually was at this moment. Whipshot was not looking so good. If she lost her position at the school, Margaret would be at the mercy of a whole crowd of students who had reasons to seek revenge. Emily actually felt sorry for her now because she knew how hard it would be for Margaret if Whipshot was suddenly released from her teaching job. Emily used to hear the things the other kids would say about the girl and how they would like to pay her back for the misery she caused them.

The ropes and harness were all clear now, and the question that was on everyone's mind was an intuitive sense of *What now?* After all, no one on the scene had ever been part of anything like this. After Castlethorn laid Whipshot on the floor, he made sure she would not fall through it again. He stomped all around her and probed for weakness in the floorboards.

When he was satisfied with the strength of the rest of the flooring, he busied himself with his machine. Some kids came too close, so he chased them off with his spinning lantern and cackling routine. He peered into his lantern. "Hoomin, says I. Dey's all hoomin beans here, 'cept fur *one*." He was also muttering about the voice in his head. Only Emily overheard him. She wondered now if he really did hear a voice. She kept this all to herself. She believed now that someone—or *something*—was guiding Castlethorn.

This was all very intriguing in spite of what "reason" told her. She *knew* what she saw. She saw the nuts backing out of the chair legs. She saw the chair leg roll from a standing position to trip Miss Whipshot. Later, during the rescue, she saw sharp boards avoid the teacher of their own volition and knew Whipshot's foot got moved out of harm's way to avoid being crushed. She knew what she saw and did not doubt herself. She seemed to understand, even at her tender age, that to doubt one's own inner self will lead a person down a very confusing, gray, and frightening path in life. In Emily's world, there was enough darkness and confusion. So Emily always made sure that she developed confidence enough to believe in her own senses and intuition above all and to never let anyone take that away from her.

She had seen enough to think that there actually was a *ghost* involved in this somehow. But why would some deceased person's soul want to first *injure* Miss Whipshot by sending her crashing through the floorboards, just to then *save* her foot from injury? Could it be that there was one harmful spirit and one helpful spirit? Or could it be that there was a whole team of spirits on the sides of good and evil? Like God and the devil? Well, now she certainly had something to muse over in her own head. For now, though, she did not have time for any of that. She had to get this situation under control before the students got into trouble with the principal. Who could know what cruelties Miss Coffenayle would dream up for the students?

The classmates had now surrounded Miss Whipshot and were starting to joke and giggle. They were growing bolder, seeing the source of their collective misery on the floor, helpless in front of them. Principal Coffenayle had Margaret by the arm and was reading her the riot act for not telling her about the whole event sooner so that maybe she could stop the "maniac" from bringing *his* machine out to make a mess in *her* school! Miss Coffenayle became so involved in the dressing down of Whipshot's pet that she failed to see what the other students were up to. They were inching ever closer and closer. They were beginning to quietly chant, "Whip-*snot*, Whip-*snot*" and "We're happy the Whip-*snot*'s dead!" They were not yet caught but would be if something did not change.

Miss Coffenayle was shaking Margaret all around and telling her what an *ugly beast* she was. Emily thought dryly to herself that it was pretty obvious who the *beast* actually was, but she said nothing. She did not want to add fuel to the fire. The kids were becoming more and more bold and were getting louder. Emily knew that this had to stop and actually felt a surge of…something that told her she needed to step forward and encourage the students to get control themselves. That this was wrong.

No matter how abusive Whipshot was, being mean back to her was only making things worse. With a burst of courage, Emily stepped into the middle of the ring of students surrounding the unconscious schoolmarm. She stood between Whipshot and the students and shouted, "*Stop it! Now!* And I mean it!" Emily stood firm, almost majestically. Firm and resolute, jaw set, head up, perfectly postured almost like a soldier from that war movie stood Emily. Though she was not hardened in the furnace of combat, she exhibited a different kind of hardness. It was an indignation. A *righteous indignation*. Something like a man of the cloth would have when standing between a violent dictator and some humble righteous little village. She stood alone. Alone and unafraid.

In her heart, Emily knew that if the students all tried to rebel against her all at once, she would be finished. Despite the impossible odds, an unusual courage that seemed to come into her from the outside. She was *told* to not be afraid. She knew that she was to just simply stand still as she was…that it would be all right. So she did that very thing. All the students stopped. They all looked at her. She turned around and set her gaze upon every person in that circle, glaring into their eyes individually, one at a time.

Everyone froze in their very tracks, and there were even a few mouths that fell open. The only sound heard in the room was Miss Coffenayle still blasting Margaret for being such an uncivilized, no-good savage. Once she knew everyone was listening, Emily spoke quietly in a very soothing voice. She used words that were not her own. It surprised even her, the speech coming out of her mouth:

"Now, everyone, Miss Whipshot may be what she is, she may be who she is, but we cannot become cruel like her. That would be wrong. If we can be cruel to her, we can be cruel to anyone. We don't want to do that. Besides, we are stuck here in this school, and this is where we live. If we are mean to Whipshot, we will be punished and feel wounded again. So after we got over our punishment, we would likely again seek revenge, get caught again, and end up being punished again in a never-ending cycle. 'Us against Them' is a situation of one-upmanship that just never works out for anybody and never ends until people are dead. This is why we do not want to be cruel people. Our only best option is to help Miss Whipshot, obey the rules, and *not* cause more chaos!" *Emily could not believe her own words.* She played it perfectly, though, just like she meant to say those things.

The students could not believe it either. They all knew and respected Emily, all the more so now. They had realized long ago that she was the most mature student of them all. This is something that students always know about their peer group. Children always know who their natural leaders are in the classroom. This, though, was something different. Emily was not only getting after them; she was teaching a lesson somehow. They felt in their hearts, as a group, that she was right. Even if they did have power over a teacher, power to harm an abuser, it would be wrong to do this thing. Not only that, but it was not practical to believe they could win in the end. The enemy was unconquerable in a head-to-head fight. So Emily was right in both moral and practical terms. They reluctantly backed away.

Other teachers were out in the hallway, simply watching the drama unfold. None of them seemed eager to intervene; it was sort of like a school of sharks where one of their number had been cornered by shark hunters. They were watching but not interfering. Many of them, though nasty people themselves, thought that Whipshot probably deserved what she was about to get from those kids. Besides, they all had their own worries, their own problems, and their own forms of illness infesting their own bodies. What did they really care about anyone else in the midst of their own suffering?

Some of the teachers had to agree with Emily's insight for this situation. It was impressive to hear her speak. They were about to interfere, to get Miss Coffenayle's attention, but it was not necessary now. Emily had diffused the students' need to do harm to Whipshot.

There was no need to punish these kids now. Everything was calm. Secretly, the teachers preferred it that way. They were mean, yes, but aggression always has its point where it burns out. Anger cannot stay focused forever because it wears out the aggressor. It breaks down the person who owns it.

Miss Coffenayle had pretty much finished berating Margaret as "The odd goddess of every toad, horror, and everlasting rot (TOGETHER)." This was the new social identity Margaret now bore. So when Miss Coffenayle said Margaret had it "together," she did not mean that as a compliment. This principal, one who molded young impressionable minds, would literally would sit up at night thinking of sneaky and mean ways of degrading the children in front of the authorities without getting caught. If a school authority was on the grounds, she could now bring the toady Margaret to them and say that this student has it all *together.* They would never know that she had just insulted poor Margaret. If Margaret spoke up, Miss Coffenayle would just play it off as a misunderstanding.

This principal believed that she was so very clever. Indeed, she had become a legend in her own mind. After all, she was a member of the Coffenayle Family line. She was not of a blood watered-down descent by marriage either. She was a *literal heir* of the Patriarch himself, a blood descendent. This meant little in her teaching career because she was currently not within the best graces of the Clan. She would one day be back, though, and they would see things *her* way. She would *make* them see things her way. She would show them how bright and talented she was, and they would *beg* her to come back.

Miss Coffenayle finally came to her senses and released Margaret's arm to send her off to sulk. She immediately knew that she had to get back to the matters at hand. She noticed right away that Emily was in the center of the student body, defending Whipshot. She also knew that Emily might not last long there if the students' anger continued.

The principal marched over to the fallen teacher. The moustache was mostly wiped away, and Miss Coffenayle did not really notice it. She just assumed it was more black shoe polish that had run out of Whipshot's oily sweaty and—*ugh!*—smelly locks.

She removed the teacher's glasses and asked someone for a damp towel. "*Please.*" She began cleaning off the crumbs, dust, and cake gunk from Whipshot's face. Though she was performing a compassionate act, her big blue eyes were just as steady and cold as always. Her mouth was set in that determined way, unique to the terminally mean people in the world. She was certainly one of them. Whipshot was snoring now, making her "snawking" sounds and seemed to be dreaming.

By this time, someone had called the nurse who was standing by and awaiting the principal's command to take over. Coffenayle looked up and seemed ready to holler something into the air but then saw Nurse Shadyknight, RN, who was now approaching the fallen teacher. Coffenayle stood up with a curt nod and not a word of gratitude for the nurse, concern for Miss Whipshot, nor anything else. She simply stood, nodded, and backed away from her star teacher.

Castlethorn was working hard at gathering cables and straps with his lantern right beside him as usual. Coffenayle noticed the lantern, even as she cursed him in her mind as a crazy old fool. He was too busy to notice her. Or at least he pretended to be; no time to deal with her, whether he noticed her or not. He had Jimmy help him untangle everything. Then they went outside, and Jimmy helped Castlethorn work on the machine. They withdrew the boom from the classroom and settled it in place, chaining it down. As they turned wheels and pulled levers, the machine slowed its whining, roaring, clanging, and sputtering by degrees. In due time, the racket stopped.

The students who were outside were now headed back to their classroom drudgery, a few of them glancing over their shoulders with true regret. The fun was over. They were all quite entertained, and a few of the kids even got to take cheap shots at Miss Whipshot! This was an opportunity they would never get again, a day they would remember for the rest of their lives. This school had a way of wearing on people, including the teachers. Some faculty actually contemplated suicide from time to time but were too lacking in will and courage to ever do anything like that.

7

Introducing the New Teacher

Now it was time for Miss Shadyknight, RN, to enter the picture and to perform her duties. The nurse looked much older than she truly was. Her life had aged her; she had seen the ravages of man's inhumanity to man. She was at one time an Army Nurse during the Great War via the American Red Cross. While serving as an active combat nurse, she learned to perform medicine far beyond traditional nursing expectations. She was more capable than her physical form would seem to indicate. She was short, hunched over, had a raspy voice, and her neck seemed to crane her head at odd angles at different times as though a muscular spasm was taking place.

Shadyknight knew Miss Whipshot well and knew her to be the cruelest of the teachers. Many beds in the infirmary were occupied by one of Whipshot's students at one time or another. Normally, the students were bruised and welted and just needed time to heal. There was an occasional broken bone, but that was not daunting to the nurse. She was, after all, a combat nurse, and she was there to fix people. She knew how to set bones and cast them properly. She had botanical remedies for bruises and knew how to properly stitch gashes to leave minimal scarring. It was all business as usual to her. Miss Coffenayle never realized how lucky she was to have Nurse Shadyknight around.

The nurse looked over the fallen teacher, took a pulse, counted her respirations, lifted her eyelids, and saw her pupils. She looked up at the students and asked what exactly had happened. She immediately was flooded with all kinds of excited chatter! She could not tell one student's voice from another. She looked from face to face, hoping to find at least one reasonable person in the room. She had been briefed somewhat by the student Tommy-Whipshot who had slipped out of the classroom without anyone noticing and ran to fetch the nurse. Tommy could not really tell her what happened. All he heard was a crash, and he saw the teacher sunken into the floor. The nurse stayed calm despite the bedlam around her and then saw one reasonable face: Emily-Whipshot's demeanor was rather calm.

"Emily," the nurse began, "perhaps *you* could tell me what happened?" She remembered the girl's name because she would frequently visit the infirmary and check on fellow students.

The whole story was too much, so Emily started with the most believable story she could. "Well, the teacher's chair fell apart, and she slipped on one of the chair parts and fell through the floor. She was stuck there for a while until Mr. Castlethorn pulled her out of the floor with"—she nodded over her shoulder—"that special crane he built. He brought the arm of the machine through the wall. He tied her into a harness and lifted her out of the floor. He laid her there. A crazy as it sounds, Castlethorn was quite easy with her, and I don't think that she was at all injured."

"Well, young lady, *crazy* describes the whole situation," responded the nurse as she glanced over to the raven-clad principal. "Principal Coffenayle, I need to take her to the infirmary. She seems stable enough for me to treat her there. No need for a hospital. No way to get her there anyway, unless we use a hay wagon to haul her over the next town. No way I can see that she would she ever fit into an automobile."

"Permission granted," Coffenayle responded with her face ever stoic and unchanging. The principal also thought to herself, *Fat chance*, at the idea that the nurse even *suggested* care outside of the school. There was plenty of room on the grounds to bury Whipshot, even if she did die. There was going to be no hospital or outside doctors. Even at the cost of "collateral damage," no one would be given the opportunity to contact outsiders and tell the story of the Happy

Valley Vocational School. Coffenayle had too much vested interest in keeping things quiet. Even the Patriarch of the Clan did not have a foothold to get information on this school; now *that* was saying something, she thought to herself proudly!

The nurse got the nod from Coffenayle and then turned to Emily. "Emily, I will need you and Tommy, the boy who fetched me, to grab a third student and run over to the infirmary. Bring me back three sturdy blankets. They are in the closet near the back of the infirmary marked '*Bedding*.'"

Tommy looked at the principal who said, "Don't look at me, you little simpleton toad-rat! Do what the nurse ordered you to do!"

Tommy immediately left with Emily and another boy about his age. They did not look back.

Castlethorn, meanwhile, had hauled all of his ropes out of the area. He and Jimmy then pulled the crane free of the wall and were getting ready to take everything back to the shop. Shadyknight was preparing the patient for transport by removing Whipshot's remaining shoe and spectacles. Someone had brought a clean wash rag, and the nurse continued cleaning Whipshot as best as she could. She gave special attention to cleaning up her face. She made note of the dampness—*and burn marks?*—in Whipshot's bloomers but did not announce it. No need to stir up the crowd with any such nonsense.

In short order, the students returned with the blankets. The nurse formed a makeshift soft stretcher on the floor by folding and layering the blankets just so. Then, with the help of reluctant volunteers, she rolled the overly abundant fallen teacher onto it. It was a like moving a six-hundred-pound lump of bread dough, but they got it done. Whipshot was breathing much easier now and was still unconscious, laying centered in the makeshift stretcher.

They had several people surround the stretcher at the feet, sides, and head. The nurse asked all the students to lift all at once on the count of three, but they could not get her very high off the ground. With the addition of four more students and crossing their arms over each other to get a solid balanced grip on the blanket stretcher, they managed to pull the teacher up and off the floor. They hauled her soggy form to a place where she could get some proper treatment and rest. She was still snoring and "snawking" away, having been sedated with sufficient sugar to get her to the infirmary.

Tommy Littleton followed the cortege with a box that contained Whipshot's glasses, both of her shoes and some treats from her coveted collection of well-frosted goodies. No point in letting her become fully awake, was there?

Castlethorn and Jimmy were still busy with the machinery outside. Jimmy had already become a sort of capable assistant. Not that he actually *knew* what he was doing, but *he did follow orders* to the letter. He had a special knack for what he was doing, too, needing to only be shown a task one time before he could do it alone. This pleased the old man to no end. Emily noticed that a type of rapport had developed between the two of them, and they made an odd pair. Odd or not, *a pair* nonetheless. An exotic-smelling old janitor filled with mad genius and his young protégé. What did the future hold for them? *No way to tell*, thought Emily. At least for now, things were calming down.

The principal wandered over to the big tiger-pit hole in the floor and began to quietly ponder. Some of the broken stakes still jutted upward. That would take some work to repair, obviously. It seemed that Castlethorn had found "hisself a noo accomplish" or "accomplice" as someone else might say. Not only that, but the "accomplish" was "hoomin," and Castlethorn seemed to tolerate him well. Miss Coffenayle figured that he would not need any more help than that.

The boy could read and write; she knew that much about him. He seemed capable, so she would see about setting him up as Castlethorn's genuine apprentice, to actually learn the trade of becoming a school engineer. It was high time to train a new engineer anyway. One never knew when Castlethorn might *really* lose his mind or drop dead; he was looking pretty old and tired these days. And his "episodes" with that silly lantern were increasing and getting worse. Even in all of her studies, she had never heard of those "beans" he kept talking about. She knew they were not magical nor even existent as a plant or foodstuff. Ah, well! She broke the man down and made him a harmless follower in her cause. That was truly the bottom line for she and Malovent.

All that said, Miss Coffenayle was still left with an even greater problem. It was time to assign a new teacher to this class. There were no true grades or graduations. There were only classrooms with students in them. There were some rough divisions by age group. The teachers did the best they could with what they were handed. Each classroom was already filled to capacity, so she could not reassign Whipshot's students to the other classrooms. Besides, that would mean intermingling dormitories.

She did not like doing that because that gave students the opportunity to talk to other kids from outside their own homerooms. Such talk could easily lead to a loss of control! Losing control even to the smallest degree would likely lead to trouble for the principal and her own purposes. Conversations about situations and people arriving at conclusions of what she was doing was not acceptable. This could undermine everything that she stood for. Black magic could certainly hinder people's minds, but it could not rob them of all their freedom of thought. Thus, the physical controls and mental/emotional intimidation were vital.

Now, Miss Coffenayle began to seriously consider her options. With her greatest weapon sick and possibly to soon die, she really needed to get a replacement, even if it was temporary. She *could* hire a new teacher from the outside, but that would not work. It would only take minutes for someone with outside contacts to expose her school and ruin her plans.

She could bring a in a criminal with nothing to lose as she did at other times. As long as they could passably read and write, she did occasionally harbor criminals as teachers. She did not mind their being sociopaths or persons of generally low standards. Thieves, charlatans, drunkards—all were welcome as long as they were not so violent as to create a huge problem. There was only one teacher who tried to cross an entirely unacceptable line.

That new young teacher simply...died. This happened one night after he had confided his intentions toward an older female student, one of legal age, to a friend of his, a fellow teacher. The young man said he intended to court this young lady, and if she were willing, they would run away and get married. The eerie part of this was that his pal did not tell on him but wished him the best. Before the young man even had the opportunity to express his feelings to the young woman, he was found by fellow teachers on the ground early the next morning. His body was smoking and stinking, partially charred. He was laying outside the faculty quarters on a path that led to the student dormitories!

A sudden lightning strike on a clear starlit night left morbid entry and exit wounds. Malovent certainly outdid himself on that one! Nobody dared asked any questions, not even about the burn marks. The body was simply taken out and secretly buried in a proper but unmarked grave. At the makeshift funeral, the dead man's friend revealed what he knew. That day, everyone understood just where the line was, and none dared cross it again. All of the teachers knew that Miss Coffenayle had something to do with this, even if they could not prove it. None of them knew about her powerful ally; they simply knew that she had something to do with this.

The teachers all made an unwritten law on the spot that they would not allow anyone to cross that line ever again. They were afraid to do so would bring the wrath of Miss Coffenayle down on all of the teachers. By one man's execution, whose only crime was to fall in love, she created a new way of doing things. She had managed to set up a self-policing group of well-educated child abusers and criminals. It was an odd dynamic but one that worked well in Miss Coffenayle's psychotic world.

The principal had to keep this order among the teachers intact. So she could not hire someone in a hurry. She did not want any wildcards in the bunch that might mess things up for her. If she slipped up, it could bring her fragile system down like a house of cards. There was no time for a proper hiring, no time to check someone out thoroughly. No, she needed to hire a teacher from the inside. She was contemplating an option already, an option that was entirely unheard of...

"Miss Coffenayle?" a voice asked from behind her.

Well, now, isn't that handy? There she was: the unheard-of option!

"Yes, Emily?" Miss Coffenayle answered sweetly, her hands behind her back as she turned toward the student.

Emily was a bit taken aback but recovered nicely. She wondered what the principal wanted from her; this did not seem like the normal Miss Coffenayle. She knew that Miss Coffenayle was this kind to people, only when it was to her advantage. The principal usually wanted a favor when she smiled *that* way. Emily continued, "We can help clean up this mess, but what are we going to do for a teacher now that Miss Whipshot is in the infirmary?"

Miss Coffenayle begged Emily-Whipshot's pardon and turned toward the students.

"Class! I want all of you to begin picking up wood and rubble. Haul it outside. Castlethorn will provide all the brooms and any wheelbarrows you might need. I expect all of you to stay busy! We shall return shortly!"

"We?" Emily stopped short of asking too many questions, something that annoyed Miss Coffenayle very quickly. Practically any questions at all annoyed her. She expected full obedience, complete and unquestioning at all times.

"Come along, child," the principal cooed as the students set off to work on cleaning up the mess. The room looked like a bomb had gone off. There was plenty to do, and Miss Coffenayle knew that the students would not dare step out of line. "I have a new role for you at our school. I will explain as soon as we get back to my office."

Emily was understandably concerned. Good things *never* happened at the principal's office. They walked to the office, slowly, and Principal Coffenayle was quite *pleasant* to Emily, which not only surprised her but worried her as well. Miss Coffenayle was one of those types of people who just should not smile. She managed to somehow emanate a grim feeling, even when she appeared to be happy enough. It was her *eyes*, Emily decided. Her expression was certainly kind and pleasant, but Emily could not see any compassion or warmth in those eyes!

Miss Coffenayle was actually quite good at small talk, and it took some of the nervousness out of the journey for Emily. They arrived at the office door and entered the lobby area. There was normally only an assistant there, named Patience, but today, there was someone else sitting across from her at the desk. Today, there sat a curiously plump man with a very fancy suit, vest, tie, and a silk top hat. He even had spats on his shoes. Emily knew this because his feet were resting on the desk. She could not place the dark-haired, goateed, and sweaty man at first, but then she realized that this was Mr. Simon I. Doesbad Esq., the school attorney. He sat back in the chair, grinning like the Cheshire Cat.

The principal was not pleased to see him, apparently. She instantly changed from the pleasant woman she was in the hallway into her usual crone of a self. "Blast you, Doesbad! How many *times* have I told you to not put your smelly feet on that desk?"

Emily looked at the dilapidated old desk. The top once had a nice finish, but age had taken its toll. Faded, oily, and covered with dirt, she could not possibly understand why it was such a problem for Miss Coffenayle to see Doesbad with his feet on the desktop. His shoes were clean; the greater risk was for him to transfer grime onto his shoes from the desk! The attorney simply refused to budge. He just sat there, grinning at the principal. She was clearly becoming more and more agitated by the moment. Emily instinctively moved back just a little bit.

"Wait," said Miss Coffenayle, "why are you so happy? The last time you looked this joyful was when the opposing counsel died in that car versus train accident! You must have some really good news...am I right?"

"Right you are, Miss Coffin-*nail!* Whoa, sorry." Doesbad held up his hands in a mock defense as though she might strike him with a fist. "Miss Coffenayle! Sorry, I know you hate being called 'Coffin-*nail.*' Ha! ha! Yes, indeed you do. But I am sure even you will be in a more forgiving mood when I tell you what *I* just did." He smiled a sly knowing smile and twitched his eyebrows.

"*No!* You didn't! Don't tell me! You did not do it already!" Miss Coffenayle was now smiling again, but Emily noted that this smile seemed to be one of great joy! This was not the phony smile that the principal presented in the hallway. No, this was real enough. Emily wondered just what the attorney could have done that would make the old vulture *so very happy* just now.

"That's right, Principal Coffenayle! I just got the judge to throw your case completely out of court! I found a loophole, and I was able to bar the school board and all its officers and representatives from coming near this place for a *very* long time! 'The Judge' is not any honorable Jon Doe. The judge is *the judge*, the one who stands in the highest court over our municipality. Believe or not, the stretch of desolate land where dwells this school actually was granted its own municipality, which is wonderful news because now, here presides the Honorable Judge Parschall."

The principal's eyes immediately lit up with recognition! This was "her" judge. Sometimes Miss Coffenayle would call him the Honorable Judge *Partial* when consulting behind closed doors with her lawyer.

While eloquent of speech and excellent at oral arguments, the attorney is only part of the reason that Judge Parschall did his best to find ways to continue cases and dismiss suits and charges against the school. Doesbad was very thorough, yes, a very good attorney, true, and Miss Coffenayle his only client, certainly. But there was something off about the Honorable David George Parschall. Nobody could quite put their finger it, not even his own staff or the judges who worked with him. As much as they respected the man, his verdicts and judgments were highly questionable, and some even considered them *suspiciously favorable* to the school.

"Yes, yes, yes! I came through for you again, Principal." Doesbad did not seem to mind tooting his own horn, Emily saw, as he punched at the air with his fists. "I was able to spar, parry, and jab my way past the plaintiff with such conciseness, such precision—keen as a freshly stropped razor, I was! I twisted him up in his own arguments so artfully that even the old Lawyer Jaggers could not have done better! Like Artful Dodger, I picked that attorney's pocket so clean that he did not have so much as a crumb to hide up his sleeve! Yessir, you should have seen me! Then the judge was about to say something, got that odd look in his eye, and *Wham! Wham! Wham!* went the gavel and *case dismissed!*"

What the lawyer did not know was that inside His Honor's black robe dwelt a minor league imp who was nonetheless very persuasive. The little beast came to Miss Coffenayle to help influence the courts. It came to work for her, compliments of Master Malovent, who taught Coffenayle how to conjure up the creature. Malovent's only purpose on this earth was to force the agenda of evil; he was a practitioner of the darkest possible magic. Miss Coffenayle was one of his favorite pupils!

The imp was a tiny twisted creature, entirely black as a moonless night, about a foot tall, thin, and spindly. Sometimes he looked furry, sometimes scaly, and sometimes smooth and oily. No matter his appearance, he was all the time evil. His eyes were tiny, his limbs thin and overly long. He could adhere to about any surface like an insect. He had short batlike fangs and needle teeth. He made no sounds when he moved. He could wisp around on ground, skim the surface of water, or float in the air like a gaseous cloud. He could dart about on all fours, faster than a jungle cat. He could hide nearly anywhere, changing shape and thickness so that he would only appear as a fleeting shadow. He had a long froglike tongue that was sticky. But not for catching insects. No. The tongue was for trapping *minds*. He could transfer energies through that tongue, and as we all know, *thoughts are energy.*

So this imp would be able to transfer thoughts and ideas into the head of his intended victim. He would present his thoughts with the highest, most educated vocabulary or in the lowest and crudest of terms, depending upon his host and how they preferred to use language. It could adapt to the person's mind and say what was most pleasing, even going so far as to using actual humor!

This type of creature was one of Malovent's favorite tools. This was a species that is only seen on earth when evil magic is afoot. The only thing that Malovent did not like about this particular type of imp was its vanity. It could, at times, be hard to control, but it was also cowardly and could be easily frightened back into line. The vanity of these creatures indicated a type of self-will that is very rare in such beasties. Oddly enough, they would rarely try to escape. Their particular desire was to have a name. They would work hardest for anyone who gave them a name of their own choosing. It was just a peculiarity of the species.

When this creature first heard of his assignment, he loved the idea of hiding inside a judge's robe and affecting the destinies of people in a significant negative way. Since he was black as ink and was to hide in a judge's robe, he demanded to be called "InkRobe." Malovent allowed it because to please the vanity of these creatures was to capture their will. He knew that the name of their choosing made them subservient. So InkRobe was sent to visit the Honorable David George Parcell, inside the pocket of Miss Coffenayle's blue suit.

When Miss Coffenayle visited with the judge to bribe him, she was successful. She presented gold bullion to the old judge who would soon be forced to retire on just his pension. She tempted him, he said yes, and that was all it took for Miss Coffenayle to own him. All she needed to bring him under the power of Malovent was for him to knowingly and willingly give consent for just one wicked act. No matter what now, he could not take it back.

He immediately began to regret his decision; he was a good man and a good judge. The offer, though, of *that* much gold, enough to care for his wife's medical problems, was something to which he had to say yes. He would be unable to afford her treatment after retirement. What else was he to do? Let his beloved life partner die?

Now that the judge was bought, Miss Coffenayle sweetened the pot by offering more bullion but with a condition. She opened her pocket, and out jumped InkRobe, right on the judge's desk. He nearly stabbed it with a letter opener, mistaking the furry imp for a *starved rat*. Coffenayle stopped him by grabbing his old frail wrist, and she pulled him close. Quite close. She said, "You and InkRobe here are going to be the best of friends. You get the gold, but he comes with it. He will hide in your judge's robe, and you won't even know he's there."

"Wh-What's he going to do to me?" the trembling justice asked.

"Nothing, love. He's just going to give you some...*guidance* on how to rule in the court. Now you can say 'no' and I go right to the newspapers about our little discussion of the gift I offered you for your services. The public will believe it, I will see to that, and you will be publicly disgraced and lose your job. No pension *and* no gold." She allowed that sink in.

The judge suddenly looked like a sad and sullen old man. She knew she had him.

"Or you can allow InkRobe here to 'assist' you in your rulings concerning Happy Valley Vocational School, keep your crummy old pennies worth of pension, and become a rich man besides. Think of your poor ailing wife and how much medicine costs. Doctor's bills… that vacation she always wanted to—"

"No! No! I've changed my mind! You cannot come in here and bribe me like that! I don't care how much money you have!" He was angry now and very scared because of InkRobe. But it was too late. He already gave consent to the deal, and that was all Miss Coffenayle needed. He belonged to her now. She already had one wrist, then grabbed the other and held him fast. She stared deeply into the old man's eyes, and he froze in place, under her black-ice blue-eyed gaze. She did not even need to cast a spell; her look was enough to frighten him without magic!

"InkRobe! Show him the way!" yelled Coffenayle. The long sticky tongue lashed out and connected neatly to the judge's neck. Immediately, his eyes bulged, and he wanted to resist. That desire was lost in a split second. His eyes then grew sleepy and dull. His face lost all expression. He lost himself; he lost his own identity. He was no longer his own person, now a partial slave to another's will. All because he agreed to a single corrupt act.

"I will work with you," said the judge sleepily. "I will take the gold. I will work your trials as you say. Praise to Malovent."

"Praise to Malovent," echoed the principal with a smile. InkRobe ran up the man's arm, curled up on the judge's shoulder, and purred after retracting his tongue.

"How's it going, buddy?" the imp squeaked at the judge. "You like Castor Oyl comics?"

Miss Coffenayle gave an evil smile. "I think he likes you." Thus ended the meeting; thus began an era of evil for the students of Happy Valley Vocational School. Such is the true origin of the attorney's success in court. As eloquent as Doesbad was, as much as he knew, as effective as his arguments were, only the power of temptation, corruption, and obedience to evil influences could ever win these cases consistently and hands down. Even with InkRobe affecting the judge, Doesbad was necessary because it took a lawyer to do the legwork, file motions and other papers. She needed a warm body, someone for the courts to see in front of them. Miss Coffenayle could not possibly run the school and appear on her own behalf. There simply were not enough hours in a day.

Besides, not having a lawyer would look out of place! Maybe people would start to ask questions. The fewer the questions, the better. This way, they only questioned the judgments. Plus, even if Parschall got himself impeached, well, there was always another judge for sale. Everyone has a weakness; everyone has a price, even if threats had to be made against family members. Such was the way of the Coffenayle family.

The principal's office was now an oasis of joy in a desert of misery! "Well done! Well done, indeed, Simon I. Doesbad, Esq.! Happy I am for another victory for you, the school, and for *us!* Huzzah!" shouted Miss Coffenayle. The principal threw her shadow-clad arms in the air, and Simon jumped up from the filthy desk, surprisingly fast for a man of his girth. A puff of dust emitted from what passed for a cushion on the chair. He jumped up and shouted, "*Huzzah!*" right along with Coffenayle.

Patience, the office receptionist, simply watched from her desk, passively accepting what was going on. She seemed to be so used to such behavior that she did not flinch, smile, nor blink at them. She knew that the "us" Miss Coffenayle referred to was not she and Doesbad. She meant herself and her *other* partner, the one she would talk to in her office while burning incense. Patience did not know the whole story; certainly, she did not want to. She accidentally overheard enough. Patience felt sorry for Mr. Doesbad. *She believed with her whole heart that he deserved better.*

The pair danced around the room in a most ridiculous manner ill of rhythm and out of time. They never really actually touched hands, though it appeared to Emily that Simon may have tried a time or two. He never really seemed terribly disappointed at his failure to touch her at the same time. Emily also saw, in her perceptive way, that Doesbad glanced her way for the barest of instants. In that brief span, she saw pain and regret in his eyes. But no, she decided, a man of his character could have not a shred of decency in his heart. In that instant, she had a conflicting impression as though someone said, "Never be too hard on someone in terrible pain." Emily regretted immediately her harsh judgment of this pitiable man.

The two continued to dance about and hum some simple nameless nonexistent tune they both somehow knew. Emily knew that this party could not last long, not with both of them visibly overweight and becoming winded. Emily wondered at how that dress could hold Coffenayle's ample form for as long as it did with her dancing and cavorting with the attorney. He began to sweat, and she was huffing and puffing. Soon enough, the dance ended with both of them leaning on the desk, gasping and trying to recover their wind but still smiling at each other. One would think that they had just fought and conquered the Kaiser all over again! Patience pretended to read a scheduling book, trying to look busy. Emily noticed that she never turned the page, idly scanning the same words over and over again.

After they caught their breath and composed themselves, Miss Coffenayle turned toward Emily and said, "Simon, I would love for you to meet our newest *teacher*—Miss Emily Keller, formerly known as Emily-Whipshot. She will be restored to her birthname on the school's in-house records and installed as Miss Whipshot's replacement."

The lawyer looked at the principal as though she had just lost her *mind*.

Emily thought it was joke of some kind. All she could do was stand there with her mouth open, eyes aghast, completely in shock.

Miss Coffenayle, with her patented warmest smile and soulless blue eyes, gently took the student, now a teacher, by the hand and settled her into a chair. One teacher had already fallen down today, and we did not need to dig another from the floorboards, now, did we? Emily sat there in that straight-backed wooden chair and just looked around the office, trying to find something, anything to focus on that would help her make sense of things. She now wondered if anything would ever help her ever again. This was just plain madness.

8

Now It Gets *Really* Interesting

Coffenayle dismissed Emily after the introduction and asked her to wait in the hall. She even said Emily could take a *padded* chair with her—this was unusually kind. The new teacher picked up the chair, still stunned, and took it out into the hall. She sat in the hall, wondering if this day could become any more impossible.

With the student-now-teacher gone, it was time for a meeting of Coffenayle and her attorney. Simon had gotten ahold of himself by now and was back in the role of barrister. He stood straight, tall, and solemn in his three-piece suit, complete with his spats and silk hat. One arm was smartly held behind his back as though he were hiding something, and the other hand held the lapel of his suit coat. The man, though portly, gave the illusion of one completely and solemnly in control. He had the appearance of one who had presented over a thousand arguments during hundreds of cases in his career.

The truth was, though relatively new to the profession of law, he instinctively knew when to adopt this posture of the man of the hour. He knew when the witness needed his steady assurance that they were going to be just fine. He knew when someone needed to know that there was nothing to worry about, not even from the witness stand. He stood as he did when he was perfectly in control, and the court was eating out of his hand. He was one of the rare breeds of truly talented and gifted lawyers.

At this moment, though, such was hardly the case. He was not in control of the situation. Under his firm, solemn, professional, albeit rotund appearance was a man trying desperately to not scream, *"Coffin-nail! Have you completely lost your evil mind? A student to be promoted to teacher?* Think! Think for a moment. You have a great thing going here! Forget that. *We* have a great thing going here. You run the school with an iron fist and have the will to back it up! You have the teachers cowed, the students in complete control, and you have somehow managed to even run the very *courts* themselves! And now you want to wreck it all with a student sitting in the teacher's seat? She will gain the sympathy of the students! They will start to turn on the school! You will lose control, Coffin-*nail!* You will completely lose control and these kids will run you out of town on a rail! Arrrrrrgh!"

Despite the undercurrents of his mind, there he stood, the commensurate professional completely caught off guard, completely stumped, dumbfounded, at the same time appearing completely control of himself—unruffled, calm, self-assured. He could not believe his ears, and yet it seemed to the esteemed Juris Doctor that the principal was convinced that she was correct in this action. If nothing else, Doesbad had learned by now that when Donatienne Coffenayle made a decision, and it was firmly decided, it normally worked out very well. Not that there was to be any talking her out of it anyway. He had learned by some very hard experiences that he should not push any contrary thoughts of his own. He could give a "suggested" course of action, which she would generally promptly dismiss. He would not fight back when she did. He made that mistake once. He still felt the sting of those boils he suffered when he contradicted her that one and only time so long ago.

Doesbad did not particularly believe in magic, but he had to admit that some things with Coffenayle were very *coincidental.* The boils affected him as soon as she was angry with him for contradicting her ideas but suddenly disappeared when her anger was averted upon his agreeing with her two weeks later. To this day, his best doctors still had no medical explanation. So being wise, if not superstitious, he at least chose to err on the side of caution. Seeing some of the creepier people on the staff also made him shudder and wonder just a little about where she found such a collection of freaks. He did not want to become one of them. He thought it was possible for that to happen.

Now, completely under self-control and in his best tone of meekness, he suggested that perhaps Miss Coffenayle may reconsider. "After all," said he, "we would not want to drop a boulder into such a calm pool. Things are going so well. Why change it up? Why use a *student?*" Doesbad saw the expression on her face and immediately regretted prompting her. She smiled in his direction, but this time, it was different than the joy she had just expressed in his job well done. This smile was that of a hungry shark eyeing its prey. The smile was broad and normally would be considered as a pleasant expression, but those *eyes—good heaven above,* those eyes! Dark and cold with anger. *Cold* with anger. Different than hot or fiery with anger and so much worse! It made him sorry he challenged her, regardless of his reason for doing so.

This coldness in Coffenayle's eyes was dark and dreary as though Hades itself was waiting for Doesbad in the depth of those blue eyes. It froze him to the bone, and he actually wondered for a moment if she truly had learned dark magical arts. Being a man of reason and logic, though, he shook that thought off and accepted only the idea that she was just a terribly cruel and unempathetic person. There was no such thing as witchcraft; it was only the stuff of legends.

Witches did not truly exist, and the stories made up about them were crafted to manipulate politics in superstitious societies of over-wrought Christians. Better listen to the Cotton Mather because the devil will drag you to hell for making herbal tea! Witches were created to frighten children from running off into the woods or into other dangerous places. Don't go into woods at night because the witches will grab you, and we will never see you again!

Try as he might, though, Doesbad still had the memory of his boils. The boils that afflicted his entire body from head to toe for thirteen and half days! That look, the one that she was giving him right now, was the same look she gave him that night as she muttered under her breath and made the motions with her fingers. His affliction with boils from head to toe started within minutes. At first, skin felt dry. Then he had an itching crawling sensation. After that, the red blotches on his skin. Then the boils began to break to the surface! He went to several doctors for treatment, and even the best medical science to offer was helpless. He hoped that the prickling itch rippling under his shirt just now was just a psychosomatic delusion, even if his heart of hearts told him it was not.

"Do you *truly* want to *question* my judgment in this matter, *Mr. Simon Ignatius Doesbad, Esquire?*"

Not the full name, he thought. She was really mad when she used his full name. She knew he *hated* his middle name. He was not even sure how he got it. He stood there, though, helpless. He was suddenly afflicted with this unsettling urge to relieve his bladder right there in front of her. No matter how painful it was, he was not going to give her the satisfaction of doing so. She would delight in his wetting the best court trousers he had in his collection. He was not about to give her that pleasure. Not to mention the discomfort he would feel the long drive home, though he would never *admit* to ever experiencing that in the past.

"Well, no," he began, "I don't want to question your judgment in this matter. You are, after all, the commensurate educator." He stifled the urge to call her "Ma'am" because he knew how much she hated that; plus it gave him pleasure to not speak to her so formally. Not that he would have ever challenged her if she demanded that formality. Any victory, even a tiny victory, is better than no victory at all. So keeping his pants dry and not calling her "Ma'am" was all he had, and he would accept that. "That being said, are you certain that you can keep control of the classroom? After all, the new teacher may have sympathy for the students. You would not want the teacher to lose control of the classroom, would you?" His question was almost sheepish. He held his breath while Miss Coffenayle paused to consider his query.

"Fair enough," stated Coffenayle. "I understand your concern, particularly in light of the recent hard-earned victory in court today. So, this one time, I will explain to you my exact thoughts on the matter."

Simon could not hide the relief in his eyes. Coffenayle saw this and though his eyes betrayed him, she admired his overall stoicism under such intense pressure.

"We don't have time to find a teacher. This was not a planned retirement. This was a sudden injury, one that occurred in front of all the students. This is a mystery that must be solved, Simon. I get the sense that there is something off about this whole situation. We could try and bring a substitute, but that would add a wildcard to this whole thing. We would need to be certain that the new teacher would play ball our way, and we don't have the time to perform the proper interviews.

"Furthermore," she continued, "Miss Emily Keller is familiar with how things are run here. She does not need any training in my ways. Emily is known to us, and she can be more easily controlled than anyone else we might hire. There is no chance that she could leave and tell the authorities what is truly happening here. We have control of the courts, yes, but not the coppers.

"If the county sheriff started poking around here, that would be very bad, don't you think? Would it not make things more difficult for us if the police began asking questions? Our strongest defense, by your word, is that the state has little evidence with which to prosecute. Right now, we can't have county officers we have nothing on poking around here and seeing things they might question. I suppose we could bribe them, but what if they were honest people? We could stir up some serious problems."

Doesbad had to agree. There was no time for a proper vetting and interview process. The seat had to be filled immediately and with someone they could keep under their absolute control. Doesbad certainly did not want the *gendarmes* getting into his files, obtaining warrants for searches of the school grounds and the "secrets" buried in the school administrative office. He knew that Miss Coffenayle was a dangerous woman, and certainly, he was not in favor of eliminating authorities or anyone else. He believed Miss Coffenayle might be capable of that very thing to get her way.

He hoped to never have to tell her that he would refuse to be a party to murder. So far, it had not come up. Not as far as he knew.

He seemed to recall a time when bribery was not acceptable to him either, but that somehow changed when he started working with Donatienne. He was already corrupt. He hoped to not become a murderer under her tight control. Already, so much seemed to have changed according to his foggy recollection.

For example, he knew that for a while he was gaining weight at a phenomenal rate. It was bothersome to need a new wardrobe every couple of weeks. That problem was nothing his doctors could treat, and his weight gain seemed to level off after he nearly doubled in size. He never really felt good anymore. Not since becoming her attorney. And why were his memories about certain things so jumbled?

Their conversation continued, and she poured him a cup of tea. He loved that tea because it smelled like the leather of his new car and tasted like fine cognac. After a few sips, he was in a better mood, and they began to discuss the particular and vital qualities the new teacher must have for the school to continue.

They needed a teacher who was familiar with school operations, one that was easily controlled, who would not ask too many embarrassing questions; they needed someone already familiar with the system. An event as serious as Whipshot's accident could not be kept quiet! A new teacher would certainly be informed of the accident by the other teachers and perhaps students. That could start rumors. Plus, the students would more likely acquiesce to a familiar face. So who better than a student?

"Okay, I am beginning to see your reasoning here. A student would be the perfect fit. Now, do you think that Miss Keller is capable of controlling the students? A whole class full of kids has just seen a spectacular event occur before their very eyes. They are bound to be shaken a bit. They may become unruly," replied Simon, relieved that Coffenayle seemed amenable to conversation.

"Yes, I understand that concern, but I have a plan for that. If things start to get out of control, we will have Miss Ladlepot from the cafeteria drop a bit of some special herbal blends I have concocted into the food of Miss Emily's students. They will hardly know it is there, the way that woman cooks. The students will be mildly sedated and more pliable to suggestions. I will instruct Miss Emily there"—she made a motion toward hallway—"on how she should explain things to the students. Besides that, she showed remarkable leadership today in that out-of-control scene in the classroom. She brought order to it, showing great initiative. The students were willing to follow her."

"I agree. If Miss Emily has shown initiative and the students have already followed her, then that is a good thing. Plus, I have seen your herbals at work before as a backup plan. Not too much in the food, I trust? I don't want any accidents."

Coffenayle's eyes narrowed just a bit, but she chuckled. "No, you silly fool. There won't be any accidents. The herbs are not truly poisonous, not like...well, anyway, this concoction will not harm anyone."

"Very good. So we have a classroom full of safe suggestible students. A familiar face teaching them. One who is familiar with not only the rules and regulations of the school but also the recent history in the classroom. I like it. Do you really think that she can handle the responsibility of being an educator?"

"Ha! Does that really matter, Doesbad? Does it truly matter if they are *actually* educated? All we need is to continue controlling the situation and maintaining status quo. In the meantime, we can look for a properly vetted and sufficiently corrupt teacher to join the staff and eventually take over the classroom. Miss Emily will not be in the teacher's seat for very long. Not only that, but that little toad, Margaret, is very easily bribed. I can use her to monitor the classroom activities. All it takes is a few clean linens or some special treat now and then to keep her in line. Whipshot has already used her very well as a classroom 'monitor.' As a 'snitch' if we want to be honest about it. Margaret is *well*-experienced in getting information on students and giving it to the faculty."

Doesbad actually smiled at this. He took an extra thought and stopped himself from saying, "Why should we start to be honest *now*?"

"Excellent!" he said instead, beaming. "I like this plan. I don't see any flaws in it, barring further injuries in that classroom. So how do we get started?"

"'We' don't do anything more. *You* return to your normal duties of our legal counsel. I will handle all of the arrangements in the classroom from here."

"Very good," said Simon I. Doesbad, Esquire. He slugged down the rest of his tea, tipped his hat, and grabbed his cane. He was very happy now and thankful for leaving her office. He was always glad when their meetings ended on a happy note, particularly after a generous cup or two of her brew. Time now to get back to civilization, his office, a stack of mail, and a nice nip of a suitable adult beverage. Never too much, though, for one never knew when Simon I. Doesbad, Esq. might be called back into service.

He knew Coffenayle hated it when he would show up for a meeting unflatteringly lubricated. He never could figure out how the seat of his trousers burst into flames that one particular day. Dismissing that unpleasant thought, he whistled his way down past the receptionist and out the door. What a wonderful day to be so very happy and alive!

Patience could always tell when he had extra tea. She was very glad to know that this meeting went well. Bad meetings invariably ended with a cannon shot "across the bow" as the attorney left the office. He was never hit by a grapeshot; near misses served well enough to remind him of who was in charge. It always made him jump, and who could blame him? Patience would put cotton in her ears whenever the meetings ended with yelling. She could not understand why such a fine man would put up with such treatment. She hoped that one day he would start to see that he was truly better than that and deserved better.

"Emily, dear. You may come in from the hallway now," invited Miss Coffenayle in an uncustomary gentle voice.

Emily entered the office again, and to her relief, the principal had changed to her more familiar Napoleonic uniform, spotless and starched as always. The uniform was tailored precisely after Napoleon Bonaparte's famous portrait. The coat was blue with a white vest, brass buttons, tight pants, and matching white stockings. The only differences in her uniform were the mirror-shined black knee-high combat boots, ruffles on the breast, and she did not add the gold epaulets to the shoulders for general wear. Those would be worn only at the highest of fashionable events, such as the annual Coffenayle family reunions. Those always came about during the fall solstice. Her straight blonde hair was pulled back from her broad, though not unpleasant, face into an exceedingly tight and neatly tied ponytail. She never took the time for a braid.

Emily had always preferred this uniform to her black dress which made Emily shiver. In fact, that dress made Emily feel positively *dreadful* inside. It seemed like something was wrong or perhaps even unnatural about Miss Coffenayle when she was dressed up like that. Not that the principal ever made anyone feel particularly good at any given time, but that dress was just…wicked. That was the only word Emily could come up with that seemed to fit. No time to worry about that now, though. This meeting required all of Emily's attention.

Emily was already seated across from Coffenayle's desk. To her great surprise and mild discomfort, the principal did not sit in her customary desk chair. No, no, no. This was a special meeting that called for special closeness. In an effort to put Emily at ease, she came around her desk and grabbed a chair just like Emily's and sat directly across from her within a couple of feet. This gesture of social mingling had the opposite of its intended effect. It set Emily on edge. She would have felt better if Miss Coffenayle was in her chair behind her imposing desk. As intimidating as that big desk was, she felt more comfortable sitting out of the principal's reach. At this distance, Emily could be easily grabbed or slapped.

"Now, Emily, you know I have watched you for a long time," started the school administrator.

I bet you have, Emily thought quietly to herself, not daring to say it. She sat there silently with a neutral posture, hanging on every word.

"Emily, darling, it is so very important that you feel comfortable in your new position. This is a huge responsibility I am granting you. You are no longer one of the students. You are now a teacher. At least for the time being."

"What do you mean, Miss Coffenayle, for the time being?" Emily measured her words carefully. She did not want to ask the wrong question or use the wrong tone of voice.

"Well, you see, Emily, we don't have a proper teacher to take poor Miss Whipshot's place. And our budget simply won't allow us to pay anyone enough money to come into this situation all of a sudden."

"I see," Emily said carefully, doubting that the school was really in financial trouble. She just kind of knew that Miss Coffenayle was lying about the real reason she wanted a student to teach. "So how long will it be before we hire a proper teacher?"

"Oh, Emily! Don't you see that you *are* a proper teacher? You are an excellent student and a natural leader in the classroom. I saw how you behaved during Miss Whipshot's accident," said the falsely earnest principal, taking Emily's hands in hers. "You stepped up in ways that far exceeded your years. I want to see you bloom into the beautiful flower I know you to be." Coffenayle cringed inside, regretting the remark about the flower. She could see in Emily's eyes that she was laying it on a little thick. She backed off and released Emily's hands. The budding teacher was glad that the principal was giving her some appropriate space.

"I am happy that you trust me, Miss Coffenayle. But to be a… teacher…that is so big," stated Emily.

"Yes, dear. And you are the only student I know of that I am willing to trust with this," Miss Coffenayle spoke truthfully.

"Well, I guess I can do it…for a little while…until you can find someone more qualified," Emily said pensively.

"Oh, that's the spirit! I *knew* I could count on you!" gushed the female Napoleon. She stood up out of her chair, slid it back into place, and invited Emily to stand. The new teacher held out her arms as the principal, her new employer, laded her with books and materials. When the books proved too heavy of a load, Coffenayle rolled a cart over to Emily, and they both stacked books and supplies onto the cart. She sent Emily down the hall, stunned at her promotion, on her way to the classroom. "Miss Emily" had left the classroom as a scared student and was returning as a terrified teacher. Emily knew that Miss Coffenayle was following her. She was stunned, knowing that she was about to be introduced to her former classmates as their new teacher.

When they approached their destination, they heard quite a commotion. It sounded like Whipshot's former students were...celebrating? Miss Coffenayle had Emily pause in the hallway, and she, as the principal, entered Miss Whipshot's old classroom. She made her way to the desk and just stood there quietly; dangerously. She was clearly not pleased with what she was seeing.

The students were basically rioting! They were hooting and hollering, dancing and prancing about, laughing and singing made-up songs about "Whipshot Eats Monster Snot" and so on. The desks were all in disarray, some of the students had tears in their clothing, papers were scattered everywhere, spitballs, airplanes and wads of paper were being thrown back and forth...and was that *food?*

Students pulled Whipshot's snack drawer entirely from the desk, left it on the floor, and whatever they did not eat was splattered on the walls. Colorful splatters covered the floor, the walls, and some students.

Coffenayle could not believe this! A food fight? In her school? Certainly, this was not possible! The students were disciplined, not unruly. How could they *dare to even dream* of such actions, much less carry them out?

Emily had stopped at the threshold, aghast at what she was seeing. She could not believe their behavior! Her normally quiet and reserved classmates seemed to have lost their collective mind! Even Margaret and Jimmy were participating. Emily stood there with her mouth open, especially concerned when they did not notice their principal, their dreaded disciplinarian, standing there in the front of the room! Miss Coffenayle's face was beginning to redden, the crimson tone of her scalp bleeding through her blonde hair, and her fists clenched with rage. Emily saw Coffenayle draw a deep breath, ready to blast the classroom with terrible shout. The newest teacher knew she had to act fast and beat the principal to the punch. Who knew what she might capable of doing?

"Stop it! All you! And I mean now!" screamed Emily who had rushed up to the teacher's desk, banging the cart into it. She *slammed* her teaching books and materials from the cart down onto the desk so hard that it even made Miss Coffenayle twitch just a bit. She looked at Emily in near disbelief, wide-eyed, but she was pleased at the same time. Now *this* was a teacher! The students all froze in place, some of them with their arms cocked to launch another cupcake, paper wad, or some other projectile.

The first thing they saw was Miss Coffenayle at the front of the class, but that was not her shout. Then they noticed Emily, standing there confidently, boldly, body erect with her jaw set, simply *daring* anyone else to make a move. Coffenayle was proud of her new teacher, and she stepped forward to make the introduction. She made quite a show of it too.

She first paced back and forth a couple of times, staring at the classroom, her hands behind her back, never taking her eyes off the students. Her uniform of the classic blue jacket and knee-high, black, mirror-shined boots was even more impressive to the students than usual. They held their breath. Literally. She walked slowly and intentionally, the metal-capped heels of the boots tapping out a cadence as she prowled back and forth.

The classroom was stunned and silent. The kids who had projectiles dropped them. Those eating Whipshot's pastries set them down. They scarcely dared to chew. All terrified eyes were up front now; the students were either seated or standing at attention. Coffenayle paced long enough that all of the students were following her with just their eyes, back and forth. Back and forth. When she would stop, the eyes would stop. Students swallowed hard. Then she would resume her pacing. Finally satisfied that the students were completely under her control, she began to speak.

"Well, *this* was most unexpected," she said quietly. Every student heard her because they were scared not to hear. She had their complete attention, and she knew it. "I have obviously failed in my duty as a principal." She began pacing again as though she were thinking about what to say next. The students expected her to scream at them or begin to look for Whipshot's missing ruler. She did neither. "In all my years as an educator and disciplinarian of young minds, one who molds young people into responsible adults, I have never seen such a display of riotous behavior! I am, though, willing to *overlook* this display on the condition that all of this is cleaned up."

She looked around and noticed that the broken floorboards from Whipshot's accident had been patched by Castlethorn, but they still needed to clean up the black marks made by the crane. Oh, and there was the hole in the wall, too, where the boom came through to save the teacher's life. That hole, she was certain, would also be repaired and cleaned up by Castlethorn. He was an odd duck but very efficient. She noticed too that having fresh air from the outside was rather pleasant. She would not allow windows; that was too much light and hope for the kids, but maybe she would have the engineer install some vents. Not a bad idea!

"Now, do I have a solemn promise from every one of you that you will clean up after yourselves? Hmmmm?" she asked with her nose slightly elevated, scanning the whole room with her eyes.

The entire classroom nodded in unison as they knew was expected. There was more than one dry mouth in the house, and the tension in the room was so thick you could dig at it with a spoon. Her stare, that arrogant, frighteningly self-assured stare of those cold blue eyes, pierced everyone in the room.

She knew she had them right where she wanted them. Yes, she did. "Now that you have had your degraded moment...now that you have engaged in your pigsty hoe-down of debauchery, I expect only the best from you. I am here today, gracing you with my personal attention because I have an important announcement."

The students continued in rapt silence. You could hear a pin drop.

Emily had set her things in order at the desk. She was arranging them while the principal was strutting about, showing her stuff. By the time Coffenayle had gotten around to introducing her, Emily was prepared to start class. Her drawers were set up the best she knew how, and the desk was neatly arranged in her best of idea of what a teacher should do. Coffenayle noticed this sincere if incorrect effort immediately and was very pleased. She nearly smiled at the new teacher and continued speaking.

"I know how upset many of you are at the accident. There is no need to be. Under my capable leadership, your teacher was successfully rescued, unhurt! Miss Whipshot, by the way, sends her best wishes and tells you not to worry, that she will recover as soon as possible."

This was a bald-faced lie, Emily knew. Whipshot was unconscious when they left her with Nurse Midnight. And what *leadership* anyway? She spent most of her time sitting there, looking bored and hiding behind human shields!

"So in the interest of continuing your education, we have arranged for a temporary substitute teacher."

The students noticed that Emily was setting things up for the new teacher. This did not surprise them. After all, Emily being who she was, should help to set up the new teacher's desk, etc. But the students wondered, who would be the new teacher? Visitors were never allowed at the school, except for deliverymen and that nutty fat man in the silk hat. No one had seen anyone new on campus; they all knew the procedure for the new teachers.

The new faculty members were always led around campus for the first couple of days to become familiar with the place. Miss Coffenayle always paraded them before the students. The kids all knew who the new teacher was, no matter where the teacher was assigned. This was highly irregular to not meet the teacher ahead of their being introduced to the classroom proper. So what was up?

"Of course, all of you understand," the dictator continued, "that these are highly unusual circumstances. Never have we had an educator the caliber of Miss Whipshot be taken out of the classroom so suddenly. This is a very difficult time for us all." She paused to wipe a perfectly dry eye. "That being said, in light of the difficulty presented, we have to take *extraordinary* measures!" She paused for dramatic effect.

The students were literally holding their breaths this time. Who, after all, knew *what* she might do? Her "measures" generally were over-the-top extraordinary. How severe must be the plans that

Miss Coffenayle considered *extraordinary* in her extreme views? How much worse could things get? *Heaven help us!*

"So, students, we have made a difficult decision. An unprecedented historic decision. A decision whose effect will reverberate down the halls of our beloved institution for the next thousand years! *Miss Emily*! Will you please come out from behind that desk and be presented to your new class?"

"Miss" Emily left her materials neatly in place and walked quietly, tentatively almost, but with every appearance of confidence in her abilities. Miss Coffenayle introduced her as "Miss Emily" so that they could all call her by a formal but still familiar name. That would make things easier for the kids to accept Miss Emily's rule.

The students' eyes all grew wide in unison. Castlethorn, who was about to enter the classroom, stopped dead in his tracks. He hovered in the doorway, somehow sensing that he was about to witness something of tremendous significance. He stood quietly with an air of respectfulness that belied his gruff exterior and custodial aura, one that could stand a good scrubbing and comb, quite frankly. He just watched. No commentary, no snide remarks. He even put his lantern down, gently leaning the pole against the wall and out of sight of the classroom. Miss Coffenayle seemed to be completely unaware of his presence, which was unusual.

"For a hoomin bean," Castlethorn once said, "Miz Coffenayle certainly had an uncanny sense for knowing when peoples wuz around." All that aside, Castlethorn stood quietly, his greasy hands folded formally across his belt buckle. He would have been described as almost "serene" or "peaceful" had anyone actually seen him at that moment. All eyes were up front, though; none of them even glanced at the doorway.

The students stared. They were not sure of what they were about to witness. All eyes went back and forth from Coffenayle to "Miss" Emily and back again. What was going on here? Was the impossible about to occur? No, not impossible. Unheard of. Unthinkable. Unspeakable. "Impossible" did not begin to describe what was happening here. Is there a stronger word than *impossible*? Because if there is, that would be the better way to describe this situation from the students' perspective. The students did not dare to believe that one of their own was about to become their instructor, their teacher. The only time the principal ever called anyone by Mr., Miss, or Mrs. was in reference to a teacher or perhaps some distinguished visitor, if the school ever had one.

Emily stood quiet and composed. Her eyes were straight ahead, mouth and eyebrows set in a perfect unreadable poker face. She did not dare allow anyone to see what she was really feeling—terrified; nervous; sick. Yet, somehow, she was able to remain perfectly stoic and calm. She felt a kind of emotional support inside her, like someone was telling her to not worry, that all was as it should be. It may seem completely insane at the moment, but all is well. All was well, all is well, all will be well.

This calming assurance came, and it felt almost like a friendly, even grandfatherly arm across her shoulders. This enabled her to endure this strange turn of events...as if seeing the fasteners come out of the chair, Whipshot falling, her subsequent rescue and injury, students entering Castlethorn's lair, etc., were not enough. Now she was being promoted to become a *teacher!* This certainly was not what she bargained for when she showed up to class this morning!

Emily had to suppress completely a surge of revulsion when the principal laid a hand on her shoulder. She could not let her emotions appear on her face in front of the students. Not at this moment. Not now. She could not let anyone see how frightened she truly was, how heavy this burden felt.

With a great flourish, as though she were introducing an act from *The Greatest Show on Earth*, Principal Coffenayle made a slight bow and put a hand on Miss Emily's shoulder. She waved her free hand toward the new teacher with a magician's flair and stated for all to hear, "Allow me, class, to introduce the newest addition to the faculty—*Miss Emily! Your new teacher!*"

Emily felt the principal's fingertips dig into her shoulder with an air of "Don't you *dare* let me down or there'll be a price to pay," even as she smiled a broad beaming grin at the classroom. The reaction of the students was universal. Emily had heard of a "stunned silence" before, but his was far beyond any of that. It was as though a hole had been torn in the very fabric of time and space itself. They were in a vacuum. No one really knew what to say. The principal looked around as though she was expecting some praise or exclamation of congratulations...or something, at least. Instead, some the students who were standing just sort slumped into their chairs, one or two at a time. Others just stood there, their mouths sort of working like they were at a complete loss. Indeed, they were.

Her hand still firmly on the new teacher's shoulder, Miss Coffenayle was looking around, looking for some reaction. She was smiling and nodding like an inventor who brought rust to a science convention, expecting it be received as a grand new thing.

The students were not sure of what to do. Then, Jimmy, sensing that if she did not get some happy, wonderful reaction to her new idea, rage would quickly follow, said, "Let's hear it for Miss Emily! Yay! Hooray!"

On cue, the whole class erupted in applause, standing, some even cheering. Someone whistled.

The principal simply beamed with delight. What a wonderful thing she had done! She released her too-tight "motherly" grip on Miss Emily's shoulder, stepped back, and started clapping. She did so in feigned praise, the light palm-tapping clap of a losing politician to her victorious opponent. She smiled as she did so with no praise or joy behind it. Just business as usual with Coffenayle. Already, she was scheming upon what she could do next. Her next move would yet be another unprecedented act, one that would be certain, absolutely certain to win the hearts and minds of the students. She needed them to love their new teacher. They would be that much easier to control. With Whipshot out of the picture, that's exactly what was needed. A nice manageable classroom full of controlled, compliant students.

Emily was unsure of what to do. After all, she had never been a teacher before. So she stood there, accepting the applause and adulation. She was self-conscious, even embarrassed, but she did not blush. She did not dare. She was not about to show the principal what was really going on inside of her. She had butterflies, stomach-churning butterflies making butter in her belly! Her heart raced like Castlethorn's machine. Why would they not stop cheering?

Please, please, please stop it! I have never been a teacher. I don't know what Miss Coffenayle will expect of me, guys. You may not like it, and you may not like me anymore. I am not your friend. I have to teach you and discipline you the way she says. This could go horribly wrong in so many ways!

Emily was scanning the room and glanced in the direction of the old janitor. Castlethorn was standing there, respectful and...*smiling?* There stood one of the most fearsome members of the staff, his hands folded in front of him, a nearly pleasant look on his face, and a trace of a smile. His head was nodding slightly.

Castlethorn knew he "jist seed" something good happen, something important. He could not figure out why, but he knew this was important. Something like a memory of his was trying to surface, but he could not quite recall it. It involved...wait a second...oh! That fog! That blasted fog always got in his way when he was thinking of stuffs "dat maht be importants!"

Castlethorn stepped out of view, away from the doorway. He heard the principal trying to quiet the class. He looked around and saw no one in the hallway. The lantern! He heard it buzz faintly. The alarm was going off. He grabbed it immediately and gave it a quick spin. Then he checked one of the glass panels. "Hmmm," he muttered quietly, almost a whisper. "They's *not* all hoomin after alls. Nots today, anyhow." He stood there, silent. Just a man and his invention. An invention that could detect trace amounts of energy.

Then the principal screamed, "Silence!" at the students. It was time to settle down now. Castlethorn took that as a cue. He jumped and quickly walked away but past the door. Emily caught a glimpse of him, not smiling anymore and in a hurry. He was staring at one of the panels on his lantern.

"Now, all of you have behaved abominably!" Miss Coffenayle continued.

The classroom was silent now and somber. *Here it comes.* She was really going to let them have now.

"Look at this mess! You should be ashamed!"

Emily did not dare move. She watched Coffenayle closely. What was going to happen now? It had already been such a rough day. Emily's head was already reeling. *Please*, she thought, *no more. I can't take any more of this.*

"Students, learners, all of you! Here is what I demand of all of you for the rest of the day!"

What could it possibly be? Writing sentences over and over for hours? Standing at attention until their feet and knees ached? Whipshot was not here to threaten them with any of her favorite abuses. So…what could Principal Coffenayle have in mind?

"First of all, every one of you get these desks in order. Now!"

The entire student body slid desks and chairs back into their accustomed spaces. They did this immediately, quickly, and efficiently. Then they stood beside their desks, ready to stand "inspection" as Whipshot used to call it.

They expected the principal to go desk to desk the way their teacher would and then blame the students and punish them individually for the deplorable condition of the old broken-down desks they were issued. The desks were something over which they had no control. Even so, the teacher would still berate them, threaten them, put them in the time-out closet or whatever she thought to do.

Emily was behind the teacher's desk now, quietly arranging her things, again fiddling around, actually, but keeping an eye on the situation as it unfolded. She wondered if she ever looked as terrified as her former fellows now appeared when she was student. She must have. How does she look now? Any less afraid? She was worried about the expression on her face because she was now even more terrified than she was as a student. Under Whipshot, things had become predictable, even if they were awful. At least Emily knew what to expect then. Now things were different, new, unprecedented, and *completely unpredictable*. Everyone was off-balance.

"Very good, students," said the Napoleonic principal. She paced the floor as if in deep thought. "Hmm, hmm, and hmm. What to do with you? What to do?" She kept pacing, back and forth. Back and forth. Emily arranged her things again, and she was watching Coffenayle closely. She believed that the principal was going to think up something terrible and then cause Emily to carry it out. That would be *fine* first day, wouldn't it? All of her former classmates turning on her. Even Whipshot's prized pet, Margaret, looked nervous. She was about as nervous as everyone else because she was Whipshot's. She had no relationship with Miss Coffenayle.

Then the principal stopped dead in her tracks. She perked up a bit. She smiled. "I know what to do. This is perfect," she stated wistfully. Everyone in the room held their breaths. "First of all, you are going to clean up this mess. Get water, buckets, and rags from Mr. Castlethorn. I need two volunteers. Who? What's your name, young man? Jimmy? Yes, very good Jimmy. Very fitting since you seem to work well with Mr. Castlethorn. Now let me see. Who are you, young lady? Out with it! Margaret? Ah, yes, I remember you from my office recently. A lovely meeting that was. Now both of you run up the hall and get the things I asked for. *Move!* As for the rest of you—"

Jimmy and Margaret wasted no time in getting up the hall, walking as fast as they could without running. They drew casual attention during their trip from a few teachers who were not preoccupied with yelling at students. None of the teachers demanded a hall pass, which was a cardinal law in this school. They knew the principal was in Whipshot's old classroom and would handle any strays running the halls. Jimmy and Margaret soon arrived at Castlethorn's office. They had that same creepy feeling from before, and they slowly, carefully, opened the door.

9

The Plot Thickens

The hideous gargoyle was still perched over the latch, awful as ever. Margaret and Jimmy opened the door, which did not squeak; Castlethorn must have oiled the hinges. Possibly repaired them. Maybe even replaced them? There was no noise, whatever the cause. The cautious pair eased their way into the old janitor's office. They were not nearly as fearful this time. They walked quietly, carefully into the museum of horrors. Then they heard a sound. It seemed as though Castlethorn was in but somewhere in the back of the workshop.

They never knew how far back that place went. They could not see Mr. Castlethorn, so they ventured further and further back. Then Margaret spotted a mop sink, such as it was, all filthy and greasy. She opted to wait here and try to find a bucket and rags. She suggested that Jimmy might go further back to find Mr. Castlethorn and at least let him know what they were doing.

Jimmy agreed and somehow knew that he *should* do that. So he did. He carefully made his way through the dust and dim lighting. An occasional window did help light the way a little better.

Jimmy worked his way down the aisleway to where he found Castlethorn. The old man was muttering and tinkering with something. Then Jimmy saw the familiar pole from the lantern. Castlethorn was deeply engrossed in whatever he was doing. The screwdriver in his hand appeared to be very small and delicate. Jimmy froze but not in terror or even fear. He was *fascinated* suddenly. This man who barely seemed to be a real person was now leaning over a workbench, working on something that Jimmy could sense was quite delicate, maybe even intricate.

Castlethorn's hand moved deftly, changing delicate oddly-shaped tools from a pouch he had unrolled onto the desktop with precise movements that belied his appearance. He scarcely looked away from the project as he would put tools down, tuck them away, and pick up new ones without looking. He seemed to know *precisely* where each instrument was. Deeply engaged, he was wearing a headset of some kind that protected his eyes.

It consisted of goggles the likes of which Jimmy had never seen before and which required adjusting from time to time. Muttering and murmuring to himself, he was writing with one hand, and the other was selecting tools. Jimmy heard strange words like *exponent, cosine, valance, proton,* and so on as Castlethorn continued to mutter. Jimmy did not want to disturb him, somehow sensing that the work was important. The boy looked around for a moment...then he saw something that drew his attention.

There, on one of the cluttered, dusty, grimy shelves was a picture frame tucked into a cubbyhole. The frame had a cracked crystal. That would not have normally been of interest to him, but Jimmy felt drawn to it. He carefully walked over and saw there was a piece of paper inside of the frame. It seemed to be very important, something of great significance. He looked over at the old janitor who was still busy with his lantern. Jimmy picked up the frame by one corner and gently dusted it off. He found himself captivated and whispered, "Har-vard Uni-ver-si-ty... Doc-tor-*ate*...the doctor ate what? Degree... Phys—"

"Boy!"

Jimmy jumped and shoved the picture frame back into the cubby. He felt a harsh hand spin him around, and he was suddenly staring into two huge human eyeballs. They were bloodshot, the whites were yellowish, and the retinas were deep brown and cloudy. Jimmy could see the terrible movement in these eyes, like the boiling of thick clouds in the terrible winds just before a storm. Castlethorn did not appear human. The boy was petrified at the sight!

"What yees be doin' in my workshop, ehhh...boooy? What be yees lurkin' about, hmm? Be yees hoomin, yesss?" the bug-eyed janitor asked.

Jimmy swallowed hard. "Yes... I-I mean, no. I am not sneaking around. I, um, I was sent by the principal—"

"Ye says, but how doeses I knows that?"

"M-Margaret is here with me. We are trying to get some water and buckets and rags to clean up the c-classroom. I came here to... to let you know." His voice choked off at that point. He stood paralyzed in the gaze of some horrific creature within its grasp. Jimmy sensed great strength in the hand that was on his shoulder. Or was it a pincer? He was afraid to look and find out. Those terrible huge eyes certainly did not appear to be human!

Castlethorn lifted his goggles. Much to Jimmy's relief, the old man's eyes went back to their normal size. These were not the same goggles he wore in the classroom while running the crane. These goggles had magnifying lenses in them, big ones that made the janitor's eyes appear huge. "Waaaait a minit... I remember yees. Yesss. Yees was dat one to help me in the classroom. Yees helped me run mah machine to get ol' Whipshot out the floor...hmmm?"

"Yes. Yes, sir. That was me. Jimmy. You remember me, right?"

Castlethorn released the boy's arm. "Yesss, I remembers yee." He looked around and back at Jimmy. "Yees seemed to be pretty handy around machines. You dassn't seems to be scared of beingz here. Seems only a little skeered of me. What think yee, boy, about coming ta help me sometimes?"

"H-Help you?" stammered the startled young man.

"Yeahhh...ya sees, Jim-boy, I needs me a helper from time ta time. An...ap-appren-um—" Castlethorn's voice trailed off, and his eyes wandered as though he was trying to find words to say.

"An apprentice?" Jimmy squeaked out, barely.

The old janitor's eyes lit up. "Yes! Dat bees the word, Jim-boy! Ap-ren-tis. Yes. I needs me one a dem. You up fer it, sonny boy?"

"We-well...can I think about it after getting some rags?"

"Rags? Rags? Boy, I bees offern you da chance to be more dan pickin' rags. More than pulling a fart-makin' teacher out da floor!"

"Um…okay. I will do it. But we have to get the rags, anyway."

"So…yee saays 'yes' to Castlethorn's jobz offer?" He moved closer to Jimmy, leaning down, almost nose to nose. Jimmy was almost but not quite used to his breath by now, among other odd smells.

"Yes. Yes, I will be your apprentice," said Jimmy, hardly believing his own words. He turned to look at the picture frame and ask his new boss about it, but then—*crash!*

Something hit the shelf. Then something else fell. Then something else! Was it an earthquake? Castlethorn left Jimmy and ran to his lantern, which was now completely buttoned up and ready to go. Castlethorn twirled the lantern around in a circle as Jimmy had seen in times past, only he did not cluck like a chicken. Things were flying now from all directions, aimed at *them.* The old man seemed very somber. He peered into one of the panels, and Jimmy noticed that it was lit up, glowing red.

"Jimbo," Castlethorn began, "wees not all hoomin beans…*run!*"

"Gladly!" responded the new apprentice. Castlethorn did the best he could to lead Jimmy out of the back rooms. They ran as fast as Castlethorn could with the old man carrying his lantern.

Jimmy could have run much faster on his own but did not dare. He prayed that the old janitor knew what he was doing. Then Castlethorn stopped in front of one of his machines. Two machines, actually, one across from the other, spanning the aisleway. Jimmy watched as some invisible force was knocking things over and throwing objects in their direction. It was advancing quickly. Jimmy was stunned.

"Stand yese back, boy!" yelled Castlethorn. He turned a dial and grabbed a lever, watching things fall off the shelves. As soon as it seemed that the invisible force was dangerously close, his grimy hand pulled the lever. Jimmy could not believe his own senses. First there was a reverberating hum. Then the smell of ozone. Then a winding noise that grew higher and higher in pitch and intensity. Finally, a burst of lighting and fire! Jimmy winced and turned away, seeing stars and flashes now, even with his eyes closed. Castlethorn turned off the machines, and as quickly as it started, it was all over. "Bee yees okay, Jimmy-boy?" asked the old man with his reassuring hand on the boy's shoulder. It smelled weird. Even so, it was a comfort.

"My eyes—" Jimmy said, holding both eyes with his palms.

"Ye'll be okayz, boy," Castlethorn said soothingly. "Looksee up herez." The old man had what looked like a household lamp in his hand. Then he turned it on. The bulb glowed with a strange swirling light, a very soft light of multiple colors, and immediately, Jimmy's eyes began to feel better. After about ten seconds, they were no longer sore and completely restored.

"Wow, what was that?" Jimmy asked. He blinked two or three times, and he was completely fine again.

"Never yese mindz it, boy," the gruff old man answered. "I'se been experimentin', and that's all you needs ta know."

Jimmy was not sure he wanted to know. Castlethorn turned back to his lantern. He made a few mumbling sounds and then announced, "Well, Jimbo, looks we got rid a that one. We's all hoomin beans here now."

"What *was* that?" Jimmy asked, suddenly remembering *why* Castlethorn nearly blinded him with that crazy machine.

"Dey's, uh...well, you know, I can't rightly say, Jimmy. I s'pose if'n I was to guess, I would say they was some kind of ghosts...likez a...um...polterghost o' sum kahnd."

"Ghosts," Jimmy pondered and decided he was not going ask any more questions.

"Now, youse lookee here, Jimbo. I'se trusted you with some things that I don't want the school to know. Specially ol' *Coffin-nail.*"

"The principal? She's the last one I would want to deal with. She scares me. Besides, what am I going to say? That you've made a machine that kills ghosts? That you can fix busted eyeballs after they were struck by lightning? Ha! She'd have me tied to a tree and beaten for lying. Nobody would believe this story. I just lived it, and I'm not sure *I* believe it. What is going here, anyway?"

"Well, Jim-boy, let me tell yese something... Ah ain't goingz tuh tell you *nothin!*" He paused and let Jimmy take that in. "Not until

Ah's can figger dis all out for myselfs. Ye sees, for a long time, Ah ain't been feelingz good. Some dayz iz betterz than others...somes is werser dan others..." His voice trailed off.

"So do you still want me as your apprentice?" Jimmy asked meekly.

"*Ha!* Boy, ye're talkin' like we gots a choice. We dassn't. Not now. Not wiff what youse knows. Yese hasta keep things quiet, and that means I has to keeps you close to me"—Castlethorn leaned in really close to Jimmy ominously—"to make sure yese keepin' mees secret stuffs *very secret*. Yese hearin' me?"

Jimmy shuddered, gulped, and promised that he would never tell anyone what he saw here today. He meant it too. Who would he tell anyway? Who would believe him? And just then, he heard Margaret stirring around. Margaret! He'd forgotten.

"Mr. Castlethorn! Quick! We need some rags and buckets so I can meet Margaret with them. We can't let her see all this stuff!"

The janitor and the student suddenly were just their plain selves again, no longer ghost-fighting experimenters. Castlethorn gathered some rags and showed Jimmy where the buckets were. They managed to intercept Margaret just in time. She was getting worried and showed visible signs of relief when Jimmy and Castlethorn showed up with the rags and buckets.

"Jimmy! My gosh! Where the heck were you? I was getting worried because I heard a lot of noise!" exclaimed Margaret.

"Never you mind. It just took a few minutes to find this stuff. We had to bang around a little to get to it. I'm just fine," replied Jimmy. "Mr. Castlethorn has offered to help us take all this to the class, so we can get it there faster by saving two trips. Right, Mr. Castlethorn?"

Margaret just looked at Jimmy the way girls look at boys when they know they've just been lied to. She said nothing.

The old man grumbled, "Ah reckons Ise kin do that." Then off they went to classroom to help clean up the mess.

When they arrived, the principal was just about ready to make a great announcement. The students did the best they could to get things wiped off without any proper rags and water. With the arrival of the Castlethorn cavalry, now they had both. The small band of adventurers came into the classroom and set down the water buckets and rags. Castlethorn realized he had forgotten his lantern but really did not have room to carry it with a bucket of water in each hand. He would have to do without it, but he really hated to with the action they had just seen in his workshop. Good thing he built the machines when he did. The school had become active with paranormal happenings, and he was glad that he could save Jimmy.

10

Emily and the Big Announcement

"Well, isn't this nice," said Miss Coffenayle. "Thank you, Mr. Castlethorn, for joining the students. We could use your help."

He immediately tried to make some lame excuse to leave; he really wanted to have his lantern close. It was back in the office because he was helping the kids to carry things. But Coffenayle would have none of that. "Piddle-twaddle!" she said. "We need your help *here!*" she exclaimed. She looked right at him. The old custodian had seen that look before and would not challenge her any further. Last time he did, that look cost him a couple of weeks of sleeping out in the weather, the only sheltering option being the old lean-to in the school's pigsty. When it rained over the next two weeks, he could either risk the pneumonia or stay in the pigpen. He was not going to challenge her like that again. The time in the pigpen was unpleasant and smelly, but after a while, the pigs got used to the smell.

"Well, then, ma'—Well then, Miz Coffenayle, I supposez Ah kin stays an' help." He was relieved that he caught that "Ma'am" before it tumbled too far off of his tongue. She hated "Ma'am," and he was not about to provoke her with that one either. It had been too long of a day for that.

The kids were all gathering around, getting wet rags and cleaning up the walls, floors, and bookcases. Mr. Castlethorn was more than happy to get a ladder. Jimmy noticed with a smile to see the old man bring back his lantern along with the ladder. He even winked

136

at Jimmy. The boy really wanted to know what that old lantern truly was! Now, since he was the engineer's apprentice, he would surely be able to find out.

The principal never got around to making her grand announcement. She had insisted that she would wait until after the cleaning was completed. She had other things that she needed to do in her office right now. She said that she would later return and make her announcement. She left the students at that.

Before the principal left, though, she instructed Miss Emily that since she was now a teacher and not a student, she was to instruct and observe, not to clean. She was not one of *them* anymore. *Miss* Emily Keller had assumed a different role today and lived by different rules.

Emily said that she would gladly keep the rules the principal just outlined for her, but secretly, she wasn't very happy about it.

Her displeasure at the new arrangement was a secret she kept to herself. She could not let Coffenayle know that she had different ideas about a how a teacher should behave at times like this. It was too soon to try and rock the boat. So she assumed the role of observing and suggesting different ways of doing things, more efficient ways. She would offer praise when things were done properly the first time and corrective suggestions when there were issues with the work that needed to be addressed. There was no degrading the students in any of it.

Castlethorn made himself busy with getting the floor repairs done. He even asked Miss Emily during a quick side discussion if he could borrow Jimmy for his side of the project. He also let her in on his decision to make Jimmy his apprentice and use him on different jobs around the school. Emily thought that was a wonderful idea as long as Jimmy kept up with his studies. Not that Emily was worried about Jimmy. She knew he was smart and could keep up just fine. In fact, she thought he might even make the better teacher of the two of them. Even if she thought that, it was not what the school administration wanted. Miss Emily was determined to toe the line. She would do whatever she was told to do.

She was concerned, though, about what the future held. She would become a student again, eventually. How would that affect the relationship she had with her fellow learners? There were not many, if any at all, friendships in the class. There was not much friendship in the whole school for that matter. The cruelty and abuse of the teachers prevented that. Coffenayle intentionally engineered the society of the school so as to prevent the students from making friends or having kids pair off in relationships. Love, above all, was *forbidden!*

Emily was supervising the cleaning and Jimmy, sent by Castlethorn, returned with the lantern. Then suddenly, Castlethorn started his routine of twirling his lantern and clucking like a Rhode Island Red. He was spinning his lantern furiously on that pole. The students all stopped to stare at the spectacle. Emily was concerned because she did not need any disruptions, not now. Not when things were just getting put back together. "Buck-buck-buck, ba-kaw! Buck-buck-buck, ba-kaw!" he hollered as he twirled his lantern. He kept this up for longer than usual, it seemed. He made his sing-song chant. Then he stopped and stared at the lantern. "Hoomin beans most is, hoomin beans one ain't." He returned to work after making his cryptic pronouncement. What on *earth* was this man talking about?

"Mr. Castlethorn, sir," Emily began, "are you quite finished with your 'hoomin beans?'"

Castlethorn laid his lantern and pole against the wall. "I'll jist leaves this here for now. Ah ain't near finish with them dat's *not* hoomin beans."

Whatever he wants, Emily thought to herself. *As long as he's quiet and not disrupting things.* She could not understand his affinity with beans and did not understand either what a 'hoomin' was. She just accepted that he was an eccentric but capable man, and he was very good at what he did. The way that he rescued Miss Whipshot out of the floor was certainly unconventional, but it was effective. He seemed to be very good at cleaning up things too. He was busily working on the floor and walls, efficient and confident in his work. She just hoped he would not have any strange effect on Jimmy, his new apprentice.

Emily was quite satisfied with how things were going. She was still not comfortable with being in charge, but she had to admit that she was much happier with Whipshot out of the picture. Everyone was. The room even *felt* different. Everything seemed to feel different now, and she could not quite put her finger on why. Something dramatically changed, for sure. She was not supposed to help the students, and she did not want Coffenayle to catch her in the act, not on her first day "teaching." Since Emily was not an expert in what Castlethorn was doing, and she could not help the students, she decided that she would get to the business of being a teacher. She turned back to her desk and…*what on earth?*

Emily looked at her desk and found that her things were completely rearranged! What had been a somewhat neat arrangement, simply and casually laid on her desk, without her knowing how to organize things, was now laid out neatly. Books were in stacks by subject, pens and pencils in place, and even a lesson plan book, which Emily did not notice in the pile when she was carrying it, turned to the proper page to begin planning! She stifled a startled shout. No point in stirring things up any more than they had already been. This was a very strange day; it was time for the strangeness to come to an end.

The new teacher sat at her desk and began her lesson plans but was rather distracted by the arrangement of her books. She could not understand why her things had moved. Mr. Castlethorn had nothing to do with it, but she could not help but think that *something* was up with him. He kept talking about 'hoomin beans,' whatever those were, and how everyone was a hoomin bean, or not. That lantern, the clucking noises, his seeming genius, and now these books. What did he have to do with this? She could not understand how these events had to be related. At the height of her preoccupation, a sudden thought entered her mind accompanied by the familiar sensation that a friendly loving arm was across her shoulder. Words rang through her mind, *Now, shouldn't you be busily engaged in teaching your new students?*

This thought gave Emily great comfort. She was able to focus now, realizing that just maybe, these strange events were really not her concern at the moment.

Emily began her lesson plans for tomorrow, starting with the first course of the day: English Literature. Math and history could wait. She needed to teach her first class and make a great impression on her students. They were getting ready to do a survey of the major works of Charles Dickens, a brilliant author whose family was flat broke and nearly ruined him with bad spending habits. Thoughts, again, with the friendly sensation entered her mind: *Why don't you link Dickens' creative genius and lifestyle to a lesson in life economics? Why not teach the students that success is more than just living a high lifestyle, that money must not be squandered?*

Emily knew that to be a brilliant thought. It seemed to be almost audible. She could practically hear what was being...dare she think...*suggested* to her?

She wrote the idea down and thought it important enough to work in. It just seemed to her that there was so much to do all at once. She could not do it all at once, but still, all of the priorities seemed to be top priorities. Everything needed to be done at once but could not be. She had to plan her lessons for tomorrow, being Friday, but then for the whole next week. She would have her normal chores to do over the weekend; the students were kept incredibly busy, even on their off times. They were tasked with keeping the school grounds in order, weeding out by the old field, hoeing, working in the school gardens, etc. How could she possibly get this all done? It was impossible. All of this was impossible. She and her fellow students had been through so much.

"But you have already seen the impossible," said the friendly *voice* in her mind. "I know that you saw how Miss Whipshot truly fell down. If *that* impossible thing did indeed happen, then what prevents *this* impossible thing from happening?"

Now Emily was becoming concerned. She had heard of "crazy people" hearing voices talk in their heads. But she somehow understood that this was different. This voice was not strange or demanding or angry. Plus, it always was accompanied by a sort of peace. For certain, she did see that chair get taken apart and that part roll right where it would cause Whipshot to fall. She *knew* that happened and she knew it was *impossible*.

On top of that, with those things that she saw Castlethorn do, she knew that something certainly seemed to be afoot.

"So," continued the voice, "if those impossible things are happening, and you have seen them and know them to be both impossible and happening, does this not mean that other impossible things may also happen? Imagine the possibilities of the *im*possible."

Emily sat quietly, sort of frozen in fascination at what she was just told. This very gentle but masculine and manly voice, like a well-seasoned grandfather, was teaching her. How could this be?

"Don't focus on the how or the possibility. Focus on what is," he continued. Then came a sense of urgency, but not panic. "Oh my! Get yourself together. Miss Coffenayle is coming, and she has something to say. Don't worry. I will still be here, even if you can't hear me. You are fine. She has good news."

Emily quickly surveyed the room. All was being placed in perfect order. The floor repairs were progressing fine, the students were done cleaning up all the goo, cake, frosting, and general mess of the celebratory riot. They were becoming exhausted; she was too. Even Castlethorn was showing signs of weariness. It was a surprising, long, tiring, and for Emily, a most fascinating day…one that ended with the most impossible circumstances. She was now a *teacher*, of all things. Plus, it seemed that she had a ghostly ally…or something like that. She stood and made sure all of her books and supplies were aligned. She called out an order. "Students! All of you! Place your buckets and rags in the corner by that closet. Straighten your desks. Then please be seated."

"Are we starting class now, '*Miss Emily?*'" A student asked in a mocking tone. The classroom laughed, and Emily allowed herself to smile.

"Okay, all of you, that is enough. We need to be seated because the room is cleaned up rather nicely, thank you, and while we won't have class today, obviously because we need some rest, we will go over tomorrow's schedule." The class seemed to ignore her and started gathering, but not in their chairs. They were standing around and chatting, laughing, socializing. Emily did not blame them, but she had to be in control of the class when Miss Coffenayle arrived or she would lose creditability and trust. She did not know what to do but then had an idea that did not seem to be entirely her own. She felt inspired by her "teacher," that kindly old man-voice.

She walked up on the students quickly and said rather quietly, "Everyone, I have a game for us to play."

That got their attention. They all gathered in excitedly. "We are going to play a trick on the principal!"

"On the principal?" asked one student.

"We can't do that!" exclaimed another.

"We'll be punished," stated Tommy Littleton, the boy from the closet. Tears began to fill his eyes.

"Oh," stated Emily. "Well, instead of playing a trick and getting punished, what would be better?"

"Strict obedience," said Margaret with some air of cockiness. "We must obey or get whatever we deserve. All of you know that *I* will see to it that the principal knows who was planning the trick if one gets played." She lifted her nose in the air, inviting a challenge.

The other students groaned. Yes, the teacher's pet. Nobody liked her, but nobody dared lay a hand on her either. She was Whipshot's favorite. Things would sometimes happen to Margaret, petty little things that she could not prove. A tug at her hair in a crowded hallway, a spitball to the back of her neck; sometimes she may even find her desk vandalized with caricature of her drawn as a sewer rat with her face on it—things like that. These things were petty and annoying but effective in letting her know that she was not liked. No one went beyond that kind of pettiness. They knew where the line was. They saw a frustrated classmate slap her one day. Perhaps it was well-deserved, but that student was severely punished by Whipshot. He was sent to live with Nurse Shadyknight for about ten days.

"Well, then," said Miss Emily, "*I* certainly don't want to do anything to get into trouble. I don't want to be punished. Do any of you?" She looked around. All eyes were to the floor, except for Margaret who was looking rather pleased with herself. Emily wanted to say something, but now was not the time for that. She would pull her aside later. "Then," stated Emily simply, "don't we need to have the classroom in order when the principal arrives? Didn't she say that she had an important announcement? Yes, she did, and when has she ever missed an announcement? A chance to tell us how wonderful things are? Would it then not be to our advantage to have all of our things in order? Shouldn't we be ready to receive her?"

The students eagerly agreed, straightened the room, and took their seats. Some sat with their heads down, and Emily allowed it. It seemed reasonable. Some students actually fell right to sleep. They were understandably exhausted. Emily took her place at the head of the class and sat at her desk, prepared for tomorrow. It was at that moment that Miss Coffenayle walked in. Emily looked up. "Class! Please come to attention! Principal Coffenayle is here!"

Even those students who seemed to be deeply asleep suddenly stood to attention. Emily also stood up, poised and formal, with her hands folded neatly in front of her. She appeared every inch the stately educator.

Miss Coffenayle looked down her nose at her new teacher. She was obviously pleased and gave a condescending nod to Miss Emily. Apparently, she had chosen her new teacher very well.

The children, the students, *her wards*, all in her hands, appeared completely ridiculous standing at attention, their clothes covered with muck. Castlethorn stood too, back to the wall, his lantern pole in hand. Emily desperately hoped that he would not start with that whole "beans" routine right now. She almost held her breath in anticipation, but Castlethorn seemed calm for the moment. Even if he was glancing from time to time at one of the windows on that lantern. He was looking around and seemed to shift the lantern to a new orientation while studying its window. A strange impossible thought occurred to her, one that she was becoming open-minded enough to address. But later. This was not the time; other business was at hand.

"Well," Coffenayle started with a smile that would freeze a bonfire, "it seems as though you have responded to Miss Emily's *discipline* very well." Margaret seemed to be especially pleased with herself, Emily noted. "It seems that you are actually ready to be taught." She seemed to perhaps mull over the idea of having class but thought better of it. "However, not today. No, not today. I see that you have cleaned up the mess you made of my classroom. It was done correctly, I see."

The principal paced the room, touching surfaces as though she were checking for dust, every inch the general making an inspection. She spoke as she was walking and looking. "Everything seems to be as orderly as you could make it. I am pleased." That frozen smile again. Those condescending eyes, looking all around, stopping occasionally at a random student's desk, causing the students to each tremble slightly. *Perfect*, Coffenayle thought. *They are scared enough to be subjected and kept in order but not so scared that they cannot learn. Perfect!* This greatly pleased her arrogant mind.

Emily knew the principal was up to something, as did every student in that room. But what? What could she possibly conjure up this time? Had the school not seen enough activity for one day? All of the other classes had been dismissed to dinner a long time ago. Dinner was almost surely over. Not that they worried much about the normal fare granted them by the cafeteria lady. Greasy, starchy, bland with cold food served warm, warm food served cold, stale bread, milk that had almost, but not quite, turned sour…yuck! Who needed it? Even so, at the end of the day, hunger was hunger, and the kids had to eat.

"Some of you," continued the pacing Napoleon, "no doubt, are wondering about dinner. Well, does anyone here *actually* feel hungry?"

Silence.

"Well, now, I *do* want an answer. Do any of you students feel hungry?"

Slowly, tentatively, some of them shook their heads.

"Now, students, as ladies and gentlemen, shaking the head does not answer the question," she continued quietly. "You have my permission to speak. *Does anyone here actually feel hungry?*"

"No," answered several nervous students.

"I see. So you spoiled your dinner with treats and such that you *stole* from Miss Whipshot, then?"

Even Margaret's eyes went to the floor on that one, Emily noticed. She was eating cakes and treats right along with the rest of them.

"Well," the principal made an overly dramatic sigh. Then she paused. The classroom held its collective breath. Even Castlethorn was leaning forward a bit. He seemed...perhaps...*concerned* to Emily. She was surprised that the old man really had room in his heart for empathy. He was one of the people the class feared most. All the same, here he was, worried about the students. Or maybe he was just worried for himself, afraid to be caught in the net. Actually, though...it seemed to be more than that. "I suppose, then that some form of discipline is in order." Miss Coffenayle paused, pretending to be in deep thought.

Here it comes, the classroom thought in unison. This was going to be terrible. A week without food? Endless sixteen-hour days in the gardens, drinking minimal water out of a community ladle served out of a bucket wielded by Goliath? Being sent to the lockdown room with no chair, table or bed, and nothing but dirty white walls to stare at for days at a time? What was it to be? Emily was becoming terrified.

Castlethorn was attentive, watching the principal's every move, his eyes not glancing at his precious lantern even a little bit. Jimmy was hoping that he could serve his time with Castlethorn. Even that creepy, smelly, haunted engineering room was safer than any discipline Coffenayle could dream up.

"The punishment must fit the cr-r-r-rime," Coffenayle said in her most stately voice, rolling the 'R' in crime. "Time in the gardens, maybe? Hmmm? No, the gardens I think are well-tended for now. A *different* classroom of our best and brightest, not *you,* just spent a week out there. Maybe we should go to the time-out room." She paused for dramatic effect. "Perhaps, but those are all currently occupied by other unruly students. I should have you clean the room top to bottom." She looked around in mock study of the room. "Hmph! On second thought, that appears to be done. Well," she continued and sighed yet again, "it seems that there is only one thing left to do."

Everyone really was very worried now. What could be worse than the gardens or the time-out room? She was certainly not going to let them off easy for this one. A few of students tried to convince themselves, unsuccessfully, that whatever punishment they were given was worth it, that the price was worth the riot they started. It was fun, yes, but now it was time to pay the piper, and if the punishment fit the crime—

"I have decided," decreed her highness, "that this *entire* classroom and every student in it, shall be..."

They all waited. Some kids had tears in their eyes. "Thoroughly instructed on how to throw a *proper celebration! Ha!*" She clapped her hands as she leaned forward with the smile of someone who had just played the ultimate prank.

The students were stunned, mouths open, some blinking their eyes and shaking their heads. *What? What did she just say?*

The principal looked around the classroom, eyes wide, broad open-mouth smile. She was waiting for them to say anything, but they were all stunned, too terrified to say a word. She had them entirely in hand and knew it. After all, this was out of character for her, and she knew it puzzled the class. "Students! Stuuu-dents! Are you with me, hmmmm? Are you paying attention? I said for punishment, you are going to be taught the *proper* way to *celebrate!*" She looked around again.

Emily glanced over at Castlethorn. He was apparently stunned, his mouth half open. In all his years, however foggy his recollection of those years might be, he did not ever see Coffenayle behave this way. Emily sensed his surprised look was completely genuine... very human...and that pleased her. It seemed that there was more to this weird eccentric-acting old man than anyone really knew. Poor Tommy was sitting there in tears, not daring to wipe them away, not caring if anyone saw them. He was so shocked at this roller coaster of a day. Why would Miss Coffenayle tease them like this? Why, Tommy wondered, did she not simply announce the cursed punishment and get it over with?

Emily knew now that something had to happen. She did not want the principal to believe that the students were not grateful for being taught the "proper way to celebrate." Somehow, as far out of character as it was for Miss Coffenayle, Emily understood that the class was about to have a real party! Before the dictator had an opportunity to turn barbaric at a perceived lack of gratitude, Emily decided to take a chance and interrupt.

"Pardon me, Principal Coffenayle?" Emily gently ventured.

"Yes, Miss Emily?" the principal answered, never taking her eyes off the classroom, her smile beginning to fade at the perceived ingratitude.

"Perhaps you might explain your *generous* offer more clearly. We have had a long day, and the students are bit tired." She did not want to mention that the students could not possibly believe that a howling wretch like Miss Coffenayle could ever be suspected of something as trite and old-fashioned as human decency. She did not want to say that something like a party would be so far removed from Miss Coffenayle, that it would never cross the minds of the students, unless it were explained to them clearly. She could not say that seeing Whipshot nearly kill herself by falling through the floor was the *only* cause for celebration they ever had under the school's "gentle tutelage." So Miss Emily said, "Maybe they don't quite understand what you are getting at."

"Ah, yes. It has been a hard day, hasn't it, Miss Emily? I could see where someone might not be able to digest this idea on a belly full of cake and hands reddened by our homemade lye soap." Several of the students' hands were actually reddened by their efforts at cleaning without the benefit of gloves to protect them. The little Napoleon composed herself, renewed her devilish smile, and held her head high. She began to strut a bit around the classroom.

She continued with, "Yes, a very hard day indeed. Perhaps a joke would ease the tension a bit. So, class, why did the student cross the road?"

No answer.

"To avoid a beating, get back to classroom, and have a *party!* Baw-ha! Ha! Ha!" She bent over again, laughing this time, clapped her hands in front of her, and held them there. "Ha! Ha! Ha!"

The students started to wake up a bit. Tommy quit crying and freely wiped his eyes. A party! Is *that* what she said?

Emily saw the response from some of the students, and she started laughing too, even if it was forced a bit. She shouted, "A party! Yay!" and clapped her hands. Then the classroom started to brighten with genuine relief and laughter and applause as though the axe man had just released them from the chopping block to go home and have dinner. The classroom was cheering and laughing, and the principal seemed genuinely delighted! The gleam in her eye was nearly maniacal, but Emily did not dwell on that. She was happy that the students were happy.

Emily looked directly at Castlethorn who just sort of stood there, appearing rather calm and half-smiling. His eyes looked pleased. He peeked at his lantern and looked back at Emily. He held up one finger. She did not quite know what it meant but suspected that maybe one was there who was not…a bean? Well, time for that later.

The principal basked in the adoration. Hands at her sides, chin aloft, her closed lips stretched in a very proud pleased smile. She let them have their way for a couple of moments. They all knew that they could not get out of hand and knew better than to leave their desks. For all of that, they restrained themselves and were very excited but contained the excitement. Even poor targeted Tommy smiled. Margaret smiled too but seemed to wonder at what was really going on. She seemed to almost resent the party. Perhaps the thought of happiness in the class offended one who helped support the misery and profited by it. This could end her usefulness, her favored status.

Almost on cue, the students sat quietly again, awaiting further instructions. The principal was certain that she had their full attention when she started speaking. "Now I want all of you to go back to your dorms and clean up. Bathe yourselves out of your buckets as is our common practice. Wash your clothes so those stains don't set in," she began. Not that it mattered, those rags the kids wore were so stained by their hand-me-down status that a few more stains made little difference. "Then retire to your beds. Sleep an extra hour, skip study, and exercise. But do *not* be late for breakfast."

She paused for more applause and felt as though her ego may burst the buttons on her blue jacket! Such adoration! All from a room of impoverished beaten curs. It doesn't get any better than that! This was the effect that small favors had upon helpless captives deprived of even the most basic human needs. When the captor restores one of those needs, the captive believes the captor to be "not so bad" or perhaps "heroic." Professors, many years hence, would call this "Stockholm Syndrome."

Miss Coffenayle could get used to this but knew better than to spoil them. Free will was very difficult to crush, and she would not want them getting out of hand and actually start *thinking for themselves*. She could not have that. Independence of thought could lead to…self-esteem, friendship…*love*. She nearly grimaced at that thought but still managed to keep her aloof grin.

"Now, all of you, enjoy your night. Remember to arise at 5:00 a.m. sharp, instead of the customary 4:00 a.m. Your half hour of study and half hour exercise period before breakfast is suspended for tomorrow *only*."

The students smiled at that too but did not erupt into applause. They seemed to sense that might be too much of a good thing. "Eat your breakfast at 6:00 a.m. Then come to class as usual."

The principal turned neatly on her heel and headed for the door. "Miss Emily shall dismiss you at her discretion," she stated at the ceiling on her way out. When the door closed behind the principal, Castlethorn left his posted position at the wall and began fussing around with that strange lantern. Emily noticed that his back was to the classroom, and he seemed to be tinkering a bit, his hands out of sight.

Emily knew it was high time to get everyone to their dorms. "All right, everyone! All arise."

The class stood in unison, as they always did at the end of the day. It was time for their pledge.

We pledge allegiance to our school,
Happy Valley be she named.
We are happy, not in a valley,
But happy just the same.

We praise the prairie that keeps us here;
That barrenness is heaven-sent.
Too far to walk, too far to run;
Escape to die a dissident!

We love our teachers, and our staff,
We eat our food with a laugh.
We love Miss Coffenayle, our leader true,
We love Miss Coffenayle through and through.

All hail Happy Valley!

11

Emily's New Life

Emily allowed everyone to leave in an orderly manner. She was surprised at how they obeyed so fully. The students knew that they had to make Miss Emily look good as a teacher to keep her. Even if this was just a temporary thing, they figured that anyone would be better than Miss Whipshot. They also understood that Miss Coffenayle was watching them closely, surveying them secretly. No one wanted to get on the wrong side of her either. The students each smiled on their way out, all of them chatting quietly about their good fortunes of late.

Margaret locked eyes with Miss Emily, unsure of her position with this fledgling teacher. She and the student Emily-Whipshot had locked horns before. Miss Emily gave her a smile and a nod to convey that all was forgiven; things were different now. Margaret halfway smiled back, uncomfortably, as though to say, "*We will all soon see what comes of this.*" Emily herself was very unsure; in fact, uncertainty was the *only* thing of which she was certain.

Miss Emily then approached Castlethorn who was still out in the hallway, muttering to himself, his back to the room. He was engrossed in something, so deeply, in fact, that he did not seem to know that the room had just emptied. Emily approached him carefully and saw in hands...*a slide rule?* No mistake about it, that was a slide rule! Emily said "Mr.—" and he jumped with a shout, instantly concealing his tool!

He glared at her.

"Sorry for frightening you, Mr. Castlethorn. Class was just dismissed, and I think that all of us, including you, should get some rest."

Castlethorn's visage softened. He did look tired, even for him. He seemed sad. He looked at the newest teacher and nodded. "G'night, Miss Emily. Gones off to mees bed now." He slumped away sadly. Tired. Worn. He was certainly going to sleep well. The pole to his lantern dragged along behind him, his lantern in hand. Miss Emily turned out the lights and turned to secure the door. She was in the hallway with the key in the lock when she was startled by a familiar voice.

"Well, you are very impressive, Miss Emily. I am most pleased." Miss Coffenayle had crept up silently, somehow, even in her combat boots. Normally, one could hear her, but not this time.

Emily was startled but suppressed a shout. "Thank you, Miss Coffenayle. I did try my best."

"Yes, dear, and you certainly were extraordinary in your performance. Walk with me, and I will take you to your new quarters."

"My...quarters?" Emily asked, more than a little surprised.

"Yes. Now that you are a teacher, we can't have you bunking with the students anymore. What if they were to get into your lesson plans or see the answers to a test?"

That made total sense to Emily. It would not be fitting to have a teacher living in the student quarters. They already had security on staff at night watching the students for attempted runaways, so teachers were not needed overnight. The principal walked side by side with the new teacher. They were both quiet. They left the main school building and walked to a part of the campus beyond the gardens. There was a neighborhood of small *houses*. Emily had expected to be in another dormitory situation. Instead, she was in a place where all the homes appeared to be the same. They were all in neat rows with gravel roads surrounding them.

Each road was marked with a letter on a signpost as A, B, C, and so on. Each house was marked with a number. The roads were built on square angles; each house had a small dirt lot that was fenced. Some of the homes had tufts of grass and weak scrubby shrubs growing in the tiny yards. The homes all had chimneys, indicating wood-burning fireplaces. They arrived at a home that was nicely seated on F-Street, lot number 1. "Here you are, Miss Emily," said Coffenayle. She waved her arm as though she was presenting to Emily a room at the Taj Mahal.

Now, to Emily…this *was* like a Taj Mahal. She wondered *how many* people were going to live there with her.

Coffenayle produced a key and unlocked the door. She held the key out to Emily and smiled. The smile seemed almost sincere. It was not unlike a parent's smile who was showing a toddler a butterfly for the first time. Indeed, it was much like that. Much like that indeed.

Emily looked at her principal quizzically, not quite understanding why she was being handed a *key*. Students were forbidden to lock up personal effects, leaving them open to frequent and unnecessary inspections. Personal space was not only a luxury at Happy Valley; it was *forbidden!*

"Go on," said Miss Coffenayle. "Take the key. It's all right. You are a teacher now, Miss Emily, and with teaching come certain… advantages. You have access now to things that you are not used to having," she said kindly and gently.

Emily slowly took the key from her boss's hand and looked at it; she did not quite yet understand what was being presented to her. Yesterday, she was in a dorm, crowded and smelly, with very little privacy. Perhaps there was some time in the bathroom alone; even that was compromised by the number of students all rushing to use the facilities at the same time. She could not really understand the idea that she was now a member of the school faculty. She was not a student, no longer a member of the ofttimes *literally* unwashed masses.

"It's okay, Miss Emily. Your life at the school here is different now. Certainly, it will stay different if you continue to perform as you did in that classroom today. I was very impressed with the way you handled yourself and those students."

Miss Coffenayle seemed almost friendly, but Emily knew not to drop her guard. That grandfatherly voice seemed to whisper in her ear just now…something about trusting snakes in a garden? She took the key and tentatively placed her hand on the doorknob, turning it. She looked back at Coffenayle and opened the door.

The little home was dimly lit with no lights on. The remaining daylight beaming in through the windows reflected off the free-floating dust and gave the effect of sunbeams through a cloud. Emily looked around at the living room, the dining area with a stove, a small sink, bare wood floors, and what, she supposed, was a door to the washroom. To her right, another closed door. What could that be?

Miss Coffenayle gave her a moment to soak it all in. Emily stared wide-eyed, barely comprehending what she was seeing. The cunning woman, the lead educator, the illustrious Miss Coffenayle was bursting with joy. She was manipulating Miss Emily. The thought was to give her a better life, and she would fall into line. Otherwise, she could become dangerous and lead the students astray. She was not so concerned about that after Emily's performance today because she saw in her a potential dictator. She could easily replace Whipshot, once a little more meanness was trained into her. The tea would, of course, help with that.

"Um," Emily began, unsure of what to even ask. Then something occurred to her, almost panicking her. "Where are my things?" She had so little material to work with, like all of the other students. A comb, a bar of lye soap, a towel. Each student was issued just one each. That plus two changes of clothes, no real uniform, just random clothing that more or less fit. The clothes were all hand-me-downs. Each student dorm was filled to capacity with beds. There was no privacy at all. That way, there was no way to have time alone to think. They would not have time for pondering or reflection, which are sources of inspiration and ideas. Ideas often lead to rebellion.

"I took the liberty of having your '*things*' recycled back into the system, Miss Emily."

Emily spun around in horror. He eyes were wide, her mouth open! Her things! Oh no! She was left with absolutely nothing now! What would she do? The others that lived here would never lend her, the new girl, anything. How would she get by? How would she appear in class in the same clothes every day? How would she bathe? No soap! No comb!

Coffenayle smiled, reading Emily's panic perfectly. She knew what the child was thinking. She had carefully programmed the students to think just like that. Deprive them of any decent living. Keep them preoccupied with daily survival. Make them count on you for all of life's necessities! Deprive them of any and all culture, art, joy, and elbow room. Keep them crowded and dependent on the system for their living. Do this with them, and something as simple as a toothbrush becomes a luxury item. They will praise the system for the simplest items of living and will obey subserviently for the slightest comfort. They will rat out a fellow student for a clean towel. They will labor for hours on end to have five minutes of music. Then they will thank the system for it!

In this case, Miss Coffenayle *was* the system! Ah, the power of deprivation! The power of oppression! Miss Coffenayle was gaining more and more power every day! She loved that feeling.

"Let me show you around, Emily, if I may call you that outside of the classroom?"

Emily nodded. The principal *asking permission to call her by name?* Emily never even knew that was possible.

"Here," she said, taking hold of a doorknob, "is the bathroom. Not a washroom like the dorms." She opened the door, and there was a toilet, a sink, and what was that? A *bathtub?* Emily's mouth was open, hardly knowing what to say.

"But what about my towel? My washcloth? My comb? Oh... okay. Is that my towel on the floor then?"

"No... Emily," Miss Coffenayle explained while stifling a chuckle, "that is your *bath mat*. It helps keep the floor dry. You climb out of the tub, and you stand on it while you dry off."

"Wha?" Emily could hardly understand. "How will I ever have time to do that?"

"Now," continued Coffenayle, intentionally overlooking that question until the end. "Let me turn on some lights." She turned on the bathroom light first, then the living room, and they ended up in the kitchen. The place was bright as the sun in Emily's eyes. It was like a miracle! The dimly lit dorms barely afforded enough light for students to read. She led Emily to the sink and showed her the lower cabinet where the cleaning supplies were. Scrub brush for dishes, soap for dishwashing, a rack to place the clean dishes—

"Is that my bath towel?" Emily asked eagerly, pointing at a towel neatly folded near the sink.

This time, the principal chuckled aloud, unable to stifle it. "No, that is your *dish* towel. We will get to the bath towel in a moment."

Emily was stunned and stayed quiet, mulling over everything, her head practically spinning. *Certainly, there is a community towel then,* she thought. *But...a dish towel? A towel just for dishes? How is that possible?*

"Now," said Miss Coffenayle, "above here in these cabinets are your plates, cups, bowls, etc." She opened the cabinets, each revealing treasures greater than the one before it. Dishes—all her own! Forks and spoons, pots and pans! What a great place! And how was she ever going to use all of these things? She hoped that her roommates would be able to teach her how to cook food and such. Every drawer held some new wonder, some new thing that Emily had never known could possibly be! After all, the student meals were always provided by the cafeteria. She had never cooked on her own.

She barely remembered how her mother used to cook. This was expected. Coffenayle provided a special cookbook. There were recipes with clear and comprehensive instructions. They started with how to light the stove, setting the flame just right, proper storage of food, etc. Miss Coffenayle flipped through the book and showed her how to look up basic instructions. There was even a suggested menu page of breakfast, lunch, and dinner ideas with differing combinations.

"Speaking of food," said Miss Coffenayle, "here is your icebox."

When the principal opened the refrigerator, Emily nearly fainted. It was loaded from top to bottom with vegetables, meat, cheese, and so on. Emily had never seen so much food all at once! She had never really seen food of this type either! No more brown nasty paste splattered onto a tray! This was all food that they could cook as they saw fit? Such luxury! This was all a bit overwhelming to her.

"Are you hungry, Emily?" asked the principal when she saw the expression on Emily's face. "Here," she said, "have a bit of cheese. Go on, reach in there, grab a bit."

Emily looked at her and then reluctantly grabbed a chunk of cheese and broke it in half. She put the rest back for the others.

"Very, very good," Miss Coffenayle smiled. "Feel free to eat that on our tour."

Emily knew what cheese was but had not eaten any in *years*.

Emily was eyeing the living room for a place to set up with her blanket to sleep. She did have the community bed back at the dorm, but it was not very comfortable. She would be willing to make do here in the living room. Not a problem; not with all the luxuries she now possessed. Sacrificing her bed was a small price to pay! She followed her guide to the area where the bathroom was. Next to the bathroom door was a cupboard Emily's guide had intentionally skipped. Miss Coffenayle placed her hand on the door and with a quick motion yanked the door open.

Emily was again wide-eyed and nearly in tears this time. She could not believe it! Towels! Washcloths! A drinking glass with tooth powder and a toothbrush! Amazing! Everything here was clean and folded, not just hung on a hook. No more transporting her own bar of soap back and forth to the dorm room. How many roommates did she have? At least two from what she saw. There was three of everything except for the glass and dental hygiene. That stood to reason, though. They could each keep their own glass with their own supplies, toothbrush, hairbrush, etc.

Emily wondered what teachers would be rooming with her. Were they going to be kind? Would they accept Emily as young as she was? Why were they not here? Dinner was hours ago. What would she use for clothing since Coffenayle took the liberty of redistributing her things back to the dorm? These were concerns that crossed Emily's mind as she followed Coffenayle down the hall. At the end of the hall was a door. *That must be the dorm room.* She hoped that they were not being too noisy. Since everything was so quiet, she figured that her roomies must be asleep or perhaps studying. After all, teaching was a big deal, requiring lots of study. Even in a place like this.

Coffenayle opened the door and could not help but smile as she turned on the light. In this room was a single bed, a chest of drawers and a...was that a *desk*? Emily could not believe her eyes. This room was beautiful with a well-made bed, hospital corners all pulled and tucked perfectly. The linens all seemed clean. The room, though a bit dusty as must be expected in a harsh prairie climate, smelled so fresh! Nice, fresh, and clean! How could this be with the two others in here with her?

Oh my! The dresser! The dresser had all the intimate apparel, socks, everything that a proper young woman would need! Emily was astonished. That, though, was not the all. Coffenayle opened a door that Emily had missed and… What? More clothes? For work, there were skirts, blouses, and sweaters, exactly the apparel Emily always tried to wear…and *extra shoes?* On the floor were three pair of shoes that were in different colors but the same low-cut style that Emily just loved to wear! *Well, these shoes must belong to other people. Certainly, one person could not be expected to have so much footwear. That would be just plain greedy.*

The unselfish young woman could not believe that this was happening. Just this morning, she was a student with a teacher trapped in the floorboards. Now she was living in the lap of luxury! Now what about roommates? Where were her roommates? She thought that they must be here by now! Of course, they were teachers. Maybe there was some kind of special meeting they had to attend. She hoped that she would meet them soon. She wanted to chat a minute before retiring; you know, to work out a schedule for bathing, dressing, cooking, and such.

"Now, Emily, if there is anything you need, let your staff members know." Coffenayle spoke as though Emily would know exactly what she was talking about, but her eyes had the glint of a tease about them. She let that sink in.

Emily's wheels were spinning, Coffenayle could see it.

"Staff?" quizzed Miss Emily. "Do you mean my roommates?"

"No, your *staff.* The people who set up your room. The ones that helped get all these groceries and clothing here. They made the bed, stocked the refrigerator and dresser. *Your staff.*" Miss Coffenayle knew that this was going to be a real challenge for Emily to take in. She was patient but was also feeling the hour. It was getting late. "You have staff members, Emily, to take care of you now. They will do your laundry, bring your groceries, or anything else you might need. I will send someone to cook breakfast for you tomorrow. After that, you will need to cook all your meals on your own via the instructions in your cookbook."

Emily reeled physically, literally. She was on the verge of collapse. Miss Coffenayle caught her with a chuckle and led her carefully by the arm to her bed. She let the student, suddenly teacher, sit on *her own* bed, stunned. She gave her a minute to stabilize. To take it all in.

Miss Coffenayle stood there with her arms folded, pleased with herself. This would be a good report to give her master. Miss Emily was completely overwhelmed as she tried to understand her change in fortunes. *People would come and take care of things for her?* Such a thing was unheard of, much less understood. Surely, this new teacher would work very hard to please the system, to please her principal, lest she should lose her life of luxury.

"Listen, Emily, I think that you have had enough for one day. I just want you to take a bath, set your alarm clock over there on the nightstand, and get up in the morning. I will assign someone to fix breakfast for you on your first morning *only*. You just get yourself dressed and ready to go. That same staff member will get you to class on time. They will lead to the building and help you get oriented as to where everything is. After that, while you will cook on your own, they will come by during the day, wash your dishes, take away your laundry, and keep house for you, generally. That way, you don't waste any time cleaning. Do you have any more questions before I leave?"

"Yes. What about my roommates? Can't they just show me around?"

Coffenayle cocked her head a bit, perplexed. She stared at Miss Emily for a couple of seconds. Then she understood. *Of course! The child thinks she has roommates! She has never, since her arrival several years ago, lived any other way!* She smiled again at Emily's complete lack of understanding of her new circumstances, then laughed again, this time with true joy, and explained, "No, Miss Emily. Your roommates can't help you find the way to class."

"Why not? Don't they want to help? We all have to work together for the benefit of the collective. They should all know that, the way of HVVS. It's all in our Welcoming Handbook."

"*You have no roommates, Miss Emily.* You are a teacher now. The dorm life is over for you," stated Coffenayle with an uncustomary gentleness. She knew that this would actually come as quite a shock. She waited.

The shock came. Emily sat for a moment, mouthed silently the words "no roommates," and her face lost all expression.

Then she suddenly burst into tears. The whole day, the accident with Whipshot that now seemed like months ago, Mr. Castlethorn and his wondrous machines, her sudden promotion, now this complete change of lifestyle, not to mention her kindly new and invisible friend. Not knowing what else to do, she wept. Unashamed, unabashed, she just let it all out. The panic, the fear, the relief, the joy, the pain of it all. She did not know what else to do. So she just let it all out at once.

Miss Coffenayle looked on with a bit of understanding. She knew the young woman had responded to this day with a toughness that belied her years. She was poised, mature, and took control of a classroom full of her peers. This was more than one could reasonably expect from any of the other *adult* teachers. This girl stood up remarkably well and performed under circumstances that would make many adults just cave in. Emily, though, did not. Here was one of the most mentally strong people Miss Coffenayle had ever seen. That being said, however, Miss Coffenayle did have her own work to do. She had her own purpose and knew that she could not allow this girl to soften her resolve.

She let Emily for a couple of minutes. The she cut it off. "Now, Miss Emily! Get ahold of yourself! Come on now! Enough!" barked Coffenayle, assuming her role once again as the school's chief educator. "Let's not be ridiculous!"

Emily immediately turned off the waterworks. She swallowed her own tears. She sat up dutifully, attentive, the student once again. Yet, she was a teacher at the same time. Coffenayle was right. This was no time for tears. She was in a new place with a new way of life, and that was that. "Yes, Miss Coffenayle," Emily stated through her tearstained eyes. "I will be ready in time to be led to class."

"That's better. Now goodnight, Miss Emily."

"Goodnight."

12

How They Spent Their Night

The principal thumped her way out the door in her shiny black boots, heel caps tapping on the floor. The door slammed behind her. Emily took her key to the living room and locked the door. She then proceeded to the bathtub. She filled it with warm water, not cold; she gathered her very own commercially made bar of non-lye soap, her clean washcloth, and just soaked in the tub, scrubbing at her feet and legs which suddenly seemed very filthy to her in this new sanitary environment. She washed her hair, which truly needed it. When she climbed out of the tub, she was appalled at how brown and icky the water actually was. Not only was there the normal bodily dirt, but there was the grime and dust from the accident in the classroom. She drained the tub, rinsed it, scrubbed the ring, and then did the unthinkable: She refilled the tub part way and rinsed herself off a second time. That water was dirty but not as filthy as the initial wash water. She felt satisfied this time that she was clean after thoroughly rinsing her hair.

She toweled off with her very own clean towel, wrapped herself in it, and headed off to the bedroom. She opened her dresser, found appropriate, even if secondhand, nightclothes and put them on. Everything smelled so sweet and...and, well, *clean* to her. She sat on the bed and dried her hair. She wanted to braid it, but it proved too difficult, so she settled for a good combing. She would comb it out again in the morning. So this was what being alone was like. She sat there, just enjoying the quiet. She loved the quiet and freshly-scrubbed feeling of a true bath, and she could take one every day if she wanted to! This was not like the communal showers of the dormitories, one shower a week, dirty and crowded. The rest of the time, they washed in their buckets. She did not know what a queen would actually feel like, but she imagined that it would be close to something like this.

She thought briefly about her roommates, her classmates, and how much things had changed. What would Margaret say if she could see Emily now? That dirty little sneak! Always getting one up on someone, finding out secrets so she could go tell on them. That was just so bad of her! Well, Emily was in control now, and there would be no more Margaret snitching on everyone. No, there certainly would not!

She set her alarm and then moved across the room and turned off the light. She made her way back to the bed and pulled the covers back. She crawled into the bed and under her clean linens and blanket on her very own sweet-smelling pillow. She drifted off to sleep.

*****

Emily suddenly found herself in a room like an office. She was sitting there with her lesson planning book in her hands. She looked around a bit, and then a man walked in. He was old enough to be her grandfather. He was white-haired, bald on top, wore funny-looking round glasses, had a bobbed nose, and a full beard that was well-trimmed. He was a man who believed in grooming and appearance. Even his bowtie was neat and trim. His shirt was bleached white and starched. He wore a brown jacket of wool with a matching vest and very proper watch chain neatly looped to his pocket. His trousers were of a different shade of brown, but the color matched well, and they were perfectly creased. His oxford shoes were a perfect match to the suit and keenly perfectly polished. He was the picture of the absolute gentleman; a man's man, certainly.

Despite his dapper appearance, there was nothing cocky or arrogant about this man. He had stoic good looks, very few wrinkles, but there was evidence of his life's roadmap. He seemed very strong, fit, and maybe even what boys would call "tough." He gave the impression that he could throw a ball or chop wood with the best of them. He was apparently a very learned man; it was just something you could tell about him. Yet, he was wise and had a half smile on his face, one of good humor. He was the living picture of the perfectly balanced man: masculine, tough, gentle, kind, serious, and yet playful. He was a high-energy type; he could probably go for hours on end but sleep like a baby and start it all over again the next day.

He came in with his leather briefcase and a bundle of books and papers. "Grades! Grades! Grades!" he shouted in good humor with a smile on his face. He dropped his briefcase and load of books and papers on the desktop with a thud! "That's all anyone cares about is grades! Not how well they did the work, not what they learned, but the *grade!* What are my marks, Mr. Mentor? What will my average be? Not 'How well did I do on the assignment?' Not 'Did I really learn the material I am to be tested on?' All they want to do is get the right marks; they don't care what they learned or how essential it is to their character!" He stared right at Miss Emily with a smile on his face as he spoke as though she knew exactly what he was talking about. Then he abruptly changed the subject, like a fish changing direction to catch a bit of food.

"And how are you today, Miss Emily?" he asked directly to her.

"Um—"

"Well, out with it, child, how are you doing? Good? Not so good? Fine? Rich? Poor? Hungry?"

"Confused."

"Ah! Yes! Finally! An honest answer to that question. Almost everyone says 'fine' when actually there is nothing 'fine' about them. That is careless communication, Miss Emily! Careless! That kind of communication between world leaders, whom we call 'great,' but who are at the end of the day just people is what causes *wars,* Miss Emily! Careless communication causes wars! That tragedy we just passed through—World War I we call it—was so unnecessary! So tragic because we called it a 'world war' as though *everyone* was fighting! But I was not fighting. I was teaching. Myself, I was trying to teach people how to improve themselves with academics, human studies, and culture so that they would not want to fight. After all, if all the soldiers, sailors, and pilots on every continent of every land simply all at once refused to make war, refused to shoot and bomb one another, refused to raise a sword to his fellow man in the name of any leader or cause, if people refused to become oppressors but would learn to get along and share the world's resources, then what would we have? Why, *peace,* of course! Peace! And it would be so much nicer, don't you agree?"

"Um...yes," replied Emily reluctantly. *War? What war?* Emily thought to herself.

"So, Miss Emily." He sat down across from her behind the desk. He leaned in on his elbows. "What are you confused about?"

"Where am I?"

"At your new home in your new bed, asleep, of course! Where else would you be?"

"Oh. So this is...a dream."

"Absolutely not."

"What?"

"It's not a dream. This is so much more. This is a meeting of minds."

"Huh?" Now she was more confused than ever. How could she be in a meeting if she was at home, asleep? This was an office, not her bedroom. This was a chair, not her bed. She was not in her bedclothes, thank goodness, because that would truly be just inappropriate. But, for real, what was this, really?

"For real? You really want to know?"

"How did you know I 'really' want to know?"

"It's very simple, Emily. I heard you think it."

"You what?"

"Yes, I hear your thoughts and the thoughts of all living people when I am trying to help them."

"You do?" She thought that this was completely ridiculous.

"Ridiculous, you think. You think this is *ridiculous*? After you watched me, an invisible being, take apart a chair right before your very eyes, you call *this* ridiculous?" the man replied indignantly but with gentle humor.

Emily was stunned. How did he know about the chair? How did he read her thoughts?

"I told you, I know about the chair because I am the one who took it apart! I already said that I am able to read all people's thoughts when I am there to help them!" he said with feigned exasperation.

She just sat there, stunned. She did not know what to say or what to think.

"Maybe we should just meet in your room. You can stay under your covers, properly concealed. I won't look at your bedclothes, I promise," he said gently. "I was hoping to just meet in the dream world so that your body could rest, but I can see that you are not quite ready for that yet. No problem. You will have to learn at your own pace." He walked over to the office door and opened it. Emily, with all her things in her hands, left the room, then back to sleep. Her sleep was dreamless, but before her alarm went off, she heard a voice call.

"Emily? Emily, are you awake?"

She sat up with a start. Her room was dark, but in the dim moonlight through the window, it seemed like there was no one there. Even so, she distinctly heard a voice awaken her. She called out, "Who is there?"

The voice, with no person visible in the room, responded, "Just relax a minute. No harm will come to you. I am here to meet with you because you were resisting our dream meeting. Remember when I said that you should let your body rest? When you were sitting in my office?"

"What? What? Wait...are you *really* the one that made Miss Whipshot fall through the floor?"

"Yes. Unfortunately, I am. I had to stop her, though. She was about to do something terrible with that ruler of hers. You know very well what that ruler can do to someone."

Emily was very familiar with that ruler. It was hopefully gone now, and hopefully, Whipshot was gone too.

"Don't think that, Emily. Don't wish harm upon your teacher. You don't really know her, so you cannot judge her."

"How do I know this is not a dream right now? It seems real, but so did your office."

"My office *is* real. That is really my office. You were really there, or at least part of you was. Just not your mortal part."

"What? My mortal part?"

"More on that later. Right now, we have to meet. Can I show myself without you being afraid? I promise that I won't hurt you."

At this point, Emily was getting curious. Curious about whether or not this was a dream. Curious about how this man knew so much, about how he could read thoughts. "Well, I suppose—"

"We will do this in steps. First, watch me perform an act you are familiar with. What object in this room would you like me to move?"

"My alarm clock," said Emily, unsure of what to expect. She had seen the chair parts move, so she believed it may be about the same thing. She was not disappointed. The alarm clock floated upward, the face tilted like someone was looking at it, and it gently settled back down on the dresser. She was a bit mystified, not frightened, and actually giggled a bit. It sort of tickled her that she was dealing with a real…whatever he was.

"Now, would you like to have another sensation which is familiar to you?"

Emily smiled in anticipation. "What might that be?"

"Do you recall any warm, kind feeling, like a friendly arm across your shoulder?"

"Um…yes…was that—"

"Would you like to know for certain?"

"Yes," responded Emily and braced herself. Suddenly, but calmly, it was there again, that warm grandfatherly feeling of comfort. Like a good person, her best friend, was sitting there with an arm over her shoulders. "That *was* you!" Emily exclaimed.

"Yes, it was. Now you can hear me in your ears instead of just your mind, right?"

"Yes."

"Okay. I will only speak to you in your ears, like I am right now, when we are alone. Other people can hear me right now, but I only want you to hear me. Understood?"

"Yes. So…in the room, when I heard you, the others could not?"

"That is correct. I was communicating with your mind only. Not with your ears."

"So you are actually here but invisible to me right now, correct?"

"Yes, Emily."

"Could you appear if you wanted to? Do you have that ability?"

"Yes, I could. Right now, I could light myself up in this dark room, but that is a little overwhelming. I would prefer to appear to you in the light. With the lights on, that is."

"Would you be transparent or very white, like the ghosts I read about in stories?"

"No. I would appear to you as I did in your dream."

"Can we do this now? I would love so much to meet you."

"Are you scared?"

"Only a little bit."

"I sense more that it is natural nervousness. You are not really truly afraid. If you were, you would be trembling or sweating. Since you are not, yes, I think are ready. Oh… I sense a question. You just thought that you want proof that I am the same man from your dream. Okay, that is very simple. I told you about World War I, something you knew nothing about when we met in your dream. Ah! You remember! Ha! I knew you would. So do you believe now that I am that same man, that same teacher, and that I am harmless?"

"Yes. I do, and I am going to turn on the light. I could not sleep now anyway, even if you paid me to."

"Very well."

Emily left her bed and turned on the light. Then she went back into her bed and properly pulled her sheets up over her bedclothes. One must guard one's reputation against unseemly behavior! "All right," Emily said, "I am ready."

A figure slowly came into view, fading in carefully. She could see a wavering outline first, then a shape, then the shape filled in. There stood a man now, the same one from her dream. Only his back was turned, and he was covering his eyes with his hands. "Emily," he said, "I am here now in full appearance. Are you quite covered up?"

"Yes," Emily giggled. "You must know that I am if you have been watching me."

He straightened up and put his hands to his sides. His back was still toward her. "We don't look when we should not. We allow you your privacy," he stated. "May I turn around now?"

"Of course!" Emily was excited now.

The teacher turned around—glasses, bowtie and all. Same impeccable brown suit, etc. He looked just a real as he did in her dream. "Well, what do you think?"

"I would think that I am dreaming, but I know that I am not," she said with a thoughtful tone. "Why don't you appear to others?"

"There are rules we must follow. That is all I can tell you for now. I am here for a specific purpose, and I had to get special permission to appear to you. I will not be allowed to appear fully to anyone else without special permission. I can I only stay in this particular state for a little while at a time. It takes a lot of energy for me to do this. It is very rare that we are allowed to do this sort of thing. Since I come on urgent business, an allowance was made."

"I see. Can you shake hands?" Emily inquired sincerely.

"Not in the sense that you are thinking," he replied.

"How then?"

"I have no flesh, so I can reach for you and make you feel the presence of my hand, but you cannot feel it like you would flesh, blood, and bone. Your hand will feel like there is nothing there, except for that warm feeling, similar to the one you got when you thought you felt a grandfather's arm on your shoulders. That made me feel quite honored, by the way. Please realize, though, that I would never appear to anyone and try to shake hands. I must not give anyone the impression that I could do something like that. Such would be a deception, and I am not in the business of deceiving people."

"I understand. So what is this all about?"

"All in due time. You will have to have accept some things I will say…purely on faith."

"I see. So…who are you?"

"I am a ghost. The ghost of Mr. Mentor."

"Well, yes…a ghost. I sort of knew. But who were you when you were alive…as Mr. Mentor?"

"Another question for another time," Mentor stated matter-of-factly. "All you need to know is that I am a fellow teacher and will help you in your classroom. You may or may not know when I am present. I cannot be present all the time because I have other things to deal with on the Happy Valley Vocational School's campus. I want you to know, though, that I will be there when you need me most. I will help you with your books, your lesson plans. I will speak to your mind when you need inspiration. Know this too: you can block me out or quit working with me anytime you decide that you have had enough."

"Enough what?" Emily was perplexed. She was certain she could not get enough of whatever this was.

"You shall soon see," he said with a smile. "I must go now because I want to be in class with you, but I have something else to do first. Get used to knowing only what you need to know about my activities. Don't look to me for every answer about the future. We will meet often, too, in the dream place. I must go now." Mr. Mentor smiled and slowly faded the same way he came into her room. Then she was all alone. She yawned and went to sleep.

*****

The night was an eventful one for Miss Coffenayle. She had finished "coddling" Miss Emily and hurried back to her office. In the principal's office closet was a black dress and matching cloak. This was her formal outfit; it was different than the one she wore around the school during her daytime study sessions. It was nicer, and the cloak gave it quite the look. She never appeared publicly in this dress; this one was strictly for her to show herself to her master, Malovent.

She could appear in any attire she chose because the master was not that picky about her appearance. She was the one who chose formal wear because she wanted to display her dedication to their cause. She wanted to become his favorite pupil. Even without the clothing, she actually had earned the distinction of being among the most dedicated disciples Malovent had in his following. She may have even been *the most* dedicated.

She took off her favorite blue coat and hung it on a specially designed hanger. It was custom-made to support the padded shoulders. She took off her long black boots and replaced them with knee-length black leather moccasins. She learned a long time ago what footwear was most comfortable for occasions such as these. Her ruffled shirt might be a tad warm under the robe, but there was no time change it. She had plenty of replacements in the office, a couple more blue jackets too, all the same style. She was seen around the school in only two outfits: the Napoleon and the less formal dress. She had extras of both, just in case of any kind of accident, tear, spill, etc. She would not ever be seen any other way. She was not ordered by anyone to dress this way; she just simply preferred it.

This, though, was her one formal dress; it was very expensive, and she wore it carefully.

Her office was just dark enough to make contact. She was well-practiced at this ritual; everything had be just so. She turned on the lights and arranged the black candles on the floor around her geometric design. It was a very intricate design, and she had to align the candles perfectly. She gathered her incense burners from the drawer and carefully chose and arranged the ground up dry leaves in the burners. Then she ignited them with a plain wooden match. When the burners were smoking sufficiently, she lit the candles and doused the light.

She was wearing her amulet, a ten Karat gold disc with a geometric pattern etched into it by hand carefully and precisely. A smooth stone adorned the precise center. The stone Malovent gave her. This was another thing that she never wore around the school. It was too powerful to allow it to be seen by just anyone. She knelt on the floor in the middle of the design and spoke unintelligible sentences in some strange tongue, throwing her hands in the air or sometimes waving over an incense burner. Her words became faster and more intense. She was throwing her body around more and fervently. She put her whole heart, her whole being into the spell.

Then the room became positively electric! Static seemed to fill the air. Suddenly—there "he" was. He appeared in the middle of the room, as was his custom, in a black cowl and robe. He hovered in the air. Around his waist was a thick golden belt adorned with small polished white human skulls, the belt about the same width as a human hand. The skulls spanned across half the belt and perfectly centered. The air was foul for a moment to Coffenayle's nostrils, as it always was whenever she and the master would meet.

He stood at least nine feet tall and was about four feet across the shoulder. His face was intentionally obscured by the cowl. His arms were draped in the ebony robe with his hands tucked away into the sleeves which were draped and flowing. A great key on a gold chain dangled from what would be one's left wrist on a human. Black fire surrounded him, a fire that appeared as flames but emitted no heat, no light. The flames seemed to draw light *into* them. This caused the room to become even darker.

The flames on the candles also turned from the yellow-red of normal, natural flames, to something unnatural. The flames burned black, and they too seemed to draw light from the room. Coffenayle had once burned her hand, testing the flames to see if they still were hot. That was the great mystery. How could flames burn hot but not emit light? The candles melted like normal, and the flames produced heat, but the darkness of Master Malovent took all the light away!

To Coffenayle, this meant that her master's darkness and evil was more powerful than the light and the good. She was on the winning side, destined to become a queen of evil, one of many, to be sure! She was taught that the queens and kings, they were there to rule in the darkness and not suffer from it. They would become the tormentors, never to be tormented. This was the teaching of Malovent; this was what she believed in, what she wanted to do, and why she did all that she did.

The master's entire robe, including the cowl, seemed to be moving about in what we could call a fairly steady breeze, yet the air in the room was perfectly still. The smoke from the incense surrounded him and swirled about among the folds of the robe, attracted to him. The smoke then actively formed patterns that mimicked the design on the floor, flowing, swirling, moving around, seeming to obey some silent command. Coffenayle bowed deeply; her beloved had arrived. Master Malovent was here, and she was at his service.

"Master," she cooed, smiling but with eyes to the floor.

"Long has the one of the Coffenayle line served me well," said Malovent in a deep, rich, and dramatic baritone voice. "Long have you served me well, Donatienne Coffenayle. I am pleased with your progress. What have you to report this night?"

"One of our finest was injured this morning, very badly, Master. I have not been able to check on her since I sent her to the infirmary."

"Oh? Who? And how so?" Malovent asked, leaning slightly forward.

"Miss Whipshot, Master. Whipshot fell through the floor and was hurt. She slipped on a chair leg that had fallen to the floor. An apparent accident."

"Apparent?" he inquired.

"We are still investigating, trying to find out what happened for certain."

"I see. I assume, then, that she is in the care of one of our own?"

"Yes, Master. Nurse Shadyknight."

"Ahh…yessss…the one referred to as 'Nightshade' since the Great Event, the night we took power. You will check on Whipshot, then get her back into class as soon as possible?" the shadow asked.

"Yes, Master. That is the plan," she stated, her face still to the floor, eyes averted.

"I am pleased. You may rise to a more comfortable position, if you like. The ritual is complete. You may address me now as a friend."

"I am your friend, Master, and you are mine. So be it," she said, sitting now with her knees bent, facing her friend.

"So be it. So I say," he responded richly. "Now, Friend Coffenayle of the Coffenayle line, what is your plan?" the baritone asked in a less formal way.

"Friend Malovent, the suffering is great. We are quite able to maintain it among the students. We have our attorney, Simon I.

Doesbad, Esq., who successfully argued, yet again, before the courts in favor of keeping the authorities out of Happy Valley."

"Excellent. We are in control of the courts, then. That fool attorney thinks that his brilliant arguments win the day, but it is our friend, InkRobe, who turns the tables more than the lawyer ever could. The lawyer is simply a pencil pushing pawn. He is a useful fool, and that is all!"

"Friend Malovent, should I tell Simon I. Doesbad about InkRobe?" Coffenayle asked hopefully.

Malovent froze in time and space. The air in the room changed. Coffenayle knew that this meant he was looking into the past or the future to determine the proper course of action. He was in that stasis for more than a few minutes. Even the very smoke from the incense and the candles' flames were locked in place. Smoke froze in the air. Flames were static and did not flicker. Coffenayle waited patiently for him to give her an answer. Then, smoke and flame began to move again naturally.

"No, not yet. He is not yet ready to join the Friendship," said the shadow.

"Yes, Friend Malovent," she responded, again disappointed at Doesbad's lack of progress. How was she to build an army at this rate?

"I know that you have desired a male companion to join us in our Friendship. Dualism makes our magic stronger, our evil becomes more powerful when there are two, male and female, joined as one in our ways. Remember, however, that his motive must solely be a quest for power and not a quest of love. Be you patient, and a dualism may come for you. So be it. So I say."

"Yes, Friend Malovent. As my master, I will obey you. I will wait," responded the principal.

"Who continues the suffering in Whipshot's place?" inquired Malovent.

"I have chosen a student from among their ranks," replied Coffenayle.

"*What? What have you done!?*" shouted Malovent. The very walls seemed to tremble.

Coffenayle's face immediately went to the floor in devotion and obeisance. She had stirred his anger before, and it did not usually end well. This time was going to be one of the better spats between them, she knew. She had a very good reason for promoting Miss Emily, one that would help preserve Malovent's power. "I need permission, Friend Malovent, to explain why I have done an apparently foolish thing," she said very humbly and deeply bowing.

"So be it. So I say. *Explain yourself well!*"

"We needed an immediate replacement. The class was getting out of hand. We were losing control. They were beginning to discover confidence and...*free will*. Adding the students to other classrooms would have caused too much confusion, too much chaos and disruption. We could not recruit a professional teacher from town because we need to keep our activities a secret from the world. A professional teacher would almost certainly see what was going on here and call law enforcement officers. Even if the cops are powerless to enter the property by Judge Parschall's order, they would eventually find a way to investigate. Nurse Shadyknight, Miss Ladlepot of the cafeteria, Castlethorn the engineer, our other staff members... I believe none of these are capable of teaching. They could not drop their other vital duties in any case. We had no choice but to bring in a student." She stated all this in one long breath. She spoke quickly as to appear confident and make her point before the master lost patience.

He hovered. He raised a cowled arm to his chin; no hand was visible. He seemed to be thinking. He froze time again and looked backward and forward. Even he found no viable alternatives. Coffenayle was still bowed, nose to the floor.

"Friend Coffenayle," he began. "I see considerable risk with this plan, but the alternatives are worse. There is nothing else that we can do for thirty days' time. You must keep control of this student-teacher for thirty days. Then we will have someone that we may use as a replacement. No replacement is available until then. Not even your idiot lawyer. He is more valuable to us in his current position. You are using him well. Be cautious. You know the laws about love interests. You must abase and degrade him, keep him at bay. He believes that he has feelings for you. You must not nurture his love interest but allow him to believe you might one day be his love, to keep him interested. You may arise. So be it. So I say."

Malovent was looking as grand and horrifyingly awesome as ever. Coffenayle's loyalty to evil was strong enough to defeat any love interest, not that she ever had one. Each and every friend or companion she had in life was just a tool, a mere transactional being to forward her evil ambitions. Once she discovered Malovent many years before, Coffenayle's only ambition was to bring his darkness into power. Now, finally, it seemed that she would succeed; the road had been long, hard, and filled with intent.

Coffenayle rose again to her normal sitting position, her black robe and dress getting coated more and more with that infernal dust! She was ashamed to present herself coated with all that gray powder. It looked terrible on her dress. She wanted nothing more than to please her master. He never mentioned the dirt nor was it sufficient of a distraction to cause her to lose focus on her spell to summon him. As masters before her time served, so she served. She was bred and raised as a Coffenayle, which gave her tools to serve Malovent in this critical time. Her dedication would allow Malovent to become the undisputed master of first the school, then the county, the state, and so on. She wanted the same thing he did: *for darkness and evil to rule the world.*

"Now, Friend Coffenayle, I see in the course of our future together one who may be annoying. I cannot tell who it is for certain. It could be your student or someone related to or working with her. Exercise caution in everything that you do. Be sure to discourage all the people you meet and make the students believe that there is no hope, no future for them. This keeps them easier to control, even as it adds to my power. I caution you to keep your foot on the neck of all persons you work with, even those who contribute to our cause. Do not let them have any optimism or hope for anything outside of the work they do for you. Have you anything further to report?" he finally asked in his rumbling voice.

"No, Master. Nothing else."

"Then I shall release you and take my leave. Farewell, Friend Coffenayle."

"Farewell, Friend Malovent," replied the principal, bowing with her nose touching the floor.

With a sudden turn and flipping of his robe, Malovent turned away and seemed to walk into nothingness. Just like that, he was gone. There was always that gust of breeze and darkness that usually blew out the candles, leaving Coffenayle in complete darkness. She arose and turned on the light. There were papers strewn about the place. Papers and dust. *Tsk. Malovent is a mighty being, but he certainly does not know how to keep house,* she mused with gentle reverence. She could never truly complain against him. She had grown up knowing that she was chosen to bring evil to power. The last three of Malovent's chosen had all been male. She was proud to be Malovent's witch, descended by magical ties from a line of warlocks. If only she could convince the Patriarch of the Family that magic would be a powerful addition to the Coffenayle line. Magic could then enrich the Coffenayle bloodline; the Coffenayles could then rule the world without restraint!

By the time the ritual was over, the communication was completed, and she cleaned up after both herself and her master, it was time for school to start. She put on her coat and boots, hung her carefully brushed formal dress inside the closet, and started a new day. So much to be done, so much power to gain. Hopefully, today she would be able to study some more spells and potions instead of babysitting Emily.

She did have a vested interest in the child, though. Miss Emily's success in teaching that class was important. Besides, if the master was right and someone who was somehow related to Emily was going to become a thorn in their side, it was critical that she keep an eye on her. Emily being a teacher gave Coffenayle the perfect reason to get close to her and to be on her good side. She could not be too good to Emily; she could not make Emily truly happy because that would weaken Malovent. This party she was planning would cause some happiness, but the joy would be short-lived enough to not do serious damage.

The principal was up all night between Emily and Malovent, but that was really not a problem for her. She knew that Malovent could make her strong enough to bear the fatigue. He had done so many times before; once, she even went a full week without sleep and was fine after a full night's rest. That was quite the situation that week. No time to think about that now, though. No point in pining over mistakes and regrets. She had to be strong; evil would not tolerate shame, guilt, love, compassion, joy, happiness, etc.

Any feeling or emotion that gave a person hope for better things in life, any light that was brought into one's day was a threat to evil. That is why she had to be so careful about having this party. It was only to earn Emily's trust and cause the students to be all the more loyal to her. Such a party would not happen ever again. In fact, she would have to think of something to counteract the joy this party would create. She had plenty of time to do that, though. Plenty indeed.

*****

Down in the school's basement, Castlethorn's night was spent sleeping for a few hours, then tinkering with his equipment. The crane that he had taken into the classroom to rescue Whipshot was now in need of some basic maintenance. The filters and oil certainly needed to be changed with all of the dirt and dust that he picked up during the demolition of that wall. It was a lighter job but dirty. The crane itself seemed fine; the cable was plenty strong and did not unravel. The boom was a big concern. He lubricated it and then extended and retracted it many times to make sure that it was not bent and, therefore, ruined. He was glad that there were not major repairs to be made. He would see if he could get "Miz Emily" to release Jimmy to him, and he would have the kid do the filter and lube maintenance job tomorrow; closely supervised, of course.

The old janitor then went to his miraculous machine he once called the PCD or Phantom Containment Device. This was the machine that he used when the resident poltergeist had threatened them earlier. He hated to use it because it blew out tubes every time he did, so great was the energy discharge. He thought he knew how to fix the problem, but every time he tried to remember, that blasted "brain fog" clouded his mind. It frustrated him. He could be on the very brink of a very important thought, inspiration, or idea, and *wham!* It escaped him. It came on without warning, that fog.

He stood in front of the machine, wishing to set it up for the next inevitable attack, but instead, he sat down into a dusty, creaking, wooden chair. He looked around the shop. He couldn't understand so many things now. He thought that he once had a clean and orderly place. He used to care about his appearance and hygiene. So much to think on, things to try and remember, but he could not. He was not even sure who he was anymore. Everyone called him Castlethorn, so that is the name he went by, but it did not sound correct to him. He was stunned still, even in his condition, at what happened just yesterday. To see Whipshot jammed in those floorboards was completely insane. This was so far removed from anything that he had experienced at the school that it was still on his mind. That memory was worse than the ghost attack. But that ghost was something he was becoming used to.

Then to see that young woman...what was her name again? Edith? No, Evelyn? No...again. *Come on, man! Clear the cobwebs! You can do this! Umm... Oh yes! Emily! Emily was her name.* Well, yes, that was something to see. Watching a student be promoted to the role of *teacher* by the hand of "Old Coffin" herself. He chuckled at the thought, thinking himself very clever to have come up with that private nickname he had for her. *The Old Coffin! Ha!* It seemed to Castlethorn, though, that quips used to come much easier. He seemed to remember a day when he was much smarter, a time when he took care of himself and had somebody to care for.

These days, he did not even understand where half of this equipment came from. He could not remember. That machine that repels the ghost..."the polter-ghost"...was a very clever invention. Whoever thought it up was very smart indeed. Castlethorn knew that he had some engineering skills; he even knew how to use that sliding ruler thingy he kept in his pocket for some stuff. He used to know more. For some reason, he did not want anyone to know he had it, and he sure did not want anyone to see him using it. There was no need to stir up a bunch of questions and make that foggy thing happen in his brain. That's what happened to him when he used his thinker too hard. Sometimes the brain fog would just cloud him up. Sometimes it would block his brain entirely, and sometimes, what he hated most, when he would try to think his way past the fog, it would *hurt!* Paralyzing agony would pierce his brain, and he would have to stop thinking. It was terrible!

Why did it hurt? Why did it happen? He seemed to sort of recall different ways around the school. Students used to come here long ago. *To muh shop*, he thought. *But they can't now, not really, not since that polter-guy came.* Now Castlethorn got mad and just ran the students off, like he did yesterday. Curious thing! Why would he do that to students? To protect the kiddees, he supposed. It made no sense for the ghost to get so angry when students came too far back into the lab. These were curiosities that certainly bore investigation. Indeed.

Something else. Castlethorn realized that the words *curiosities* and *indeed* were part of his thought processes, but he could not make the words come out of his mouth. He could certainly think them to some extent, and he even had his moments of brilliance. Even when he was brilliant, his words could not come out of his mouth that way. He sounded slurred and coarse. He knew that his speech was that of an idiot, but he could do nothing about it. That was why he never spoke much to anyone. He was secretly ashamed.

In his shame, he became a recluse; a recluse that was somehow compelled to not shower or shave regularly. A recluse that grew long, ridiculous, greasy unwashed hair. One that did not care for cleaning his equipment, tools, nor for general housekeeping. Something that kept coming to mind: a piece of paper with something written on it. Something important. He leaned forward in his chair, trying to think past the fog, but the effort exhausted him. "Makes me tireds, it do—" Aw, there he went again with diction of a drunken *sot*. He even knew what *sot* meant. In spite of knowing, he could not say the word, could not make the word come out of his mouth.

He dropped his head into his hands and wept for a moment. He knew he was different than all of this. He was a different man entirely. He was not happy to be this way, but he could not help it.

He also knew for certainty that he was happy at one time too, in a much sweeter time, a much better day. He indulged his tears for a few minutes and just wept out loud. *No one to hears mees. No one to care to come to sees mees.* He wept for the dirt and filth. He wept for keeping his sliding-thing a secret. He wept for Lantern. How pathetic was that? He named an invention. He called it by the proper name of Lantern. *So I coulds haves someones to speaks to. Blast this fog! Curse you! Stop it an' leave me alone! I beg you! Leave me!*

His shoulders heaved with heavy sobs and sighs. Then it was over. The good cry was over. This happened to him every few months or so. Things would just get to him. He was okay for now. He dried his eyes and blew his nose on a filthy gray rag and just carelessly dropped it on the floor. *Gots to get the bidness done. Den afters dat, have some o' dee tea. Dee tea seems ta takes the edge offa thingees.*

He found Lantern. He greeted it with his usual good morning pat on the top. He asked Lantern if he wanted any breakfast or coffee or something. He never did. The old janitor wondered occasionally what he would do if Lantern ordered an omelet! He would laugh at the thought but realized stranger things were happening at Happy Valley, so maybe he should not tempt the Fates. Fates? Where did he ever learn about Fates? Some book. *Aah!* He stopped in his tracks. The pain again. He reached too far past the fog. That pain was unbearable, sometimes making his head tingle. He would have to sit again but just for a moment. He sat and let the thought go, whatever it was. Then pain went away. He went over to his jug where he kept his cold tea. *Somes lahks it hot.* He drank his cold. He found a nearly clean container and poured some tea. *It tastes lahk the ocean. Smells lahk it too. When I was a boy, ta sees dee oshun was good fer me. But Ahs culds not meremberz why!*

He went back to his machine, "the ghost repeller" or whatever he called it. He opened a panel on the side and found the burned-out tubes. He pulled them out from that side, then went to the other cabinet and performed the same exercise. He put all of the tubes in an old broken crate. It did not matter which one; there were many crates, all of them old and broken. Half of the tubes shattered as he dropped them in. It did not matter to him; they were no good anymore anyway. He replaced the tubes with new ones that he got from a cabinet that was not as old and broken as the rest of his shop. In fact, this particular cabinet, one that only he secretly knew of, was full of things that he could not understand. He had to be careful how long he looked in the cabinet because the fog would hurt him again.

That chore done, the panels all buttoned up and ready to go, he needed to turn the machine on again. He would not turn it all the way on until the next "polter-thing" attack, but he did have to leave it on, ready to fully energize on a moment's notice. Only when it was fully energized did it repel the spooks. It was sitting there, ready to go, like a cocked rifle, and Castlethorn checked the meters and gauges. He was satisfied that the readings were correct and normal. Not that he could remember why; they just seemed that way. The machine worked every time the readings were just as they currently were, so that was good enough for him. No point in asking brain-pain types of questions. Now to Lantern. It was good to keep Lantern in order too; he had to know how to read whatever might be in the room.

It really bothered him that he could not say "human beings," that it always came out "hoomin beans." Then again, that was clever, he believed. It helped him keep his reputation for being strange. How he loved clucking like a chicken! He made that one up by himself. He could not let anyone know what Lantern and he were actually up to. They were reading the energies in the room, it seemed. Clucking like a chicken, saying "hoomin beans," and behaving strangely in general laid to rest all of the suspicions. He did have one technical term that did not cause brain pain and the fog to stop him. That was "ectoplasmic spectrometer." That is what Lantern really was. He managed to retain some mathematical methods that were not affected by the fog or the pain. But it was only enough math for him to be able to do his job with his slider-ruler thing.

This was the most suspicious thing. It was like he was permitted to access only so much of his mind's information. The rest he could not access. He, at times, almost thought that someone or something was controlling him, preventing him from remembering things. Now, how could that possibly be? Of course, who was he to be rational at this point? He was dealing with *ghosts! Ha!* He laughed at the thought that "witches" might be next. He would have to come up with a spell-detector of some kind. *Ow! Pain again! Oooh…that is rough.* He sat down again for just a minute. He had to check Lantern, but he would need to take a minute.

*****

Across the campus, Nurse Shadyknight was busy throughout the night as well. Normally, she did not have to stay with a patient in her infirmary all night long. Most of the time, she could sleep in her own room. Injured students had no place to run, even if they could. In Whipshot's case, she was ordered by Coffenayle to stay beside the patient, in one of the beds. The ugly, cruel, obese teacher-woman scowled, even in her sleep. She snored and "snawked" her way through the night. After a really *thorough* sponge bath, Whipshot had quit stinking up the place.

The nurse made certain that the patient kept breathing and was hydrated. She had the glass bottle of saline hung over the bed, and the surgical rubber tubing with a needle at the end was taped securely into her arm. The arm was taped to a flat board to keep it from bending so the needle would not perforate the vein. The teacher's glasses were on a nightstand along with a bedpan. Shadyknight had learned through the night what noises to listen for to keep Whipshot from wetting in the bed. For a well-seasoned nurse, this task was challenging but not overwhelming.

Shadyknight wore a traditional nurse's uniform complete with a pin that designated her status. She wore it proudly on her traditional nurse's bonnet. She was middle-aged, and her body was crooked, but she stayed energetic. Her expression was sullen with unspeakable burdens, but she was a diehard and gave the impression that she was not to go down easy. She had cared for many students. She had seen much during her tenure at Happy Valley.

Oddly, though, while she recalled meeting Principal Coffenayle when she first came to the school, she could not remember much about the events surrounding Little Napoleon's arrival. It seemed to

Shadyknight that there were some significant events that just escaped her memory. She could remember, of course, nursing school and being hired by her all those years ago. She even remembered something about being…happy…and standing *taller*, but that is where it all ended. She poured herself a cup of the school's tea; it was excellent to sip at while she pondered the events of her life. Strange how it tasted like her mother's chocolate pudding but smelled like her home-baked bread.

In spite of her personal challenges, she was the school nurse. It was her duty to take care of the ill and injured, no matter what. So that was what she did. She was not a doctor, but her years of experience trained her nearly as well as a doctor who just graduated medical school. She could not perform surgery—not legally, anyway—but she did understand well enough the procedures. She could confidently amputate a limb and have the patient survive. She hoped to never do that, but she could if the occasion called for it.

She was up all night with only a light doze. A "twenty-minute blink" she called it. She would sit down, check the clock, blink her eyes, and suddenly, twenty minutes were gone without her even realizing she had dozed. Not a deep slumber, the blink would allow her to awaken in an instant. She found this to be largely automatic, and it was sufficient rest to keep her self-aware, to get through the night, and do her job effectively.

She was not very comfortable with taking Whipshot into her infirmary in this condition. Shadyknight was afraid she was critically injured and still believed she may be. She believed that the teacher should be in the hospital with a real doctor looking after her. Be that as it may, there was no way to contact anyone and no way to get the patient placed into more capable hands. Besides, people in this generation were of the general consensus that hospitals were places to go and die.

The general public believed that staying at one's own home with a doctor dropping by was the way to be cured. That being said, the school *was* Whipshot's home, so…well, there just was not much else to do. They would not be able to contact a doctor with the phones all locked up, and even if they did, Miss Coffenayle would never allow him to "trespass." Strangers were rarely allowed to encroach on the Happy Valley Vocational School.

So Nurse Shadyknight did all she could by keeping the fluids dripping, seeing to patient comfort, etc. There was no one else staying in the infirmary. She had a decent budget, so she could keep plenty of painkillers, equipment, and supplies on hand. All in all, she was treated fairly well as the school nurse. Coffenayle even had her keep some sulfur-based drugs on hand for occasional infections.

For now, Whipshot's pulse was strong and steady. She was breathing well enough. Her saline IV was dripping at the proper rate, and she seemed comfortable. It was time for Shadyknight to freshen up a bit, then she would check on her supplies and replenish her inventory where it was needed. She turned and left the room. She did not see any of the unusual things that were about to happen.

As soon as she was gone, a hairbrush picked itself up off the nightstand and began gently stroking Whipshot's hair. After a few moments, the brush seated itself back onto the nightstand, precisely where it was before. Then Whipshot's hand lifted up slightly off of the bed, and her wrist hung limply as though someone were taking a pulse. Next, her glasses lifted themselves into the air, and a gauze patch dipped itself into the water pitcher and cleaned them thoroughly. The glasses folded up and set themselves neatly, carefully back on the nightstand. The sheets and blankets were then rearranged lovingly along her chin. Lastly, her hair was slightly disturbed in a pattern that suggested gentle stroking.

Whipshot sort of cooed, and her permanent scowl straightened out just a bit, not into a smile exactly, but her whole look softened for just a moment. The tuft of hair around her ear seemed to have a bit of a breeze disturb it just a little. One could imagine that there was a whisper in her ear just then. But why would that be with a living embodiment of cruelty in that bed? Who could care about Whipshot to take care of her like that? Nonetheless, that is what happened. Then all was quiet again in Whipshot's room.

Shadyknight returned and stopped short. *Something* seemed to be different. Something was a little off. She looked around the room, circled the bed, and peered at her lone resident. Hmm. Her hair?

Something about that hair looked too neat. Everything else seemed to be in order, seemed the same. Oh, well, it's been a long night. Long indeed, and she was certain that no one was in the room. They would have had to pass by her to get to Whipshot.

Shadyknight had been certain to place the patient in a room where some person with a grudge—there were plenty of those—could not get to her in her helpless state. But…didn't she look different somehow? More peaceful maybe? Well, even one such as she deserves to have a pleasant dream now and then. The nurse did not give it another thought. However, she did set up a cot for herself in the room across the doorway to prevent anyone from sneaking in, and she got some daytime sleep.

13

Miss Emily's First Day

She jumped! Her alarm went off. Emily got out of bed and immediately put on her clothes, getting ready for the day. There was a knock on the door moments after she was dressed. She answered it and found someone dressed in a maid's attire on her doorstep. She was an older woman, tired, hunched to one side, and forlorn looking. "I was told to come help Miss Emily with her breakfast. Are *you* Miss Emily?" she asked without a smile.

"Um...yes, I am Miss Emily," she said, surprised, until remembering that Coffenayle was going to send staff to help.

"Well? You gonna let me in or do I need to produce an invitation? I ain't got none, ya know."

Emily stepped aside and beckoned her to come in. She pushed past Emily and without ceremony or even an introduction and immediately started to speak. "I'm going to clean your house and take your clothes to the laundry. Make sure your name is on the clothes so you can get them back, especially socks. Name and house number is the best way to make sure that your stuff stays your stuff. I don't do windows. You will find ammonia under the sink. Clean your windows with a little ammonia in a bucket of water. You'll figure it out," she said as she was digging in the icebox, getting out food. She did not bother to ask Emily what she wanted for breakfast. The maid correctly assumed that whatever she made was fine because this was a student, and anything homemade had to be better than that greasy swill they served in the school cafeteria.

Emily went back to her room to finish preparing for the day. By the time she was finished, the maid was gone with the dirty laundry that Emily set outside her door in the laundry bag. On the table place was a wonderful-smelling breakfast of sausage, eggs, and toast. Emily sat down and ate too fast, but who was there to see? The breakfast was wonderful! It tasted as good as it smelled. She had actually forgotten what good food tasted like! She was in heaven!

She had an amusing thought of whether or not the maid was a ghost sent by Mr. Mentor, if a ghost was sent to clean up and get her started on her day. She had to dismiss it, of course. It did not work that way. At least she did not think it worked that way. So little she knew right now. She picked up her books and supplies, put some of the things in a bag she found in the closet, the went outside...her first official day as "Miss Emily."

Miss Coffenayle had told her that the staff member would guide her to class. That did not happen, so Miss Emily stood there, looking around. She knew that someone else had to leave the houses soon. She saw a group of teachers after only a few minutes. She knew they must be going to the school. She followed them but did not try to catch up. Emily did not want to press her luck too much on her first full day of teaching. They were a generally unhappy lot, speaking very little but walking close together. She could not hear what they were saying when they did speak. She did not really want to hear because she was certain that word was getting out about Miss Whipshot.

If they found out that she was Whipshot's student, the one that got promoted to be a teacher, well, they would have a lot of questions that she was not about to answer. She would let the principal field any questions about her promotion. She did not want to let anything to slip about Mr. Mentor. That had to be kept a secret for so many reasons! There was no way that she was going to talk about him, not ever!

There was something "off" about all of the teachers, Emily noticed. They were walking, yes, but with a slight limp. Each of them was walking as though their backs hurt them. They were like the maid and Mr. Castlethorn. It was hard to describe other than say that they were just not shaped quite right. Something disturbed her at the core. She knew that this was not natural; Emily knew that people would be injured from time to time, but to see *every one* of the staff and faculty members limping along like this was just not normal. Why she had the sensation that their injuries were actually *caused* by something, she could not really tell. It was very strange. It was as though she knew that they should not appear that way or have any pain. Yet, here they were, looking miserable and seemed accustomed to it.

She followed them at enough of a distance that they did not notice her; this was exactly how she wanted it. She followed the sullen, somber group until the school was in sight, then she broke off and went her own way. She came in through one of the main entrances and went right past all of the classrooms, never looking in, studiously avoiding eye contact wherever she could. None of the students were in yet. Emily imagined them in the communal washrooms, trying to get cleaned up as best as they could. The washrooms were so disorganized that one was lucky to emerge from them with one's own towel and soap! Not to mention toothbrush for those who were fortunate enough to have them. Sad, but no time for sad memories. She began to organize her books and materials for their day.

Miss Emily was first in the room, as it should be. She arranged her lesson book, her texts, and supplies on top of her desk. Then she sat in the teacher's chair and just gazed across the classroom. She still could not believe what had happened. How could she ever be a teacher? Well, no time for that now. She had to get things in order for her day. She arranged her pens and pencils inside her middle desk drawer and found where Whipshot kept student files. She did want to eventually go through these, but now was not the time. She did pull a couple of them out and scanned over their contents. The files were predictably sloppy, poorly organized, and generally a mess. The two that she looked at had notes scribbled in them, such as "worthless toad," "dimwitted fool," and so on. Emily could not stand any more of that, so she replaced the files and closed the drawer.

She did take the liberty of writing her name, "Miss Emily," on the board along with the day, month, and year in big friendly letters. She wanted to make a good impression on her fellow classmates… um…on *her students*. She felt so fresh and clean and pretty that it seemed like she had a whole new life. In fact, yes, it was a whole new life. She was ready to see what the day had in store. Things had changed so rapidly in such a short time.

Then she thought about Mr. Mentor! Talk about change. Her most trusted confidant was not only older than her, but he was a little *deader* too. She could not wrap her head around this whole situation! It was beyond belief; if she had not experienced it herself, she would not have—

"Believed it?"

Emily nearly jumped out of her skin. She looked toward the sound of the voice. There he was. He was standing right there, looking just like a normal person! It was Mr. Mentor.

"I just wanted to let you know that what you saw was real! I am real, and you must not start to doubt your own senses. Darkness awaits you on the path of doubt, Miss Emily. You must not start to believe that any of this is unreal. Last night, I introduced myself. That was a very kind meeting, one that I enjoyed. Now, today, we must get down to business.

"The next several days are going to be very difficult for you. However, you will have me near you almost all the time, helping you along. For now, know that Principal Coffenayle is talking to Miss Ladlepot, placing an order for the party. Don't worry. It won't be cafeteria fare. They are sending the lawyer to get some good food from town. Miss Ladlepot will just get it ready, if even has anything all to do with it. Here come your first students, Miss Emily. Miss Coffenayle will be here immediately after the class recites the pledge."

And just like that, he was gone. Brown suit, beard, shoes, proper watch chain—all of him exactly the same as last night, but now he was gone. Just as he faded out of view, the first students came in.

This group was of about six kids in all, ramshackle and dirty as they always were, doing their best in the conditions they were handed by the fickle finger of fate. They were a little unsure of how to deal with their fellow student turned teacher. She was one of *them*, now. She was one of the enemies. Miss Emily would be the one giving the beatings. She would now be the one berating them. The insults, the curses—their fellow student was now one of the teachers, and she was the talk of the student dorm last night.

Since the school did not mix classrooms in the dorms, none of the students outside of Whipshot's class knew much of anything about this situation. The teachers didn't know much, most likely because Emily did not introduce herself to them on the way to class. This promotion happened after class hours, so there was not time for teachers to find out. Emily's students all took their seats, books in hand. They did not have homework, obviously, so that was one thing Miss Emily would not have to worry about.

They all sat in their respective chairs and just stared with their eyes forward. No one seemed to know what to say or do, so they just kept as quiet as they could. After all, Miss Emily was a wildcard; no student had ever seen a teacher so young, and certainly never one from their ranks. Emily was equally quiet, smiling and nodding at each student as they came into the room. She did not want to just stare at them, so she busied herself with her lesson plans. Slowly, the room filled in the customary manner, the children all entering the room and nodding to or somehow acknowledging their new teacher. No one said much. Some of the students seemed to take this in stride as just another odd occurrence in a place known for its weirdness.

Then Margaret came into the classroom. She hesitated at the door, so very slightly that one would not have noticed unless they were studying her closely. Her expression was sullen, almost grim, even for Margaret who was not known for being chipper. A career as Whipshot's henchman had taken its toll, and she seemed to know that there was going to be payback. She dreaded this moment and would have run away if there was someplace to where she could run. There was no place for her in the class. There was no one to protect her from the wrath of her peers, and she knew it.

Immediately, Emily saw the puffiness and rings under her eyes. She knew that the class snitch had a hard night before coming to class. Probably sleepless. Maybe even a night of some harassment from the other students. Emily could only imagine how it must have been. She also knew that since she, Emily, was an unknown, they probably did not dare harass the toady too much. For all they knew, Margaret might be Emily's snitch as well. Teachers held positions of power. They were ones who could do great harm. At this school, they loved doing it. So how much would Miss Emily love it?

By the time Margaret had reached her special seat, the more comfortable chair that was one of her perks, Emily started to feel angry. She recalled the unjust behavior of Margaret, how she made so much trouble for many of the students, in particular poor Tommy. The stoolie made sure to always bring up something Tommy Littleton had done or failed to do. It could be something as small as an expression on his face during a lecture or complaining about a class assignment.

Emily was recalling everything that Margaret had done and was becoming angry. Suddenly, she felt that grandfatherly presence that seemed to say, "Do not hate Margaret or her actions. Hating the sin is the same as hating the sinner. Hate never goes anywhere good. You may disapprove, you may believe her actions are wrong, yes. Even so, you must be anxious to forgive her because hatred in any form pulls a person away from doing good and toward the darkness."

Emily immediately felt better as though some burden had been lifted from her shoulders. It was not for her to judge the wrong actions of Margaret. "Yes, Emily, that is correct," said the good presence. "You don't know Margaret, really, or how she truly feels about what Whipshot had her doing. She could prove to be a strong ally if she somehow believed that Whipshot's ire would not affect her anymore. She needs to feel protected. She is actually a very softhearted and vulnerable person whose tender feelings are easily hurt. Because of this, she sees herself as a very weak person. She believes that every other person can better endure the abuse that Whipshot hands out."

Emily immediately could see that *fear* in Margaret! The fear— oh the terror in that girl's heart! The new teacher did not dare express her newfound insight to the class. She would prejudice them and lose their trust. She could not allow that, not on the first day.

Soon, the classroom was filled with students, all with their books in hand, all with the same expressions of wonder in their faces.

Every one of them, without exception, looked to the broken floorboards that had been repaired piecemeal but effectively. The boards had been meshed together into a sort of patchwork quilt of shambles yet orderly and well-fit. One could say that there was sort a schizophrenic genius at work, almost like a Van Goh painting. The boards were a latticework of parts and pieces that did not match, did not coordinate, and yet somehow…they did. The boards still needed to be sanded and polished, but the work looked solid. It was sort of like a mismatched jigsaw puzzle that pieced together perfectly to create an off-center and juxtaposed picture. A picture that somehow worked. Such was the mind of Castlethorn.

The wall was also not patched, sanded, nor painted. When Jimmy walked in, he noticed right away the progress his new boss had made on the floor and that the wall still needed work. The boy figured that his work was cut out for him as the new apprentice… whatever Mr. Castlethorn was. Janitor? Carpenter? Mechanic? Maybe a combination of all of these. Jimmy took his seat after nodding a "good morning" to the new…teacher? He was not yet used to the idea. None of them were, including Happy Valley's newest educator.

The classroom filled up, the last student was in place, which didn't take long, given the school's strict rules about tardiness. None dare be late because the whole dorm would be punished for even just one student's indiscretion. Peer pressure kept the masses in line. For Miss Emily, this was showtime!

She stood up, all eyes glued on her. The pressure was immense, but she knew she could do it. She somehow knew Mr. Mentor was there for her. With his support, she was convinced she could do almost *anything*. So she started with, "Class, all of you come to attention, please." The classroom all stood in their attentive stance. Again, they recited the school's anthem:

We pledge allegiance to our school,
Happy Valley be she named.
We are happy, not in a valley,
But happy just the same.

We praise the prairie that keeps us here;
That barrenness is heaven-sent.
Too far to walk, too far to run;
Escape, and die a dissident!

We love our teachers, and our staff,
We eat our food with a laugh.
We love Miss Coffenayle, our leader true,
We love Miss Coffenayle through and through.

All hail Happy Valley!

Then right on cue, the principal walked in. The walls were still ringing with words of praise for their prison. The students remained at their best attentive stance. Miss Emily had fully expected the principal, due to Mr. Mentor's timely warning. It would have been strange for her not be there at any rate. Miss Coffenayle stood there, regal, stoic, and firm. The very picture of discipline, arrogance, and absolute power. She was tired, but she would never let it show. Malovent was particularly exhausting, but she had his magic to counteract that. It was a very simple spell, really, but nonetheless effective. "Everyone, I have a surprise," she said, "Well, I suppose it is not really a surprise since all of you are expecting a party today. We are to celebrate both the rescue of Miss Whipshot and the promotion of Miss Emily. You may applaud."

On cue, the whole class applauded obediently and politely but with little enthusiasm, much the way a whipped dog may fetch a stick.

"I want to let all of you know that I have heard from Nurse Shadyknight," she continued, "and Miss Whipshot is resting comfortably. She woke up for a moment this morning and wished all of you the best. She is warm, safe, comfortable, and happy." This, of course, was a bald-faced lie. She had not checked in on Whipshot. She only knew that she was still alive. She would intuitively know if death were coming, that she was sure of. It was one of the benefits of her powers.

"Miss Whipshot left Miss Emily with well-organized and comprehensive notes to continue your education. Miss Whipshot is a champion of justice and mercy, as all of you well know. She is also a champion of education and wisdom. As an instructor, she was so well-organized that she left everything that one would need to continue your education in a seamless manner. The transition will be so smoothly *executed* that you will hardly know the difference." She looked over at Emily from time to time with her chin aloft, giving a sidelong glance that seemed to tell Emily, *"Don't you dare foul this up… I don't care how you do it or what you do or don't have. You don't want to know what I will do to you if this goes badly."*

Emily's knees began to weaken. She was suddenly overwhelmed by the power of the principal's thoughts; somehow, she could feel what the principal truly thought of her, the class, the world. Too many years of being beaten down. Too many years of being taught by cruelty that she was a big nobody, a big nothing. A mangy cur that deserved only what she had, and even that was too much! Emily began to visibly flinch, and the corners of her mouth began to turn downward, like one who suddenly realized they were in the wrong place at the wrong time with the wrong expectations. Her mood darkened. She became suddenly depressed, and her heart started to race.

Then came the words, "Easy… Easy, Emily. Do not believe a word of all the bad feelings you are having. These feelings are very bad, from the wrong side. Do not listen to them. Listen to me. Believe in yourself, Emily. You were chosen for this work. You are to be their teacher. You will succeed at what you have been given to do. Take a deep breath and remember how you feel when I am with you, and know that I am with you all the time. I am here to help you do things that you do not believe you can do."

It was Mr. Mentor yet again to the rescue. Emily gave a confident smile and nod to Miss Coffenayle, even under her cold, cold stare.

The principal seemed to be pleased with herself; she had chosen wisely! "Now, class, I understand the limited nature of past celebrations. The food from the cafeteria is both nutritious and great-tasting, the best we can offer," continued the principal.

The class all knew better. The food was terrible, for the most part. It was greasy and stale. Most of the foods were covered with gravy, and the gravy was always there, they suspected, to cover the appearance of what they were eating. No one dared protest or flinch. They did not dare to give the slightest indication that they would counter anything that the principal might say, standing there proud in her Napoleon uniform, lying through her teeth—a true master of propaganda.

Miss Emily had now stepped over there beside the principal as she had seen Miss Whipshot do many times. She was playing the role of the teacher perfectly, now at ease with herself and her position. Emily did not really like supporting Miss Coffenayle, but she knew that this was expected. She had to play the role flawlessly, even deceptively. She somehow understood that she might even have to do things that would violate her conscience to keep up the appearance. She understood that the ultimate good was at stake.

"However," the principal continued, "I have decided that we have a few spare pennies in the budget, and we can afford to have special food and treats brought here for the party."

The class stood there, stunned. They did not know what to do. Never in any of their memories had they experienced even the very idea of food being brought to the school for a party. The silence was deafening; some of the students were slack-jawed. Before it had a chance to become awkward, and possibly a trigger for Miss Coffenayle's unpredictable fits of temper, Miss Emily prompted the students.

She stood just out view of Miss Coffenayle's searching spotlight eyes with a pantomime of polite applause. The students in the front of the class caught on immediately and began to applaud. It was infectious, and the whole room erupted in applause! Emily gave a quick upward motion of her hand, hidden from Coffenayle, and the class escalated their applause to a standing ovation, and they were smiling, a few of them saying, "Hooray!"

Coffenayle placed her hand on her chest, closed her eyes, and bowed so very slightly with pleasant nod. Perfect. They were eating out her hand. They were right where she wanted them.

14

Simon I. Doesbad, Esq.

Simon I. Doesbad was driving far out of his way, out of his routine, and away from things he would rather be doing. At least he was in his Nash Touring, a very fine car. He was grumbling and complaining to himself about his morning. He had to cancel both breakfast and lunch appointments with "important clients," or that was at least what he would tell people. The fact is that he only had *one* client, a client that paid him very well. The disadvantage to that was being under her thumb or perhaps even her heel continually.

Coffenayle paid him in gold bullion, as well, and while he made a lot of money that way, he had to be careful about how he handled himself. His gold was not in the form of coin, so daily trade was nigh impossible. He needed to trade it for dollars, and the only men who would not ask too many questions about the amount of gold he was cashing in were of questionable character. He made certain they saw his firearm tucked handily inside his belt, under his coat while transacting business. The understanding was mutual. He saw their guns under their coats too. They were all friendly enough but cautious.

Doesbad led a difficult double life. He would leave his house every day dressed as a custodian, complete with a cheap cap and a broom. Then he would go up to his office before hours without being seen, enter, lock the door, and put on his lawyer suit. That was how he would dress to entertain his wealthy friends during the day with chess or backgammon, high-dollar cognac, and expensive cigars. In the evenings, after coming home dressed as the poor custodian, he enjoyed playing cards and smoking cheap hand-rolled cigarettes while drinking cheaper homemade beer. It was true that the Eighteenth Amendment had recently been passed, prohibiting alcohol, but most of the local citizens—and cops—took "a little home brew now and then."

Truth be told, he actually liked his evening pals better than his day companions. The trouble was that he was too vain to let go of the wealthy appearance. He felt like he "made good" when he was acting that way. He felt that he had arrived at some wonderful place far, far away from the impoverished world of the unwanted orphan he used to be.

When the phone rang early this morning, he thought he was perhaps dreaming. But he was not. No one had his home phone number for safety reasons. It must be Coffenayle! Drat! He checked the time, could not believe the hour, then answered the phone. He thought he misheard her at first or that perhaps she was joking. She was not! He was on retainer, and his client needed him *right now*. This was an annoyance to him, but truth be told, he would go to the ends of the earth for that woman. There were any number of honest women in his home neighborhood, and there were finer women where he "worked," playing the part of the wealthy attorney. Somehow, though, there was just something about Miss Coffenayle's…strength that kept him interested.

So the not-so-wise attorney got up, shaved, talked to himself in the mirror about what a fool he was, how much better he could actually do in life, and then got dressed. He put on his coveralls, his cheap cap, donned his broom, and wandered out the door. He waved to a couple of his card-playing friends and walked out of the neighborhood.

Closer to downtown, he hailed a cab, and it took him to his office building. He entered, went upstairs to his suite, got dressed in his lawyer clothes, and came back down as *Simon I. Doesbad, Esq.*— an important man with important things to do. He called a limo to meet him at the office and take him to the place where stored his car. He paid the limo driver. Then he retrieved his keys from the man at the parking lot's pay booth. "Busy day, eh, Simon? Must be. You're in early," stated the parking attendant over his newspaper.

"Indeed, my good man, *busy I am* today!" shouted Doesbad as he threw the man a generous tip. He got into his fine car, and the motor turned over just immediately as it always did. Ha! The electric starter was a far cry from that hand crank model he traded in. While the engine was warming up, he looked at the list of things "that woman" wanted from him. Cupcakes. Soda pop (cola no less). Custard puffs. Napkins. Delicatessen sandwiches. Potato salad, and more! What a spread! He had attended wealthy weddings and funerals that served less food than this.

He thought back to how he ended up being general counsel for Happy Valley Vocational School—one meeting! That one meeting was all it took for HVVS to become the exclusive client of Simon I. Doesbad, Esq. To this day, he does not remember the details of the meeting. He did remember signing the contract. He did remember sitting with Principal Donatienne Coffenayle in the lobby of the school. He recalled that at some point, he was starting to question some of the things he was seeing.

He was unhappy about the way the school was difficult to contact. He had heard that all vocational and extracurricular activities had been cancelled. These used to be the backbone of the whole program. The appearance of the school itself was highly questionable. It was not at all the way Mr. Mentor, his personal friend, would have wanted it. In fact, it reminded him of his own boyhood in an *orphanage*. This was not an orphanage. It was a school for young men and women, orphans or not, to gain the tools they needed to make their way in the world! He was certain that Miss Coffenayle was violating the wishes of Charles and Edna. She should know better. He remembered that when he started asking questions, Coffenayle suggested a more private place to talk.

They went to her office. She offered him some tea, and he accepted. Then everything got cloudy. He could not remember how they came to an agreement, but they did. There was another room they entered during their meeting. He saw odd shapes and a very tall man wearing a robe. The room smelled sweet but funny. A candle.

More tea. The memories were very disjointed and strange. It was sort of like, well, a nightmare. Almost as though the things he was remembering were impossible but at the same time very real. On that day was the deal that changed his life. Strange, though, how his memories were spotty and disjointed.

So lost he was in thought that he nearly missed the turn onto the road that led to the General's General Store. It was owned by a tough and fierce old man with a heart of gold. He had lost both legs in the Great War and was a bit of a legend. He claimed to be a general in that war, but no one bothered to try and substantiate that claim. To them, it did not matter. He was just the old shopkeeper, everyone called him "Pap," and almost no one knew his real name, Aloysius Childerbaum. Everyone embraced the old boy, war stories and all, because they respected him. It was very well-known that he was a WWI veteran and that he had lost both legs in the war during a heroic act. He had medals to prove it, but there was no evidence of his actual field rank one way or the other. He certainly had the town's respect, general or not.

He had his medals that he kept at the store in a small chest. He would pull them out for the little boys in the neighborhood who would come by for penny candy. They would get candy whether they had their pennies or not as long as they stuck around to hear his wondrous tales of smoke, fire, bravery, and blood. His favorite was of how he personally once slapped the Kaiser himself in the face with a leather glove and called him a "dirty chicken-livered coward." True or not, no one cared. The stories were a lot of fun, and he enjoyed telling them.

Doesbad parked his fancy car outside and waited for just a moment. He was always mobbed by the kids in front of the store, and the people in the neighborhood would come out to admire his car. Once in a while, he would treat the boys to thirty cents each so they could go see the latest moving picture show and have a treat while they were there. This was not one of those days, though, and even without the cash payout, the boys would still crowd around in admiration and ask to touch the shiny wonderful car. The kids came out from wherever they were playing or milling about, and there were always more kids to be found. They came from every direction. Strangely, though, some could not be found by their mothers who were calling for help with chores.

Doesbad told them that he was there to buy some food and treats for some friends of his who were throwing a party. They could have a cupcake apiece if they would pitch in and help him load up the car...*carefully.* He once forked out a substantial amount of cash to Pap one day because his "helpers" were a little too enthusiastic and broke a couple of lamps and a grandfather clock. That was a financially rough day for Simon. Though he forgave "his boys" almost immediately, he learned his lesson about youthful enthusiasm. Thus, he introduced the strict controls over their behavior.

Doesbad entered the place with three boys at a time. Their hands were crammed fully in their pockets as they meekly walked ahead of Doesbad. He was not going to lose sight of them for certain. They found old Pap in his cane-woven wheelchair, his pants neatly pinned up over his stumps. Today, just to be funny, he put large boots on the stumps with the toes pointed upright to make himself look like he had tiny legs. He looked up and was glad to see his old friend.

"Simple Simon!" he quipped. "How are things going with you? Well enough, I hope!" He wheeled quickly over to the well-dressed attorney.

"I am well enough, old friend! I see you have...new feet?" Simon responded with a grin.

The old man thought that was hilarious and laughed until he coughed.

Simon continued, "I am here to place a rather large order, and I hope you can fill it! These boys are here to help me, and they *promise to be careful*, don't you, boys?"

The boys removed their hats and nodded in agreement. That cupcake was really important to them.

"Well," smiled old Pap, "they ain't never bothered me none. Heh! I could always stand to sell another grandfather clock!" He winked at Simon who simply smiled and shook his head, silently indicating, *Not today, old friend, not today.*

"All right then, Simon, down to business! What can I get'cha?" He pulled a pencil from the back of his ear and produced a pad of paper. He licked the tip of the pencil and sat there at the ready, looking at the attorney.

Simon read off the list of cupcakes, candies, bottled sodas, and handmade sandwiches, etc. The list got longer and longer.

Pap could hardly believe his ears! That was the biggest order he had gotten all year, maybe even since he first opened his doors! This would clear out his sandwiches, which he would have to pack on ice if Simon was taking them anywhere! "Martha!" he hollered to the back of the store. "Clear the icebox of sandwiches! We just sold them all! Then we'll need to make new ones for the lunch rush!" He turned back to Simon. "You taking these somewhere?"

"Yes, I am taking all of this to a client out of town. A very *important* client. There is big celebration, and we are feeding about forty people. Hungry people." He failed to mention that this was his only client at a crummy orphanage. "I have a ways to drive, so I will need to keep them cold. Can you pack them on ice?"

"Why, certainly! Martha! Put them on ice! Simon has to travel!"

They packed the sandwiches in a hurry, and old Pap got the boys, in very careful shifts of three each, to carry the other stuff out to the car. The ant trail proceeded without incident; all grandfather clocks were spared. By the time all of the food and supplies were organized and packed into the Nash, there was barely room for Simon I. Doesbad, Esq. to drive. Once satisfied that everything was in order and that none of the boys had stowed away in the car anywhere, which happened once, he thanked everyone for their help and support. Then he jumped in the driver's seat and left the scene.

As always, he had paid his account in full, in cash. Simon was glad Pap could fill his order. Simon chuckled to think that the ol' boy was torn between feeling so happy to sell so much and feeling anxious about restocking for the lunch rush. Soda pop and candy he could replenish easily, but the sandwiches would take some time. The boys in the neighborhood would be talking about this for weeks. Doesbad felt…proud of what he did for the neighborhood!

He drove off with roar and a generous sounding of the horn while the boys jumped up and down, cheering and hollering. He loved showing off for the crowd that way. He really loved remembering how he felt as a boy in that orphanage whenever he was given a special task to do with a guest's car. He liked doing anything involving cars. He hoped that some of the boys in that crowd felt as inspired as he did as a boy, seeing this big, wonderful, magnificent car and being a part of something bigger than themselves. Ah, yes! What a day it had already been. He was actually relieved about not having to engage in overstuffed conversations with overstuffed men about being overstuffed!

*****

Back at the school, Emily and Miss Coffenayle were just finishing up their business. The class was very happy about their party, rejoicing and excited. Emily was excited for them. Miss Coffenayle felt puffed up, very proud of herself, and she loved the adulation she was receiving from the students. She also knew that she could not let these positive, happy emotions get too far out of control. She would have to drop by the other classrooms and reassure them that business as usual was not changing throughout the school. Miss Coffenayle *must* remain in control.

Speaking of control, she had to report back to Malovent and assure him that she was not going to let this spark of hope get too deep of a root in the children's hearts. Malovent was reluctant about the party but agreed to it. Coffenayle said it would help relieve the pressure in the student's minds and would make them more compliant.

When she was first being tutored by her master, she learned an important lesson. The mistake that most tyrants make is to give the people absolutely nothing to lose. The tyrants, through history, some of which Malovent himself dealt with, would get so carried away with themselves that they would forget under whose authority they operated. They would go off on their own, believing that they could handle the masses. They would then go overboard, as in "Let them eat cake" overboard. When that happened, the peasants would finally realize that no life at all would be better than the one they had. Even in death, they had nothing to lose.

When they would finally hit that tipping point, well, *"Reign of Terror, anyone? Don't lose your head, Marie!"* Miss Coffenayle learned that all great revolutions in history occurred when the people began to realize that they had everything to gain and nothing to lose. Malovent also taught her that tyranny could indeed last forever if the dictator handled things properly. Forever! Imagine that…being a dictator under Malovent forever! *What bliss*, she thought. *What joy! A tormentor in his name forever!*

15

The Lunch Party

This party would be the perfect safety valve to give the kids a break from the intensity of Whipshot and transition into whatever Emily had to offer. So far, so good. As far as she could tell, Miss Emily had perfect control of the kids. The orderly desks, the school anthem. No sign of rebellion from Miss Emily. She seemed to be doing very well so far. Maybe she was not quite the wildcard as she and Malovent had originally feared. She may even get her own steel ruler eventually. Time would tell if this Emily person was indeed worthy of a ruler. They were custom-made, expensive, designed to be weapons, and not all of the teachers possessed them.

"All right, everyone, all right!" the principal spoke out loudly over the din. "Class will resume as normal until the time for the party is announced. Right around lunchtime, I suppose. That will depend upon when the delivery of food arrives. I will leave you now to Miss Emily. Teacher, resume your instruction." Upon that announcement, Miss Coffenayle turned smartly on her heel and marched out of the classroom, business as usual.

The classroom was now still. All eyes were on Miss Emily. Now was the time for Miss Emily to shine. She somehow felt inspired that these first few moments of teaching would define her in the eyes of the students. She knew they would either admire and respect her as their new teacher or they would see her only as a student that was put in place as a mere Band-Aid. So what would it be? Band-Aid or teacher? Not much of a choice. An unusual courage welled up inside of Emily. Teacher it was.

She continually felt as though Mentor was helping her along. She began to speak without really knowing what she would say. These next words were not rehearsed or even thought of beforehand. She literally did not know what she would say next, but the words came. It was almost like stepping off of a cliff, only to have a bridge form beneath her feet. One step at time, each time she stepped off the edge, a panel of bridge suddenly appeared to support her foot. One sentence at a time, the words came to her. To top it off, she somehow *knew*, not just supposed, but *knew* that Miss Coffenayle was just outside the door, listening.

"Class! I am here now not as your fellow student but as your teacher. Those of you who even start to think that I am somehow going to go easy on you because of my age or that I will somehow be a fellow student to you on any level can think again!" She paced smartly around the room. "I know that there are those among you who would love to get on my *good* side." She stopped and stared directly into Margaret's eyes. "I don't *have a good side!*"

Miss Coffenayle stood outside, nearly snickering with pride. She had chosen well! Malovent would be so pleased with this.

Emily continued with her rant, pacing the room. "Forget trying to get special favors or treatment out of me! Anyone with a special chair will lose that chair immediately, and I will have Castlethorn take it this morning! There we be no praising one student over others. There will be no earning of special favors. There will be no *snitching!* The one thing that will happen, when the rules are broken, the whole class will be punished *together*. The entire group will suffer as a unit for the transgressions of the *one!*"

At this, little Tommy seemed to brighten up but not too much. He did not dare because Miss Emily stared him down. She did feel bad for doing that, but Mentor seemed to be telling her that this abuse was important and necessary. She had to give the impression that she was a tyrant. When posing as a tyrant, one must do tyrannical things. "I know that you are having a party today. Now in *my* classroom, we *earn* our parties! We don't take handouts from anyone!"

"But Miss Emily, we earned our party. Coffenayle said—" protested a student.

The new teacher quickly moved over to the student's desk and hovered over it. She looked stern. She felt terrible, but she maintained her stern look. "Is *Miss* Coffenayle here right now? Hmm? No! She is not. Does anyone see *Miss* Coffenayle? It think not! She is absolutely not here. Who is here right now? Hmm? Who? *Answer me!*"

The student reared back in the chair and trembled just a bit. "Y-you are."

"Oh yes! Yes, I am! *I* am here! Miss Coffenayle is not! You will never refer to her as 'Coffenayle' again. Well, no point in delaying. No time like the present. Class! Stand attention!" They all stood up as a body. "Because Billy Bonn here failed to call Principal Coffenayle by her appropriate title, everyone gets to repeat the name 'Miss Coffenayle' one hundred times, lest Mr. Bonn should ever forget again. Begin!" Emily moved to the chalkboard and drew a hashmark for every time the class repeated *Miss* Coffenayle.

When the class finished their recitation, she put the chalk down and asked, "Who is here now? That's right, *Miss Emily* is here now. Who is not here now? That's right, *Miss* Coffenayle is not! Who is in charge then? That's right! Miss Emily is charge! I am here! I run this class! When *Miss* Coffenayle is here, she has the floor, but when she is not, understand that she has given me absolute power over your lives here in this classroom! Is that understood? Well? *Is that understood or not?*"

The class was in shock. They never knew Emily…um… *Miss* Emily had the kind of energy needed to be this way. Some of them could not believe it. There had been some speculation at the dorm that Miss Coffenayle was going to be the true power in the classroom. They did not believe that Miss Emily had the strength to handle them. Some also thought that she would go easy for the exact reasons that she just stated she would *not*. So much for getting a break. This new tyrant may have a different style, but she was just as bad as Whipshot; perhaps even worse.

"Y-yes, Miss Emily," stuttered Billy Bonn.

"I didn't ask just Mr. Bonn here who finally seems to have grown a brain!"

"Yes, Miss Emily!" the class shouted in unison.

"Do you want to have that party? Or should I have the food taken to the teacher's lounge?"

The class answered both yes and no, confused at what part of the two-part question they should address. Emily paused and then said, "There seems to be some confusion! Do you want that party?"

"Yes, Miss Emily," the class stated.

"Do you want me to take the food to the teachers' lounge?"

"No, Miss Emily!"

"Very good. So far, Billy has been the only one to endanger your party. I suggest you keep an eye on him."

Margaret perked up a bit.

"Not *just you,* Margaret! The whole class! *You* get to lose your special chair!"

The girl hung her head, completely deflated.

"Now that we have a few things straight—" Emily had Margaret stand up, and she changed the girl's chair out right there in front of everybody.

Miss Coffenayle walked away with her head held high. Emily was the perfect choice, the perfect dictator. She did not even need to use those screeching scornful insults that Whipshot was so fond of, the very same ones that Miss Coffenayle grew tired of. Miss Emily was there, constantly reminding the students of what they had to lose. Those reminders would keep them in line. Offer them a carrot, but put it on a long pole, perpetually within the distance of them smelling it! They never quite reach it, pulling the wagon the whole time. She was perfect! Coffenayle was quite pleased with herself. The class would have their carrot today, though, if that fool Doesbad would just hurry with the food. In the meantime, Miss Coffenayle would busy herself with the cafeteria lady. Miss Ladlepot was one strange duck but great at her job.

The principal entered the kitchen area and, as expected, was washed over by a head of steam and smoke. Odd odors filled the air. Everything was running normally for Miss Ladlepot's kitchen.

Anyplace else, this would have been a serious situation, one that needed to be addressed. Not at Happy Valley, though! Coffenayle walked through the steam and the odors, past the many wondrous machines and such. She found Miss Ladlepot in her customary state, screaming at her cooks. "Dadblast it, Polly! I don't cares about'cher lame excuses! You get dems eggs cooked, and you do it right *now!* What? I dassn't care! Scrape 'em off the floor and cook them! Scramble 'em! Cover them with gravy! Those kids are lucky to eat anything at all!"

"Miss Ladlepot!" called Coffenayle. "I need to see you right away!"

"Who? What? Who come inta mah kitchen? Is that you again, Castlethorn? You bring me another stoodint?" There was a rattling of ladles.

"Miss Ladlepot, it is Principal Coffenayle! Drop those cursed ladles and get *over* here! I have to talk to you about the number of students for lunch!"

"Oh! It's you!" shouted Miss Ladlepot. "Okay!" Ladles crashed on the floor. Ladlepot emerged from the steam and noise; she was in her normal grimy uniform. Miss Coffenayle was pleased. *No ladles in her hands, thank goodness.*

"Can we go someplace quieter to talk?" Coffenayle hollered over the banging of Goliath chopping up something new. He was laughing with every blow of his cleaver.

"Yes, we can," replied Miss Ladlepot. She wanted to holler at Goliath to keep it down but knew it would not do any good. She would only yell at people when it was productive. Miss Ladlepot took the principal into what passed for an office. It was just a little nook of a room, one with a folding card table for a desk, an empty file cabinet, a portable fan, and two very uncomfortable chairs. They sat down at the card table, and Miss Ladlepot sat sideways, her feet aligned with the door as though she could not wait to escape the meeting. There was gruel that needed her full attention this morning. "So," started Miss Ladlepot, "what is—"

"I'll not keep you. I know that this is Gruel Day at the cafeteria and you need to get back to it. I have a request. Very simple. Before you make your count for lunch and dinner—not that leftovers matter much because you throw them in with whatever you cook the next day—you will be missing some kids."

"T'wazn't *my* fault! If them kids gots the delicate stummacks, then they kin just stay hungered and go to the nurse!" Miss Ladlepot shouted. "You got no—"

"Miss Ladlepot, *please!* I am not here to blame you for anything. You are going to be missing Miss Whipshot's entire class because she had an accident!" stated the principal forcefully. "They are going to be busy with me for lunch and dinner. I am throwing them a party and—"

"A pardy sez ye? A *pardy?* Principal, we ain't had no pardy here in so long that leftovers from the last one jist got used up last month!" shouted Miss Ladlepot as she jumped up out of her seat, nearly tipping the card table over.

Last month? The principal thought it over and wondered for an instant how long she kept leftovers. This is the first party the school held since *he* died. She left that thought where it lay, thinking it best that she doesn't know everything that goes on in the kitchen. She never ate the food from here anyway.

"Well," continued Miss Ladlepot with her red frizzy locks starting to bounce with excitement. "There's tuns o' stuff I kin do for that party. It's a little short on notice, but—" Her eyes grew wide. But before she could come out with some idea for roadkill this or that, Coffenayle cut her off.

"Miss Ladlepot… I appreciate the offer, but the school is paying for food to be brought in."

Miss Ladlepot paused and let that sink in. She was not going to cook for the party? Outside food being brought in? Whipshot's kids are going to eat food from the outside? "Are you shore that's wise, Miz Coffenayle? Youse wantin' gives 'em the screaming bowels? Theys will be on the privy all night long! Wiff the dormitories set up the way the way they are, there's gonna bees a pow'ful mess to cleans up for the dorm attendunts."

Miss Coffenayle chuckled. "Oh, Miss Ladlepot, I'm sure they will be fine."

"I'll leaves ya to it, then!" barked Miss Ladlepot, seeming in a bit of a huff over this whole thing. She did not like it when she did not feed the kids her own self. "If there's nuthin' else, I'm leavin' ya to find yer own way out!" She stormed off back into the smelly steam.

Coffenayle left the little room, luckily knowing her own way out. Unbeknownst to her, as she left Miss Ladlepot's little office, a ladle came whizzing through the steam with a sniper's precision, and it stopped just inches from the back of her head.

Miss Coffenayle was preoccupied, mumbling to herself, and there was too much noise and steam for her to notice the soup missile whizzing toward the back of her head and how it suddenly stopped, hovered and then was set down gently on a countertop. Goliath looked up and saw the short spectacle. He froze with his cleaver in the air, mid-chop. He shouted, "Ah ha! Miz Coffin near nailed. No hoomin stop it!" and immediately returned to chopping up whatever furry thing now lay on his cutting board. "Ha! Ha! No hoomin stop it! No hoomin stop it!" he chanted. Coffenayle was completely oblivious, busily thinking of the next steps for the party.

Mr. Mentor was glad he caught the ladle in time. The party *had to* happen. The kids needed that break. He left the kitchen area through the wall with another errand on his mind. He had to be quick about things if he wanted to accomplish his mission. Many lives were at stake!

Castlethorn had returned to the classroom to finish his repair work on the floor but saw that class was already in session. He knew that a party was planned, and he hoped it would be outside. Or that at least part of it would be. I mean, why not? He had some sanding and varnish work to do. There was still that hole in the wall he temporarily covered with a tarp, and the kids would be better off without that *stink* of him working. Besides that, the *varnish* might be offensive too. He chuckled at his jab at himself. The only safe target for humor is one's self, someone from long ago once taught him. He was surprised he remembered that. The memories that came through naturally for him did not hurt. It was when he tried to force a memory to surface that he was pained by the headaches and green fog in his brain. He decided to put on a little show for the class. Maybe that would inspire a picnic on the grounds.

He burst into the classroom with, *"Buck-buck-buck! Ba-kaw!"* and twirled the lantern. "Be's they's all hoomin?" he asked loudly as he twirled Lantern and continued to cluck like a chicken, moving about the classroom.

"Mr. Castlethorn! Please!" barked a startled Emily as she was writing on the board. A precious large piece of chalk broke in her hand as she was writing a story problem for the students to solve. She was so startled that she crammed it into the board, and it shattered. "Must you do that *now?*" She turned to him with her hands on her hips, the way she saw other teachers do when they were upset. "We are in the middle of class, sir! I don't know what you were accustomed to with Miss Whipshot and how she did things, but this is *my* classroom now. You can return to her routine as soon as she is better and resumes teaching and not *before!"*

The old janitor froze, Lantern clinking away, expending the last spin's energy.

"Ahs be sorry, Miss Emily. But you mus' know that they's all hoomin beans, 'cept one. All hoomin...but one's not," Castlethorn stated softly. He checked Lantern, gave it a turn, rechecked it, and started to head for the door. He seemed mildly ashamed, and his head hung down.

"Well, I am sure that the class is most impressed to know that," she retorted with less hardness in her voice. "Understand, sir, you may come back during the party if you wish to entertain us. Perhaps you could join us for some food and treats," she said to him with a slight smile. She could not help it.

He stopped at the door. He was facing the hallway but then turned around. He looked at Emily, his jaw agape in surprise. "Whu...what? Miss Emily...yous invited me to-to tha pardy?" He could not believe his ears. "If'n youse kids don't mind, I... I would loves to come by and joins fun stuffs wif you." He was fighting back a tear. He could not believe this might actually happen.

"Well, students? What do you think?" she asked the class as she gently nodded her head with a "Please say yes" expression on her face.

The students knew better than not to. Besides, old Mr. Castlethorn did a lot of work, and he even had them help him, which was a really great thing of him to do. So the students began nodding and saying, "Yes, sure, why not?"

Emily turned back to him. "Well, that settles it, then. Mr. Castlethorn, I will send Jimmy when the time for the party arrives. We may need help setting up things, if you don't mind."

"Aw, Miz Emily, dat's what ah'm here for. An' I will be gladz to attenden youse party. I gots to go now, but I will wait for yese party to start. I willz be dere in mees office," he said and left the room. He ambled down the hallway, drying his eyes with Lantern in hand. He was anxious to check his readings; he could do that in his office while waiting for the party and gathering materials for the floor and wall. Plus, he had not changed his coveralls in a while. Maybe he could find a spot of polish for his old work boots too.

*****

Meanwhile, Coffenayle was at her own office, mopping the cafeteria steam off of her brow. She was expecting that moronic Simon Doesbad anytime. Her receptionist was in the receiving lobby of the office, typing something. The door between the two offices was open. Coffenayle sat at her desk, just taking a break. Then the shadows started to grow long; the natural shadows of books that were cast along her shelves grew darker and larger. She knew what that meant—she was being summoned.

She jumped up and closed the door. Then she placed her candles in the correct position on the floor and lit them. He was coming! She lit the incense and threw her black dress on over her school uniform. She knelt on the floor with her head bowed.

She sensed the electrical charge in the air that meant Malovent was soon appearing. So soon! She had just spoken to him. What could it possibly be? She quickly lit her candles and incense. No time to dress up, though! The shadows grew longer and darker as they creeped across to join in the middle of the room. The shadows formed a dark puddle in the middle of the floor. Then he began to take shape! Oh, how enthralling to her was the mystique! The puddle then began to grow taller and taller, forming a thick black column. Then the column became rounded at the top, and tentacles of energy began to twirl around it like the stripe on a barber pole. Then, suddenly, he appeared, covered as always in his cowl. He was not completely formed yet. He looked a little fuzzy. This was not a full appearance, so it was likely an update on something. These types of appearances were always less formal.

"Coffenayle," stated Malovent.

"Greetings, Master," stated the principal, her head still bowed.

"You may rise."

"Yes, certainly. What may I do for you?" asked Coffenayle.

"Beware the new teacher. I cannot foresee what, but she may present some danger to us."

"Danger?" she asked, perplexed.

"Yes. There is much good in her…and something else…but I sense corruption enough to keep her in line. Miss Emily could go either way. I am here to remind you to be cautious of how much 'fun' you allow the class to have. We don't want to generate too much positive energy. Positives only serve us if the students are brought to a high, then crash to a depressing low. We discussed earlier how you know what to do. Just beware of Miss Emily getting too great a foothold in the classroom." Malovent paused for just a moment. "Ahh…yes," he resumed. "It is time for you to go now. I sense that idiot lawyer who wants to be your boyfriend is on his way. Ha! Ha! Ha!" The laugh was bland and humorless. He stopped speaking and turned to Coffenayle.

"Yes, Master," she answered. Then the shadow began to melt back into the floor, just in time. She thought she heard Doesbad pulling up outside. It was time to start the party. She extinguished her candles and incense quickly and cleaned up. She opened a window to flush the smoke. When the air was fairly clear, she opened the door. The secretary did not even look up. She was used to Coffenayle talking to herself in her office. The principal brushed by the desk without a word, the secretary not missing even a beat on her typewriter. Just another day, another normal day in the most abnormal show on earth.

Doesbad had pulled up outside in his exceptional car. She had to talk to him one day about parking that thing outside of the school. It might draw attention. For now, it was the best place to park it because they needed to unload the food and treats. He got out of the car and opened the back doors. He told Coffenayle that they had better hurry because the sandwiches were on ice and might get wet. She told him to bring the boxes into the main lobby and leave them on the floor, that she would get some assistance. She hustled to the engineering office and kicked the door quite hard. Knocking never seemed to work. "Castlethorn? Castlethorn? You in there? We need some help with the party, and bring a hand truck. Hello? Hello?"

She heard someone coming and figured it must be Castlethorn. The door opened, and the principal waited to see the old janitor. But it was not; it was…one of the…students? Oh yes, she knew about this, the one who was to be Castlethorn's new apprentice, that sharp young man who did so much in the rescue of Whipshot. "Oh, hello! You must be… Johnny?" the principal stated pleasantly.

The student was startled and started to tremble a bit.

"Oh, no, dear boy," Coffenayle reassured him, her hands folded pleasantly in front of herself as she leaned forward slightly. *The show must go on,* she thought to herself. "Don't be nervous. We are not here to have a teaching moment or any such thing. I hope you did not forget the class party?"

"N-no, I did not forget," said the young man. "But if I may say so?"

"Oh, yes. Yes, dear boy. Go on indeed." She listened intently, looking for anything at all that she could use against him later.

"Um…my name is Jimmy and not Johnny…um…that is all I wanted to say, Miss Coffenayle," his voice trailed off, and he hung his head.

The principal was secretly amused. She had trained this one *very* well. He would never be one to give her trouble, stand up for his rights, or any such nonsense. She loved seeing his subservience, his beaten countenance. The whipped little beast knew his place—beneath her heel.

"Oh, yes. Of course, Jimmy. How silly of me." *Yeah*, she thought, *you could drop dead, you little rat, and I could not care less.* "Is Mr. Castlethorn here? Um…by the way, why are *you* here?" She was a bit concerned to see a student in the engineer's office. Anything unusual could be a threat to her.

"I came to talk to Mr. Castlethorn. I had to let him know that the party is about to start. Miss Emily sent me. Also, I am his new apprentice."

"Oh, yes! That is right. I nearly forgot about that in all the excitement. It has been an exciting two days, after all, has it not, Jimmy?" She wondered if this whole apprenticeship thing was a good idea. Having a student around all of this stuff was probably dangerous. But, no, she thought better of it. Let Miss Emily have her way, and besides, what was the harm? Maybe Castlethorn might actually clean up his ac—She froze in mid-thought. What on earth was going on here? "Mr. Castlethorn? What?"

The old janitor had appeared in the door. He had shaven. He was relatively clean. He smelled like soap and water instead of… whatever he usually smelled like. He had damp hair pulled back into a ponytail. He stood taller, though still bent at the spine, and really had cleaned up rather nice. He had changed and actually pressed his coveralls. And he had the buttons undone to reveal a…*shirt collar?* Was that a *necktie?* No! That could not be! But it was. The knot was sloppy, yes, but it was a tie! What on earth? She had not seen him look anywhere near this good since…the funerals.

"Mr. Castlethorn?" she asked, staring at him, wide-eyed.

"Miz Coffenayle…how are yees doing ta-day?" he responded.

Yes, she thought to herself, *definitely him. Diction that sounds like a slobbering fool.* She composed herself, then she spoke aloud, "I take it you are coming to the party then?"

"Yes'm… I bees plannin' on it, if yous dasn't mind," he said sheepishly. "I dun gots the floor all dun except fur the varnish and dem wall holes is gonna be patched. I gots old Jimbo over heerz to hep me. So Miz Emeelee dun invahted me." He let his eyes close and his head bowed low.

The principal watched this man nearly grovel, ashamed of himself for daring to ask. Just like the frightened, timid savage she knew him to be. His abject humility pleased her. The party would be harmless. She could double his workload later and really break his soul, but good. Malovent would be *proud*. "Well," she began slowly, savoring the old janitor's bowed head. She enjoyed the fact that she could tolerate his presence; he really did clean up. "Is your work *all* caught up?"

"Yes'm." His head bowed lower.

"Is there anything left to do in that classroom?"

"Yes'm. Wahl repairz, sandingz, payn'tin, and varnishez. Muh matereeyulz is awl gazzered ups."

"I see. That sounds important. Should I move the party elsewhere while you work on it?" He did not see her wicked smile. It was a loaded question. As meek as he was, he was still wise.

"Th-that'd be up ta you'n, Miz Coffenayle." He winced slightly, and his voice quivered the slightest bit.

"I see." She was pleased. Very pleased. In fact, that was the *only* answer that would get him into the party. So it did. "Very well, Mr. Castlethorn. You may come to the party…as our guest support staff member."

He looked up, and his eyes were wide, surprised, and grateful. They nearly watered with gratitude. He could not remember the last time he got such a break. He could not remember his last sponge bath or hair wash. He could not remember yesterday very well either, much beyond what he could scribble in his activity log. Writing did not give him many headaches, usually.

"I thanks yee, Mis Coffenayle," he said quietly with his head bowed. "Ye thinkees Miss Emily maht lets me bring Lantern?"

Miss Coffenayle chuckled. "I think that might be arranged. Oh, yes, Mr. Castlethorn, could you possibly round up some students and a handcart? There are food and goodies in the rather large car out front."

"Yes, I certainly will do dat, Miz Coffenayle! Thanks to yee agains for makin' me a party guest," Castlethorn said with a huge smile.

Miss Coffenayle glanced at his smile. His black tooth was still there, but... *Did he actually brush his teeth?*

"Very well, I will leave you to it, then. Run along! Lots to be done."

Castlethorn and Jimmy went to the classroom first to a retrieve a few other students. Tommy came along in the group. Emily smiled to see Tommy willfully get involved in something. He actually volunteered. He was normally so timid, but not so much now. He seemed to get along well with the classroom. The students were not actually friends with each other, but they did seem to get along in their own way. No one really gave anyone else a hard time; Miss Emily watched to be sure that Margaret was safe too.

Out at the car, Castlethorn was impressed! He really liked that Nash Touring, all decked out and shiny! All of the kids were impressed. Doesbad was busily unloading the car, telling the kids to be careful, to not scratch the paint, don't drop this or that, etc. The chubby lawyer tried to look stern and stately, but he was having too much fun watching the kids have fun. He remembered his younger days and how excited he would have been to see such a sight as this grand wonderful car! He made his living as a boy washing such cars for pocket change. That pocket change, plus tips from influential men who appreciated the boy's initiative, really added up. In the hands of a wise investor who was fond of Orphan Doesbad, that money put the boy through law school.

They began hauling things into the room, and Miss Coffenayle was there at the door, beaming with pride at what she had done. They would sing praises to her name for this. She knew they would. They brought in the ice box sandwiches first, then some plates showed up from the cafeteria at Emily's suggestion. There were forks and spoons, no knives. Miss Coffenayle had a rule against knives, remembering Caesar's demise, but they did have small spatulas for the mayonnaise and so forth. Emily had provided her desk to act as the buffet serving table. She had some of the students move their own desks together to hold the sodas and snacks. The students were very excited. Talking and moving around the table, looking at this or that. Nobody touched anything, and they were all on their best behavior. They did not want for the principal to suddenly end the party. Besides, after that mess from the riot, they had their fill of cleaning!

When they were finished setting up, they had quite the spread. All of the foods and snacks, the drinks, all of it was lined up and presented neatly. There were sandwiches, potato chips, pretzels, candies of various descriptions, bottles of different colors of pop! Root beer, colas, fruit flavors! Most of the students in this room literally did not remember the last time they ate such foods. When the setup was complete, Miss Emily called the class to attention. Miss Coffenayle and Doesbad, Esq., stood at the doorway, smiling.

Castlethorn was over near the place where he had to do the varnish, studying one of the glass panels on Lantern. He was muttering to himself, but no one could hear him say much. At least he was not clucking like a chicken, which got a smile out of Emily. She had never known that he could clean up this well. He was still a wreck of a man to look at, but Emily could easily imagine him doing other things. She seemed to feel that he was greater than all of this. She just sort of…knew it. She overheard a word or two about something "not hoomin" in the room. She began to wonder if—no, that was silly! No one could find a ghost by looking into a lantern. Could they? She thought Mr. Mentor was in the room because she was getting those impressions about Castlethorn from somewhere. She shook off her thoughts. They were getting too weird. This was supposed to be a *party!*

The invisible Mr. Mentor chuckled to himself.

"Class! Come to order! Attention please!" shouted Miss Emily.

The students immediately stood by their desks at their attention posture. Castlethorn leaned Lantern against the wall. He stood pleasantly at attention too, his hands folded in front of him. They were actually clean, even if his nails were a mess. The room was very quiet.

Miss Coffenayle could see delight in the children's eyes. She was wary, remembering what Malovent said about too many joyful feelings. She would have to do something about this. Something that would make her master proud. But later. For now, there was all of this wonderful food; was that potato salad? Yes, it was! A personal favorite of hers. She would stay for lunch *and* dinner!

Emily spoke, "I just wanted to bring to your attention, class, that this party is happening because of Principal Coffenayle! Give her a round of applause!" Emily joined in the clapping too. So did Doesbad and Castlethorn. "And to her friend who did so much for us today... Mr.?"

"He was just leaving," stated the principal.

The lawyer looked at her with astonishment. She moved close to him and whispered, "Don't worry, Simon. Go to my office lobby and talk to the secretary. I will have food brought to both of you. I don't want her to be alone for the party." The secretary was an excuse. She wanted to share the spotlight with *nobody!* With that car and the food, the man was becoming a folk hero. He would not be around to steal any more of her glory, that was for sure. Yes, it was time for him to go and keep company with a secretary who much preferred to be alone. What fun that would be! Doesbad could hardly wait. When the humiliated lawyer quickly left, his silk top hat in his hand, she returned her gaze to the classroom. "Now where we?" she asked.

The class began chanting, "Miss Coffenayle! Miss Coffenayle! Huzzah!" as they stood by their chairs.

Ah, the glory of it all! The students chanting her name over and over again. She basked there, chin aloft, looking down her nose upon the unwashed masses, the uninitiated, the well-educated but unknowing students. These kids had no idea what was about to hit them. Let them have their cupcakes, soda, and sandwiches! Let them praise their principal! They may be shouting praises and song now, but she would put an end to that. For now, though, it was time for food and fun. Miss Emily let the chanting go on for a couple of minutes and then asked Miss Coffenayle how they should proceed.

"Ah, yes, how to proceed. Well, I think that the present staff and faculty should fix a plate first for the office staff and for themselves.

Then the students will be sent row by row to take a plate, fill it with what they like, grab a spoon, a fork, and then return to their desks. Everyone may begin to eat as soon as they have their plates. That way, the front row might be ready for seconds as the back row starts eating. There is plenty of food, so no one will be shortchanged. That arrangement would keep the students busy eating or getting food at all times. The model of efficiency, this will be. If that is okay with Miss Emily, of course!"

"Certainly! Class, you may begin after Jimmy and I take food down the hall to Mr. Doesbad and Miss Coffenayle's secretary. Principal Coffenayle, would you like to serve yourself first?" Emily did not have to ask twice. The principal stacked her plate high with a sandwich and lots of potato salad. She grabbed a cola to drink. Emily motioned to Mr. Castlethorn who gave a quizzical "Who? Me?" kind of look and then came over, not terribly sure of himself. He stacked his plate, grabbed a cola as well, and then set his food on a sill beneath a bricked-up window. He looked at Miss Emily, and she motioned for him to eat.

Coffenayle had already dug in; she was shoveling it in like it was her last meal and was a bit noisy. Emily was surprised and even mildly disappointed. No wonder her boss was on the heavy side. Maybe Miss Coffenayle did not have all that much class after all.

Emily sent Jimmy down the hall to get a food order from Doesbad and the secretary. Miss Emily announced to the class how she wanted them to proceed in the food line. Coffenayle was into her second helping, then she noticed that the class was not eating and suddenly realized it was likely because of her. She did not care, really, but why stir up resentment? She piled onto her plate to fill the vacancies with her second helping, grabbed a couple more colas, and left the room unceremoniously. Apparently, thought Emily, she was still hungry. Disgusting.

Jimmy returned and reported to Emily the food that Doesbad and Patience wanted. Emily looked at him quizzically.

"Patience?" she asked.

"Oh, yeah. That's the secretary's name. I learned it from her just now."

"That's odd," said Emily. "That is really her name?"

"Yes," Jimmy smiled, then Emily smiled and neither was sure why. Something felt nice about the name. Patience.

"All right, Jimmy," said Emily. "Are you able to handle that food order?"

"Ah kin he'ps me apprentish," said Mr. Castlethorn who was sitting on the bricked-in window's sill, daubing his lips with a shop rag. It was a clean rag, though, and Emily thought it was sort of cute. "I is finish wiff mah foods, dem's goodly viddles."

Jimmy and Castlethorn walked down the hall together with plates of food. Jimmy could not wait for his turn at that buffet table, but he was willing to help. Castlethorn looked almost...content. Jimmy noticed this but said nothing. He did not want to jinx whatever was happening.

"Patience, ye says?" asked Castlethorn.

"Yep. Patience. She was happy to see somebody come and look after her. Doesbad was there, but who knows what that fat lawyer man was doing?"

"Hoomin beans is funny critters," replied Castlethorn. "Yees never knowz whatz dey maht does next. Things is not ahlways wut they's be lookingz like—" Then a mild headache hit him. Another memory failed to surface, lost in the clouds of his mind. Why did that keep happening? He was silent for the rest of the trip, and Jimmy did not seem to mind.

They arrived at the office, and there sat Simon I. Doesbad, Esq., with a peculiar little smile on his face. Castlethorn paused at the door, cocked his head a little, and then moved to the desk with the food. Jimmy followed. They put their offerings on the desk with a cold root beer for each person. Patience was especially kind, and Doesbad seemed to be in a disposition unlike any other Jimmy had seen. It made the boy curious, but he somehow knew that asking questions was not the right thing to do. Castlethorn seemed to be affected by the situation as well, feeling the need to retreat from the room as soon as possible. Patience and Simon thanked them both and seemed strangely silent, looking at them as though asking them to leave. They did.

Jimmy was giggling a bit as they walked back down the hall. Then he stifled himself when Castlethorn looked at him. "Ids all raht, boy, I seed 'em too," he stated simply. No more conversation was needed. They both knew what might be afoot, so they left it that. It did make them smile to themselves, though.

They arrived at the classroom door, and Jimmy saw the long line at the buffet table. Emily noticed Jimmy's expression, and since he normally sat closer to the front of the room, Emily excused herself to the front of the line and motioned for Jimmy who did not hesitate to get at the buffet table.

Jimmy could not believe the spread; the amount of food that was served was incredible! It was amazing! Jars and bowls and bottles galore! He hardly knew where to begin. He dug in and made sure that while he would be fed, he did not overdo it. He was not the only student in the classroom after all. The students were all happy and excited about this whole thing. Was it really just yesterday that Miss Whipshot fell through the floor? So much had changed so quickly. They talked of their studies and of how it would be wonderful when they all graduated and got to see the world. They wondered what the world really was like. Some of the students had seen Doesbad's car and could only guess at what waited for them "over the fence" as they started to call it.

Miss Emily finally got something to eat for herself after Mr. Castlethorn indicated to her by a gesture with his hand that she needed a turn at the buffet table too. She fixed herself a plate and selected a bottle of orange pop. She sat on a chair, her food neatly on her lap, caring for her new clothes that Miss Coffenayle had just provided. It would not be fitting to make stains on them the first day she worn them. Emily mused over things silently as she ate.

Jimmy chatted with his fellow students and told the tale about becoming Castlethorn's apprentice. Tommy Littleton was also involved in the conversation and expressed over and over his relief at Whipshot not being able to hurt him anymore. At least not for a while. Margaret was also talking to her fellow students. She smiled and laughed a couple of times. It seemed that the herd had accepted her back. Emily was glad to see that. She believed that poor Margaret deserved a second chance.

The class was done eating. Emily was finished as well and stood up. She spoke quietly with Mr. Castlethorn for a moment. He called Jimmy over quickly, and the two of them left the room. The new teacher took her place at the front of the classroom and got their attention. "Everyone, please. I need your attention." They immediately stopped talking and put all eyes to the front and listened closely. "Jimmy and Mr. Castlethorn have left to go to the cafeteria to get some tubs of soap and water. We are going to wash our own dishes and have them ready for dinner. I know that you have had a big lunch, but dinner will follow at the normal time in just a couple of hours. I need some volunteers to come forward and cover the food. Please put the cool things back on ice."

A few students stepped up and helped with the food, including Tommy and Margaret. They were busy getting things put together. The rest of the students were quietly chatting. When Jimmy and Castlethorn returned, they seemed a bit shaken. After all, it *was* Miss Ladlepot's kitchen. They both stated that they were fine, that the ladles *mostly* missed them. They would explain later. They did have the tubs of soap and water, though, on pushcarts. Emily noticed a trail of drips and immediately dispatched two students armed with some cafeteria towels from the buffet to wipe up the drops all the way down the hall. No need for an accident.

The remaining students pitched in, and each washed their own plates and then stacked them back onto the table, just as way that they were before. They hung the towels to dry, and Miss Emily had them return to their own seats. She asked them that they now be quiet and get ready to resume class. This was a party, yes, but schooling must continue. They would finish cleaning up from lunch and then go outside for some fresh air. She wanted to get them outside for a bit so no one would get sleepy. It would be a good time to tour the grounds, like Miss Whipshot used to do with them on *very* rare occasions. After all, she was not built for walking very much.

16

Meeting Nurse "Nightshade"

Meanwhile, back at the infirmary, Nurse Shadyknight was still tending to Miss Whipshot. The treatment was going well; in fact, almost *too* well. It was very odd, really, because the nurse felt that she was almost *receiving thoughts* about what to do for Whipshot. For instance, she would consider a certain position into which to move the patient, but then a clear thought would occur to her. She thought someone was talking to her at one point. Things like "Roll that foot to the right and be careful of her knee." Or "Tuck pillows under her hip and back." Such things as that. Each time Shadyknight would follow a prompting, it seemed that Whipshot would breathe easier or was more comfortable in some other way. She was even being prompted on how to manage IVs with "Increase the saline." Or "Watch for infiltration on that arm." None of these actions she was moved to perform could actually do harm, and there were improvements in Whipshot's condition at the same time. This was the first time she had ever experienced such a thing in her career as a nurse.

Miss Coffenayle never even took the trouble to check in, and this bothered the nurse. She knew the principal depended on Whipshot for a lot of things. She even referred to the teacher as her friend several times. Now, however, when her "friend" needed support, the principal was nowhere to be found. There was something that Nurse Shadyknight was trying to remember about Miss Coffenayle, something important, but every time she tried to recall it, she could not.

Her head fogged over, and sometimes she would end up with a headache. Very strange, that.

All of the nurse's self-monitored vitals were normal, but she would have these odd symptoms with no apparent medical causes. She could never understand this, and there was no doctor around to consult. She could take some aspirin, but that was about all she had for treatment. She did not bother because the aspirin never helped the headaches, and she did not want to use morphine. It was too easy to form the habit, and for headaches, it was simply not worth it. In any case, the headaches always went away on their own as quickly as they started. It was just a mystery, and that was the end of it.

Another odd thing: materials sometimes seemed to just appear as she needed them. One time, she went to fetch an IV bottle and found that it was already on the bedside tray. One moment, the tray was clear; the next, there was an IV bottle, complete with hose and needle, ready to go. She was busy and could not retrieve one. She certainly did not have an assistant helping her that day or any other day, for that matter. Still, there it was. Plain as day. It was the same with bandages and other supplies. Because she had just the one patient and was becoming very curious, she thought that she would put this to a test. She would intentionally leave things behind and then see if they would appear at her beck and call. They never did. Things would only appear if she would accidentally leave them behind or had a sudden urgent need. It had to be a real need that was not intentionally created for it to be filled. She was grateful for the immediate help.

There was no one else around with whom to share her "miracles." Shadyknight did not get students or faculty into the infirmary daily or even weekly. She did well with those she did treat, but people avoided just sitting and visiting with the nurse after the rumor started. Oh, that terrible story! The poor tired nurse sat down by her patient and tried to read something. She couldn't, not with that false story weighing on her mind. She sat back and just ran it through her mind yet again.

There was an innocent man in her care, and she poisoned him with no less than nightshade berries. When his widow fainted, the nurse brought her to the infirmary and poisoned her too. Shadyknight was already her faculty name, and one can see how easy it would be to change that to Nightshade. That became her new name in private circles and the not-so-private circles as well. Miss Coffenayle had forbidden anyone from calling the nurse that to her face but that did not stop the backstage rumors.

She was an excellent nurse! Why would anyone even think to persecute her that way? She could not recall any such event even close to that happening in her career. Her efforts at remembering much, though, were still strangely impeded. What if she actually *did* do something like that? She did not think herself capable of murder, of course not! Even so, what if there was some kind of tragic accident or a medication error? What if she had taken care of someone who just simply was going to die anyway, but she promised to keep them alive? Something like that would actually be enough to trigger the stories. It might make people believe that she was not capable of proper nursing. They might even start to believe she was capable of murder. She thought and thought and thought over it more...and then she dozed off to sleep.

She found herself working her way through a crowd of people. Everything was tilted at odd angles, like she was having a hard time focusing on the dream. She found a man on the floor in what seemed to be part of the school. She looked at a mirror someone held up to her, and she noticed to her astonishment that she was lean and trim again. She looked much younger and less haggard in appearance. She was standing straight, no crooked spine, no slight limp. Then she noticed that there was this green fog everywhere. She turned back to the man on the floor. Helpless people stood around, wringing their hands. No one seemed to know what to do. She had them lift the patient and suddenly found herself tending to him at the clinic. She could not make out his face, but she knew all of this was very familiar. She knelt and touched his wrist to take a pulse.

The scene changed again very suddenly. She was now on one knee with her hand on a casket. She was in black mourning clothes, at a graveyard in the same green fog. The grave was freshly dug. The people surrounded the casket. Some were crying; others were scowling at her. Nurse Shadyknight stood and faced the crowd. One man suggested that they fire her for being such a poor nurse. Somebody else said that they should kill her like she killed him. She tried to tell them that she did not kill anybody. She couldn't! She was a nurse! A nurse! Miss Coffenayle came out of the fog and defended Nurse Shadyknight. It was not her fault! This was just one of those unfortunate things in life. Shadyknight fell to the ground by the casket and tried to open the lid and see who died, to see if there was some mistake! She was a nurse, a nurse, a nurse!

But no one would listen. They became angrier, slowly approaching her, forcing her back. She was standing at the edge of the grave! Then they pushed her into it, and she felt shoveled dirt fall on her face. She was a good nurse! A good person! But they would not listen. Then the pallbearers appeared, all of them wearing black hooded cloaks that were girthed about with belts of small human skulls. They lowered the casket on top of her, all of them chuckling, some of the mourners weeping; others were calling for her death. She was screaming, begging for her life! "No! No! Please! I'm not a murderer! I'm a nurse! A nurse! *A nurse!*"

*****

She woke up. Oh, what a horrific dream! Oh, how terrible that was! She looked over at Miss Whipshot who was resting peacefully. Her expression was different now somehow. Something about the light in the room maybe. The unconscious woman seemed to be more serene, more at peace. Odd thing that. Maybe the rest was doing her good. The nurse went to the sink and washed her hands. She put some water to her face and looked in the mirror. What? How could this be? The lines in her own face were not as deep as they used to be. She really started to wonder now at all these odd events. It was a good thing that she was alone. She would have a hard time explaining this to another nurse or an assistant. She could not even explain it to herself. She did not even know what she was trying to explain. All she knew was she appeared...younger...and her body did not hurt as much.

There was a knock at the door. Shadyknight did not answer it at first because she thought she was imagining things again. The knock happened again but was more persistent. She answered the door and found Miss Emily standing there with her class. One of the students was holding a bouquet of freshly cut wildflowers. "We came to check on Miss Whipshot," said Emily with a smile. The nurse could not believe her eyes! Visitors? Really? She invited them in immediately. "Are you okay in here?" asked Miss Emily. "We thought we heard shouting. Something about a nurse."

"Oh," replied Shadyknight. "Not to worry. Don't give it a single thought. We are fine. Miss Whipshot is right this way. Now remember, everyone, this is a place for the sick to recover. We must be very quiet. And please, please, please do not touch anything."

"Students, we all heard the school nurse. Be quiet, and don't touch anything you find in here," said Miss Emily.

The class followed the nurse, and Miss Emily stepped aside to let the students pass her. She would head up the rear of the line and supervise the students from behind. With her supervision, she knew for certain they would behave. They followed the nurse, and she found them a pitcher of water for the flowers. They carried the pitcher of flowers to the infirmary section where the patient beds were. The students were all impressed with how clean and white all of the linens were, nipped and tucked with hospital corners on all the beds. Everything was neat, orderly, clean, white, and smelling fresh.

Miss Emily was also impressed. This was not at all what she expected. The rumors about "Nurse Nightshade" abounded. She killed a poor defenseless vagrant by doing experiments on him. She let a teacher die after eating bad food in the cafeteria. She used to torture animals to process in the cafeteria kitchen, and that's why the grounds were so quiet—all the wildlife had run off in fear. The students told each other all kinds of stories. Naturally, each story was believed no matter how outlandish. And who knew what rumors Miss Emily might hear from teachers?

They finally arrived at Whipshot's bedside. She was sleeping and no longer experienced all that horrid snoring. She did not seem to look as mean when she was asleep. That is probably true for every person who is found asleep. We all seem harmless when we are napping. This case seemed unusual, though. Emily and the students noticed differences in the appearance of their former teacher. Were some of her moles *missing?* No one said it, but everyone seemed to think it. She looked nice too, all things considered, peacefully asleep with her hair actually *combed.*

Since the pitcher of flowers was at the side of her bed, Emily thought it might be time to leave. Shadyknight was not in such a hurry to dismiss them. "Well, before you go, does anyone have questions for me?" asked the lonesome nurse. The students did not seem to know what to ask, but one spoke up. It was Tommy Littleton. He asked about how long it might be before Miss Whipshot came back to class. The students all looked at each other. A great question! They all then looked to the nurse for answer.

"Well," the nurse began, "it is hard to say. These situations vary from patient to patient." Finally! Some company! An audience! "Miss Whipshot had quite a shock to her system. She was injured, as you know, and when a person is knocked unconscious, it may take some time for their body to heal."

And to lose some moles, thought Emily.

And to lose some wrinkles and bitter facial expressions, thought the nurse.

Neither of them expressed these thoughts to the students. "Anyone else?"

"Did you actually *kill* somebody like the whole school says you did?" somebody—they never really found out who—asked.

This took the nurse aback. She stood there, slack-jawed and stunned. Her eyes were as big as saucers, and she could not believe the audacity of such a question! She did not know what to say. However, as good manners would seem to dictate, Miss Emily came to the rescue.

"Class! Everyone, it seems to me that we have worn out our welcome," said a shocked Miss Emily.

"Well...did you?" asked another student.

Shadyknight had been given a moment to regain her composure by Miss Emily's timely intervention. The second time she was asked, the question seemed to be more a challenge. Well, challenge accepted! She stood up tall and held her shoulders back. Her back crackled with the effort; her spinal joints felt full of sand. "No, I most certainly did *not!*" She may not have remembered everything, but one thing she did know: she did not attend nursing school to become a monster. Her posture was strong, shoulders back, chin out, just daring anyone, anyone at all, to try and prove that she did this horrible thing. "Those things you hear about me are nothing more than damaging rumors! That is all! Rumors! I don't care who says it. I don't care who thinks they know it. It simply is not true! I never killed anyone! Do you *understand me?*"

The class fell silent.

Miss Emily saw the courage of that nurse's conviction etched into her face. If she ever had doubts before about the nurse's ability or integrity, they were all settled here and now. Emily knew that the nurse knew that she never killed anybody. Something told Emily that what was being spoken here and now was the absolute truth. She no longer believed that there even was a shred of truth to the stories. Emily now knew for herself that Nurse Shadyknight was an excellent nurse. How she knew it, well, that was a bit of a puzzle. The puzzlement did not take away from her knowing, though. She just simply *knew.*

The students all became timid, their eyes cast to the ground. Emily looked Shadyknight, the "infamous Nurse Nightshade," square in the eye. She said, "I believe you."

The nurse stared at her for a few seconds, searching her eyes. Somehow, she knew that Emily now knew the truth, and it formed an instant bond between the two of them. Two women, both with responsibilities and duties, understood each other and formed an unspoken—indeed, an *unspeakable* trust between them. Theirs was a bond of two people suddenly unified by some unseen, unknown force. It seemed impossible, but their bond was nonetheless there, nonetheless very real. Shadyknight's eyes welled up, and all she could do was softly say, "Thank you."

Miss Emily took the lead in the class again. She was about to show everyone there that learning was not just a tool for the classroom. Lessons, perhaps the most important ones, were learned outside too. They were learned among the people. Certainly, now, the students would understand that education was not meant to be kept caged up in the halls of academia, inside the ivory towers of fools attempting to appear wise. Education was supposed to be used to teach knowledge, logic, and moral principles that can carried into the world for the best benefit of all the world.

Miss Emily spoke her thoughts, "Class, we have just learned something very important today. We have learned that what we may accept as ultimate truths inside the classroom and school may not be the actual truth as applied in the real world. We see here today that *what is commonly spoken may not always be ultimately true.*" Emily stood there, shocked at her own words! Where on earth did she get that from? She never read that anywhere, to her recollection, and yet she spoke it like it was her own knowledge. She felt very calm, though, assured that what she just said was actually the very truth that was needed by her students.

They needed to hear that truth. They needed to see what effect words, "mere words" can truly have. For words convey ideas and explain one's motivations. Words misspoken start wars. Words properly spoken convey messages of peace and understanding. There was a type of empathy that was formed here, a kind of understanding that every one of the students now had but was unspoken. All of them, even Margaret, the least empathetic one in the class, understood what had happened to this poor nurse, this poor woman. All because of words!

Nurse Shadyknight was now sobbing, trying to be "brave," but failing miserably. This was just too much. Too many years. No one to talk to. No one was willing to listen. Certainly, some staffers would come by once in a while for aspirin or minor first aid. Students would appear with an injury she would fix or some ailment or another which she was helpless to treat for a lack of supplies; but they were all there to *get* something. Even when someone had to stay there for a couple of days, it was all about getting something from her. They were not giving to her or to anyone else. This classroom of children was there to *give* flowers to a cruel tyrant. That very act was of tremendous importance to the nurse.

As it turned out, they gave something else very important. They *gave an ear* to a hurting, mistreated, and misunderstood servant to the people. She had, for too many years, been afflicted by the vicious monsters of gossip, rumor, and innuendo. These three, this deadly trio, had destroyed more lives than all the aforementioned wars put together. Now the students understood why.

Miss Emily suddenly found herself being tutored, even as though Mr. Mentor was standing right in front her. In her heart and mind, she heard and felt that he was saying, "Everyone is fighting their own private battles. Even the ones that work so hard to appear so lovely and perfect on the outside. No one is exempt from the terrors of humanhood. Not the poor, not the rich, not the neglected. All have their own wars to fight. Those wars are too often lost because of the words and opinions of the others around them. Some appear so perfect because they are putting a screen around themselves formed by pride and vanity. In that pride and vanity, they are constantly looking for victims, for people to step on. By doing this, they think they are elevating themselves.

"Mere possessions—clothing, jewelry, cars, etc.—mean nothing in the war for souls. Remember that while gold is highly valued on the earth, it is used to pave the streets in heaven. The war is being won and lost right here in our everyday lives. *Some who appear to be down and out are among the most valiant. Others who appear to be on top are really the lowest and have the most hurt inside.* On the same token, some on top truly earned their distinction and are among the finest of souls, and they are people who seek to share their successes. Some who are down have indeed earned their poverty and misery by selfish living. Be cautious, therefore, of whom you leave lying in the wallow and whom you venerate as a great person. *Look to the heart, not to the appearance.* End of lesson."

"Miss Emily?" asked Jimmy "Are you okay?"

Emily jumped. She was startled. The class was staring at her, and the school nurse was approaching her. "You…were sort of gone there for a minute. You were staring into space or something," continued Jimmy.

Emily shook it off. That was a real teaching moment by Mr. Mentor, but she could not tell the class that. Not now, maybe not ever.

Shadyknight looked at her, concerned, now with her hand on the teacher's shoulder.

"I was just thinking about something, everyone. I am just fine," replied Miss Emily.

The school nurse looked at her eyes, and her pupils were fine. Her eyes were moving normally. Nothing seemed to be amiss. Then she looked *into* Emily's eyes as though she understood something significant was happening. She saw in those eyes of that girl, that young woman, something that reminded her of...of...oh no. Green haze again...no use fighting it. No need to get a headache. The important thing was that there was some message transferred from heart to heart in that one moment. For now, that was enough.

17

Touring the Grounds

"Class," Miss Emily said, "I think it is time to continue our tour of the grounds. Nurse Shadyknight has a patient to attend to." She knew it was a lame excuse, but it was the best one she had at the moment. It was time to go. Whatever they had been *sent(?)* to do had been accomplished. Why she felt they had been sent, she did not know. Things were getting stranger and stranger but feeling better and better. Why was this? The class and their teacher bade a good day to the nurse, and she resumed her duties.

The class walked on, continuing their exploration of the school grounds. Near the infirmary was a field overgrown with weeds. It was rectangle-shaped and had two structures at each end shaped of wood and metal, like the letter H. What appeared to be tiers of big benches, places for people to sit—Emily was not sure what to call them—surrounded the field. Everything was in terrible disrepair from neglect. The class stood and stared at something that seemed to be very significant at one time.

"What is this?" asked one student.

Emily did not know and said so. They could almost see in their mind's eye that people crowded here at one time. This seemed to be a place of great importance. It was felt more than seen. As a class, they all walked onto the field, ignoring the weeds and avoiding the stinging nettles. Two H-shaped structures made of wood and metal piping at either end were a bit of a mystery. The students in Emily's classroom, including herself, had never been exposed to much outdoor recreation, other than then occasional walks around the grounds. Emily determined silently that she would find out what this was.

She would talk to Jimmy later and have him speak to Mr. Castlethorn. If *anybody* knew, it would be him. She felt impressed, deeply, that Castlethorn knew much more than he was willing or perhaps able to admit. She was willing to bet the school nurse had a lot more to share too. But Shadyknight, never again "Nightshade" in Emily's mind, already had too much of a day.

After standing there for a few minutes, taking it all in, Emily decided it was time to get back to the classroom. She was getting hungry, and the students probably were too. They had been gone for a while.

That was when someone noticed a dog on the field. It was just running around, chasing its tail. It seemed to hover around the H-shaped post. It would randomly bark and pant. But when it looked at the students, it would wag its tail. One of the braver boys started to approach it, but not too closely. Emily almost said something but stopped herself. She wanted to see how this would play out. The student tried to call the dog over to him but got no results. He threw a stick to play fetch. Nothing happened. The dog just stood there, his tongue hanging out as he wagged his tail. He leaped into the air and just bounced around, randomly and aimlessly. The dog seemed overjoyed about nothing. He would play and pause, bark playfully at the kids, run in a circle like he was glad to see them, but would not approach the kids. He'd just stand there stupidly and wait, but when the boy would walk toward him, the dog would run away.

"Aw," said the boy, "he's just stupid. Stupid dog won't let us pet him, won't fetch—he's crazy. I'm surprised he has the good sense to feed himself." The whole class seemed to be a little let down, but they did not say much. Everyone just gave up on the stupid dog.

Emily announced that it was time to get back. As they walked away, some of students were still looking over their shoulders at that mysterious field of great significance with its stupid dog. They followed their teacher back toward the school. They passed several buildings that they had seen in times past. Lately, the buildings seemed different to Emily somehow. She was paying more attention to things. She noticed the weeds, the nesting places of rodents inside of the buildings, the decay. Roofs were caved in due to age and disrepair. The structures they covered were seemed to be usable at one time. It was as though everything here was just...abandoned. Suddenly. She thought this because there was a garage with a car in it with the hood still up and tools on the fender.

She kept these new observations to herself. The class was, of course, oblivious. She saw other broken-down motor cars and machines. She saw tractors and tools of a manner foreign to her. Each building seemed to have its own purpose of some kind. Things were different for her now that she was not focused purely on her own survival. This might be an important principle. *Maybe keeping people distracted and focused on their own selves prevents them from seeing beauty.* Just another thought to keep to herself. Mr. Mentor seemed to remain silent on all of this, but Miss Emily instinctively knew that everything they saw today was of great importance.

They walked quietly back toward the main building of the school. The whole class was deep in thought. They approached the building, and Emily stopped suddenly. Something seemed to be wrong. She was being watched...she felt it! Then, instead of having a calm and gentle prompting, there was Mentor's voice in her head that said, "Yell at them! Now! Tell them they all look terrible! They cannot go into Miss Coffenayle's school looking like that!"

"All of you stop! What is wrong with you? Didn't you see me stop? You in the front, you almost ran into me! Are you daft in the head? Are you an idiot or something? *Answer me, now you slack-jawed toad!*"

The kids all froze. That could not be Miss Emily, the polite and kind teacher. She sounded and acted like Miss Whipshot!

They could not believe their ears! What was wrong? What just happened? "All of you acting like idiots! After your quality education at this fine establishment, you are all acting like fools! A bunch of toads! Morons! Miscreants! Shame on all of you! Look at those pants and those skirts! Ladies and gentlemen, this is unacceptable! You insufferable slobs!" She picked up a stick she found on the ground, and with her back to the school, she swung it.

No one could believe it! They backed away from her, eyes wide in fear and disbelief. Kind, sensitive Miss Emily! Their fellow student who once was among the abused masses had now given in and become something terrible, the same kind of crazy person Whipshot was!

They all backed away from her and immediately started cleaning off their pants, skirts, and shoes. Emily stood there, watching them closely and berating them. She leaned on her stick like it was a walking cane. "Come on, come on, you moronic little fools! At least *act* like you've got brains in your heads!"

One of the students started to protest, and she raised the stick over her head and brought it down on his shoulder but pulled the blow. It did contact his shoulder but for just a tap with no pain or damage. He hardly felt it.

Emily whispered, "Act like it hurt! Now!"

The student instantly grabbed his shoulder and dropped to his knees. He cried out in pain. The other students recoiled, and Emily swung the stick toward their heads as she told them quietly to duck. Students bent at the waist, and some fell to their knees, hollering in fear. They caught onto the game now and played their part well. Miss Emily wanted to appear to be bad but was not going to hurt them. They somehow understood this immediately and knew to not *be* afraid but to *act* afraid.

From the behind the window curtain in her office, wearing her black dress with fragrant smoke filling the room, Coffenayle was pleased. She turned back to Malovent. "It seems, Friend Malovent, that we have chosen well."

With his dark energy swirling about him, his cowled arms folded across his chest and his face covered by the hood of his cloak, the mysterious Malovent rocked the room with evil laughter. He was pleased, and Coffenayle was relieved. She did not want to incur her master's wrath again.

Out in the secretary's office, the reception area for the principal's office, Patience sat quietly over her empty plate. Simon I.

Doesbad, Esq. heard the laughter from the office and immediately jumped out of the chair. He did not even know anyone was in there inside the principal's office. He did not see the principal move past him to get in there. This was the only entryway that he knew of. Was that incense he was smelling? Odd…but…*familiar?*

"Don't worry about the things you are sensing here, Simon," Patience said kindly. "Miss Coffenayle has…um…her *ways.* You'd probably be better off not knowing."

"Yes," said the lawyer simply in agreement. He smiled at Patience and gladly sat back down. They resumed their discussion.

In the midst of the beratement of the students, Coffenayle walked up to Emily who pretended she did not see the principal's shadow come up behind her. The students were all sitting on the ground with their teacher occasionally pacing as she continually told them how much they had to be ashamed of. Their clothes were a mess, their lives a mess, they were so very lucky to have this school here to take care of them, etc., etc., and so forth. She used Miss Whipshot's words which had rung in her own ears many, many times over. It was easy to use her memorized insults. She threw an occasional wink at the students as she would call them out individually for having freckles that looked like smallpox or a belly that looked like a sack of pus hanging off a scarecrow. She went off script for that one, actually, and had to stifle her own chuckle.

"Miss Emily," Miss Coffenayle said as she touched her on the shoulder, and Emily pretended to be startled and whirled around with the stick at ready. She immediately lowered it when she was facing the principal.

"Oh, Miss Coffenayle! I am sorry for the stick! I did not see you," she fibbed.

"No, no, no, not to worry," she smiled. "I am glad to see you have things well in hand. How are the students doing?"

"We just took a tour of the place and took some wildflowers to Miss Whipshot. The nurse is watching over her."

"Ah, yes, the nurse. Do you know why they call her Nightshade? She killed a man, once, but we could not prove it. Without proof that his death was intentional, I could not fire her. He died under her care, all the same, supposedly of natural causes. So I am glad someone is checking up on her. Excellent initiative," said the lead administrator. "Is your class about ready for dinner? We don't want food to start spoiling. Everything seems to be cool enough, but we don't want to take any chances of it going bad," she said as though it made a difference. Her potato salad was waiting.

"Well, yes," said Emily studying the students with a penetrating gaze, "they have learned enough for now." *Boy, had they ever*, she thought to herself. She told the students to get back to their class and finish stuffing themselves before she knocked the stuffing *out* of them. Coffenayle loved that one and smirked but said nothing. As the class walked back toward their party, Emily singled out Margaret. "Come here, you little snake!" she shouted at her and grabbed her by the arm. "Miss Coffenayle, would you mind escorting these miscreants? I have to have a *conversation* with little missy here."

Coffenayle lifted her chin in pride. "Certainly, Miss Emily! Things are well in hand. Class, follow me!"

Margaret looked terrified as though she knew what was coming. All of her misdeeds were now being accounted for, and payment was due. She had tears in her eyes. She was terrified and trembling. "Margaret," started Miss Emily, "I need you keep looking scared, but stop being afraid, okay?"

The girl looked at Emily like she was out of her mind.

"Listen, and please listen good. I don't think you really like being the class snitch, do you?"

Margaret shook her head.

"Good. Keep shaking your head and act like you are pulling away, trying to fall on the ground. Excellent. I don't want anyone to know about this conversation. Not yet anyway. *Do you understand?*" Miss Emily shouted for the benefit of anyone watching. "Now this is very important. I have a feeling, a very odd feeling, that things are starting to change here at the school. I cannot tell you why. Now, you know me as a classmate, right? You know that I can be trusted, right? Good. Now I need you to resume your role as the snitch. I will give you your cushy chair back, and I need you to play the part. No one is actually going to be punished, but we cannot allow the principal to find that out. We have to all act our part. *You little toad! You ugly red-headed fool!*

"I know that you were doing things for Miss Whipshot because you feared her, and it was easier to obey her than it was to get punished, right? Yes, I understand. I don't hold any of that against you, but I need your help. Or I can really start to abuse the class just like Miss Whipshot did. Would you like that?"

Margaret shook her head.

"Okay, good. Keep shaking your head. Now we are going to work together and make things look good. Bear in mind that if you rat me out, I will deny this whole conversation ever happened, and I will be forced to make things just as bad under me as they were under her. If you understand, try to pull away from me and tell me to stop it. Good. Now I am going to yell at you. I don't mean any of it. And *that, you worthless little twit! That is what I think of you! Now you work for me the same as Whipshot! You understand me?*" she yelled, and she gave Margaret a good hard shove. That shove, regrettably, had to be real for the benefit of the audience. Margaret understood and worked hard to not smile as she picked herself up off the ground. After all, she had much to smile about. All was forgiven, and she was part of the master plan.

*****

The dark and evil Malovent, alone now, and still peering through the curtain, floating in the air laughed again, but not as loud. He was quite pleased with what he was seeing. Donatienne Coffenayle had chosen well. He did not know for sure at first; the future cannot always be read accurately, not even by one of his stature. For now, his doubts were laid to rest. He floated back from the curtain. He returned to the design on the floor. As he appeared, so should he return. This was the way of things. He folded his arms and dropped his key out of his sleeve which dangled by a chain. In truth, there was no particular reason for the key; he just liked to give humans something to be mystified over. It increased their awe and aroused their curiosity. Such things served to encourage a study of his mysteries. He lowered his hooded head. He slowly melted into the floor as a breeze blew out the candles. Waste not, want not.

The conversation in the secretary's office continued. Doesbad was chuckling loudly, having an immensely good time. Patience did not seem to mind so much either. They spoke of all sorts of things. Their lives, themselves, their hopes for the future and the future of the school.

*****

Miss Coffenayle entered the classroom just ahead of Emily and Margaret. She saw that the students were sitting at their desks, eyes forward, hands folded neatly, all feet to the front, and nobody moved a muscle toward that buffet table. This pleased her. She had been tossing around the idea of canceling the rest of the party for fear that she might help create too many positive feelings. She knew how her master felt about positivity. Even so, both he and she knew that they could not keep the students negative all the time. It would burn them out and make them completely useless.

Miss Coffenayle had been lectured by Malovent on the Dark Ages and how evil had become so strong in the land that even learning ceased. Without learning, there was no progress, and society was destroyed from the inside out. This led to famine and pestilence, which in turn led the dictators being overturned by sheer force. So, yes, there were some positive moments that were given to the students but just enough to keep them hopeful. Miss Emily was playing into their plans…and into the hands of evil very nicely. She was abusing Margaret right in front of the other students, at the same time demanding that she be the snitch. Now the brats have no idea what she might do next. Neither did Miss Coffenayle, for that matter. What an interesting game!

18

A Second Party! Yay!

Emily and Margaret returned to the room. Emily gave her a slight nudge from the back, but Margaret played it up perfectly. She nearly stumbled into the classroom. The class dutifully stared straight ahead as though they were each afraid they might be next. Emily went over to the wall where the cushy desk chair was sitting and restored Margaret to her seat. The class snitch was now restored to her former glory. The class did not move. Miss Coffenayle was both surprised and thrilled to see that Emily had adopted another practice of Whipshot. After all, the class snitch was Miss Coffenayle's idea to turn the students on one another. She needed them to not form alliances.

Taking one from their ranks and turning them into a ratfink was one of the most effective ways to do it. It worked in most of the classrooms, and in Whipshot's class, the idea excelled because she added the comfortable chair and overtly special treatment. This made everyone hate the collaborator and caused them to also mistrust one another. A very effective program indeed, and Whipshot perfected it. Miss Emily was following suit. This experiment with Miss Emily was going far better than Miss Coffenayle had anticipated.

After all, Emily restored this policy without so much as a word from Miss Coffenayle. This pleased the principal to no end. She loved it when people participated in her little games without her coaching them. It showed how much control she had over them. The fools often participated in their own destruction with the hopes of just getting a couple of favors in return. Oh, how easy they made it for people like her to win!

"Class," started Miss Emily, "we have had a busy couple of days. Yesterday was especially harrowing. Understand that this party is at the good graces of Miss Coffenayle and myself." She held up a plate of cupcakes and said, "This is how easily I could end your party." She stared right at the class and very intentionally dropped the whole plate into the trash can. "Do all of you understand?"

"Yes, Miss Emily," the class responded in a unified monotone.

"Good. You may proceed row by row to the buffet table." The plate of cupcakes was the least favorite of the students. They were made of carrot cake, and it was not baked very well at that. She had taken a quick poll while they were outside. No harm done! But Miss Coffenayle loved it! Emily, in her own way, had become quite cunning but for good purposes. She did it to the benefit of those she was trying to protect. This was certainly not what Miss Coffenayle thought!

"Miss Emily, my dear," Miss Coffenayle said as she approached the new teacher. With her back to the class, she took Emily by the shoulders and quietly said, "You made me so proud today! Keep this up, and I will make you a permanent teacher, and you will never have to return to that *awful* dormitory again." She winked, turned to face the class, and announced to the class that she would not be joining them for dinner; she had other duties to attend to. The class bade farewell in unison. No one was that disappointed, not at all. The principal walked out the door in her most self-important march. There were things to do.

The class proceeded to the buffet in order, as they had been told. There was plenty for everybody still. There was no need to rush. They were all very content at the new class arrangement under Miss Emily. Even to see the snitch restored was not upsetting. They all understood the score now. Miss Emily was working the system and keeping the class onboard with her plans. They were all a bit worried at first, but her explanation set them all at ease.

*****

Castlethorn was busy in his office. He had to admit, it felt pretty good to have cleaned up some. That was a good party, it was. He remembered two things all at once: there was a second half to the party, and he still had a project in that room. He was normally making excuses to avoid people; now he was making excuses to join them. The food was good, but that was not the only reason. He wanted to take more readings with Lantern. There were strange readings. *Somethun's going on.* But he could not put his finger on what. He wrote in his greasy journal book his findings from today. At least one person in that room was not "hoomin." He knew it. Sometimes he could see the "nonhoomins"; they were somewhat "glowish" and white but transparent. Mostly, he could not see dem. That was where Lantern came in handy. *Cuz when deys were inbisible, Lantern could he'p wiff dat.*

There was a knock at his door. He was suddenly reminded of some poem he once read that talked about rapping, tapping on the door, only that and not more, or something like that. Too much fog, too many years. Why could he not remember? So who could that be? He hoped it was not crazy Miss Ladlepot. He ducked enough ladles to last him the rest of his life. He approached the door after checking the machines that kept the "polterghost" in check. If it was a student, he did not want them to be attacked. The machines were working just fine across the aisle from one another. He could not understand why that "nonhoomin" was so crazy whenever someone got too close to that back room. He dropped his shop cloth on his way to the door, right on top of a very important piece of paper in a frame, one he could not remember. He opened the door slowly, carefully.

"Mr. Castlethorn? Are you coming to eat?" Jimmy asked while standing there, smiling.

"Jimbo! Why are you asking me thet?"

"Well, Miss Emily hoped you would come. I wanted to see you there too. We have a floor and wall job to look at, don't we?"

Castlethorn rubbed his chin and pretended to think it over. Jimmy actually got a little anxious. Then the canny old janitor said, "Sure, whys not? We gots da wahl an' floor to fix, affer all, now, ain't we?"

Castlethorn stepped out of the door, locked it, and Jimmy took the lead. They went to the class to eat. There was still plenty. The truth was Castlethorn felt better about things than he had in years. Wild horses could not have stopped from going to the party as long as he had permission.

*****

Miss Coffenayle walked into the secretary's office. Doesbad and Patience heard her coming, so he got out of the chair and was getting the lunch dishes together when she arrived. Everything looked perfectly professional and innocent. They did not want to get caught in their "conversing," which was actually flirting. The principal would not like it. Patience wanted Doesbad to come back, and he wanted to be back. So they played the best parts they could and seemed to be successful. Miss Coffenayle did not suspect a thing.

"Well!" she shouted. "Things are moving forward and according to plan. We have much to celebrate!"

"How so?" asked Doesbad as he stacked plates and threw away bottles.

"Miss Emily, whom you doubted"—he let that remark slide—"has proven to be the perfect replacement for Miss Whipshot. Between that and the court case you were able to argue before Judge Parschall, we are cooking right along!"

"Excellent!" shouted the lawyer as he clapped his hands together with his best lawyer smile. "So things are going according to plan! That is wonderful!" He did not know what the plan was but had to act enthralled because it was what she expected. Besides, and this he did not understand, he had feelings for Coffenayle. But, he must admit, it was not the same as what he was starting to feel for Patience. Ohhh...what was that foggy sensation in his head? He shook his head to try to clear it. He closed his eyes for just a second, and the world sounded hollow. Everything echoed in his ears. Then he was fine again and able to hear.

"Simon? Simon? Are you okay?" Miss Coffenayle asked.

"Huh? Oh…yes, I am fine. I was just lost in my own thoughts for a moment—"

"But, yes, everything is working according to plan. We are doing just fine."

"Good, good. I am quite excited. So what are the next steps?"

"For now, we need nothing more. Let's go join the students at their dinner party. You will see what I mean about that new teacher I promoted."

They walked down the hall and ran into Castlethorn and Jimmy on the way. The four of them walked as a group with Coffenayle in the lead, the firm and furious leader. The three men lagged behind just a bit with no particular desire to keep up with Little Napoleon. Jimmy was glad to be around Castlethorn now. He seemed to be somehow *different*. As for the creepy lawyer, well, he was not so creepy after all, Jimmy decided. The man brought them their party food, and he drove that really fantastic car! Maybe he had misjudged him. Miss Coffenayle had done so much to keep the students isolated from school staff while the teachers kept things so stirred up in the classroom that students did not trust anybody. They even turned upon each other, but that was changing, and he hoped things would continue in this new positive direction.

They arrived at the classroom just as everyone was digging into the food. There was quite a dent put in the buffet, but there was still enough left for them to eat generously. Miss Coffenayle greeted Miss Emily and surveyed the classroom. The students were happy to be eating, yes, but they were eyeing Miss Emily. What? Was that *the ruler? The steel ruler?* Oh, this was even better than she had thought! That young lady certainly had initiative! Emily was standing at the head of the class, arms folded, brandishing the ruler in one hand. She looked over and saw Miss Coffenayle with the others.

"Hello! Class, we have visitors." The class stood up and greeted Miss Coffenayle, Mr. Doesbad, and Mr. Castlethorn. "You may be seated, everyone. Enjoy your lunch. We will resume classes immediately after we get cleaned up," commanded Miss Emily. She then turned to the three guests and said, "Please feel free to join us, of course. The buffet is open."

"Wese thanks yee, Miss Emily," Castlethorn said with a smile.

"Yes, certainly. You do host a glorious party," stated the principal. "Mr. Doesbad," Miss Coffenayle continued, "I think you better understand now what we were discussing earlier, correct? Good. Perhaps you could take a plate for yourself and for Patience back to the office?" She was still determined to not share the glory with her lawyer. Doesbad was more than willing to have dinner with Patience again. Miss Coffenayle never even noticed his delighted countenance as he made up two plates and left the room, practically on air.

"Miss Emily, may I be excused to work with Mr. Castlethorn on the wall and floor after dinner?" asked Jimmy.

"That would be fine. I don't object to you staying here after class is dismissed."

Miss Coffenayle had already started heaping the potato salad onto her plate. Castlethorn and Jimmy hit the buffet hard as well. They took their generous plates, two each, since there was plenty, to the bricked-up window sill where they could discuss their plans for the repairs. Miss Emily sat in a chair with her plate, the ruler on the chalk tray where she could reach it. Coffenayle noticed this and was pleased, just as Emily thought she would be. It was a stroke of genius for Tommy Littleton to suggest that he retrieve the ruler from the schoolyard where he had tossed it during the "Great Uprising," the name the students gave their riot. They sometimes joked about how they should have had war paint and headdresses like the ones used during the Boston Tea Party.

Miss Coffenayle began to think of how to best manipulate the situation to her side's advantage. She had Doesbad right where she wanted him. Check. She had control of the courts with InkRobe who would contact her occasionally. An irritating little troll, but Malovent swore by his effectiveness. Check. The other teachers were slowly being warmed up to the idea of a student teaching Whipshot's class. Miss Coffenayle went out on a limb to tell them so soon, but Miss Emily's performance was spot-on. The perfect replacement. The principal was pleased with her own stroke of "genius." Double check!

Malovent was pleased as well. Coffenayle's latest decisions kept the work of evil moving forward. So what were the next steps? She could not really think of anything that actively needed to be done. So, now, she could safely sequester herself to her office and let Patience field her calls. She was behind in her studies; she did not want her power to wane. The arcane arts were difficult to manage. Violating the very laws of nature itself required constant preparation. The very thought of devoting herself entirely to her studies made her quite happy. After all, studying and dissecting the powers of *L'Gremoire* was the ultimate education.

*****

Back at the infirmary, the school nurse was watching over her only patient. Whipshot was sleeping soundly. But she looked... well, different. Nurse Shadyknight thought it was her imagination before; now she was *sure* of the changes. The lines of her patient's face were starting to soften, and she looked, um, *thinner*. She seemed to breathe easier too. This was mysterious, but not as mysterious as Shadyknight's own condition. The nurse noticed that the lines of her own face were changing in a manner similar to her patient's changes. She thought it could just be her own vanity, her own desires for youth and beauty; but no, it was beyond that. Whatever was happening, she could not understand, but she was glad for the miracle.

The wildflowers that she had in the pitcher by Whipshot's bed were a welcome addition to the otherwise bleak and sterile environment. She liked a clean place, but the bleakness made the color of the flowers welcome. They were mildly fragrant too, and that was a nice thing. Yes, it was. She only hoped that she did not drive away the students with her rousing speech earlier that day. Strange how things were suddenly changing. Things were becoming visibly better and better.

She wondered what else may be in store.

19

Miss Coffenayle's Assertion

After dinner, Castlethorn and Jimmy retreated to his office to get some supplies. They needed sanders, varnish, brushes and so forth. On the way to the office, Jimmy wondered how they would find the things they needed and what they might uncover in that terrible mess. Castlethorn opened the door to the office, freshly oiled hinges hardly squeaking at all. Jimmy was pleased at that. No loud noises, no screeching of rust on rusted metal. They started to walk down the corridor, and Castlethorn stopped. "Ye'd best wait here, Jimbo. The polterghost is quiet, and Ah wants tuh keeps it that way."

Jimmy was fine with that idea. Yes, sir, he certainly was! While the old janitor wobbled down the hallway, Jimmy's natural curiosity took over. He began nosing around at the dusty, dirty, old, and fascinating things that lived in Castlethorn's world.

He was just aimlessly poking around, looking at things here and there. Then something caught Jimmy's eye. He saw that picture frame that he found earlier. He saw it more clearly now and looked over his shoulder to make sure that his new boss was not watching him. Moving the shop rag and picking up the picture frame, he saw that it was fancy and made of very pretty wood. The glass was dusty and cracked. Jimmy carefully brushed the dust off of it and saw something amazing! This paper was addressed to a "Doctor of the Physical Science of Engineering," and it was awarded to a Cassius Lawrence Thorne. What? Did he really see that?

Jimmy had spoken to Miss Emily about this earlier when the class was distracted by the buffet. Emily asked him to quietly find out more if he could. He found out all he dared to at this point. Jimmy quickly put the frame back out of sight in its own cubby, which was easy to do on that messy workbench. He was onto something, and he knew it. But how did he know this was important? He would have to report this new information to Miss Emily.

"Come on, Jimbo," called Castlethorn. "I findses all wese needed." The old janitor was pushing a dolly that held a large wooden barrel full of various things. He beckoned Jimmy to follow him, which he did, and the two of them worked their way out of the shop and up the stairs. They went down the hall to the classroom where the students had just finished up clearing the room of all of the buffet items. The plates, and so on, were on a cart heading back to the cafeteria, going the opposite way of Jimmy and Castlethorn. "Say, where yee be goings withs those plates and such?" asked the old man.

"We're going to the cafeteria. Why?" said the student in the lead, pulling the cart.

"Dassn't youse go intuhz that kitchen. Jist ye knock on the door and waits fur Miz Miss Ladlepot ta screams at'chu. An' she will, no doubt. Den youse needs ta run."

"Why?" asked the student who was pushing the cart.

"Becuz ye needn't ducks the ladles."

The students both looked at Jimmy incredulously.

"Believe me," Jimmy replied, "you just do what he says. It gets pretty crazy back there...unless you guys have not had your fill of crazy for this week."

"No, no, no!" both students shouted. They had their fill of crazy. "I think we'll take your advice," said the lead student. He looked back at the boy that pushed the cart who eagerly nodded. Then they went on their way. The student who was pushing just kept shaking his head.

*****

Miss Coffenayle caught up with Doesbad, just as he was leaving the office. Patience had left for her own home long ago. He asked the principal if she needed anything else for the night. "Just one more thing, Simon," she said as she moved past him toward her office. He followed her, wondering what else she could possibly want. He was growing irritated because he was tired. It had been a long day. She stopped in her tracks and spoke into the air, facing away from him, and said, "In case you are irritated at me and wondering just *what else I could possibly want* after tiring you out today—"

He stopped dead in his tracks. He hated it when she read his mind. It always made him wonder what else she might know.

"I brought you here for your own benefit, you *idiot*."

Now he felt insulted as indeed he should. Anger snatched him out of his self-pity. The pair now in her office, his boss knelt down and did something in front of a little box. She turned around with a pouch in her hand. "Good. I *like* your anger," she said. Anger, rage, frustration, depression—all of these and every other negative emotion made her powers grow. She had been using the despair and frustration at the school for many years now to grow closer to Malovent. The more negative emotion she was able to generate, the more easily she could communicate with her master. She tossed Doesbad a pouch, and he caught it with a clinking sound. Gold bullion. It felt like about three one-ounce ingots. A bonus! She tersely dismissed him with, "Get out of my sight now, you toad! And don't return until I demand it!"

Simon I. Doesbad left in a huff. No amount of gold was worth all this. Not from her, not from anybody. He jumped into his big car and roared away. He loved the lifestyle that his only paying client afforded him. Or at least the one half of the lifestyle anyway. Now he needed to secrete his car, change, hire a cab, and get himself home to his dingy apartment. Maybe the boys would still be up for some cards and home brew. Something to look forward to, at least. That and maybe one day dining with Patience again. He knew they must not become too obvious. Coffenayle would not like it. Honestly, he had to admit, it did feel like he was betraying his one true love.

He could not understand, though, why he loved that abusive blonde overly-fed cow of a woman. But he did carry a torch for her! Oh, yes, he did. He sat back in his leather seat and smiled. He did love her. So how could he feel things for Patience too? Oh my! What a tangled web he was weaving. It was on his mind all the way home. Even the boys that night noticed that his mind was not on the game. "Just a little too much of this fine quality beer," he told them. Compared to his finest cognac, it tasted like boiled cat urine. For beer, though, honestly, it was pretty darn good! Plus, he did so enjoy their company more and more lately!

*****

Jimmy and Castlethorn arrived at the class just in time to see Miss Emily giving out the homework assignments. She stood there, tapping her foot, ruler in hand, and then looked over at the janitor and apprentice who were hovering, unsure of whether to enter. Miss Emily nodded to them. "Come on in, please. I was going over with the class our plans for tomorrow. Jimmy, I will stay after and talk to you about the plans personally. Mr. Castlethorn, will you spare Jimmy for a few minutes?"

"Why certainly, Miz Emily. I won't interferes none wiff the boy's ejucatin'!" exclaimed Castlethorn as he proceeded to the repair site at the front of the classroom. "Go on, Jimbo. Ah's gonna get ever'ting all set ups."

Miss Emily dismissed the class after a rousing chant of the school's anthem. "Hoorah, Happy Valley, yay." The students all left the classroom in an orderly single-file line under the watchful eye of Miss Emily and that mighty scepter of power, the steel ruler. They exited the classroom silently, and only out in the hallway did they begin to chatter. The other classes were letting out as well under the watchful eye of their teachers.

Once the classroom was finally empty, Miss Emily checked the hallways to be sure they were clear. Since she was a teacher, she was allowed to stay over, particularly if she was with a student. She stayed because she needed to talk to Jimmy. She took him aside, excusing themselves from Mr. Castlethorn's workplace. He was getting the sanders all set up, preoccupied with how to get the job started and what steps he needed to take.

The pair sat in a far corner desk, hopefully out of earshot. But there was something about Castlethorn that told Emily she did not have to fear him so much. "Jimmy," said Emily, "I have Margaret on our side. Before you say it, yes, I know. She could rat us out to Miss Coffenayle. But I don't think she will. She has been changing a lot with all that has been happening. She was never that bad, really. She just did not know what else to do. Being at the devil's right hand was better than being in his path in this case. She does not like the abuse any more than any of us. But she had to keep up that front to avoid getting punished. It was simply self-preservation. She understands what I am doing, that I am keeping up the appearance of abuse, but only in front of others."

"But, Miss Emily, they will eventually catch you being nice," complained Jimmy. "I don't want to lose you as a teacher because we don't know what will happen if they get someone else or even if Whipshot gets better. Then again, maybe Nurse Nightshade will kill her," Jimmy stated wistfully.

"Jimmy! Shame on you. You saw Nurse Shadyknight not very long ago. Don't you believe what she said?"

"Yes…yes, I do. But you can't blame a guy for trying."

Miss Emily chuckled softly. "No, I guess I can't. So here are the lesson plans for tomorrow." She outlined the usual regimen of Math, Science, Literature, etc., and Jimmy nodded in agreement. He understood that the class might actually learn more now. They did get some education under Whipshot, but that was really difficult learning. The class did learn to read and write. They did understand math. So it was not all wasted effort and beatings after all.

"Say, Miss Emily," started Jimmy.

"Yes?"

"I saw something today in Castlethorn's office—"

"I bet you did. What was it?"

"A piece of paper in a frame. It was a 'doctor-*ate*' degree."

"What is that?"

"I don't know, but it belonged to someone named 'Cas-ee-us Lawrence Thorne.'"

"That is so odd."

"Yes…somehow, I knew that this was important, and I knew I had to tell you. It was almost like—"

"Like what?"

"Well, it was like the framed paper fell where I was supposed to see it. Almost like someone moved it there. I don't blame you if you don't believe me…" Jimmy's voice trailed off.

"Oh, Jimmy! Yes, yes, I *do* believe you. I have seen some odd things lately, just like you have. We might be able to share them sometime," said Emily hopefully. She leaned a little closer to Jimmy. He did not seem to mind, and he might have moved in toward her a little bit himself. "Well," Miss Emily said, "I had better let you get back to work. You have a lot to do before class."

Jimmy took his leave of Miss Emily and joined Castlethorn as she gathered her things. She looked back at Jimmy on her way out the door. She smiled briefly.

"Wahl, Jimmy," said Castlethorn. "Ye may haves you a new friend thar." He winked and chuckled.

Jimmy denied knowing what he was talking about, and Castlethorn just laughed all the harder. Then he suddenly stopped and turned a bit grumpy again. "Let's get to sandin' dis floor. We got lots tuh do tonight, and yees got da schoolin' early in the morning."

Jimmy put his mind right back on business and did exactly all that his new mentor taught him, exactly as he was shown. Castlethorn was pleased. Jimmy and he would work out just fine. He let the boy work on the floor, and he started on the wall.

*****

On her way back to the teacher's dorm, not surprisingly, Miss Coffenayle caught up with Miss Emily and offered to walk back to her new home with her. The new teacher accepted and knew that Miss Coffenayle wanted to talk. She just had that *look* about her. They chatted about this and that, small talk, until they arrived at her little home. When she opened the door and turned on the light, she was shocked!

Her clothes were scattered everywhere. Her dishes and kitchen wares were all over the floor in the living room and hallway. Furniture was turned over, her bed mattress was pulled off and lying haphazardly against a wall. The bed frame was turned legs-up, and the place looked terrible. Leaving Coffenayle's side, she ran to the kitchen and opened the refrigerator. It seemed that all of her food was untouched. Thank goodness!

She looked at Miss Coffenayle who did not seem at all surprised at this terrible mess. Emily did not know what to say. She asked, "What on earth do you think happened here?"

Coffenayle smiled that evil grin Emily knew so well. "Well, child, I had your fellow teachers give you a 'welcome aboard' party. While you were feasting with your students at dinner time, I sent them here to remind you of where you came from and how easily you could *lose it all!*"

Miss Emily stood there with her mouth wide open, unsure of what to say.

"Don't worry, dear. All of your personal effects are still here, and nothing is damaged. No real harm. There is just a cluttered mess. You clean this up, and I want you to think while you are cleaning up of how quickly your position as a teacher could go away. You need to always remember who is in charge of this school and everyone in it. Remember, I could have just as easily said, 'Burn this house down.' Now understand that this is a one-time warning. Consider it your shot across the bow. This will never happen again if you behave yourself. But if I think action of this sort is needed again, it will be much worse for you. Now clean this up! You *think* of the power I have over you while you pick up every scrap of this mess. I will inspect it tomorrow. You had better have this place cleaned up just the way you found it on you first night! Need I say more?"

"No, Miss Coffenayle, you need say nothing more," said Emily with firm resolution. She had collected herself and immediately made up her mind that she was *not* going to allow Miss Coffenayle to win. She was not going to break, crack, or even chip. She would not show remorse.

"Then I will take my leave of you, young lady, and you may think about what I told you this evening." Miss Coffenayle walked stiffly out the door, begrudgingly admiring the girl's ability to gather herself and adjust to circumstances. *Emily is a survivor and a rather tough one at that. She will prove quite useful once I turn her*, she thought to herself with great intent. Just to top it off nicely, she slammed the door as she exited. *That* would show Emily who was in charge!

20

Mentor's Clues, Malovent's Warning

After she was sure Miss Coffenayle was out of sight, Miss Emily checked the house. She looked out all of the windows to make sure there were no trespassers around. Then she laid on her soft mattress after dropping it to the floor and put the pillow over her face. She sobbed softly at first and then began crying loudly, huge crocodile tears, into her pillow. She was finally overwhelmed by the whole situation. She could not take anymore. This was it! She realized that she was in an impossible situation. The deck was stacked against her, and Miss Coffenayle held all the aces. Emily felt terrible. She felt cheated, tricked, vulnerable, and naïve. She was helpless. How could she overcome the meanness in this place when everyone here was against the good and loved the evil?

"Everyone?" asked a familiar voice.

"M-Mr. Mentor? I-Is that you? Are you really here?" Emily asked, sitting up and drying her eyes. She felt ashamed now for feeling sorry for herself. She had this powerful ally, this friend who had not let her down so far, and here she was losing faith.

"Yes, of course, Emily," said Mr. Mentor. He slowly faded into sight. She was getting used to this now. He was standing there with his cane, his wise face turned up into a wonderfully cheerful smile. Same brown suit with starched collar, bowtie, and proper watch chain. "Come into your living room. I have something to show you."

Emily finished drying her cheeks and composed herself. She went into the living room and could not believe her tear-stained eyes! Oh my goodness! The living room and kitchen were all cleaned up and in perfect order again! All of her clothes were back in the closet; all of her utensils were neatly stored in cupboards and drawers. Everything was back exactly as she left it this morning. Emily was stunned, awed, and thrilled all at the same time. Then he fixed her bedroom the same way, much to Emily's amazement!

"Oh, how wonderful! Mr. Mentor! Oh, how did you—"

Mr. Mentor cut her off, "How did I do this? Ho! Ho!" He gave a hearty laugh. "How did I do this, you ask, after you saw me drive Miss Whipshot into the floor and then help Castlethorn pull her loose? That's a good one! How do you think I did it?"

"Um…" Emily was at a loss for works. "M-Magic…perhaps?" she stammered, not know what else to say.

"Oh, dear me, no!" said Mr. Mentor. "Not magic. I work by spiritual power which may appear to be magical to some. Watch this." He tapped his cane on the floor, and the bed, mattress, and clothing all were a mess again. Then he tapped his cane once more. All simply returned to their correct places. Emily was flabbergasted!

"What's the difference between what you just did…and magic?"

"Well, it is simple and yet complicated," the master lecturer began to explain. "Magic is a matter of trickery, illusion, and forcing elements to do your will. Magic is manipulative and evil in nature. But spiritual power? That is different matter. Spiritual power gives me the ability to, in a sense, become a partner with the elements, to sort of…make friends with the power of creation that is inside the elements of all objects. Then I use that power in partnership with the objects, to convince them to reset, I guess you could say. To come back to order. It is *possible* for elements to disobey, but they almost never do. Not unless they are under the influence of evil."

"So…my clothes, bed, and dishes just…*obeyed* you?" Emily asked in fascination.

"Yes, precisely. Very impressive, you catching on immediately like that. We knew you were a bright and virtuous young lady, and that is why you were chosen."

"Chosen? Me? For what? By who?" Emily really was in shock now.

"By whom," Mentor gently corrected her. "All things you need to know will be shown to you in good time."

"Okay, Mr. Mentor…but this is all so confusing."

"Naturally! You should be confused. If you were not perplexed, it would be because you were not thinking. We are glad you are thinking because we need you to learn. You and I do not have much time."

"For what?" Emily was getting excited now.

"Well, again, dear lady, this will have to wait for another time. Just continue as you are doing. Having Tommy retrieve that steel ruler for you, that was a stroke of pure genius. Miss Coffenayle loved to see you with your 'scepter.' She believes that you have become corrupt and that she now controls you. Your instincts tonight, dear Emily, were correct. Miss Coffenayle does want to *break* you. She wants to weaken you enough to do her will and her will alone. Now, I think you understand that I am here for you for real, correct?" Mentor asked and waited for an answer.

"Yes. I know you are here for real," Emily spoke with great resolve in her voice. She was standing up straight and true now. "I know that you are here to help me. I will do whatever it is that you need me to do."

"Oh, that is such a good girl! A fine young lady you are. I knew I chose wisely," Mr. Mentor said with great delight. "Now I need you to keep on doing exactly what you are doing. Convince the principal, the lawyer, and the other teachers that you are as bad or worse than Miss Whipshot. That will keep them off guard while we go to work."

"Speaking of teachers, Mr. Mentor, what about Mr. Castlethorn?" Miss Emily asked. She moved over to a chair and sat down.

Mr. Mentor sat on the floor, resting his hand on his cane.

"Oh, how rude of me! Would you like a chair?" Emily asked.

"No, no, no." Mr. Mentor waved her with a smile and a gesture of his hand. "I am never uncomfortable. I am sitting on the floor because I choose to, and it is easier for you to look me in the eye from down here. And I need to know that you are paying attention. This man you are asking about… Mr. Castlethorn. Do you trust him?"

Emily thought for a moment. She then said, "He is very strange. He scares us kids quite a lot. He makes me nervous sometimes."

"I did not ask if he scares you. Please also remember, Miss Emily, you are not a 'kid' anymore. You are an adult now. You may be too young for the role, but you are in the role nonetheless. Now that we have that cleared up, do you *trust* him in spite of your fears?"

"Yes, I do. I *do* trust him. I just never realized it before. Mr. Castlethorn is pretty strange, but there is more to him than that, isn't there?"

"Are you asking me or telling me?" Mr. Mentor smiled as he relaxed on the floor, legs and arms extended, cane in his lap, leaning back on the palms of his hands.

"I am telling you that he is strange, that I believe there is more to him, but I want to know if my belief is correct."

"Ah, yes. Why is this suddenly important?"

"Because Jimmy told me about something he found in Castlethorn's office."

"And what was that?"

"A picture frame that had some piece of paper in it. It must have been terribly important from the way Jimmy described it. He said that the paper was a 'doctor-*ate.*'"

"Oh." The old man smiled wisely. "This 'doctor-*ate.*' Did it state a name?"

"Um...oh it did! Caw-see-us Lawrence Thorn, I think it was."

"I see," said Mentor. "And you believe this to be important?"

"Yes... I know that it is important. I just don't know why."

"Well, Miss Emily, you have strong insight. I would do you a disservice by telling you more. All I will say for now is that you are on the right track. You are safe with Cass—ahem, Mr. Castlethorn." Mr. Mentor, for all his wisdom and knowledge, nearly slipped a secret to Emily before its time. He would have to be more careful about that. He must not become too eager or relaxed around this wonderful girl. He would do her no good by telling her too much. He felt that he may have gone too far by cleaning up the place for her. She put his mind at ease after seeing her response. She now knew she was safe with him. He knew that she understood in that moment that cleaning her room would probably never happen again. She had to clean up for herself from now on, even if it was not her mess.

"Well, Mr. Mentor, what is next?"

"You and Jimmy will have to work that out for yourselves. As for me, I must be going. I have a report to make." He stood up and straightened his still-perfect suit and checked his watch pocket with his thumb. He was now ready to go. "Remember, Miss Emily, I am nearly always about. I am nearly always with you." He turned to leave, and while walking away, he spoke over his shoulder, "My advice to you is to keep Margaret close. You may find her to be quite handy if you're ever in a pickle over what to do next. Also, look after Tommy. He's a courageous boy with good ideas." The he slowly faded away, even as he approached the door, passing right into it.

Emily was all alone now but did not feel alone. She was happy and somehow knew that Mentor and others were working with her to do something wonderful. She caught onto his allusion to making a report. He was accountable to others. He was working with other people. They must be spirits like him, she supposed. This was not the time to speculate too much about that or anything else. She was tired and felt that she needed her rest. She believed, somehow, that she was in for some very busy times. She needed all the rest she could get. She, Jimmy, Margaret, and even little Tommy—what could possibly come of all this? A set of mismatched children! *How could we*, she thought, *be at all important?* But then again, she was just a student two days ago. If her becoming a teacher could happen, well, what *else* would be possible? With that thought on her mind, she changed and went to bed.

*****

Miss Coffenayle had another meeting with Malovent after leaving Miss Emily's place. This meeting was important because she needed to follow up with him after the party and Emily's promotion. Malovent was keeping a close eye on things now, and that was concerning to Miss Coffenayle. She wanted to please him, to maintain her position with the Underworld. She did not know what the hierarchy of evil actually was, but she knew that Malovent had to be a very powerful figure. To impress him was critical if she was to gain more power. Her magics and potions were already quite effective and were becoming all the more so. She was quite proud of what she was becoming, proud of her power. She donned her black dress and robe.

"Master," she bowed before him after the necessary rituals. "I am pleased to report that all is going well with us."

"Excellent," replied the black-robed figure of the tall, darkly majestic Malovent. "You have been a most faithful servant, Miss Coffenayle."

Ah! she thought. *This is to be a good meeting. When he starts with that line, it is because he is pleased.*

"We saw what you did with Miss Emily. That was a stroke of genius. As you know, when you cause the students and teachers pain and duress, the more power we have. She was particularly disturbed."

"Thank you, Master," she bowed.

"You have done well. Continue to carry out our master plans. The courts are on our side. The teachers are under your control, and we have not hired an outsider. Miss Emily is frightened and is keeping the students in line. There is much confusion and frustration being raised among them, particularly after your all-day party and Miss Emily suddenly turning on them. I have never seen someone come so close to joining our side so very quickly."

He hovered over the design on the floor, gently bobbing like a boat on calm waters. This always fascinated Coffenayle. The dark lightning bolts of evil energy flowed gently up over his robes when he was pleased, but they could lash out like angry vipers and strike her when he became angry. Oh, how powerful! How wonderful to her! How majestic was his dark presence.

"Now, Donatienne...you must see something. Something unpleasant. You must understand now why the students must never fall out of your spell, why they must be kept off balance and never rebel." Malovent waved his arm, and suddenly, Miss Coffenayle was frozen in place, standing stiffly with her arms pinned behind her back. She began to panic, not understanding why she was being treated this way. She then felt the ropes holding her in place. She was outside at the old field. She could not understand how this was all happening, but she was tied to a stake. She was surrounded by students with a couple of teachers helping them.

A teacher suddenly appeared. The teacher was wearing Miss Coffenayle's black cloak over her shoulders! It was Miss Emily! *How dare she wear my cloak! She will pay for this!*

"A jury of your peers," Miss Emily motioned to the students, "has found you guilty of abuses, witchcraft...and...*murder!* The penalty is *death by fire!*"

Students brought forward brush, brambles, and firewood. They stacked their burdens around the principal dressed so properly in her shiny black boots and Napoleonic suit.

They chanted in unison, "Death to the Coffin-nail! Death to the Coffin-nail! Burn, witch, burn! Burn, witch, burn!" The chant continued for as long as they worked.

As they stacked the wood and brush all around her, she felt the ropes pulling tighter against her skin. She felt prickles of the brambles poking her. She knew this was not real, but at the same time, it was real in her mind because it felt that way! She was going to be executed by her students! After all she did for them, gracing them with her presence, educating them, disciplining and preparing them for the real world!

She smelled burning tar and saw Little Tommy standing there with a maniacal gleam in his eye, smiling at her, and he was holding a flaming torch! She could not break free; she could not escape! She tried shouting out her magical spells, but she could not concentrate enough to cast one properly! Then upon a signal from Miss Emily, Little Tommy pressed the torch into the tinder. It lit quickly. He pulled the torch out and lit several fires all around Miss Coffenayle, looking her square in the eye. He loved what he was doing...the chanting, the fire...his principal tied there against that stake, helpless and unable to move!

She yelled and hollered curses at the children, but it did no good. She was stuck! She felt the tongues of fire licking at her boots, melting the polish, and finally searing her feet. As the flames roasted her, she began to scream! She felt her uniform catch fire! She felt the burning, the fabric flaring, the blistering of her skin! She smelled her own flesh beginning to char. She screamed at first in rage instead of pain! *The miserable brats! They should be grateful!* Then she started to feel the real pain! At that, she started begging them for mercy! Even as her eyeballs began to bubble, the last thing she saw was all of the children laughing and pointing, showing each other the spectacle.

Even the teachers were laughing now. "Burn, witch! Burn!" Her eyes exploded, blinding her as they ran down her face! She writhed about in more pain, and she literally felt her lungs burn as she tried to gasp for air. He heart sped up, charred flesh began to split; she suddenly was out of her body and looked down as the students danced around her, and her lifeless body sagged against the ropes. She screamed long and loud at the sight of the children laughing and celebrating the final consumption of her charred corpse, pieces dropping and disintegrating in the blazing inferno.

Suddenly, she was kneeling on the floor before her master. She was safe, sound, and whole. She fell flat on the floor, grateful for its coolness against her face. She was gasping at the terror of…her *vision*? That was a vision! She was safe! She brought herself to her hands and knees, and her heartbeat slowed. Her breathing normalized. She gave herself a moment to gather her wits. Then Malovent spoke.

"My disciple, Friend Coffenayle, do you understand what just happened?"

"Y-Yes, I had a vision, F-Friend Mal-Malovent. A vision of my death. Is this a premonition? Is…is this a prophecy?"

"Yes but no. This is only a possible future. I had to show you what will happen if you lose control of your students. The evil power that you have built up by creating such negativity as you have done can possibly unleash rebellion and rage in your victims."

"Can I avoid this?"

"Absolutely, but you must retain control of the school. Do not let Miss Emily gain control."

"Yes, Master," she said as he hovered over her, watching her carefully. Malovent was pleased with the control he had over her. He was using fear to control her as much as she was controlling the school by fear. He allowed her to think about things. He sensed that she was considering her own mortality. She was no longer kneeling but was sitting with her legs crossed, nodding her head contemplatively.

"Master?" she asked sheepishly, as she struggled to her feet.

"Yes, my disciple?"

"May I ask about the order of things in the Underworld?"

"You know that you are forbidden to ask certain questions—"

"This one involves the 'hierarchy.' The positions that one may attain."

"I see. You want to become a queen tormentor, am I correct?"

"Yes."

"You want to know what it takes to become such."

"Yes, my master," she said humbly with her hand on her chest, her head bowed. Her black dress seemed to begin to levitate and float around her.

"I see. This question I may answer. Only when you are rid of all weakness, of all light, of all good, and you have embraced entirely the darkness may you become one of my tormentors. So be it. So I say."

The raven-clad Coffenayle bowed again all the lower. She was enraptured by the very thought of what he just told her. She was on track. She had to be or he would have never told her what he just did. All she had to do was continue on this path, the one that she had chosen, embrace complete and total darkness, and she could become one of them. One of the tormentors.

"But beware, my disciple. Such a path is not easy for mortals. You have done well already. Yes. But you must be complete and entire in your devotion. For instance, you gave extra gold to your lawyer tonight. Such is a dangerous tendency. You should not give without getting something in return. What was the return?"

"Master," she began slowly, "my intention was nothing good. I abused him as I gave him the gold. The gold buys his allegiance, makes his soul all the more mine."

"So what good is his soul to *you*?"

"I own him. I have captured his heart with a love potion that he takes with his tea whenever he visits me here at the school. The tea makes him gain weight, and this frustrates him, adds to his poor self-image worse than twisting his limbs and spine would do. Plus, this keeps him appearing normal for the courts. His appearance is important there. He is very useful for our cause, and I use him with great spite. He serves our purposes, and he even loves me without knowing why. This causes great conflict in him, keeps him off balance.

"The fool thinks that I don't know that he lives on the bad side of town. He thinks that I don't know that he sacrifices all of his gold for vanity. He could make a decent living on the wages I pay him, but he chooses to live tottering between misery and greater misery. He never knows if I am going to help him from one moment to the next. I pay him, yes, but only after giving him a very difficult time about it. I abuse him just like I do the students, but I leave him just enough hope to allow him to think he is in control of his life.

He drinks expensive cognac with his ridiculously arrogant friends by the light of day. Then under the cover of darkness, he drinks his cheap home brewed beer and hangs around with those ridiculous factory workers, garbage men, ice delivery men, and so on. His life is not worth living, and he is the only one who does not know it."

"I see," replied Malovent slowly. "You use him well. The gold you gave him is just enough to keep him clothed in vanity, never sensing the true nectar of life that is well within his grasp. You keep him distracted enough to forget just who he really is. This pleases me. Naturally, you realize that I already knew all of this. I just wanted to be certain you understand your own position in his life. You are a very cunning and knowing manipulator. Well done. I see great power and more darkness in your future. *More than you could ever know.*" He smiled ironically beneath his cowl, out of her view.

"Thank you, Master. I embrace every opportunity you present me with great relish. I am with you, with those you follow, and with those who follow you."

"You are among my most devoted and enthusiastic followers. Excellent! Now retire. I must attend to other matters, and you have much to do." As he left her, the room was filled with dark energy as though the very heart and soul of Hades himself were there just for her. She relished in it. Darkness was her desire. Evil was her love. She disrobed, and wearing just her Napoleon blouse and trousers, put away her candles and incense. She then donned her jacket, locked her office, and whistled all the way down the hall.

She was not aware at all of Mr. Mentor standing there with his cane and his well-pressed brown suit. He checked his watch and walked through a wall to the outside of the school. He had his reports to make too. He replaced his watch and draped the chain properly. There were advantages his side had over evil. The dark ones, they never knew all that they believed they knew and they never realized how much the good side knew of their "secret" plans. Liars, murderers, and thieves never had as many secrets as they thought. Feeling certainty and great power in her false knowing, Miss Donatienne Coffenayle went home and had a good night's sleep.

*****

Goliath was asleep on the floor beside his bed, wearing only a raggedy pair of boxers. His unwashed chest, belly and body were covered with thick, curly hair. He preferred the floor over the bed. The bed was too soft, too uncomfortable. He normally did not dream much. His mind was much too foggy. This night, however, was different. He lay tangled in his dirty sheets, his unwashed body stirring about. This was not a peaceful night. He dreamt of a woman this night. A kind woman with reddish hair who brought him things to eat. She was happy to know him. She asked him questions about him day. He told her he be happy chopping meat. He liked his day work. Something was familiar about this stranger. She made him feel happy…if this is what happy was. When she spoke, he felt like he did when he was chopping the meat, only this was much, much better. She would come and go in this dream.

He grew smarter in this dream and he knew more stuff. He could not see much anymore through the fog in his brain, but he knew he knew more better things a long time ago. He was big now, but he stood taller once. He was with other men his age, kicking and sometimes throwing a funny-looking ball around. He wore a strange hat on his head. Sometimes the guys dressed like him would run into other guys dressed like him, but not exactly the same. Different colors. People were happy see him, Goliath, but not Goliath with the other guys running into each other.

The red-haired lady would sometimes be happy for him too, sometimes sad. It depended how good he kicked the funny ball. Other ladies, more like him, not old like the redhead were near him. Goliath liked the ladies. He felt bad when they went away, and the red-haired lady was old and mean. That lady with yellow hair! That lady made the red-haired lady old and mean! "Bad! Bad! Bad! Bad!" Goliath woke himself up, yelling. He was tired, wanted to sleep more, but could not. He was awake now. Almost time for bell anyway.

21

The Day Dawn Is Breaking

Goliath put on his white coveralls and apron. Then he sat on the floor, playing with a bouncy ball that was his. *All* his. *Bouncy ball fun. Not fun like cutting meat. Meat more fun. Cutting meat make Goliath laugh. Mean red haired lady not friend. Sleep time, she seem friend. Real time she not friend. She mean. Stupid soup ladle hit Goliath when he not work hard. Good for Goliath chop meat hard. Make good work. Soup ladle no hit him. Bouncy, bouncy ball. Bouncy ball never hurt Goliath. Ball be Goliath friend.*

Finally, the alarm went off, and Goliath shut it down. He was dressed for the day, already having donned his work clothes. He went out to the kitchen and opened the refrigerator which had not worked for years. He grabbed a paper-wrapped package and tore it open. *Meat. Meat good food. No cook. Better red.* He ate the raw meat over the sink and threw the bones in the trash. Flies, suddenly disturbed, buzzed around the kitchen. The giant man gave them no thought. He lumbered over to the sink and grabbed a bowl. He filled it with water and drank it. He put the bowl back into the empty cupboard. He belched loudly and laughed at himself.

Then some of the gas went downstairs. He stood perfectly still and bore down, twisting his face and bending at the waist. He made loud, terrible razzing noises! He laughed harder and suddenly grabbed the back of his pants! He had to use the toilet immediately. He did and then took time to wash his hands. He was a kitchen

270

employee, after all. He wiped his hands on his dirty towel and left the filthy, stinking bathroom.

He walked outside and closed his front door. He walked over to the school cafeteria and went in through the kitchen service entrance. Miss Ladlepot was standing over a rank-smelling pot of something, stirring it with one of her hand-rolled cigarettes dangling from her lips. She looked up at Goliath and nodded in the direction of the hacking board.

His eyes lit up with excitement when he saw a whole side of beef just begging for his cleaver's kiss. He muttered with joy as he bellied up to the counter, pulled his favorite cleaver off the hanging rack. He named the cleaver "Rusty" (because it was) and started whacking away at the meat. No rhyme, no reason, just chop, chop, chopping away. But once in a while, he would sneak a glance over at Miss Ladlepot who was busy stirring at her cauldron of stuff. He... remembered bits of his dream. Miss Ladlepot was still his mean boss. Now, though, he understood something new about her, something, well...*nice*. Miss Ladlepot was oblivious to his stares.

Flowers ripped out by the roots from the school landscaping would later appear on top of her desk, dirtball and all. She would never know the reason for this. Oddly, though, she would feel compelled to keep the "pretty parts" of the flowers in her desk drawer, out of sight. Out of sight from everyone but her. She liked them and did not even know why.

*****

Emily was back in the classroom early, and the students filed into the room and took their seats. She seemed to know that Miss Coffenayle was lurking about, sneaking a peek into the classroom. She stood up front-and-center in the classroom. "And...just *what* are you little miscreants *doing*? I have told you already that we do not simply come into the classroom and sit in our chairs like we *own* the place! We don't do that, do we? No! We don't! Tommy, what is it that we do?"

Even though Tommy knew that this was Miss Emily acting like this just to impress Miss Coffenayle, he still got really nervous. Too many bad memories and impressions from Whipshot lashing out at him and forcing him to stay in that closet. "W-w-we...um... we stand at...um...at attention," the boy replied, trembling. He was expecting a whack from the ruler to his shoulder, but instead, Miss Emily approached with a stern look and stood with her arms folded.

"Then why aren't you doing it, you little *toad?*" she demanded. He stood up beside his desk at his best attention stance. Then Miss Emily whacked the desk with her ruler. Tommy's desk now had another scar in it for him to try to write around. She bent of over and quietly said, "By the end of the day, I will hit this desk so many times it will break. Then they will *have to* get you a new one. Don't worry. Now I need you to let some tears out."

The tears came easily to a boy so traumatized.

Coffenayle stood across the hall, peeking in from another classroom. The teacher and students in that classroom were used to her presence, her sneaking about and spying. They thought nothing of it. The sadistic principal was overjoyed at her new creation. *Miss Emily! My! My! My! What did you ever say to that boy? Wonderful! Just wonderful!* Having her house torn apart last night by the other teachers was a stroke of genius. Naturally, it was a good idea. After all, it was Miss Coffenayle who thought of it.

She briefly interrupted the teacher to thank him for his hard work on the "special project" last night. He just nodded, and they shared an evil grin. Then he went back to teaching multiplication tables: "That's right, you bunch of no-account mules! You stupid toads! We are going to keep repeating the nine's until you get every one of them correct in *unison!*"

Coffenayle went back to her office. She had her own studying to do. She was soon to become a queen, after all.

*****

This morning, Castlethorn was in his office, looking things over. He double-checked Lantern after giving it a couple of solid spins. No one was present right now. He was the "hoomin" bean in the room, and Lantern showed just him. It was nice not having to cluck like a chicken to cover himself. He got tired of having to appear crazy to everybody. The fog in his head was bad, yes, but it did not make him behave irrationally. It made things hard for him to remember. He could not work as well as he believed he once could in better times. In the back room of his office, he had photographs hidden from prying eyes.

The photographs were of people he could not remember, times he could no longer understand. Letters, reports, academic awards, papers, writings from someone very smart. He knew that when he put all of these things back here and hid them. He could not remember why. Who was that in these pictures? The fog would increase every time he tried to remember. If he tried too hard, the headaches would begin. It was like a punishment. He was being punished for trying to remember things. What was his life like before the school? He knew he must have had one. He saw the photos of a wife, a husband, and a child. These people were all in many of the photos; they did a lot of things together. One of them was playing at some team sport, one that looked strangely familiar to Castlethorn.

Something else too: he knew that he built Lantern in better days but could not remember how; it was the same with that ghost-repelling machine that blocked the poltergeist. Students, teachers, everyone who tried to come back here, everyone but Castlethorn, was repelled with great violence when they started looking at things. If this dangerous ghost was guarding this room, why would it let him back here and no one else? The ghost must be hiding something from them. Since Castlethorn was so very careful, maybe he was allowed back here because the poltergeist did not know what he was hiding. The old janitor was almost certain that if he was discovered back here with these things, he would be driven out.

Unbeknownst to Castlethorn, as Mr. Mentor had taught Emily, evil spirits never really knew all they wanted to know about the righteous living souls. There were some things forbidden for them to know. This was a law that gave righteous people in overwhelmingly evil situations a narrow advantage. The poor old guy never even knew that he was a victim of evil. He certainly never knew that he was in the middle of a *war!*

In a dusty old box that he kept in a rolltop desk, one he labeled "*Odz an enz,*" he had the original plans for Lantern. It was called an "*ectoplasmic spectrometer,*" and its purpose was to read a room and tell if ghosts were present. "Hoomin beans" read normally with a white signature. Yellow or green were ghosts, and red was a very nasty thing. He did not know what the red ones were, but they were very bad. Very dangerous. There were other things in his box too. Trophies from colleges, award letters, scholarships—all kinds of things. Much to his consternation, he could not remember much at all. His slide rule was still of some use to him, but he kept that to himself. He knew it was important that he not let anyone see him working with it. Jimmy and Emily saw him, but only for a moment. Even if de kiddeez did know what he was doing, well, he just *felt* he could trust them.

That Miss Emily was some special young lady too. Castlethorn was sitting on an old worn-out stool that allowed him to rotate. He was just turning back and forth, thinking quietly to himself. He was very reverent when he saw Miss Emily get promoted to teacher. He felt like that event was very important to him; it was almost like he had seen things such as that ceremony happen before. That must have been in the days before the fog took him over. Sometimes he would just feel so sad and angry, like something important had been taken away from him. He could sense that he had been robbed. He *had* been robbed, and there was no way to reclaim whatever was stolen. He felt that he had lost his mind. He could not even really talk straight. He knew he sounded different than other people, and it embarrassed him. Even so, he had this crazy belief that it was not always that way for him. He somehow knew he was normal once. How could he possibly know that?

Castlethorn also knew that there was a ghost close to Miss Emily, one that would come and go. Not every ghost that Lantern helped him see was dangerous. A few were harmful and dangerous; others were just pure evil. Those purely evil ghosts were the red ones. He did not believe they were normal ghosts. Those things were in a class all by themselves. But the yellow and green ones? They were there around the school frequently and generally harmless. One of the green ones seemed attracted to Miss Emily. He did not want to scare her, but it seemed to follow her around a lot. That was so puzzling. Well, enough of all this. It was time to check on Miss Emily's floor that Whipshot done broke. It was time to make sure the fixing was done all proper.

He put his private things away and locked up the desk where he kept them. He put the key in a special slot inside Lantern. *That wuz good hidin' there.* He made sure that the settings on his two machines, the twin sentries that kept the "poltergoon" at bay, were correct. They were humming along nicely. Good to see. He now went to see the floor that Whipshot "dun ruint." He had to finish "fixin' dat hole in de wahl" too. He wanted to bring Jimmy back here with him one day and show the boy around. Maybe let him run a machine or two. *Yeah, dat soundses fun.* He grabbed Lantern and left the office. He walked up the stairway to fix Miz Emily's floor.

Classes were nice and busy. All the furor over Whipshot's accident had died down, even if the quietly spoken rumors had not. Some even speculated it was a student conspiracy to hurt Whipshot and let Nurse Nightshade kill her. The kids, they said, did this so they would not have to put up with her anymore. All of it, though, was just a bunch of useless, silly, hurtful talk.

Miss Emily was in control of her class, and Castlethorn watched her intently for a couple of minutes. He was fascinated by this whole new thing of a student becoming a teacher. She glanced in the direction of the doorway and saw Castlethorn standing there. She motioned for him to come in and said, "Class, we have a visitor. What may we do for you, Mr. Castlethorn? Class, say good morning to Mr. Castlethorn."

The class greeted the janitor with a monotone "Good morning, Mr. Castlethorn" in perfect unison.

"Jest checkin' the wahl an' floorboards, Miz Emily. Don' lemme disrupt your class teachin', ma'am," he said.

Miss Emily granted permission, and he walked over to the floor repair. It held up amazingly well, and the varnished finish was hardly even scratched, "even wi'f peeples walkinz on it." He was satisfied with the job he and Jimmy did, even at first glance, but he kept poking around so he could linger and put an ear to what was going on in the classroom.

Emily was having an inspired morning. She was teaching math that she did not fully understand as a student. Nothing horribly advanced, but it was coming to her easily now. Part of it she knew was her own natural intelligence coming through, now that she was relaxed and not fearing Whipshot's screaming. The class seemed to be doing better too. Even Little Tommy, she noticed, was less anxious and able to concentrate better. This was a good thing. Emily knew she needed to keep Miss Coffenayle convinced that she was the "evil" Miss Emily, though, and remembered to always play the part.

There were times when she was about to get stuck on some part of the algebra, but then she felt the answer just sort of "pop into" her head. That was Mentor helping her, and she knew it. She just had to listen intently and allow him to inspire her. She also noticed that when she did not want help or became too anxious, she did not, or perhaps could not hear him. Upon that realization, the words "profound insight" came into her mind. She continued to teach and learn math.

Castlethorn had his back to the classroom and picked up Lantern. He kept his movements hidden but gave Lantern a quick turn and peered into the little window. He thought to himself that something was going on. He was just now watching Miss Emily get stuck on a math problem, and then the response like someone gave her the answer. That, and he knew that "dey was not all hoomin beans" in the room right now. He could see a green presence near Miss Emily, nothing new, but this time, he noticed that it would flicker or flare up with white light whenever Miss Emily got stuck on a problem or question. After the white flare-up, she suddenly knew the answer. He understood that the ghost told Emily things. Green and yellow-appearing ghosts were good, for sure. Red ones were certainly evil as he learned by hard experience. But today, there were no red ones. Not in this room anyway.

Lantern could only pick up the red, yellow, and green lights within about fifty feet, he had learned over time. So, yes, something was going on. Something indeed. He could not quite understand yet what was actually going on, but now he knew that the "not hoomins" could talk to the "hoomins." They did not always do that, but he at least now knew that they could. That was enough for now. His head was starting to hurt, and he did not want to push it any harder. There were limits to what he was allowed, it seemed to him, to think. Who or what was acting upon him he did not know. But it certainly was not a "hoomin." That was enough to know for now.

*****

Patience saw her boss coming and knew right away to not even speak to her. She was in one of *those* moods again. Miss Coffenayle stormed rudely past and slammed the door. Patience knew it was to be another morning of study, the principal locked in her cave. That was fine. Patience had plenty of things to do. She always did.

Miss Coffenayle sat in her chair and pulled out *L'Grimoire*. She needed to know more about how things operated. She was very satisfied with Malovent's teaching, and she craved more. There were books that he told her to study; there were books she found on her own and received his approval to read. Not that she thought she needed his approval to study anything she chose; she just did not want to waste time. She wished to read and learn things that were going to advance her position with the Underworld and nothing else.

22

Donatienne Coffenayle's Rise to Power

L'Grimoire was a special book that was particularly important. It was bound with a very soft leather laid over a hard cover. It smelled wonderful to Miss Coffenayle. The pages were written on parchment, handwritten in a rust-colored ink, which Malovent claimed to be human blood. She did not care one way or another, but it was intriguing to her. The main thing to her was the content. She was interested in arcane knowledge. She wanted to know how to learn more. Malovent assured her that everything she needed to know to become a tormentor was there.

He should know…it was a book he had studied to become who he was. He passed it to her because her thirst for power, instant power, was so great that even he himself was impressed by her greediness for it. Today, during a brief, partial appearance of the Master, he finally admitted to her that he had never passed this book to any other student of his, ever. He told her that she was the greatest disciple of his, that he was very glad to have her. She was thrilled! Her goal had been reached at last! Since she was so eager to become evil—truly evil and not just a wicked, selfish, and greedy person—he would tutor her in *all* his ways.

She knew that ruling in the Darkness would be worth casting all good, all conscience, all regret out of her soul to have that power. *Yes*, she thought. She would succeed. She would become Darkness itself and stand beside Malovent and all the other masters before him, stand beside them as a queen tormentor. Forever there, forever in the darkness she so loved, forever evil and torturing others for daring to have any decency and light inside of themselves.

She was alone in her office now, and it was time to perform a ritual purging. She went to the door and instructed Patience to not trouble her for *any* reason and to disconnect the office phone. In total quiet, she would meditate upon the things she did to rise in power under Malovent's teaching and systematically rid herself of all remorse for doing those things. She lit a very mild incense, took off her uniform, and donned her informal black dress. She simply sat quietly in her most comfortable chair, the one behind her desk, and once again, she reviewed her own story of how she came to power.

She recalled how easy it was to murder Mr. Angelton, the assistant principal to Mr. Mentor. Angelton was a good man, a reflection of his own name, but he was in her way. That's all he ever did to her; he got in the way of the master plan she had cooked up with Malovent. In truth, it was all Malovent's plan, but she had to be the one to carry it out. To carry it out, she had to carry Angelton out. So she did. She cast a spell to cause a car crash. Use magic to dump the driver's cup of hot coffee into his lap, he spins off the road and into a tree. Simple, easy, done. Now, getting rid of Mr. Mentor was a different sort of situation.

She had to steel herself to kill Mr. Mentor because she truly liked him. Having feelings of love or friendship for anyone was a problem because it made Miss Coffenayle appear *weak* in the eyes of her new master. She had to counsel with Malovent many times before she could work up not only the nerve to kill Mr. Mentor, but she had *destroyed the love* she had in her heart for her boss. She actually performed incantations to crush her loving decent feelings for that man, just before slowly poisoning him to death, taking her time so it would look like a mysterious progressive illness. Mr. Mentor grew sicker and sicker, finally bedridden and growing weaker until the day eventually came.

On that fateful day, Mr. Mentor called Miss Coffenayle to his bedside. Mrs. Edna Mentor was already there, grieving. "Dear, dear Miss Coffenayle," he began weakly, "this school will soon be without its principal." Edna took his hand, shook her head, and wept. It could not really be the end. Not like this, could it? "I need you to do me a kindness, dear Miss Coffenayle."

"Certainly, Mr. Mentor! Anything!" she answered. *Why won't you hurry up and die? There is enough poison in you to kill a horse!*

"Please call Mr. Dozeman. He is my personal friend, and I need his services. I need him to amend my Last Will and Testament. He has nearly finished his degree and will be a lawyer soon. I would love for him to become our general counsel, if he is so willing."

Edna wept out loud. She could not bear this thought, this man, this love of her life, her best friend and counselor, her guide, *her Mentor* and teacher! Oh, how could she go on?

"Of course I will, sir. I will call him immediately. It will take him a couple of hours to get here. Will that suffice?"

Mr. Mentor sat up on the bed. He tried to appear strong in spite of being so very, very tired. "Yes. And please hurry, my dear."

Coffenayle immediately left the grieving and nearly widowed Mrs. Mentor and the nurse to tend to the dying administrator. She got Dozeman on the phone. She explained the whole story. She was in tears.

"Of course! I will be right there with all the documents we need. Are you certain that we need amend his will? Is there no hope for recovery?" asked Dozeman, obviously distressed.

Miss Coffenayle assured the nervous voice on the other end of the line that it indeed was necessary for them to finalize his Last Will and Testament. She was not sure if Mr. Mentor would make it through the night. Simon J. Dozeman, nearly "Esquire," assured her that he was getting ready as they spoke and would most certainly be there in two or three hours. She hung up the phone and made a private celebration inside herself while mourning for all the world to see. For the next couple of hours, she paced the halls, checked on the room where the old boy lay dying, she worried about the changes to the will, ran errands back and forth for the nurse, and did her best to look sad.

Then came a knock on the door. *Finally!* She met Simon J. Dozeman at the door after dabbing her eyes with some water. She stopped, leaned against the closed door, and began gasping for air, quietly, raise her rate of respiration. She opened the door and appeared breathless and frightened. Simon was alarmed at her very appearance and asked, "Are you all right?"

"No...um...well, yes, yes I am," she stammered in her best phony dither. "But he-he's not d-doing very well at all. The nurse, Mrs. Edna, and some teachers are with him. He called for you and does not think he will make it through the night. Please! Please hurry!" Without another word, she grabbed him by the sleeve and pulled him along behind her. She *really was* anxious, she recalled with a chuckle. She was anxious because she needed that will to be legal before she could take over the school. She knew that would be his wish because there simply was not anyone else! She made certain of that. A little hot coffee and poisonous magical tea helped the cause right along. Yes, they had to hurry. They had to get to Charles Mentor's room before something went wrong.

They ran up to the room, both of them breathless but safe with all the documents they would need in Dozeman's worn-out leather bag. He went to the bedside after catching his breath; Coffenayle held back. No need to crowd the old coot. He approached the nurse and grieving dutiful wife. They looked up at him. The nurse took her place beside Coffenayle, and two of them whispered quietly, the nurse shaking her head. The teachers stood at a respectful distance, heads bowed, brave men choking back their tears. Coffenayle bowed her head as well, trying hard not smile. Dozeman was hesitant, nervous, afraid. He had never been at the side of a dying man before. He swallowed hard. "Sir?" he asked softly.

Mr. Mentor's eyes shot open immediately. "Simon? Is that my beautiful friend, Simon, come to see me through to my last breath and last wishes?" His eyes were vacant and glazing over. His feet were cold and changing color. "Simon?"

"Yes, Charles...sir... I have the papers for the will. You have it completed already. Everything, including the power over the school, go to your darling Edna. I understand, though, that there are, well... changes?"

Drat! If Dozeman did not know what the changes were to be, then he was not done yet with the will. What if she was not to be the one in charge? Coffenayle remembered how much restraint was necessary for her to keep from blowing her cool and shaking the old fart right out of his deathbed at the thought! How *dare* he after all she had done for the school! That power was to be hers and hers alone! It should have already been done! She simply stood there, holding her breath, waiting for the final outcome.

"Yes… Simon. Changes." Mentor's eyes closed. He took a deep breath and blinked. He looked back at Simon.

"Sir…what is it?" Simon urged him softly, sitting on a chair pulled close to the bed.

"I am of sound mind. Do…you…believe me?"

"Yes. I do. I will certify you to the courts if you can tell me where you are."

"I am in the infirmary, of course."

"About what time is it?"

"About nine at night."

"What is your name?"

"Charles… Edward… Mentor." He stared intensely into Dozeman's eyes.

"What is happening around you right now?" he asked earnestly.

"Heh! I am surrounded by my friends and loyal subordinate, Miss Coffenayle, who is certainly more than my equal. My…lovely wife, Edna, is here. Nurse McKnight…is taking…care…of…me." His eyes closed for a moment. He swallowed hard. "Water?" he asked.

The nurse brought a glass of water, propped his head, and allowed him a sip. Then she lowered him back to his pillow.

"And," the dying man continued, "some goofy lawyer is asking me obvious questions! Ha!" He began coughing.

The nurse sat him up and patted his back. She rubbed it gently, soothingly. She was the consummate picture of compassion and caring. She laid him back down. Tears flowed freely from Edna's eyes. Coffenayle was rubbing dry eyes with her handkerchief, making them water but not become red. This was the first time she tried that move, and it worked!

"Now. I want all my money to go to Edna still. But there is to be a change. I want the powers of the school to be handed over to Miss Coffenayle. She is more than cap...cap...capable. Do...you... have that?"

"Yes, sir. I do. I have all of it. I will have witnesses around this bed sign it. I will also have them sign the certification that you are of sound mind, even if your body is not healthy. The powers of running the school will go to Miss Coffenayle. Edna will have your money and will be well cared for under the provisions of the original will. All is in good hands now, old friend."

"Good. That is good." The old educator laid back again contentedly. He closed his eyes. He sighed and allowed a little smile to pass his lips. He opened his eyes one last time and looked straight at Edna. "I...love...you." And with the last of his strength, he squeezed her hand. Then he took a short panting breath and exhaled long and hard. His hand went limp in hers, his eyes closed reluctantly, but there was nothing there to keep them open any longer. He took two more similar breaths, and on the third long sighing exhale, he breathed no more.

Died: Charles Edward Mentor.
Time of death: 21:15 hours.
Date: Tuesday, May 10, 1910.
Requiescat en Pace.

Now, Miss Coffenayle, sitting in her office, quietly recalling the man's death, started to feel regret. She knew that this memory must be preserved, but the regret needed to be destroyed. She concentrated and recalled the pain she felt has he breathed his last. She focused on that pain and rationalized it, forcing it away, replacing it with other ideas. She called on her powers to cause these other ideas to replace the light that her regret represented. She completely crushed her remorse and regret with "knowing" that Charles had gotten in the way of her ambitions. She dwelt on the feeling of revenge against Mr. Mentor for allowing himself to be good and for causing her pain as she got rid of him. She allowed—even caused—this twisted idea of good and evil to replace any human feeling she had for the man who mentored her in her education career. Yes, that was better. All the guilt and regret over this moment was now replaced with the darkness she loved. This was the purpose of the ritual, to purge herself of any decency. She was getting better at it.

Miss Coffenayle returned to the experience as she recalled Edna feel his hand go heavy in hers. There was no more warmth in it, no kindness, no anything. She shook him gently by the shoulder. "Charles...darling? Charles? Please...don't. Don't." She desperately felt for his heart, then listened for it, her ear to his chest. She put her hands on both of his shoulders and gently shook him. "No! No, I don't accept this! There is too much for you to do! Now...you come back, you open your eyes, you get dressed, and go back to work. Like before. Yes, Charles, you do that!" She waited a moment, hoping. Then she just collapsed onto his chest, sobbing. "No, Charlie-punkin. You can't do this to me. It's too much for me to bear. I just can't do this alone, punkin. Not alone...please, please, please come back. I need you...please don't..." Her voice trailed off, and she just completely broke down. She was crying quietly, but everyone present could tell that the poor woman, the world's newest widow, had just shattered completely. Her heart was broken. Her strong will was... gone. It was just gone. She had nothing left to give.

The nurse gently pulled her off of the reclining frame of the expired educator and placed her in the care of Simon who lowered her back into her chair. Nurse McKnight verified the obvious. Vital signs were at zero. Body temperature was falling, respirations zero, pulse zero, blood pressure per the sphygmomanometer zero. She recorded the time in her medical records. She pulled the white sheet over the head of her beloved chief, educator, and friend. There was not a dry eye in the room, even though one set of eyes needed a handkerchief to stimulate tears. After she settled her business with the dead, the nurse reluctantly turned her back on a man who never turned his back on her. She did, though, what he would have expected. She immediately went to the aid of the living.

"Bring Mrs. Mentor to the other room. I have a bed for her," Nurse McKnight said. She looked back and saw that Simon and

Miss Coffenayle were having a hard time with the poor woman's limp mourning frame. She quickly brought a wheelchair, and they propped her up in it. She was the picture of misery. Her mouth was open, softly moaning, and her eyes were closed. She would not respond to anyone in the room. They laid her on the bed, and the nurse went about discreetly changing her from street clothes into a proper hospital gown, protecting her modesty the whole time.

She was efficient, she was quick, but very smooth and gentle, obviously a highly competent nurse. She propped Widow Mentor up with pillows. The poor woman was silent now, her eyes open, mouth closed, and she was just staring at the wall into space, not seeming to really see nor perceive anything. Nurse McKnight snapped her fingers near her ears with no response. She gently pricked her earlobes, shoulders, hands, and feet with a pin. Nothing. No pain response. Her only signs of life were breath and a heartbeat.

She turned to Miss Coffenayle and Simon. Her expression was solemn. One could even say dark. "I fear greatly for Mrs. Mentor. If she does not find hope in something, she may herself die," she said softly. Then she was silent; perhaps having seen one death too many was taking its toll on the competent professional nurse. She felt drained. No one noticed, but there was the slightest hint of a smile on Miss Coffenayle's face.

In her office, Miss Coffenayle's face wrinkled with a bit of pain. She did not intend for the old woman to lose her mind. She again applied her magic to sear her conscience completely, to sever it, to surgically remove the light, the kindness that caused her to feel regret. Consciously and completely, the principal removed all feeling she had over this moment. *Dark was the nurse's countenance, and all the more strength for Malovent,* thought Miss Coffenayle to herself. He fed well on the misery of this moment; she knew. His dark majesty would grow stronger this day.

Her actions would bring her all the closer to becoming Underworld royalty. Her second murder was now complete, and she was all the closer to her dreams coming true. Malovent was truly pleased. Upon Mentor's death, she felt herself grow all the colder, darker, and detached on the inside. Her heart suddenly became all the more jaded. She relished in the evil that was welling up inside of her, loved it, cherished it. Power from Malovent was flowing into her. She was becoming an embodiment of living darkness! How delightful.

Relishing her recollections, the principal meditated in her office upon how that night, she put on a sad and sorry face for the deceased and his widow. She was as solicitous as could be. Ever the servant, ever the willing employee, ever the loyal and faithful steward. Yes, Coffenayle remembered all of this and loved every moment of the misery. Ah! The funerals. Yes, two of them. Mr. and Mrs. Mentor were buried properly. The dirt on his grave was hardly dry when the widow was laid to rest beside him. Wreaths for them both. The mourning, the grief, the hopelessness—all of it fed Malovent very well. The school faculty and staff fell to near total hopelessness, and the absence of hope was one of the darkest emotions humans could muster up. Broken hearts, broken wills. All of this was bringing Coffenayle closer and closer to her goals.

The principal recalled the eulogies, remembering first his…then hers. His death was expected by the masses; hers was not. Coffenayle could never express her joy at their passing but excused her smile as "remembering them fondly." The eulogies were both about the same coming from Coffenayle's lying cursed lips. She just had to put "Mrs." in the place of "Mr." and talked a little bit more about how much Charles had taught her during her tenure at the school. That part, at least, was true. She did learn a lot from him, all she needed to know to replace him when his untimely death occurred. She personally laid the wreaths on both graves. She alone held the secret of the one.

Then there was the Last Will and Testament to be read. Simon had double the duty because their deaths were so close in timing, and the will tied them together. There was a provision that in the event that Mr. Mentor died, all of his money went to the Mrs. But after she died, any remaining funds not needed for final expenses or any outstanding debts would go immediately and directly to the school. Mrs. Mentor did not have time to run up any bills or debts. She did not spend any money at all in the few hours that she was alive after his death. The way the will was written, then, put the school in possession of the considerable wealth of the Mentor estate. Since it was known that Miss Coffenayle would now run the school, as provided for in the will, that put her in direct control of a rather large sum of money.

*****

Miss Coffenayle opened her eyes in her office, sitting in her chair. She had done it! Gone was all her human regret. She had just now purged herself of all sorrow over the recollections of those moments that were so critical to her gaining power. There was nothing left to purge for now. Now she could just...enjoy her next memories.

She sat back and recalled how she immediately summoned Malovent after Mentor's death. She brought him all of the dark news and laid it at his feet, rejoicing. She had bought her formal black dress and cloak after Mr. Mentor was bedridden in anticipation of her making this very report. She had also studied about improvements on incense and candles to burn during her rituals to create more dark energy to strengthen her relationship with her master. She had everything already set up in her personal quarters to where she retired "to mourn;" she knew he would not last the night and was prepared to give her report.

Malovent appeared after the ritual was completed, and at that time, he was not very big or strong-looking. She was pretty new at this and she had not done enough evil to strengthen her perception of him. His waist was girded about with a gold belt, though, which was something new. He was about six feet tall. He was pleased with her as she outlined the events that led to her holding the most powerful position in the school. He told her that he was there to teach her the next steps to take.

"Now," said Malovent in a deep rich timbre and more powerfully than ever, "it is time for you to begin running the school. You will be surprised at the things that will happen here, and some of it may at first appear unpleasant to you. Since you will grow powerful from all of the changes, do not resist what is happening. Our magics are powerful, and you are a great witch. You must continue to do what I tell you, no matter what you see or how you feel about it. To succeed, you must let the darkness harden you."

"Yes, Master," she replied while bowing. "I will carry out your will, no matter what."

"Excellent. Take down these words. Write the steps precisely as I give them to you." He paused for her to go to her desk, then continued, "First, you must evict all of the current students. Send them to the other schools in their home districts. This school will now become a refuge for children who have nowhere else to go. They will be orphans and abandoned children. They must have no traceable family ties. The vocational programs will be abandoned. You will introduce a purely academic curriculum. No extracurricular activities. This move, though a radical change, will prevent student families from complaining about your...*new* methods.

"Secondly, you will close off all communications that outsiders and inspectors will have with the school. You will need to get a foothold in the courts. I will show you how to do that. The most important thing at the moment is for you to shut down all communications. Lock up the few necessary telephones and destroy the rest. Do not let your new 'students,' staff, or faculty have access to them. You may have a phone line for your personal assistant, but keep the phone locked and unplugged unless you need her to make calls. This will keep the outside world from communicating with the school and accessing our program until we get someone in there we fully trust.

"Your third step will be to create a self-contained system. You will grow vegetables on the grounds and use students as laborers. Recess and recreation playgrounds will be removed from this place. Necessary foods for the nutrition program will be provided by shipments from the outside, but deliveries will be received on the dock. No one will ever enter the school.

"The fourth step will be to get control of the faculty who already live here. Fire the ones who have families with children too small to work. Keep the single people or those whose spouses and older children can work here on the grounds. Fire those with children who still need to attend classes, and fire those employees who have outside family members, and bar them from returning. Give them a generous severance payment to allay suspicion. Give the excuse that things need to change now, and be nonspecific.

"Then you need to remove all support staff access to phones. This must be done quickly to prevent the authorities from shutting you down before you get control of the courts. The attorney Dozeman will be perfect for that job. We will also have an ally who will use mystical means to rule the highest judge. You will have no problems in the courts.

"You will need to keep control of everyone, so make barrels of the tea which I will describe to you from the ingredients I will reveal to you. You will distribute it after saying the incantations I will give you. Those who work for you as teachers and support staff will lose their personal identities, and you will use them to carry out your work of darkness.

"You will also cause the attorney to take the tea when you meet with him. Do not allow him to enter the school until after you have shut down communications. He will come to you to find out what is going on, and you will meet him to explain yourself. Then you will take control of him. He will be the only one who has anything to do with the school who will live off campus. Everyone else will surrender their will to your rule and will not ever consider leaving. Once someone is recruited, they must remain until you are through with them. When you are through with them or if they create too many problems, you or I may destroy them with our powers.

"You must cause as much angst and misery as you can among the people. Here is where we will gain our power. Their hurt is our darkness, and our darkness is life to us. You know this…that darkness is now your life, do you not, my faithful disciple?"

"Yes."

"And you know that your murders, your shedding of innocent blood, have condemned you? That you now are a member of the denizens of the Underworld? Without hope for light ever again?"

"Yes."

"Do you therefore pledge your soul to the pursuit of darkness at the cost of afflicting the innocent, at the cost of harming those who would love you?"

"Yes. You know that I do. I have already harmed those who loved me. You have seen my ability to afflict others. You have seen my unquestioning obedience. Have I not carried out your requests and commands, done all things, even killed people according to the letter of your rule and law?"

"I am pleased with your work. Now proceed with making the tea and distributing it to the faculty."

"What about the students?"

"Leave the children to retain their identity. Let them have free will. Then crush them. With their full freedom intact, your oppression will be all the more painful. The tea...is a tool to *suppress* free will. It will disturb memory. It will cause people to become a shell of their former selves. Their bodies will become twisted over time. They will no longer look like their old selves. You will assign them new identities. They will obey you and have less of a conscience to stop them from committing acts of cruelty since they will have lost who they truly are. The pain that we generate—again, you must remember this—is what gives us our great power!"

"Ahhh...yes, Master. I will do as you say. I will prepare the tea and place it in all the break rooms in place of coffee. Now, what if they do not like the tea? What if they will not drink it?"

"Oh, but they will. The special brewing will appeal to their most carnal senses, their most basic instincts. It will taste so very sweet to them, even as it twists their will and their bodies into something ugly. Each person will experience a different flavor. The flavor and scent will taste and smell like their fondest wishes and/or memories so they cannot resist drinking the tea. They will become something they were never born to be. They will become pathetic and so horrible that the outside world will never accept them. Then will my power take their energies from them ever so freely."

"Will I get an incantation?"

"Yes. After they take the tea in sufficient amounts. I will discern when that is by my magic. I will summon you, and you will then learn the magic spell to drain their energy. It will be the darkest thing I have taught you yet."

"Even *darker* than murder of the innocent for material gain? Even *darker* than intentionally organized criminal activity?"

"Yes. Much so."

"I would imagine you to be smiling under that cowl, Master. May I see your face?"

"*Absolutely not!*" he shouted with a roar that shook the very walls.

His devoted disciple, already on the floor, bowing, began to tremble in fear. "I shall never ask you again, Master. Forgive me!"

"*Never beg forgiveness!* You are what you are, and I will accept no apologies! There is no forgiveness in our ways! None! Do you understand me?" he roared at her. The walls continued to shake. She had never seen him so fiercely angry!

"Yes... Master... I do," spoke Coffenayle as she trembled. She vowed to never ask that question again. The master would reveal himself as he chose to, and that was up to him entirely. Yes, she remembered it all, without regret, reveling in her own dark works. She even entertained the notion of becoming more powerful than Malovent himself...then they would see who would hide their face and who would not. Ha!

Miss Coffenayle sat in her office as principal, loving every minute of her recollections of Malovent, then a smaller less-imposing figure. Everything was going perfectly. No hitches in the plan. The tea, to this day, sits in the coffee pots of the employees who willingly drink it every day. That stuff was more attractive than laudanum itself! She liked to indulge herself a bit of the poppy liquor on occasion, but lately, she needed her wits fully about her. When she was on that stuff, she became completely loopy! Ah, well! That was the past, and there was no time for apologies or for regrets. Such was a waste of energy.

That amazing tea, though, had powerful effects, the likes of which she had never before seen. She recounted the difficulties she had with Cassius when she first started as principal. He did not agree with her ways. There were some who followed him, too. Now look at them! Idiots! The lot of them! That tea really took a toll on some of them. A few were not only clouded but completely lost!

And their looks. Nurse McKnight took a big hit there. Miss Coffenayle cackled out loud about that. The once lithe and attractive nurse now had deep lines in her face and the girth of a baby hippo! Ha! Oh, yes, she had them all as soon as they drank that tea. There was no name for it, but she referred to it as "Taste-All Tea," or "TAT" for short, because the taste was different for each person. It, indeed, tasted like all things. The most addictive quality of the tea was the recollection of the drinker's fondest desires and memories, and the spell put on the tea caused the user's body to become sick and twisted.

The school field, now overgrown with weeds, it was not as disorderly as it seemed. The wildflowers, the weeds—all of it was done intentionally. The wild plants were all herbs for creating that tea. The students would gather them in season, thinking they were just clearing the grounds. The heaps of "weeds" would be gathered into the barns on the pretext of burning them eventually. In truth, though, the herbs were there to dry out and be brewed into the tea by the cafeteria. Even the very steam of the tea had powerful effects over time.

Maybe that is why Goliath became who he was. Maybe the potency of the evil brew affected him more powerfully than even Miss Coffenayle knew.

Her studies taught her much, but similar to any other education, experience was the true teacher. Power over others was her laudanum. It was her magical tea. It was her obsession. Powerful and addictive, magic was irresistible to her. She loved dark power, *intoxicating* power, through and through. She cast her lot, and her mind was firm. She was determined to become completely evil.

The one thing that she had to not allow was regret. She may have liked the Mentors and Mr. Angelton, but that was now a moot point. She could not feel regret. She had to guard herself against that. She had to allow herself to feel nothing but selfish gratification. She was warned against trustworthiness, loyalty to friends, sincerely helpful acts, friendliness or unselfish courtesy, kindness, willing obedience of anything but evil, cheerfulness, financial thrift, bravery, spiritual cleanliness, and all forms of religious reverence. These things she could no longer allow herself to feel.

To feel remorse or possess virtue would cause light to enter her, and the light was now dangerous to one who had murdered and taken the oath to evil as she had done. Were there any good or light in her when she reached the Underworld at her death, she would not be allowed to become a tormentor queen. She would instead become one of the tormented. To embrace the darkness fully and to become entirely steeped in evil was the only way to escape being tormented for all eternity. Darkness was already sealed as her fate by her actions. Since darkness was now an absolute given, the choice was clear: become a victim or a victor!

Miss Coffenayle opened her eyes. She leaned back in her chair, quite satisfied with the results of her purging. She no longer had any regrets over what she did Angelton and the Mentor's. She was ecstatic in her joy! In fact, it was time for a couple of celebratory shots from the old cannon! She yelled from her desk at the door, "Patience! Cover your ears!" Then she loaded her cannon.

Patience reached into her drawer and put cotton balls in her ears, held in place with a phone operator's headset. At least she had a warning this time.

Coffenayle primed, loaded, and fired her cannon with three distinctly separate volleys of six shots each for a total of eighteen holes added to those already marking the doorway. She was in a grand mood now.

Patience Lovegood simply continued her work, quietly enduring yet more foolish displays from her employer. She threw away the cup of school's tea, which she poured every morning under Miss Coffenayle's watchful eye. She replaced with a tasty herb tea of her own blend that was the same color. Her boss was none the wiser, assuming that Miss Lovegood's overly quiet demeanor and seeming shyness was from the effects of TAT. It was okay with her that the secretary's body did not seem distorted. Magic, after all, was not an exact science.

23

The Plot Gets Even Thicker

Back at the classroom, Miss Emily continued teaching. She had moved out of mathematics and into spelling. Castlethorn was busy in the area where the floor and walls had been repaired. He did have some things to do there, but he took his time getting them done. He watched what he was doing, certainly, but he also was keeping one ear on what Emily was teaching. Lantern was showing him the unseen story. Miss Emily *certainly* had a ghost with her, no doubt about that. Castlethorn saw green, and she was teaching fine, but when she got stuck, he saw white emanating from the green, and *answers just came to Emily*. It was confirmed far too many times to be coincidental or a mere anomaly. This thing was real! *She was being helped by a ghost.*

The janitor believed in ghosts, certainly. That one in his shop was really nasty, something he did not understand at all. First of all, why was the mean ghost there in the first place? Why attack people who started looking through things? Why did it also attack people who tried to visit that one particular part of his shop? Why did it leave Castlethorn alone? And why was he the only one allowed to be there? It was almost like that thing was a watchdog, but it certainly was not there to protect him. It did not attack people who came near him. It only attacked strangers who tried to remain in that part of the shop or otherwise look around. So there must be something that the ghost did not want people to see. He would have to try something later, but he would need the boy to do it. Jimmy he could trust. Jimmy would not tell on him. Not his Jimbo! He liked the boy as both a good assistant and a friend. Jimmy was a "good hoomin bean."

Jimmy glanced across the room and caught Castlethorn's eye. The message from the apprentice was clear: *Please get me out of here!* So when Miss Emily ended her particular lecture point and glanced at her notes, he cleared his throat.

"Ahem! Um… Miz Emily?"

Emily looked up. "Yes, Mr. Castlethorn?"

"Um…may Ah borrowz my apprentish for de rest of da afternoon?"

"Jimmy, would you like to go with Mr. Castlethorn?"

The boy hesitated, and Emily was after him like a shot. She was immediately in front of his desk. "You worthless cur! I ask you something nicely, and you *defy* me? Me? Your teacher who slaves day after day to educate your thick noggin and to try to force something into the pea brain that inhabits it? You would defy me? Would you?"

"Uh…no, Miss Emily. I was just a little surprised you wanted me to go with him."

"Surprised? Surprised? You think I actually *want* you here, you smelly toad? You stinking pile of rat pellets! Get up out of that chair and do your duty! Now! Move it, rat poop boy!"

At that last remark, Jimmy jumped out of the chair and scurried over to Mr. Castlethorn. What an actress! He had a hard time hiding his smile. Little Tommy Littleton was not so constrained. He actually chuckled at "rat poop boy" and Miss Emily caught him in the act. She pointed directly at him and demanded that he present his knuckles. His desk had already been bashed several times that day, and one more good hit should break it like Emily promised.

Tommy was shocked because she had never to this point asked for him to present his knuckles. Whipshot used to do that to him. She would have him ball up his fists, and she would hit his knuckles with the flat side of the ruler. To use the edge of the ruler would have cut his fingers off. Now here was Miss Emily with her arms folded and the steel ruler glittering in the light, demanding his knuckles. "That's it, Little Tommy! You mangy skunk! Spread those fists!

Further! Further!" When the fists were just right, Miss Emily, kind Miss Emily, raised the ruler over her head, with the cutting edge down, gripping it two-handed like a Samurai sword, and brought it down with all her might. *Wham!* And *crack* went the desktop, split right in two...with Tommy's knuckles untouched.

Tommy cried out in shock and then pretended to have pain while making sure his fingers really were all there. He did not believe that she would have intentionally cut off a finger or two, but one could never be too careful. Accidents can happen. He added to it by bouncing up and down and hollering in apparent agony to bounce the splinters of wood off of his pants. He jumped up and trotted over to his shame closet, bent over and holding his hands, and climbed in. Emily took her cue now and shut him in. She only pretended to lock the door. She suspected that Tommy needed a place to hide while he smiled to himself. She was right. He did. He made sobbing noises to make it look good and because he had to cover any possible giggles. Miss Emily composed herself as the class all looked down silently. She turned to Jimmy and the janitor. "Mr. Castlethorn, would you kindly bring a new desktop to replace the one that Little Tommy has been mistreating? Clearly, he's been abusing school equipment."

"Yis, Miz Emily. Me and Jimbo here will replace it raht away. Would yese rathers we wait until after class?"

"Yes, Mr. Castlethorn, I would prefer if you *waited*," replied Miss Emily with a cool demeanor, acting as though the man were a fool asking a foolish question.

"An' I can brings Jimbo wifs me? Ta goes work in our office? I gots to get that desktop ready, and I kin do it faster and better with his help."

"Yes. You can take Jimb—I mean *Jimmy* with you. Now if you please, I have a class to teach!" She sounded so irritated and exasperated.

Mr. Castlethorn and Jimmy wasted no time getting clear of the classroom. They hustled down the hall, pole in hand, and Lantern dangling over Castlethorn's shoulder. "Thet floor's lookin' okay, Jimmy. We dun goods job there. We gots work in the office ta do now."

"What do I need to do in the office?

"Ya needs to helps me gets to tha bottom o' somethin.'"

"Oh?" Jimmy asked no more questions. He was not sure he wanted to know; whatever it was, he would just do it.

They opened the door and walked past the creepy collection of oddball items, jars, chemicals, and rust. Jimmy noticed that either the office smelled a little better or he was getting used to it. He guessed the latter of the two. They got to the posts of the machine that controlled the poltergeist. They stopped dead in their tracks. "Jimmy, ya ever heerd of a 'polterghost?' Um...poltergust...guts. No...wait... polter*geist* is da name. Herda him?" asked the old man.

"Uh...nope."

"Yese remembers that thing that was throwing my stuffs all outta order? That thing dat tried to get'cha?"

"Yeah. How could I forget?"

"Wahl, dat's a poltergeist. It's a really noisy ghost."

"*Ghost?*" Jimmy asked in alarm. "No way. No way am I going to deal with a ghost. I know this school is weird, the people are weird, and this office is the weirdest of all! Um...no offense."

"Heh! No offense taken, Jimbo. I bese knowing I ams a purdy weer' ol' man."

"Huh?" Jimmy was surprised and puzzled at Castlethorn knowing he was strange.

"Yeah, Jimbo. Somethin' is off about this whole thing."

"Yes...so?" Jimmy asked carefully.

"So we'uns gots a mysterious thing ta unravel."

"But...well... I am not sure what to ask you."

"I don't needs ya ta ask. I need ya ta listen. First, though, can yese keep secrets?"

"Yes. I keep secrets all the time. Nobody would believe me anyway, and nobody really even talks to each other about much at all."

"Good. Good. Das a good point!" Castlethorn smiled, but not a creepy smile like Jimmy would see in the classroom. This was a smile that was more kindly and wise. It hid the nasty stained and crooked teeth. Jimmy was glad.

"Okay den, Jimbo. Hey…yese dasn't mind me calling yese Jimbo, right?"

"No, I don't mind at all. I kind of like having a nickname."

"Okee then. Dat's a good thing, Jimbo!" Castlethorn smiled again. "Now lissen up goodly. Wese in a differn sorta sichyashun here. I believes dat the hoomin beans has others living here. Others that ain't living, dey bese daid, but deys living around us. You get me?"

"D-Dead people? Living here?" Jimmy thought for a moment, and Castlethorn let him think about it. The boy worked it over in his mind, squinting and shaking his head, then he suddenly looked surprised. His eyes got big. "*Ghosts?*" he exclaimed.

"Yis. Dat's right, Jimbo. Ghosts. I dasn't understand quite all of it yet, but this place is full of them."

"What… I mean…how…how do you know that ghosts are here?"

"Well, dat's the story. Yese sees muh Lantern over there?"

"Yes."

"He's gots a name, ya know."

"He does? What is it?"

"Lantern." Then Castlethorn roared with laughter until he coughed. Jimmy had to laugh too to break the tension. Then the janitor composed himself. "Awl right, Jimbo. Times fer serious talks now. I kin sees dem ghosties with the help of Lantern. Yese, remember how I spin him round and round?"

"Of course I do. You scare the pants of people when you do that."

"Ah ain't seed no one wiffout dere pantses, Jimbo. What'cha mean by dat?"

"Uh, nothing really, it's just a silly exaggeration. But you really do scare people."

"Uh-huh. Dat's intenshunulz. I wants peoples ta be thinkin' I am crazy. Dat way, they dassn't come poking around here in all mah good stuffs." He waved his around the office like it was a big tourist attraction. Jimmy wanted to say that people don't want to come poking around here, but he didn't; better to not hurt the old man's feelings. "I don't need peoples getting into muh stuffs. I dassn't needs peoples puttin their noses around where they dassn't belong. Not until I figures out what is going on here. Sumthin' is. I just kint thots of it."

"Yes, I know what you mean. I was hoping to learn why that noisy ghost back there keeps me out of the back room."

"Hmm. Yes…yese and ever-one elseez buts me. Not many comes here, but the ones dat does, he keeps 'em out."

Jimmy thought for a second about that picture frame with the "doctor-*ate.*" He wondered if that had something to do with all this. That Cassius person. He decided to take a chance and ask his new friend, his new boss. Jimmy said "Mr. Castlethorn, I want to show you something."

He led Castlethorn to the picture frame with the important paper in it. He showed him the paper, and Castlethorn picked it up for further examination. He got a good look at the paper and started to read it aloud. "Doctor-*ate*…awarded to Cassius—*aaaahggh!*" The old janitor fell back and grabbed his head in agony!

Jimmy acted quickly and pushed a box of rags over close to him and guided him backward into it. Castlethorn fell back with a thump and lay there, holding his head and gasping. "Ohhh. It harts, Jimbo. Veery badly, me haid harts!"

Jimmy was sort of paralyzed, not knowing quite what to do. He went over to the filthy sink and turned it on. The water seemed clear, so Jimmy emptied out and then rinsed a Mason jar. He brought his best friend a drink.

Castlethorn sat up and took it. He drank deeply. He finished the jar and threw it aside. It smashed, but the broken glass would find a good home among the other odds and ends. No danger of hurting anyone anyway. Castlethorn sat up and leaned forward, feeling better. "Ohh, Jimbo. Dats was a *bad* one."

"What happened?" Jimmy asked, quite concerned.

"Wells, if yer in fer a penny, yese is in fer a dollar. Or something lak that."

"What?"

"Never mind that, Jimbo. But this beses a secret 'tween us. I gets the fog and brain pain whenses I trahs to remember somethun I'm not suppos'ta."

"Not supposed to? Well, Mr. Castlethorn, who would want you to quit remembering something?"

"I dassn't knows. I really dasn't. Sumwon, doh, knoweez. Sumwon fur sure."

"What can I do for you, sir?"

"Wahl, Jimbo, Ah'm okay for now. The pain quits immediates when Ah stopz thinkun."

"You mentioned a 'fog.' What did you mean by that?"

"Well, yese see, when Ise try to merember somethun Ah'm not suppose' to, and that's the only reason I can figure for the pain, becuz Ah can remembers stuffs, jist not certain stuffs. When I tries to remember, my brain fills wi'f this greenish fogz. And it gets ahl cloudeez in muh head."

"Wow. I am so sorry."

"Yessir, me too. I wishes I coulds merember wut dat picture frame meenz tuh mees."

"Do you minds if I takes…um, *take* it with me?" Jimmy was starting to talk like him now. And he really did not want the old janitor to think he was poking fun at him. Jimmy tried again. "May I take that paper with me?"

"Um…sure, it don' botherz mees nun. Takes it…but keepees itz ower secret."

Jimmy pulled the paper out of the frame and folded it up, then tucked it inside his shirt. Then a thought occurred to him. "Are you feeling strong enough to show me something?"

"Sure, Jimbo. The pain stops and dussn't boddeer mees nun after I quits merembering."

"If you're okay, then I want you to take me to the machines that stop the poltergeist."

"Sure, let's goes."

They walked over to the machine, and Jimmy started to walk toward the back of the office alone. The invisible poltergeist started to come at him, wailing, howling, and throwing things all over the place. Jimmy then calmly stepped back past the electrodes, he was safe. Castlethorn activated the machine. The ghost stopped right where it was supposed to. It could come no further and retreated. Then Mr. Castlethorn turned the machine off, and it came after Jimmy again. It seemed to know that Jimmy had something. So Jimmy came back in with the paper and returned it to Castlethorn. The spirit came after him but left him alone when he stepped out of the area, even without the machine coming on.

Then he asked Mr. Castlethorn to walk past the electrodes. No response. Nothing. Then Jimmy tried to join him to walk to the back of the shop and had to retreat again. Alone, the janitor could remain without stirring anything up. Whenever Jimmy joined him, the poltergeist attacked. Then they tried to cover Jimmy up with a canvas and pass him through behind Castlethorn. That didn't work. They put Jimmy on a covered cart and tried to roll him past. The noisy ghost seemed to know it was Jimmy. There was no longer any way for Jimmy to get into the office or out of the office with anything important. This experiment cost several sets of tubes, but Mr. Castlethorn thought it was worth it.

After several tries, Jimmy suggested that Mr. Castlethorn bring something from the back of the shop and hand it through to him. They did this several times with several different items. No response. The ghost was silent. So then Jimmy suggested that maybe…just maybe…there were things that he was not supposed to personally *see* in the back room. They discussed the situation and knew that Jimmy could not go back there, but Castlethorn could. They could pass things from the back room into Jimmy's hands without any problems, so Jimmy could get things that were given to him. But what about things that Castlethorn was not supposed to remember? Could they get those through to Jimmy?

What if something that gave Castlethorn a headache to look at was also something Jimmy should not see? Yes! What if Castlethorn found something that gave him a headache, and he stuffed it in a bag without looking at it and trying to remember what it meant to him but then carried it to Jimmy? Could that work for them? No harm in trying. So they did.

Castlethorn went back into the shop and clanged and banged around a bit. A few things fell over. Castlethorn said he was okay, and finally, he emerged with a small object and the paper wrapped in a cloth. He brought it past the electrodes. So far, so good. He passed the object to Jimmy, and they waited. Nothing budged. No angry howling, no terrible noises or things being thrown all over the place. No danger that they could discern. Jimmy and his boss carefully moved toward the door, both of them backing up, watching the back of the office for any disturbances. Castlethorn spoke quietly, "Okays, Jimbo…walks out da door with the ting in yer shirt, along wiffs dat piece of paperz. It dassn't knows you gots it. Walks out slows and carefuls, and keeps yers eye out. Be ready ta runs back in here and gives me that thang back if dat poltergeist wants it back. Y'hear?"

Jimmy swallowed hard. "Yeah… I hear." He put the bundle under his shirt, buttoned it, and made sure it was all tucked in snugly and slowly backed out of the door. He made it up the staircase and to the hall. Castlethorn checked the hall so as to not be seen and then told Jimmy to walk just a few steps away and wait. Castlethorn closed the door. He went back down the stairs and activated the ghost-stopping machine. "Hey, you big ugly, knot-headed, clumsy, wart-faced poop-eater! Jimmy dun went outs de door with sumfun he *stole!*"

Immediately, the ghostly force kicked up a fuss. Thankfully, the ghost could not pass the electrodes. Then he replaced the tubes, tried again, but before the creature could reach them, Castlethorn said, "Wait a minnit! Mah mistake! I gaves dat to him. He stoles nuthunz!"

Then the ghost got quiet and retreated. No more disturbance.

"Hey, Jimbo! Comes on back! I think ah figgered it out!"

Jimmy came running back into the office. "What? What did you figure out?"

"Ah kin gives youse whatever Ah wants, but youse can't stealz muh stuff. That poltergeist won't lets you goes back there an' won't let yous seez anything either. But if'n I go back and gets it, an' it dussn't knowz da thing is forbidden, den I kin gives it to yuh, an' it don' comes affer you. Duz dat make senses, Jimbo?"

"No, but nothing does lately. Not ghosts, not the poltergeist, not your nutty idea. But…it *works!* And that is all that matters, boss!

Whether it makes sense or not…it *works*! I guess the poltergeist does not know everything."

"Yis, yis, it duz works, Jimbo. We figgered it out. Nowz wut?"

"Well, one other idea. What if we have you carry the forbidden item out and give to someone at the top of the steps?"

"Hmm." Castlethorn gave that idea a good hard thought. "Wahl…okay. Ah seez what ye're gettinz ats, but wut if da polter-guts comes after you at the top of the steps? He'd be way past da machine. He could get looses in da school and kilz peeples."

"Right. No way to try it out and see, not without a severe risk. I guess we have one good way, and that's all the way we have."

"Da's right, Jimbo. Letz leaves wahl enuff alone."

"I agree. So suppose we talk a minute. There's a lot I'm curious about. One thing for sure I gotta know, Mr. Castlethorn. *Why* do you cluck like a chicken when you spin Lantern around? Does that make him work better for you?"

"No, Jimbo, it don't. What I duz when I clucks is to look completely reedikulus. I duz it to looks crazy so nobody's axes mees eny questions. They jist thinks dat the nutty ol' man is jist fooling around. Even Coffenayle does not ask. She jist shakes her head and goes away. I dassn't wants for any anyone to knows I be seein' da ghosts."

"Well," Jimmy chuckled, "you sure had me fooled. Everyone else too." He still thought Castlethorn was crazy or something, but he knew now that Castlethorn was aware of what was happening. So that meant that he was trying to get "uncrazy" somehow. That made Jimmy feel so much better! Now what to do with the things he had? "So, Mr. Castlethorn, what about these things that you have given me? What do we do with them? I mean, these things that you can't remember…what good are they to us?"

Jimmy pulled up a stool and sat down, nearly sliding off of it when the seat tilted. He braced himself with his feet. Castlethorn found a chair with the woven cane nearly broken out of the seat. He turned it around backward to sit on the stronger part of the weave and leaned forward, his arms resting on the back of the chair.

"Hmmm…dat's a good question, me boy." He covered his mouth with a dirty hand and stroked his chin. After a few moments of stroking, he decided that maybe the new teacher could help. He could not understand *why*, but he just sort of...*thought* she could help, maybe. "Okees... I gots us an idear. Youse jist takes the stuffs to Miz Emily. Ah will go to the class with you so she knows you don' stole it. Ah won'ts talkz to her but Ah will gives herz a nod to goes ahed and takes my stuffs. Dat ways, if there's more stuffs, she knows yer ondee up an up. How's that sound, boy?"

Jimmy thought it over. He trusted Miss Emily and was convinced that she was trying to do good things. So he agreed. They talked for a minute about how careful they would have to be. It could be bad if they got caught trying to figure things out. Castlethorn confided that he had a sense for a very long time that there was something afoot. He believed that it was something bigger than he was able to handle. Maybe it was bigger than all of them were able to handle. What he knew for sure was that he could not take it on by himself. He also told Jimmy about the green and white image he would get from Lantern when he took it into Miss Emily's class.

"So," Jimmy asked, "how does Lantern work? What does it look like when you see a ghost?"

Castlethorn grabbed Lantern and sat back down beside Jimmy. He took lantern off of the pole and held it in both hands where Jimmy could see the glass panels.

"Wahl," Castlethorn explained, "to makes Lantern work, Ah has to spin him a-round. That generates the 'lectric somehow or t'other. When he gets full o' de 'lectric, Lantern sees the ghosts. I looks into his little window right there, sees? It will glow differ'nt colors, depending on the type of ghost we's seeing."

"Colors?" Jimmy asked.

"Yep. Colors. Green, yellow, white, and red. Yese see, da green and yellow ones is good. De white wunz is hoomin beans, dey is peeplez. But when yese sees a *red* one, yese best be for runnin' away. Dem's are de bad ones. The brighter da red, the worstest. My pol-ter-guest? He's a red one. But that ghost whut follows Miss Emily all around the room? He's a green one. Bright green. And when he's talkin' ta her, white colors come off him, and it seems like it touches her."

At last, thought Jimmy. *I know what 'hoomin beans' are. They are 'human beings'.* Then he said out loud, "Touches her? That sounds dangerous."

"Ah thought so at ferst, but Ah finds out lader dat's not the case. She seems ta learn somethun from him when it goes white and touches her. She gets da smarter wi'f math and stuffs."

"I see," Jimmy said thoughtfully, but he really did not see all that well. He was trying to take it all in.

"So," said Castlethorn, "Ah believe dat Miz Emily is bein' tot while she's teaching."

Jimmy believed Castlethorn because he had seen this happen in the classroom. Emily would look like she was stuck, *really* stuck on a problem. Then she would sort of perk up, nod, and not only solve the problem, but she would be able to explain to the class just how she went about doing it. She could recite step by step the whole process for getting the answer. Not only that, but she taught well without hesitation! If Castlethorn's idea was not the right one, it was at least an idea and one that made sense, considering all the other madness that made sense.

"Say you are right about all this," said Jimmy, "and there are... ghosts here. One of them teaches Miss Emily to do smart things. What about the others? What do they do?"

"Well, Jimbo, I ain't quite figgered that one out yet. That is part of what we are working on. We needs to figure out what them other ghosts is doing here."

"Do you have any idea who they might be?"

"Every time I try to think of them, Jimmy, my brain goes all foggy, and Ah can't remember. I has my suspicions, but every time I try to put it together...well—"

"Yes, I get it, Mr. Castlethorn. Okay, I am in this with you. You are not alone anymore. I want to get this stuff under my shirt to Miss Emily and see what she thinks."

"Yessir, Jimbo! You duz that. And bese ye careful too, all right? We dasn't wants ta get caught."

Jimmy walked toward the door, and Castlethorn followed him. He had Jimmy wait until he went out the door and cleared the hallway, both ways. Then he waved Jimmy forward, and there was no grass growing under the boy's feet when they touched the school's wooden floor. He raced for Miss Emily who was getting ready to dismiss the class. He stopped just shy of the doorway and caught his breath.

"Class, I will need all of you to do your homework tonight and be ready for class tomorrow. Testing will start to happen soon, and you will need to be caught up. That includes *you*, Jimmy!" Jimmy's mind was blown. She knew he was there, even though her back was turned. Maybe her friendly ghost told on him?

"Yes, Miss Emily," Jimmy said with little enthusiasm.

"Jimmy, can I see you after class about your homework assignments? You missed getting to copy them down with the rest of your classmates."

"Yes, Miss Emily," said Jimmy in the same monotone.

The classroom stood at attention at Emily's command, and all of them recited the school anthem. They were dismissed; the show was over. They got through another day as a team, as a class, without being discovered by Miss Coffenayle. It was uncanny how things were progressing. The class was actually learning important things about important subjects by the methods that Miss Emily was using to teach the class. They were not only learning things, but they were remembering them and were enjoying it. By a sensible agreement, they had to be careful to not reveal their joy to the rest of the school. The rest of the classes were still being abused, still being punished, still facing up to their taskmaster teachers.

Tommy passed by Jimmy and whispered to him to remember to have Castlethorn replace his desktop. Jimmy said that he believed that Castlethorn would do it later tonight.

The class departed. As soon as they knew they were alone, Jimmy stepped over toward Miss Emily's desk and said that he had something to show her. She walked to the door of the classroom and closed it. They could not be too careful. She joined him at the desk and unfolded the piece of paper from the picture frame for further study. He also removed the bundle from his shirt, wrapped in a more or less clean shop rag. At least it didn't stink. He carefully unwrapped the little bundle and saw it was the back of...a *picture frame?* Is that what this was? He lifted it off of the rag and turned it over with both hands. It was in poor condition, and he did not want it to fall apart. The brown varnished wood was coming apart at the corners; the joints were loose.

The frame was badly affected by grease, dust, and time itself. The glass was surprisingly unmarred. There was a picture of a beautiful young lady. It said "*To Cassius, My Forever Love. From Your Darling Darla.*"

Jimmy was immediately stricken by something in his heart. Something deep and wonderful; something terribly painful. It was like a poem about true love lost and forever separated.

Emily was also awestruck. The picture was so very important. Tears welled up in her eyes. Her heart ached for this lovely Darla. She could not help but to stare at those eyes. That photo. It was just a photo, right? But it seemed to be so much more to Miss Emily. She knew there was something there, something critical. This beautiful lady was simply radiant in her life at one time. She was full of love and life and joy. At the same time, the newest teacher also knew that something terrible had happened. She knew that Darla was horribly sad and hurt. Odd. How could she know that about somebody in a picture? This was a different sort of picture, though.

Emily had not seen many photographs in her life, but somehow, this one just stuck out almost as though it was communicating something to her and Jimmy.

Jimmy sensed this too, that something was very important about Darling Darla. He could not tell what. Jimmy somehow understood that Castlethorn had obviously held onto this picture and gave it to him for a reason. This was no accident. The old man knew that this picture was coming straight to Miss Emily. They knew now that Emily was communicating with a ghost of some kind, that she was being inspired by some quiet genius. This mystery was growing deeper and deeper by the minute! Jimmy believed that they were getting into something far deeper than they could understand. He did not know what or why, but they were now part of something very important. This was, well, he hated to say it being a young man of his awkward years, a true love. He also knew that Emily knew it.

Emily looked up at Jimmy and got his attention. They could not risk standing here looking at this any longer. Anyone could wander by and catch them. This was not a risk that was theirs to take. It would not be fair if they were caught by someone because they were being careless. There was a great responsibility here, and they could not take a chance. Emily told Jimmy to get started on repairing that desk. She took the paper, the "doctor-*ate*," and carefully stacked it among her books and things. She hid the picture among her other teaching items in her box, and Jimmy walked over to the broken desk. He moved it away from the other desks to a corner of the room where he could work on it more easily. *Yeah, right*, he thought to himself. Just like he knew what he was doing. He started working to carefully pull the remnants of the desktop off of its frame.

Just then, the very moment that they were doing what they were supposed to, Miss Coffenayle walked in. She had seen the closed door and was curious. Seconds sooner, she would have caught them with the paper and the picture.

"Why, Miss Emily!" she stated with feigned cheerfulness. "I am glad to see that you are getting things ready to go home for the night." Then she noticed young Jimmy, the new apprentice. "And how are you, young man? I see that Mr. Castlethorn has you quite busy already! Good! Remember to fix that hole in my school," she said as she pointed over her shoulder to the broken wall. "Good to see you diving into your new work with such relish. How are your studies?"

Jimmy answered without apparent nervousness or hesitation, "I am doing very well, I believe, but Miss Emily is the final judge of that."

She turned to the teacher. "Well?"

"That miserable toad is doing well enough in spite of his *obvious* lack of character and general disposition to make mischief," replied Emily coolly and rolling her eyes.

"Ah," replied Coffenayle. "You are indeed a true educator and unafraid of the facts. I see that I have chosen well." She smiled a wicked grin and looked Emily in the eye. "Keep it up, Miss Emily. You know what we are capable of here."

"Indeed I do," Miss Emily replied meekly. She knew very well what Miss Coffenayle was capable of, and she was ever so glad that Mr. Mentor promised to always be near.

"Very well, then, I will leave you to it. Make sure that Castlethorn does not work this student too hard. I don't need him falling asleep in class. We need all of our students alert and learning. Goodnight!"

"Goodnight, Miss Coffenayle," said Miss Emily. She turned to Jimmy. "Jimmy, what do you say to your principal? I thought I taught you miscreants something better than rudeness!" She scowled. Jimmy looked up, actually nervous. He did not want to slight Miss Coffenayle, especially now with their mystery to solve.

"Um...sorry, Miss Coffenayle," Jimmy said and intentionally bowed his head to her. "I am very sorry to have made a mistake and I hope that you have a wonderful night," he said sheepishly.

Coffenayle put her chin up, clearly pleased at his contrition. Her arrogant, cold, and terrible blue eyes glared at him and twinkled with the most gleeful pride at having caused this student-turned-work-man to feel fear. Fear of her; fear of her great power. That boy was participating in the end of the world and did not even know it. The ignorant little wretch! How she hated these brats! "Very well then. Miss Emily, you needn't punish this student. It was only a small social slight, an accident. I am sure that it will never be repeated, correct, *boy*?" She nodded toward him. Then she just...stared.

"Y-yes." Jimmy felt a cold chill go through him. It was a like bitter ice, black and terrible. He felt it from her as though the principal was radiating something. It was like a stink, a terrible polluting odor but one that he could not smell. He could sense it. He did not like it. It made him cringe; it made him feel terrible and worthless. There was for a moment rippling through him absolute hopelessness, a feeling of absolute terror, and doubt.

He was scared and cold inside as though life itself was being torn from his very soul. He was hopeless, depressed, miserable, and wanted to die, but at the same time, he feared death. Never, even under the punishments of Miss Whipshot, had he ever felt so...*alone and useless!* It lasted only for as long as the principal stared at him with those cold, clear, and terribly blue eyes. Then she broke off her gaze. Thank heaven! It was over. Poor Jimmy had just experienced his first brush with true evil. He hoped that it would never brush up against him ever again.

"Very well then," Miss Coffenayle grinned as though she had won some great victory as she left the room. This was the kind of victory that one achieved by stepping on a crippled ant. She loved every minute of picking on a boy whom she knew was helpless to stop her. She was the ultimate bully, cruel and terrible. She exited with a great haughty step, feeling oh so very special indeed. One could only hope that her days were numbered, for such evil people do no good in this world.

Jimmy was still in terrible doubt and shame, even though Miss Coffenayle was gone. He hung his head even lower. Not even Whipshot made him feel so low. So worthless. He felt like the lights inside of him had gone out. All was darkening.

Maybe the good he was feeling just moments ago was too weak to overcome Miss Coffenayle's evil. Maybe he was beaten. Maybe he was too weak and no good. No, there…there was no doubt. He was just a boy, after all, dealing in the affairs of adults who were much too powerful for the likes of him. He was just a toad after all. No, he was worse than that. He was a useless, no-good, little wart on the base of a toad's—

"*Jimmy!*"

He felt hands grasp his shoulders and shake them gently but desperately. Someone needed his attention. Someone was touching him warmly, kindly. He was feeling aroused now, awake. Better.

He opened his eyes. Emily was leaning over him. Her eyes were scared. "Jimmy?" she asked. "Jimmy, are you okay?"

Jimmy suddenly realized that he was on the floor. He did not even know that he had fallen or when. He blinked twice and shook his head. He tried to sit up and could only do so with Emily's assistance. She sat him up and let him rest a moment. He was breathing hard, and his pulse was racing, but he was recovering quickly. He shook his head again and felt his strength return. The light was coming back on inside of him. Slowly, he stood as he braced himself against a nearby chair. He stood and wobbled, but just a bit, and then regained strength. He was breathing normally now, and his heart was no longer pounding. He looked at Emily and then sat down on a chair. She helped him down and pulled a chair over to him and sat beside him. She waited for him to speak.

"That was terrible," he said simply. "I did not even know that I had fallen down."

"What happened to you?" Emily asked with obvious concern. She was noticing his lovely brown eyes for the first time.

He looked into her hazel eyes, those elegant languid emerald pools. It was like he'd never seen Emily before. "It was really bad. I lost all hope. I was cold and dark and afraid inside. There was nothing…just nothing. I could not stand it. Everything was just…dark. I could not hear anyone or see anything. I was in a terrible empty place. I did not even know that I fell—"

"Well, you're back now from whatever terrible place you were in. Yes, I believe you were wherever 'there' was. You're not there anymore. You're safe now," said Emily. "I've got to get going." Emily gathered up the things she needed to take home and was moving for the door.

Suddenly, Castlethorn burst into the room, gasping for air. He was pushing a cart with a new wooden desktop on it. He had been running, at least the best he could. He had Lantern with him. "Wha' hapin here?" he asked between gasps. "Is youse all right, Miss Emily? Jimmy? Is youse okay heerz?"

"Yes," said Emily matter-of-factly. "I was just leaving." On that note, she walked out. She knew nothing about Jimmy's agreements with Castlethorn and did not want to discuss it now. With Miss Coffenayle about, it was hard to tell when or where she might be listening. Emily walked down the hall, greatly aware of the weight of the treasures in her teacher's box. For the first time, she began to feel just how dangerous all of this could become. She hoped Mr. Mentor was up for a discussion. She hoped he would be at her teacher's dorm. She amused herself by thinking how strange it was to *hope to meet with a ghost*. She quickened her pace and kept a low profile as she left the school. She was, after all, a girl with something to hide. She had become a spy.

"Jimbo…wha' happin here?" The old man was kneeling in front of his apprentice, his young *friend*. If something happened to Jimmy, he would never forgive himself. "Yese kin talks to me, my boy. Yese knows ye can."

"How did you know something was going on?"

"Wahl, Ah was coming over here wi'f the desktop and parts. Ah had Lantern wiff me and Ah gev him a spin, lahk I always do, just to sees what maht be happening. Then he shows me thuh dark red. In yer classroom. Bad dark red. The evil kind o' ghost. I thought muh poltergeist might a caught you passing my treasures to Miss Emily. She has them, raht?"

"Yes, she does. And she will take good care of them too. But—"

"Yes, Jimbo?"

"There was no ghost."

"Say agin?" he raised his bushy eyebrows, bloodshot eyes wide.

"There was not a ghost. No one was here but me, Emily and Miss Coffenayle."

"Hmm. Wahl, les' you and mees work and talk. Quietly."

They worked on the desk, and Jimmy told him everything that happened with Coffenayle's cold stare and how it affected him. Castlethorn made absolutely sure by asking Jimmy about it a few times that there was no evil ghost around. No poltergeist, no spook, no nothing was in the room. The thing was, Lantern was indicating the truth because Lantern was never wrong. It was like striking a good dry match. Lantern worked every single time. Never had there been a failure at it detecting a ghost, and he never had any lights show up when no ghost was present, at least not before. This was the first time in years that a red light appeared without some kind of manifestation of an evil spirit. They concluded that maybe the lantern could pick up evil power too if the power was strong enough. Maybe Coffenayle was friends with evil or something. They did not know, but they did know that Jimmy was affected by something and that Lantern picked it up.

The desk was soon finished, and so was the conversation. There was no one in the school but them as Coffenayle had left. Her office was closed, and it was time for Jimmy to get some sleep. He and Castlethorn bade goodnight, and Jimmy went back to his dorm to join his classmates. Castlethorn said that he would finish the wall on his own, that Jimmy had been through enough for one night.

There was a lot on Jimmy's mind, but tonight was shower night, and he was late. He only hoped to be able to sleep after his cold shower. All the hot water was undoubtedly gone by now.

24

Questions, Answers, and Revelations

Emily made a widely berthed circuit around her little house. She looked around for signs of intrusion. She hoped she did not have any unwanted visitors again. The windows were all intact. There was no one hiding in the bushes. Everything seemed normal. She was now more cautious than she ever thought to be at any other time in her life. She was holding onto something valuable, and she knew it. Why she knew it, she could not tell, but she did know it. She was even using an old "spy trick" she learned from one of her classmates when she lived at the dorm.

Emily put a small piece of tape over the doorjamb by the doorknob. If the tape was broken, as it easily would be, she would know someone had opened that door. She suspected correctly that Miss Coffenayle had given someone a key to get in and tear her place up that one night. Tonight, Emily inserted her key, turned the knob, and the tape broke. She was probably safe.

She entered her home and turned on the light. No mess, thank goodness. First things first. She checked every room and closet. She put her school things in order for the morning and took a quick bath. She put on nighttime clothes, something appropriate for entertaining a guest. She turned her blankets down on her bed so she could just lay down and go to sleep after her visitor left. Then Emily sat in the living room with her curtains drawn. She had arranged two chairs sitting directly across from one another. She hoped it looked inviting;

it was now time to call on Mr. Mentor, if that was possible. She felt awkward about calling out to someone, a ghost, who may or may not be present. "Um, Mr. Mentor, are you there? I would *really* like to speak with you now. I hope you can hear me."

"Yes," a familiar voice softly responded. "I am here. Thank you for this lovely seat in your home."

Emily looked at the chair and watched as an impression formed in the cushion on the seat and in the back. Then he began to appear. The familiar form of her trusted friend, complete with his cane and proper watch chain, slowly faded into view. Emily believed, somehow, that he could stop his appearance anywhere between invisible and appearing completely human. She wondered if all ghosts could do that.

"No," Mr. Mentor answered with a grin, "not all ghosts can do what you see me do. There are many who can, yes, but not all."

"Hello, Mr. Mentor," said Emily as though an old friend had just dropped by for a visit, which indeed he had. "I am glad you came."

"Do tell," he grinned.

"I think you already know something about this, but for the sake of time, I will just tell you what I have. Mr. Castlethorn gave some things to Jimmy." She was holding the gifts upside down on her lap. "I want you to tell me what you know about these things, please. I need you to be completely honest, if you would."

"Well, then, show me what you have, Miss Emily," the old man said politely.

"I have this 'doctor-*ate*' from Cassius Lawrence Thorn. And I have a picture of a lady named Darla. Both of these things came from the back office of Mr. Castlethorn."

"I see. And what would you like to know again?"

"I—that is, we, being Jimmy, Mr. Castlethorn, and myself— would like to know more about these items, why they are in Mr. Castlethorn's shop, and who these people are."

"I...understand," said Mr. Mentor. He seemed to be hesitant, almost unwilling to talk about these artifacts. "Was there some risk getting these things? Was there any danger for you or Jimmy?" he asked earnestly.

"Yes. Yes, there was some risk. There is a poltergeist in Mr. Castlethorn's office that attacked Jimmy."

"I see. From where did you learn the term *poltergeist*? That is quite an impressive word, all things considered."

"That is what Mr. Castlethorn calls it. The spirit is very dangerous. It attacks any student who tries to enter the back of the engineering office."

"Oh, dear. Jimmy…is he all right? The poor boy!"

"Yes, Jimmy is fine. There is a machine in the engineer's office that stops the spirit from attacking if you leave the area immediately."

"I am aware of that machine. Quite the invention, wouldn't you say?"

"Quite so," answered Emily. "But who built it? What is it doing in the engineer's office, anyway? Was the poltergeist there first? Or was the machine?" She sat back quietly. It was obvious that she was not going to say anything else until she had an answer.

Mr. Mentor leaned forward on his cane, both hands grasping the handle. He put his chin on his hands and even nibbled at his fingers a bit. After what seemed to be an hour, he looked up.

"Emily, first of all, know that I was aware that they found their way around that poltergeist. He is of a lower order of spirit. Think of it as a sort of watchdog, like you would find at a junkyard. He can make noise and cause injury, but it cannot think well for itself. Nor does it communicate well with its handlers. They count on the noise and threat that the spirit presents to frighten people off. Fortunately, it is not all-knowing. That is how they are able to get things past and into your hands. Our friends were correct in the way they dealt with it," he began.

His mood suddenly became somber. "Now, there is much that you must learn in a very short time. We are almost but not quite too late. There is a very dangerous person that—"

Emily cut him off without trying to be rude. "Yes… Miss Coffenayle."

The old man looked up, his eyes wide, his mouth partially open. His normal dignity left him for a moment. "What do you know about her?"

"We think she is evil."

"That's a very *strong* word to be used to describe a fellow human being, Miss Emily," he stated in a chastising sort of way. "This evil you speak of. How did you discover it?" he asked as though intrigued.

"Do you know about Mr. Castlethorn's friend he calls Lantern?"

Mr. Mentor threw his head back and laughed. "Oh, yes, that poor guy has been chasing me around with that contraption of his for years. He claims it is a ghost detector. The thing is…as you and Jimmy have guessed…is that he is *right!*"

"So…he really does see ghosts?"

"Well, not actually ghosts themselves. But he does see an energy signal that his lantern can detect. Different energies glow different colors. There are many ghosts here, but most you don't need to worry about. They are here because they refuse to move away from this plane of existence. I will tell you nothing more about them. But I will tell you what the lantern's signals mean: Good is yellow or green, white signals are living humans, and sometimes white signals may show when power is being exerted in a good way. And red indicates—"

Emily cut him off again, "Evil!"

"Yes, dear child. Evil. Now I must ask you to stop cutting me off, if you please. It is rude."

"Sorry."

"Not only is it rude, but you are tipping your hand as to what you are thinking. For the purpose of this discussion, you are fine, but if you do that in the presence of an enemy, you can get hurt by accidentally telling them your secrets. When that happens, you can give away things about yourself that you don't mean to give away. For you and Jimmy, that is a very dangerous thing. By the way, how is your nemesis, Margaret?"

"She is fine. She actually works with us to trick the principal. I won't have a teacher's pet and I have not any need of a class snitch. Margaret is working with us to makes things appear as though I am the new Miss Whipshot and that she is still the snitch. We do that to hide from Miss Coffenayle what is truly going on."

"Well, now, I impressed with everything that you just said," smiled Mentor. "You have a very sound strategy to keep Miss Coffenayle off of your back."

"Thank you." Emily blushed a bit and hoped he did not notice. He did, of course, but he did not show it. No use in further embarrassing the poor girl. Besides, there were important things at hand. He had to decide what parts to tell her. The whole story all at once would be overwhelming and might scare them out of helping him. Mentor understood that he had to lead them to the places where they could discover the truth for themselves, in their way, in their own time. This was the way of the Almighty. This was God's errand, and Mentor was naught but a servant to God. So how would he guide them without burdening them too much? He sat silently for a moment, leaning on his cane and brooding.

"Mr. Mentor?" Emily quietly interrupted his musings. "May I show you something?" She picked the items off of her lap, stood up, and set them on her chair, face down. She looked out the window, searching for possible eavesdroppers. Mr. Mentor smiled. She was careful. Good.

"You needn't worry, child. We are quite alone. I saw to that. And there is no way anyone can listen in on our discussion at all."

Emily felt reassured enough to sit back down. She handed the larger item toward Mr. Mentor first. Then she remembered that he was a ghost. "Can you hold this? Or can you just look at it?"

"Oh," he said, "I can handle objects as you have seen me do. But it takes a lot of energy and concentration. It is hard for us to move solid objects in your world, particularly when we are visible to you living souls. Appearing takes energy too. So I would rather you just hold it for me. I won't get so tired that way." She held the paper and unfolded it. Mentor looked at it and immediately nodded. He was very pleased.

"What do you make of this, Mr. Mentor?"

"The question is, dear heart, what do *you* make of it?"

"Well, this is a 'doctor-*ate*' for Cassius Lawrence Thorne."

"Yes…well, almost…it is not a long 'A' sound at the end," Mentor said with a smile. "It is not 'doctor-*ate*.' It is pronounced more like 'doctor-*it*.' Say it together quickly. Doctorate."

"Doctorate."

"Yes. Do you kids know what a doctorate is?"

"No, but I know it comes from a university. Harvard."

"Yes. Very good. The man, Cassius, holds at least one degree from Harvard."

"A degree?"

"It is like a diploma that a high school student gets upon graduation, but in college, they call them degrees. The recipient has studied to the level of either a bachelor, a master, or a doctor. Thus, we have a bachelor's degree, a master's degree, and a doctorate. The recipient of a doctorate becomes a doctor of his or her art or science. That is the highest degree of study."

"So this was a very smart person."

"Yes. Perhaps even a genius."

"I see. So…why would this be in Castlethorn's office?"

"I am delighted, Emily, that you found this. I truly am. I think that you are onto something great. I think that you will need Jimmy and Margaret to help you in this thing. Is Margaret trustworthy?"

"Yes, I believe she is. Besides, who would she rat to? Her teacher is ill."

"She could go directly to the principal, you know."

"No, I don't think she would. I think that Margaret is going to be on our side."

"So…you are choosing 'sides.' That is an interesting choice of words."

"I…don't know, Mr. Mentor…but it seems more and more like there is something evil going on here…" Her voice trailed off.

"Why do you hesitate to speak?"

"It just seems silly, now that I am thinking about it."

"What seems silly?" he asked earnestly.

"The idea that we are working against evil. But what else could it be? Jimmy got hurt today."

"What?" Mentor seemed shocked. Naturally, he knew all about the event between Jimmy and Coffenayle. For now, he behaved as though he did not to draw out what Emily knew but in her own way. He wanted to allow her to come to him with what she knew, to come to terms with it. So much was riding on this. So badly he wanted to tell her, but she had to find things out as she was strong enough to take them. She had come so far, talking with a dead man's spirit and all, but Mentor was warned to not carry things too far with the kids. The whole chair leg thing had been built up gently over time. Emily saw other things happening before the chair leg event. Certain truths had to be arrived at gradually. He had to be careful and let her arrive at her own conclusion.

"Well, he was not hurt exactly. He is okay now. But he did receive some kind of terrible shock."

"How so?"

"Miss Coffenayle called him a *boy* but did it in such a strange way that he actually fainted from the sound of her voice. This is concerning to me. I think that Coffenayle did that on purpose. So how much of that power does she actually have?"

What Miss Coffenayle did to Jimmy to make him pass out, Emily did not know exactly. Mentor, though, *did* know. He would not tell her what he knew, not just yet. She was not ready to know, but she would be soon. Things were coming to a head faster than Mr. Mentor would have liked. The opposition was quite clever, and they were trying to make their final moves so quickly that Mr. Mentor would not be able to keep up if he delayed. Time, though, was still on Mentor's side, even if by a narrow margin.

"Power, you say?" quizzed Mr. Mentor.

"I don't know what else to call it. Something knocked out Jimmy, and Miss Coffenayle seemed to be the one who caused it."

"Do you believe in 'powers,' Emily? Please do tell me the truth. This is far too important to try to impress me with what you think might be the 'correct' answer. You need to tell me exactly what is inside you right now. Tell me how you feel about this whole thing," Mr. Mentor said with a grave expression. He leaned forward on his cane as was his habit when he was in deep thought. He watched her carefully and somberly but kindly. Emily could feel a great heaviness and seriousness about him, a man who was normally light and airy in his demeanor. She weighed her next words carefully and chose them with great intent.

"I have learned a great deal lately," she began. "Even a week ago, I would not have ever dreamed that I would become a teacher. I mean, I know that this is not actually real and I know that I am being used by the principal for something. She is very selfish and only cares for herself. I grow nervous when she smiles because I know that is when she wants something. I know now that she is a...very *bad* person. I know that this, whatever *this* is, needs to end. I don't know what will happen to us students. We are all orphans and abandoned children, but I do know that most of us are good. We must be to get along in a place like this. We count on each other for our survival. I am glad that you freed us from Whipshot, and whatever I can do to help you make all of this right, I will do it."

Mr. Mentor continued to lean on his cane. He brooded a bit and then tilted his head back, looking up. His face seemed to almost have a light shine on it, Emily noticed. He remained in that state for a few seconds, and then the light faded. He looked back at Emily; he was again his normal sunny self. "I have chosen well, and so have you, Miss Emily. You and your two new friends. The three of you were chosen, but you had to make the final decision for yourselves."

"Decision?" asked Emily, a bit shocked. "I have no right to choose for my friends."

"That is correct, and you have not chosen for them. They have chosen to follow you, and since you are following me in this matter, it is only natural that they would come along. And they will. You have assessed Margaret correctly. She was the teacher's pet only for the sake of her own survival. She has a good heart, but you must very careful to not give her a reason to turn on you because she could go right to the evil side if she becomes afraid that you have betrayed her. Jimmy is a brave and capable lad. He has no idea of who he is or the good that he has done. He...well, he would follow you to the ends of the earth," Mentor said with a knowing twinkle in his eye.

Emily nearly blushed again, knowing what Mr. Mentor meant.

"So...it *is* evil that we are fighting?" Emily responded thoughtfully.

"Yes, in every sense of the word," Mentor replied matter-of-factly. "You three are about to do some very important things, things that you were chosen to do from the beginning of your lives. You were prepared for this job and put here for that very purpose."

"Put here? By...um... *God*?" Emily swallowed hard.

"Yes. By God. He knew that you would be needed in this capacity. Your lives have been hard, yes, but these things made you strong. God allowed you to pass through these things to train you for this very purpose. He sent me here to teach you, specifically how to do your jobs. How to complete this...mission, to say it more accurately. There is a very real war that began long ago in heaven, one that continues on Earth." Mr. Mentor stopped right there. There was nothing more him to say at this point.

"War?" Emily asked, puzzled.

"Yes. A war started by the devil himself, named Lucifer, who rebelled against God and became Satan."

"I have so many questions for you, Mr. Mentor!"

"Yes, but I cannot give you anymore guidance than that. You will learn what you need to know as time goes on. I am not here to preach to you or to teach you about God, other than this: God is real. He sent Jesus who died for you, me, and all of us. It is in his holy name that we are able to fight evil. That is all I can give you. The rest you will learn on your own, if you make the correct choices. For now, you are here to help me win this fight. To beat Miss Coffenayle. Do you, for yourself, accept what I have told as true?"

Emily's mind spun around and around. She thought so many wonderful thoughts that she could not comprehend them all. She felt supremely loved. Her heart felt on fire. She *knew* that Jesus, whom she had already heard of from her parents, was helping them to fight. Her eyes were wet. All she could do was say. "Yes, I will do what God wants me to do. I know He is there helping us."

"Miss Emily, you have made a wonderful choice. Tell your two friends about it, and see what they say too. Don't worry about the words. Just say what is in your heart. For now, keep all these things secret from all the other students. This battle is for you three only."

"I will, Mr. Mentor."

"Now I know that you have done a lot tonight, but there is more yet to do. That doctorate. Whose is it?"

"It belongs to someone named Cassius Lawrence Thorne or Cassius L. Thorne," she said as though stating the obvious.

"Yes. Have you heard the name Cassius before?"

"No."

"Then you don't know that the nickname for Cassius would be..."

"For short? Cassie?"

"Shorter."

"Um... Cass?"

"Precisely!" Mr. Mentor slapped his knee, very pleased indeed. He was smiling. "Now, say the nickname with the middle initial and the last name. Work it out very slowly." He trailed off and let her brilliant young mind work.

"Cass... L... Thorne..." Emily's eyes grew narrow with concentration.

Cass L. Thorne, she thought and shook her head a bit. Then suddenly, her eyes lit up with great excitement! She exclaimed, "*Castlethorn!*"

"Yes! Ha! I knew you could do it!"

"This degree, this doctorate, belongs to *Mr. Castlethorn?*" she stated as a fact and also questioned her own statement in the same breath. "But that's—"

"Impossible? Heh! You, Miss Emily, who consorts with a ghost, sees objects move with invisible help, witnessed a poltergeist try to kill people. You who recently aided a friend who was stricken unconscious by witchcraft. How have you become any kind of judge over what is *impossible?* My dear young woman, you are *living the impossible!*"

Emily sagged in her chair. She was overcome by her mentor's words. She did not know what to say. Indeed, *she was living the impossible.* So much in so little time. Mr. Mentor let her sag a bit, taking it all in. He did not have much longer; there were other things to do. She would also have to get some sleep.

"Now, sit up straight, Miss Emily," he said very gently and with perfect understanding of her situation. She had much on her plate right now, yes, but there was work to be done. He would not push Emily past her threshold of capability; he was given a particular insight into how much she could take. She had more room for learning, even now. She was a peculiarly strong young woman, a true warrior who chose her friends wisely.

"There is more for you to learn. You have a second gift here, I believe?"

Emily straightened herself and became the student again. She had experienced a great epiphany tonight, but that was not all she was here to do. This was all very, very real, and she would not back down, especially not now. If he had something more to teach her, then she was the willing student. She was now locked into this thing, completely committed. "Okay, Mr. Mentor... I am ready to know about this gift." She offered him the picture, and he exerted the effort to take from her hand. She allowed him to have it. Mr. Mentor looked at it with a heavy sigh.

"Ah, Darla! Poor, poor Darla!"

"You know her? Not that I am surprised at this point."

"Yes. We were great friends once. And I hope to be great friends with her again very soon. You can help with that. It is very interesting that Cassius—never call him that, by the way, not just yet—chose this picture to give you."

"Why is it so interesting?"

"Because this shows that Cassius is not as lost inside Castlethorn as he seems to be."

"Lost? Inside?"

"Yes. You will be instrumental, the three of you, in restoring much that has been lost." He returned the picture to Miss Emily, the warrior-teacher and his friend. "But enough of all this for now. You need to get some rest. I know that you feel too burdened to sleep, but I will help tuck you in."

They walked over to her bed, neatly made, and he raised the turned down blankets. She climbed into the bed. He covered her up. Then he did something unexpected. He tapped her gently on the head with his cane. He turned away, bade her goodnight, and turned out the lights. She was aware of nothing more until she rose for school the next morning, completely refreshed. She could not possibly know that she had only slept for an hour and seventeen minutes precisely.

25

Coffenayle's Promotion

A different sort of interview was taking place in Coffenayle's office at the very same moment as Mr. Mentor's talk with Emily. Coffenayle was, as per custom, bowing before an ever larger and more powerful-looking Malovent. She thought he was simply grand! He was taller and broader. His mighty key dangled from his left sleeve, bigger and shinier than ever! His skull belt was broader and decorated now with the heads of cruel monsters she could not identify. One day soon, he told her, his belt would be simply dripping with human souls, forever his captive and hers to torment...as queen. Yes, she would be queen! It was assured now. She had demonstrated her power to strike a person down with the mere mention of a single word spoken with evil intent. Malovent was indeed pleased!

The office was decorated in the usual fashion with the chalk outline on the floor, but the geometry was not quite as complex. And there were fewer candles. Malovent had taught her a new way of doing things. He did not need as much help from her as he used to. He was becoming stronger and stronger because of her faithful devotion to evil. Her discipleship, as she continued to study, would soon give him the ability to travel freely on the earth without her help. He even brought greetings to her from his own master who will here remain nameless. This master was one whom he, Malovent, followed on his own journey into evil.

The grandmaster of them both, the devil, stated his pleasure at having a disciple so dedicated to Malovent as to be able to turn him loose. With Malovent fighting on the earth, gathering an army, this was going to be a glorious war after all! Miss Coffenayle and Malovent were key warriors in the effort to gather evil on the face of this world. This planet would soon be theirs to rule over; the good would finally be the ones in torment!

The disciple had given her full report over the most recent events. The student/teacher, Miss Emily, was moving along just fine. She did not react with shock when Miss Coffenayle struck Jimmy down with magical power, just to show the brat what it meant to slight his principal in the least degree. Miss Coffenayle wanted to reinforce in him who was in charge. She wanted him to know that she could do with him as she would. This time, she did it by will. She did not have her amulet with her and used no other physical means. She knocked the boy down without a magical wand, a rune, a talisman, or anything else to help her. She cast her magic by pure will. After she gave her report, Malovent asked her what she would want most in the whole world right now.

"Well, Master…since you have asked…when do I get to meet… *him?*"

"Not just yet. But soon enough," Malovent stated as he hovered with his dark energy swirling about, bolder than before. Indeed, the master was growing stronger! "I have always taught you to press forward without regard for health or safety, that evil would take care of you. I have taught you to never wait for anything, to take at your pleasure, and to demand of life all you wanted immediately without regard for consequences. But now, my faithful disciple, you need be patient. You will meet our master, our dark majesty, Satan himself, soon enough. But for now, you must be patient and allow yourself to marinate just a bit longer in evil power."

"Yes, Master," stated the anxious, ambitious, and evil witch. She bowed again before her master. He hovered over her for a moment, and if she could see his face, she would have witnessed a most wicked grin.

"*Dispense with that nonsense!*" he shouted.

She trembled before him on her knees. She feared his anger. She had been smitten by him before and did not look forward to anything like that again. She believed that he could destroy her with a snap of his fingers if he wished. She was willing to die for the cause of evil, but she feared to do so prematurely before she could ascend to an Underworld throne. Because she shed innocent blood to fulfill an oath, her die was cast. Her soul was sold to the cause of evil, yes, and hell awaited her, but she wanted to be greeted as a queen, not a victim.

"N-nonsense?" she asked with great hesitation and trembling in her voice.

"Yes, *fool!* Nonsense!"

"I don't understand—" she sheepishly stated.

"You don't understand what you have done?"

"N-no." She was terrified.

"You have cast magic without a talisman! Without a robe! Without a candle! You did not have your cards, runes, or charms with you. You cast evil power at a fellow flesh-bearing human with only the thought and a single spoken word! Recall your studies before I turn you into the worthless toad you are so fond of! You speak of toads often to your students at this…*prison* you call a school, do you not?"

"My studies…" She stayed bowed in her black dress, trembling with fear and trying to think. Then she remembered! Yes! This must be the lesson:

> To cast magic is done by any fool,
> Who wishes to break the Golden Rule.
> Talismans, cards, trinkets and such
> Can cause the apprentice to do much,
> But to cast a spell with mere words and such…
> With no magical charms or potions of Aster…
> Such magical power is reserved for a Master.

"Master… I have done it!" Coffenayle raised her eyes to him and shouted.

"What? What have you done, fool?" Malovent asked with a softer tone.

"I am not a fool any longer," she stated as she started to rise.

"Oh? Then what are you...if *not* a fool?" Malovent asked with the softness of a philosopher.

"I am"—she stood up tall and faced Malovent—"I am a *master!* A master of magic! A master witch of black magic of the highest mortal order! By virtue of this, I need bow before you *no* longer!"

Malovent paused. He stood there in the air, bobbing up and down, hovering, seeming to ponder. His shaded cowled face—that dark shadow where a face would normally be—turned toward her. He waited for any shade of doubt, any hesitance at all on her part. He waited for her to drop her eyes in fear and shame. She did not. She stood there—tall, proud, arrogant, full of ego and self-assured greatness, the very picture of the perfect disciple of evil. He realized that she would not back down, so he drew back with his arm as though to strike her with his power. His draping sleeve had not a hand at its termination but a ball of black fire! He reared back as though to cast it her.

She instantly dropped back to a defensive stance and made the magical signs of a shield. A black mass of energy appeared before her in a shape that covered her from a direct attack. She stared directly at Malovent; she could see him clearly through her side of the shield, but he could barely see her. It was a very well-made shield! She was completely defended. She was obscured, but she was able to see her opponent perfectly as the shielding spell intended. She was not afraid. She was willing to fight!

And that very action on her part was the final secret test for promotion to a master status: the willingness to strike back at one's own master in self-defense without fear and without hesitation. This method of testing was never divulged to a student; it was necessary for the apprentice to counter an attack naturally and out of defensive rage. There must be no fear; there could only be the will to fight! Rare were such disciples in this world. So many disciples who failed the master degree test had been found dead on the ground by other mortals. Dead from heart failure, seizure, or stroke. While these deaths appeared natural, if sudden and unexpected, they were actually caused by the teaching master striking down a failed apprentice. In this case, the black fire would not claim another mortal life. Not tonight.

Malovent extinguished his fire and lowered his arm. He laughed. It was a throaty evil cackle but with a deep foreboding monotone. He went on for some minutes, but Coffenayle would not back off. She knew not if his laughter was a ruse to distract her and cause her to drop her defense. She would not be stricken by him, and she was determined to never become his helpless victim ever again. He moved back and forth, drifting in the air, but she tracked his movements. She followed him with her fingers and hands twisted in seeming impossible ways. He would raise his ebony fireball from time to time. She held her shield up, not giving an inch. She was afraid no more. When he tired of the game, he cast a fireball at her! She blocked it completely without hesitation…but did not counterattack!

Malovent stopped in the air. He lowered his arms and signaled for a truce by waving his arms in such and such a manner. This was not a surrender, in magical terms, but it was an acceptance of another as his equal, of not wishing for a magical battle. Certainly, yes, in a pitched battle, he would destroy her, but her destruction was not his purpose just now. His purpose was to use her as a tool, and she proved that she would be an effective tool indeed! Coffenayle understood the sign of the truce, so she dropped her shield and returned the proper countersign of acceptance.

The purpose of this ritual, this *graduation*, was not to determine the strength of the newest master's abilities. Those abilities would become stronger with time. It was to discover the inner strength of the new master. It was to determine if the disciple would follow the rules of combat. Evil had no use for renegade mortals. They had to follow the rules.

Malovent knew Coffenayle had studied the laws and knew the rules. Many of Malovent's disciples, over the ages, had fallen victim to their own vanity. Malovent had killed several of his own disciples, just like the other Masters of the Guild, his equals. To break any of the Three Rules of Combat was to suffer instant death. For this reason, only a disciple who had studied the rules was able to take the final test. The candidate for the test could not be primed or told they were to be tested. The test was to be administered without warning so that the candidate could react in complete spontaneity. In that split instant, they either passed or they were cast into torment. No second chances.

Malovent was pleased with Coffenayle as he had worked with her over the years because she was so *completely dedicated and so eager* of a disciple. She learned so quickly. Today she was tested; today she had passed! There were three requirements to survive this test:

1. To realize and immediately embrace one's own mastership without hesitation.
2. To display the will to defend one's self against their master without hesitation, but only as far as needed to preserve their life and limb.
3. To recognize and embrace the full meaning of the sign of the truce.

Coffenayle stood defiant and proud. She had done it! She had been accepted as an equal. The murders, all the distortion of lives, all of the study, the risk, the effort—it all paid off. It paid off today! She was a master now, one who had irreversibly embraced evil and all it stood for. All that remained was for her to fully purge all regret, to sear completely all conscience, all good, and light from the bottom of her soul. Once that was done, she could drop the title of Master. She would simply be known by an assigned name as was Malovent. She would be "master" only to disciples she was training. She looked forward to choosing her name but was forbidden to speculate what her name might be. That time would come later.

At that level, with her own chosen name, she could wear the dark cowl of an evil queen in the Underworld. On earth, she could use magic to torment other mortals who got in her way. She could define freely what "getting in her way" actually meant. She would exercise her own power at her own discretion without fear of punishment for misdeeds. Indeed, there would be no misdeeds. At the level where Malovent served, all that she did in the name of evil would be instantly justified without accountability. All of that was just one more purgative step away.

"Very well, young master, I am pleased with you. You have shown fearlessness, a desire to defend yourself, and you respected my truce. Only a handful of disciples have ever achieved this status. Now...now you may begin to carry out your desires. We will soon have a wave of students educated after our ways, inserted into the highest offices of business, religion, militias, and politics—all to pollute the earth!"

"Thank you, Malovent. I need not call you master any longer, correct?"

"That is correct, Coffenayle. You call me by my proper name since you are a fellow master. But—"

"Yes?"

"You are still a young master and need to follow me until you become strong enough to only use me for occasional advice. Though you are a master and powerful, you still need be guided. To leave my tutelage too soon will mean your *death*. We cannot allow incapable masters of our craft to wander the earth, making too many mistakes. I recently burned such a disciple. She spontaneously burst into flames while sleeping in bed one night."

Coffenayle chuckled. "Well, we can't have that, now, can we?"

Malovent chuckled in return, pleased with her fearless dedication. "I release you now to do your job at the school."

"Very well. Thank you, Malovent. Now you say that I may do according to my desires, correct?"

"Yes. You may...with certain restrictions as I have just expressed to you. That being said and understood, I have sensed in you some new idea. What is it then?"

"I wish to leave the school. I want to go abroad into other lands with the Coffenayle Family and convince *them* that our powers can make the family greater than they already are. With your permission, I would like to do so."

"So what of the school? Much work has been done here. You have deformed lives and bodies. You have even shed blood to take control of this place. Would you throw all of that away?"

"I would gain much more for our purposes by being a member of the Coffenayle organization. We could create much more misery for the purpose of evil and not be in competition with the Coffenayle worldwide crime and business establishments. To put our students out in the world, doing our bidding at the highest levels as we planned, would be to compete with the Clan. Their power and influence could make things difficult. I have no desire to go to war with my own flesh and blood."

Malovent hesitated but only for a moment. Even though he could not read mortal thoughts as mortal witches could, by virtue of their flesh, Malovent had become accurate at guessing what they would likely do. He had perceived this thought, this plan of hers coming, and he was not surprised. Nor did he act surprised.

"I see the wisdom in your reasoning, Coffenayle. Your power could do much in their worldwide network. Can you convince them to accept you and your ways over their objections?"

"They only object because they do not understand the full power of what we have to offer, Malovent. I am confident that I can convince them."

"We cannot leave the school as it is. You know this."

"Yes. I intend to burn it *all.*"

"That will generate much misery and death. This will make us all the more powerful. I have already discussed this among my peers when I suspected this to be your plan. Arrangements have already been made on our side. So you say. So be it."

"Thank *you*, Malovent."

She made it a special point to enjoy not groveling and calling him Master. She took her leave of her near-equal who faded in his dramatic fashion, but this time, she was not kneeling! She changed out of her black dress and left the office with a spring in her step. She was so happy that she had attained such great knowledge! A master! She was a master! This was an honor she hoped to attain but did not think she would for many more years. Her studies and dedication paid off. She knew that to reach a master's status was no easy feat. She knew so much, yes...but there was something that the Little Napoleon did not know.

She did not know was that while Malovent rejoiced in her knowledge, he also took great joy in her ignorance. There were many secrets hidden from her. Malovent inwardly grinned at her newfound identity. *Master Coffenayle indeed*, he thought to himself as he secretly despised and mocked her ignorance. Mortals were so funny that way. They loved titles, and some would sell their souls for a mere title before their name. Conscience got in the way of many through family, friends, and others in their lives that meant something to them. The support of fellow mortals has pulled many souls away from the brink of the abyss before evil could claim them. But not Donatienne Coffenayle.

No, this one was special. Malovent knew it. The devil himself knew it. They knew that they had to keep her on their hook. They saw her dedication to hard work to advancing herself in this world. They knew that she could be a terrible enemy to the cause of evil if she turned away from them. They understood that her natural charisma was a potential force for good and light. Fortunately, her weakness was their greatest strength: she was willing to only accept other people into her life on a "transactional basis," meaning that other people in her life were only a means to an end. Once she got out of them all that she could and wrung them dry, she cast them off to the side like so much flotsam.

The beauty of it all was that she felt nearly zero regret for doing it and no compassion for her victims. It was rare for evil forces to find such a one that managed to stay out of jail. Usually, such types would get so carried away that they would fall prey to justice. Prisons were loaded with such men and women, people willing to degrade their fellow humans to the status of a mere tool. At the end of the day, Coffenayle felt no more for her fellow mortals than she did for a hammer or a saw. That was the rare quality in her, that *willingness* to intentionally and fully embrace evil but do so with such cunning as to avoid the law. Indeed, she would become an excellent tormentor queen. That is, *if there really were such a thing.*

Malovent loved what they called the Great Lie. He knew that there were no kings and queens of the Underworld. He found it laughable that mortals would actually believe that he had their best interests at heart. He had no interest in their desires for money, for power, for fame. No. All that he and the brothers and sisters of the Underworld had left in their eternity was to drag as many mortals as they could after them! They wanted souls to be condemned with them, to eternally suffer the fire and brimstone. Sealing a soul to become one of their kind only required the mortal to take the Oath and then slay a fellow mortal for the sake of gain. The time was growing short; they had not much longer to chip away at the souls of men, women, and children before the End of Days. When their days ended, they would finally end up in their own chains. After that was the great suffering, never again to emerge from the fiery pit.

Some mortals were at first reluctant to take the Oath to shed blood for gain. Others were more eager. But Miss Donatienne Coffenayle? She was a wholly different breed altogether. It was almost as though she was simply born for destruction. She thrived on chaos! She truly loved to invoke the greatest misery possible. She created a pigsty of destruction and then loved to wallow in it. Yes, the Underworld had won several souls from the Coffenayle line, but this one, Donatienne Coffenayle—she was simply rife with her enthusiasm for the evil cause. It pleased Malovent to no end that she would burn with him in the eternities. She would not be a tormentor; she would be the tormented as would he be. This was justice to Malovent in his own dark heart. After all, if one as great as he would not enjoy a glorious destiny, why should anyone else?

Donatienne was willing to bring her own family members into his game. While the Underworld already owned many Coffenayles, it was hoped that many more would quickly join when she showed them the raw power of evil. They may have their petty corporate rules and such forbidding religion to be combined with family business, but the Patriarch surely would fall to the temptation to embrace magic! Once he did, Coffenayles would come pouring in willingly! They who were once sitting on the fence would fall for the power of black magic! She would be responsible for all of them. She could teach them all to become queens and kings! As for those would not purge themselves, well, she was just as content to torment them under her reign. The reign she would not ever have.

26

Miss Coffenayle's Home

Mr. Mentor, who had left Emily moments before, quietly slipped out of the principal's office through the wall. It was a very handy thing being able to approach the living and evil beings without being detected. It was all a matter of eternal laws. Beings living in dissimilar dimensions, or "kingdoms" as the Good Book often called them, cannot normally perceive one another. Lower kingdoms cannot see the higher kingdoms, but higher kingdoms can see the lower ones. All of this is for the same reason that you cannot hear all of the radio stations on one receiver all at once. There has to be an attunement to the same frequency at the same time for the dissimilar beings to see one another.

Mentor was able to watch evil beings without them knowing he was there. He did not like staying on such a low frequency for extended periods because it was offensive to his good nature. He also had to be careful to not reveal himself to them by mistake. Malovent and his kind did not know that Mr. Mentor could watch them, and he did not wish to give himself away. To be seen by them would change the whole game. It was to Mentor's advantage that he could lower his own frequency and keep it at a level that he could see but not be seen. On the other side, evil beings were not able to accelerate their vibrations to meet the higher good frequency of the kingdom where Mentor dwelt. It would be incredibly painful and very harmful for them to even try. Such would become so scrambled that they would be delivered to their final torment immediately.

Mr. Mentor and Malovent could both communicate with mortals because they *chose* to do so. Some mortals can see ghosts or spirits too, but they also *choose* to do so usually. There are cases where mortals are tormented by ghostly visions without desiring them. This is because mortals vibrate at a frequency that may tuned into by good and evil spirits. This accounts for some of what people call "mental illness." Not all ghosts are hallucinations, but not all hallucinations are ghosts.

Rare are the mortals who can actually see into the affairs of the spirit world, naturally, simply by making the choice. This is a divine gift, and Mentor had met a few such people. The majority of them, unfortunately, chose to do improper things with their gifts. They chose to take advantage of other people or they chose to make money with "psychic" tricks. *They could do so much good too,* mused Mr. Mentor, *if only they would do the right thing with their gifts.* To meet a righteous and gifted person who can see the spirit world is the desire of every good ministering spirit.

That aside, Mentor had received much intelligence from spying on this interview. Spying on the evil beings of the spirit world was not against the rules by which Mr. Mentor was bound. This gave the good side an advantage over the evil. The evil side could lie, scare people, spy on them about anyplace, other than exceptionally holy places that blocked evil out and, of course, use temptations of money and power to perform their evil work. They had all kinds of dirty tricks because, generally speaking, they were not bound by any rules. They did not fear the committing of "sin" because they were condemned anyway. They literally had nothing to lose. Good spirits, on the other hand, have much to lose. They can still choose to fall away, to become corrupt.

There is nothing decided, finally, about the eternal fate of mortals until the Last Day. The battles and skirmishes of the spiritual war cause mortals to change sides all the time. Some people leave the good to join the evil, and some leave the evil to choose the good. There are infinite degrees or frequencies of people who constantly vacillate. Some days, they are lower; other days, they are higher. The goal of the good spirits is to keep people heading in the right direction, to become just a little better each day. Such is the way of things.

The situation that came about here at the school is very unique. Mr. Mentor was told by his superiors that the level of evil embraced by Coffenayle is rare. It was not unheard of, but it is a rare thing to see someone embrace evil so fully that they actually gain real power over the living. The power to affect lives with greed, lust, malice, etc. is very common. Too common, in fact. These common sins and behaviors don't have the same impact that actual pure *evil* has on people.

Pure evil can really hurt folks, change lives, even alter the very appearance of normal sons and daughters of God. Mentor knew this all too well. Only the strongest of evil power could actually do that. He knew what he was up against, and he knew that people could suffer terribly if he did not do his job properly. This thing was starting to rev up now quite a bit. He was glad to discover Miss Coffenayle's plan to destroy the school, all souls onboard. It was very unfortunate, but at least something could still be done to stop Malovent and his little pet witch. If only she understood the truth.

Time was growing short before Mentor would have to make his final moves. He just did not know how short. With what he just discerned from the mouths of Coffenayle and even Malovent *himself,* he knew that he must not let them destroy the school. There was too much potential for the lives at stake to change for the better. There were too many good people in this place; he had to win this high-stakes chess game. He had been working on it for years. Now was the time to involve more mortal help. He had not intended to involve Emily and her two friends this soon, but now was the time because he could not wait any longer. He had to bring them into this thing fast and hard. He thought about what to do and received inspiration. God was very close to his chosen servants, and answers came to Mentor almost instantly. He needed to contact Jimmy and Castlethorn.

*****

Miss Coffenayle had retired to her home. It was a rather short walk from the school. From the outside, no one knew it was a home; the place was simply nightmarish. The wrought-iron fence that surrounded the building was falling apart, rusted, and there was a heavy iron lock on the gate. The lock's thick shank was crusted with rust. The key port in the front of the lock looked like it required one of those old skeleton keys. Even if one had the key, it was doubtful that the lock would even work. Truly, one could easily topple the gate if they rattled it hard enough. It was surprising that the winds from the changing of seasons didn't just blow it right down along with half of the fence.

The ground that surrounded the building was barren, except for some patches of intrusive weeds here and there. Signs in the outer yard indicated that the building was, in fact, slated for destruction. The signs, or what one could read of them, said that no one should enter the grounds. It was private property; it was condemned; skull and crossbones liberally decorated the signs. The signs themselves were rotted and falling apart. There were shrubs on the property surrounding the front of the house, but they were twisted and brown with only the most tenacious of leaves barely hanging onto the stems.

The backyard area had more life about it, for some reason. There were thistles and thorns, nettles and briars. There was a patch of ground overgrown with weeds. This patch was about the size of a fair vegetable garden. Ornate stones outlined the perimeter of the garden but were now covered with moss and mud. Small animals scurried about, doubtless some type of vermin that nested in the thick weeds and fallen fruit trees. Neglect had allowed nature to take its cruel course. Everything had been growing wild for a long time. The fruit trees had gone without pruning and became top heavy unto collapse. The dying barely rooted trees would still produce occasional pears, apples, and plums. The unpicked fruit would just rot on the branches. No one cared anymore for this once beautiful and productive piece of property.

Growth had overcome twin monuments near the trees, alabaster marble stones carved with affection. Now rot and decay had overgrown them. Lovely carvings once, both of them, painstakingly cut by a grieving but skilled stonemason were now left to the ravages of disease and death that now ruled this entire property. These stones were no longer white, no longer pristine or beautiful. This small scene was as sullen as the rest of the place.

There was a timeworn walkway of hand-carved pioneer flag-stones leading up to the door. There were rotting wooden steps leading up to what once was a porch. Now the former sturdy porch looked more like an aged and deteriorating apple crate. The wood did not appear strong enough to hold a person. There was a lamppost on the boards that stood tilted, ready to fall over. Its post was bent, and the cracked glass was so dirty that even if lit, the lamp would hardly glow at all.

To say the structure needed a coat of paint would be laughable. Several coats would be absorbed by the thirsty, dried out, graying wood before the paint would have much effect. Many of the boards were falling off anyway, and there would need to be extensive repairs before painting would even become an option. This ramshackle heap of wood, rot, and depression was once a beautiful dwelling place. One could almost sense that this once was the happiest of homes and very welcoming. Now, the windows were boarded up, and the door was apparently nailed shut. The once-ornate brass knob was corroded, and the designs on it were long since faded.

Above the door was a masterfully hand-carved eve but now was so ruined and rotten that the intricate flowers that once ran its entire length could hardly be noticed. In between the ruined flow-ers was what seemed to be the head of a cherub. Now it was just a rough, washed-out gray ball that had indentations where facial fea-tures were once meticulously and delicately carved into the wood. This was once a beautiful home. Not anymore. When it rained, the water would run down the former cherub's face, and it would almost appear to cry from the gouged and worn eye sockets. The opening of what seemed to be a mouth frowned and would drool the eyes' tears that ran into it. Think of a prisoner chained to a wall, starved and tortured, begging for death but who was not allowed to die, one who was fed just enough dry moldy bread and sips of water to prolong his misery but not enough to give him relief—so seemed the cherub. So seemed the home of Miss Donatienne Coffenayle.

She approached her home carefully, as was her custom. She had a habit of checking the fence for evidence of a burglar or of the merely curious. Vandalism would have been out of the question because, well, what more could one do to the place? No, anyone that came around here would likely be looking for something—shelter, items to sell for scrap, etc. Other than that, there was no conceivable reason to approach the place. That is why Coffenayle allowed it to look like this.

She had a decoy house where the other teachers lived, and that was where she would go after work if anyone was watching. She could even spend the night there if she needed to. Her place had the same type of Spartan furnishings where Miss Emily and the other teachers lived. That was a place where she could have visitors from the school board or other places. She had not done that yet but could if she needed to.

She would spend the night there when she felt that someone was watching her movements or whenever Malovent gave her the order to do so. She smiled at that thought of Malovent giving her *orders*. There would be no more orders for her, not for "Master Coffenayle." Naturally, she understood that she still had to obey him if she were about to make some mistake or another that might expose them. He could still order her about in such extreme circumstances but no longer as a matter of course. Yes, this promotion was as welcome as it was deserved!

She skirted the fence line for any sign of a break-in, footprints, bits of human rubbish—indeed anything at all that would prove a human presence besides herself was on site. Once, a long time ago, she found a tin can that had been torn open with a pocket knife. She discovered an unshaven, unkempt, and unclean man in the backyard bushes, stretched out asleep. She woke him up, looked him in the eyes, and froze him with an icy stare by the power of a dark amulet she wore around her neck. She informed him that he was on a witch's property and then cast a spell on him that made him believe that there were worms under his skin and that he was being chased by a pack of wolves.

She laughed hysterically as he writhed about and squirmed and then tried to run from the mirage pack of wolves at the same time! He eventually ran to the fence, jumped over it, and she released the spell after he was about fifty yards from the house. She knew that he would tell all of his friends to stay away! He must have because that was the last smelly vagrant she ever saw on the property. She let him live for two reasons: first, it amused her to do so; he suffered so well and made her laugh. Secondly, she wanted someone to spread the legend of the witch's house.

She reported this to Malovent who thought it was hilarious. He almost laughed his way out from under his cowl. That would been magnificent to have actually seen his face. She stopped in her tracks when she realized that she had *never seen Malovent's face, not even when he promoted her to the Circle of Masters!* She thought that was odd for a moment and then dismissed the thought entirely as she completed her patrol. Once satisfied that it was safe to enter the house, that no one was watching her, Coffenayle approached the front gate. She produced a key very similar to the one Malovent held up his sleeve, and she inserted it into the oversized lock. The key turned very easily, surprisingly so. She opened the lock, which functioned perfectly, swung the gate open smoothly, and locked everything back precisely in the same way she found it. She made her way up the flagstone walkway and onto the porch. The boards were surprisingly strong. She had to stifle first a grimace, then a grin when she remembered Whipshot being trapped in the floorboards of the classroom. How did that happen anyway?

She took the same key and opened the lock on the house. The knob turned, and the door pushed open smoothly without so much as a squeak. She was pleased with what her magic was able to do with the locks and hinges. Everything was precisely as old and rusted as it appeared to be, but she was able to work a charm that allowed her to manipulate the rusted deteriorating objects as easily as she would with freshly installed and well-oiled hardware. She entered the house and turned on the lights. She stood for a moment and let her eyes adjust to the indoor lighting. The moon provided plenty of light for her exterior patrol, but it was not as bright as the indoors.

She blinked once, twice. Ahh, yes…much better. She scanned the room with great pride: *The master magic user has returned home for her rest!* She breathed in very deeply and puffed up her chest in her self-pride. She could almost taste the title of queen on her tongue! She looked around, taking it all in. Everything. All hers. She once thought to have it shipped to her new location, wherever that would be. Now, though, she would not have time. *It will be a shame to burn it all.* Even so, nothing here even compared to the rewards she would receive from carrying out her plans.

It was a deluxe home in every sense of the word. She had a spacious living room decked out with the finest in antique furniture and art. The works of art were suited to one of her stature: statues of grotesque devils with various weapons of destruction and torture, paintings of mighty generals crushing their enemies, a couple of antique suits of armor elegantly rusted and battle-damaged, real animal hide rugs such as yak, zebra, and a giraffe, mounted heads of ferocious animals snarling and hissing. She even had an *original* portrait of Napoleon Bonaparte himself, the one she used as a model for her own uniforms. She fully intended to make his conquests pale in significance to hers. In her superior conquests, she would be more wise, for she was more well-trained in the manipulation of people than Bonaparte. World conquest was in her blood. She was bred to rule the world! Yes, she believed she could once the Clan accepted magic.

It was not that the Coffenayle line thought magic was somehow immoral; to them, it could be the means to an end, yes, but they believed it to be unreliable. Magic did not have the mathematical predictability of their other means. Magic could not be quantified; it had no material substance that could be measured by physical means. That would soon change, though, because Donatienne was becoming more adept and more precise at using magic. She would soon show them that magic could be predictable, whether by their numbers or not because magic would do precisely whatever they ordered it to do. Malovent had promised her that this could happen. And she believed him.

There was currently no provision in the family charters for punishment of their members who engaged in magic; they saw it as just another form of religion. They did not mind religion at all and, in fact, made a lot money selling religious books, icons, and images. They were fine with their members engaging in religion as long as their beliefs were not used as a basis of business decisions. They would not allow morality to begin to interfere with their ways. Family members who found religion, adopted morality, and became a threat to family secrecy were occasionally "removed from the roster" of the family; other people might call it "murdered." Then they would be buried by their religious outsider friends who did not even know their real names. Just another random crime taking another innocent life. It would hit the papers one day, selling good copy, and then would be entirely forgotten. Such was the way of the the Clan.

Donatienne, on the other hand, used her "religion" to forward her business. The family did not care one way or the other because she was on her own. They did admire her business acumen and her plan for using the entire school to increase her own power. They did not mind her murders; in fact, they found them quite clever. What they did not understand, though, was the oath she made. She told them about it, yes, but they did not care to hear much about anything unless it served to give them a greater foothold in the world. Her oath was her personal matter. Her source of power was hers and hers alone. She did not affect their business nor did she divulge their secrets. That was all they cared about.

That was okay by Donatienne. She would soon show them all the power that her magic could bring to the Clan. It would take some more time to become perfect at casting magic. She needed to have perfect results. She knew that to try to bring something less to the table would not be acceptable.

Coffenayle cooked herself some supper in her well-stocked kitchen. She had only the finest foods and had taught herself to prepare them. She did not trust a cook nor any other servants. The closest thing she had to that was Doesbad. She did a wonderful job of using him, even if she said so herself. Not even he had crossed the threshold of her home. There was only one benefit he ever received from under this roof, and that was the bullion she would pay him for services rendered. She pondered for a moment how he had feelings for her that would never be requited. No, not him, not any man. She did not have time for men, though she was attracted to them on occasion. They never could see her inherent superiority, and she would not have them near her. Besides, she did not need the burden of romance. There would be far too much to explain to a suitor.

She poured herself a glass of fine wine and rewarmed the leftovers from her latest gourmet dish. She served herself on her finest china. She even had a dessert all ready to go. She ate too much in celebration of her own cleverness. Then she washed the dishes, dried them, and put them all away. Miss Coffenayle was an immaculate housekeeper.

She left the kitchen and walked up the three marble steps to her bath enclosure. She had this installed after the Mentors died. She tied the curtains open, then she poured herself a lovely bubble bath, adding lilac water. She lounged in the luxurious bath, silently allowing herself to relax. She even dozed a little, a dark, dreamless sleep. She only had feelings of grandeur, then awoke, feeling wonderful and refreshed.

She emerged from the tub and dried herself slowly, relishing the feeling of the very soft and thick towel. She changed into her satiny nightclothes and put her uniform into the cleaning bag. She moved a picture on the wall and turned the dial on her secreted safe as was part of her nightly ritual.

Nightly, she checked the condition of her gold bullion, not trusting anything to chance where her wealth was concerned. She may be a magical master now, but she was still a Coffenayle. Several bags of gold lay in the safe. She owned gold by the pound. Her supply was limitless, given her relationship with Malovent. Then a thought occurred to her. She could now cast magic without talismans, cards, designs, or any other trinkets, yes? So what about summoning her peer in magic? What about calling on Malovent?

She opened the double doors to her bedroom to welcome him. She sat on her four-posted curtained bed and concentrated. She called on her former master. She sat and waited. Nothing happened.

She made a second attempt and called upon him again. She waited...
nothing. The third call was much different. She was more determined, demanding his appearance, but doing so with respect. That
was the final critical element—to make a demand but with respect.

The room began filling with a yellow haze that grew thicker and
thicker into smoke. Then beneath the cover of the smoke, a shadow
of a familiar tall figure began to form. As he came more fully into
view, she saw that he was bigger and broader at the shoulder than
he had even been before. He stood tall and regal, cowled head, with
the key hanging out of his sleeve. His belt, she noted, had changed
as well. This time, it was even broader, brighter, and it was decorated
this time with faces of people that appeared to be in torment. His
arms were folded. His hands concealed his head looking down, concealing his face as always.

"Yes, Coffenayle? What is it?" he boomed, sounding almost
pleased.

"Malovent," she said simply, "how good of you to come." She
could not conceal her smile.

"What do you require?"

"I was lonely," she chuckled.

"Indeed?" he asked in an amused tone.

"Yes. I thought that I might have you over for a sip of wine and
a crust of bread."

"Oh, I see. Or perhaps you might have wanted to just try out
your newfound status, not unlike a young person staying out far too
late, drinking far too much liquor on the night of their legal entry
into adulthood. We have killed many young people that way!" He
laughed loudly and heartily. She joined him.

"Oh, my friend, you know me all too well!" she exclaimed, wiping tears from her eyes.

"Yes, *better than you might imagine.* So tell me...are you pleased
with what your status allows you to do?"

"Yes, I am well pleased! I am happy to know that I can call upon
you anytime I choose."

"Yes, that is true. Always remember this: you must not abuse
this privilege. Your initial attempt at summoning me as a fellow mas-

ter without the aid of trinkets and talismans is what we like to call the 'free one.' To abuse this privilege will displease me." To make his point, he raised his arm and instantly conjured up a ball of yellow static-looking energy. He cast it at the wall, and it struck with a flash of black fire, burning a hole into it, scarring the paint and plaster. He turned toward Coffenayle as though he was looking for some response. She appeared unmoved, almost bored.

"Honestly, Malovent? Did have to resort to such theatrics? Burning my wall?" she asked calmly.

Malovent laughed again. "You are indeed a true master, Coffenayle. You have lost your natural fear of magical attack. Fire and flame no longer impress you. A mere couple of days ago, you would have recoiled in abject fear of me and begged for my forgiveness, begged for your very life. Impressive."

"A couple of days ago, I was a mere witch. You made me into a master. As such, I should behave accordingly, should I not?"

"Are you asking permission?"

"Definitely not!" she scoffed. "I was making a point, not asking an actual question."

"Yes. Indeed you were. Your confidence is a great strength to you."

"I require nothing more of you tonight. I am very pleased that I am able to summon you. This means that my studies are beginning to pay off," the new master said, almost but not quite dismissively.

"They are," Malovent replied simply.

"Then I suppose I am able to be rid of my talismans. I don't need the design on the floor or the candles."

"Yes that is true. Dispose of them by consuming them completely in flames. These are of no use to you now, and we don't want them to fall into the wrong hands. Allow yourself no room for sentiment. These are not keepsakes."

"I will do as you suggest," Coffenayle responded with a smile.

"Is there anything else then?" asked the cowled figure.

"Nothing. You may remain or leave as you see fit."

Without another word, Malovent folded his arms and disappeared in more yellow smoke. The appearance of the smoke was one thing. The smell was another. Miss Coffenayle nearly gagged on the extra dose of sulfur. She swatted the smoke away and hoped silently that the vapors and smell were theatrics that could be disposed of by Malovent. She would definitely address the issue on their next visit. She looked at the wall where he burned it with his show of force. Oddly, the wall was unscathed. Malovent surprised her with repairing the wall before he left and did so unnoticed by her. This must have been a treat, a show of respect for her new promotion. She was a peer now, no longer a mere lackey.

Coffenayle decided that she would start to study that portion of her books which covered the repair of physical objects. She could magically break them well enough, but she had difficulty repairing them. In fact, it was currently impossible for her. Repairing things was a more advanced skill she never took time to learn about. Well, it seemed to be time to do so. But not now. She yawned. It was time to go bed. She wandered over to her silk-sheeted place of rest. She turned out the lights and, in sweet repose, dreamed of power beyond even her most wild imaginings. The world of dreams was such a wondrous and magical place.

27

Nightshade Dreams and Stranger Things

Nurse Shadyknight had been asleep for a couple of hours. She was dreaming now of wonderful things. Her dreams were much more peaceful these days, though she did not understand why. She was waking up these last few mornings more rested and refreshed. She had an in-house patient to take care of—perhaps that was why things were easier for her. She was actually a nurse that was doing her real job. She was not just taking care of the bumps and bruises typical to the students and their usual accidents and abuses from staff. In this particular dream, a kindly old man in a brown suit who sported a very proper watch chain was talking to her.

He seemed somehow familiar, but whenever she tried to identify him in this dream, her attempts were obscured by a green fog. He would grow distant, somehow moving far away from her without walking; it was the oddest thing. As long as she spoke to this nice man of just general things, they conversed well. Then, when she tried to remember his name or why he seemed so familiar to her, he would suddenly appear far away, and his voice was muffled beyond her hearing.

During the day, when she was quietly keeping vigil over her patient, her mind would wander to her dreams. She knew she liked this man, and he seemed to like her as though they were somehow friends. Such a kind and wonderful dream. All of this began happening after Miss Whipshot became her patient. During the day, she

349

would entertain the ridiculous notion that Whipshot was somehow the cause of her feeling better. Because, after all, when was Whipshot ever the cause of anyone ever feeling any good thing? The woman was practically the embodiment of evil.

But still, there was something about this whole situation. The kids visiting, bringing their cruel teacher flowers, the nurse's own outburst about those terrible rumors. When did she start to care again about what other people thought of her? She had not cared for a very long time. Not since the rumors started that the Mentors both died under her care and that she had something to do with it.

Shadyknight noticed more things, medically impossible things. For one, the teacher was changing in appearance. Miss Whipshot was not as miserable-looking. Though she was sleeping heavily, she seemed to change positions every couple of hours, eliminating the need for the nurse to roll her over. So how does a comatose patient move herself about? It also seemed that Whipshot was getting… well…*thinner*…and that was about the most ridiculous thing of all. It could not be; yet, it seemed to be that way in spite of the improbability. Then to top it all off, the lines of Nurse Shadyknight's own face seemed to be easing up as though some great burden was being lifted. Simply put, she was not looking as old as she did a couple of days ago.

A common thing to the nurse's everyday practice, the bedpan, was a most necessary evil. An unpleasant chore indeed, both to the filling and the emptying of them. The patient in this case was not nearly as foul as one might expect. Her abundant stomach, so fat that it would lay beside her, would occasionally rumble, and the nurse would fetch the bedpan and allow nature to take its course. She would keep the patient clean but never had to change out her bedsheets for any reason other than good hygiene during sponge baths. There was always sufficient warning of the need of the bedpan, and such moments always occurred when the nurse was on hand and able to take care of the problem. Most peculiar indeed.

Nurse Shadyknight did believe in God, but not to a point of what she would call "superstitious." She did not believe that God openly interfered in mankind's affairs but that He was very hands off and sent Jesus to save people from themselves. She did not believe that God was in the world's affairs daily but, like a child with a top, sent the world to spinning and was amused at the results. She knew God was good but did not think that He would move people to do good. She believed that God allowed people to become good or evil, to study His words or not, to become either heaven- or hell-bound on their own, and all on their own. The end came for mankind when they died and they were consigned to light or darkness all because of what each person chose to do. Perhaps, she would occasionally think, it was time to dust off that old Bible of hers. She had not touched it since the Mentors died. Perhaps reading the Good Book to ol' Whipshot might do them both some good.

*****

At the student dormitory, Jimmy laid awake, his mind adrift in the mists of his own thoughts. They were heavy thoughts too, about all of things that he had seen over the past few days. So much had happened he could hardly keep up. The accident with Whipshot. The principal throwing the party. His promotion to become the engineer's apprentice—he never would have seen that coming. Then there was another unpredictable event in Emily-Whipshot being promoted to *Miss* Emily Keller. A student becoming a teacher of students? Yet, she seemed to be doing very well at it. Jimmy knew too, for a fact, that Emily was somehow getting help of some kind. Some sort of special tutoring or something. He knew what they had learned in class up until now in between abuses. Some of that stuff Miss Emily was teaching, though? That was far beyond anything that she could possibly know from the classroom teachings of Miss Whipshot alone.

Then the inventions. Oh, my goodness! The things that he was learning! His head was filled with the most fantastical things! He had never heard the word *poltergeist* ever in his life! Now he was not only dealing with one regularly, but he had access to a machine to *stop* one. He also had access to a second machine in the shape of a crazy man's lantern that could detect *other ghosts* merely by spinning it around and peering into the little glass windows. Not only could that machine detect ghosts, it could tell "good" ghosts from "evil" ghosts. It was recently discovered by its inventor that it also detected the presence of strong negative energy. The negative energy appeared red in the window, just like the presence of an evil ghost. Good ghosts appeared as green or yellow. He also found out that there was white energy whenever Miss Emily was having a moment of inspiration. She got stuck on a task, white energy appeared, and *wham!* She had the answer.

Speaking of the lantern... Castlethorn named it "Lantern," funnily enough. Jimmy thought that maybe he could start naming his everyday objects. He could have new friends—"Pencil," "Desk," and "Chair." He started to giggle aloud at his own cleverness but was immediately shushed by some other students who were trying to sleep, several to a bed, in this overcrowded dormitory.

Then he began to reflect on the idea of how lonely Mr. Castlethorn must be to feel the need to name objects in his vicinity and to refer to them as he would *real* friends. Jimmy then calmed himself and realized that perhaps that he should also try to sleep. His concluding thoughts were of how Mr. Castlethorn, a man who only terrified him days ago, was now concerned for his safety and was becoming his friend, to boot. *Interesting thoughts these*, considered Jimmy to himself as his eyes slowly closed and he found himself in the world of dreams, wonderfully pleasant dreams, and he began softly snoring in synch with the others in the bed. If he could have seen himself asleep, he would have noticed the trace of a smile on his lips.

*****

Margaret's own thoughts were equally foreign to her this very night. She was the most hated girl in the class, the "snitch" that no one could stand. Then the teacher that had terrorized them all was suddenly taken out of the picture. Only to be replaced by order of the principal with a fellow *student*. Then the student/teacher protected her and seemed almost to be a *friend*. Margaret was only the snitch and teacher's pet because she was trying to protect her own self.

Miss Emily understood that. At first, Margaret thought that the new teacher would abuse her the way that Whipshot had. She thought that some kind of revenge was going to happen. To her surprise, not only was Miss Emily not taking revenge on her, but she forbade the other students from doing so too.

Naturally, there were some petty recriminations in the dorm—the occasional tug at one of her pigtails, the refusal to allow her to shower until the hot water was all gone—but even these were not that serious. It seemed that she was being gently reminded that the students still remembered what she did, but they also respected their new teacher and were glad that Whipshot was gone. They almost *had* to do something to Margaret after all of the misery she caused them. It was universally understood, however, that Margaret was trying to survive like all of them. The few students that would actually speak to the former snitch, off to the side, were starting to tell the others that "she was not all that bad." It would only be a matter of time, and she would be completely forgiven.

Regarding Miss Whipshot, some of them actually said out loud that they hoped Nurse Nightshade would find the same nightshade she gave other people and would shove it down Whipshot's throat. One student had a more creative idea of where to put it, but Margaret could not bear that thought. She was too much of a lady, even if she did smile a bit at that disrespectful suggestion. It seemed that the whole class was just glad that the suffering was over.

The only time Miss Emily yelled at them or called them terrible names was when Miss Coffenayle was around. The newest teacher seemed to have the most uncanny sense to almost *predict* when the principal would show. It was rather unusual because no one else knew—no footsteps could be heard, Coffenayle did not announce herself, nothing like that at all. Miss Emily simply knew with perfect timing when to act out in nasty ways to keep Miss Coffenayle happy.

Margaret thought it a strange but sensible idea for Miss Emily to reinstate her as the class snitch. During her new tenure, though, everyone knew it was just a show for the principal. No one held it against her that she had a soft seat in which to sit; not this time. Margaret was their equal for a few days, sitting in a standard student chair, so they knew that the cushion was just part of the ruse. Everyone understood that poor Margaret was just as much of a victim as anyone else. Some of them were actually a little envious that they did not think of becoming a rat before she came up with the idea. Margaret was not always the snitch; she suffered for a long time. Then she started ratting people out to get Whipshot off of her own back.

The adventure that they had going into Castlethorn's office/lair was something completely unexpected. It was very frightening, certainly, but Margaret noticed that the three of them had built some kind of trust. She, the snitch, Miss Emily, the teacher, and Jimmy, the apprentice, had all three braved something together. It was something that served to galvanize them. It was almost as if they were intentionally thrust together by fate, destiny, or whatever mysterious force was out there, making decisions for people—God, perhaps, if there was such a being. Margaret figured that if there was something more to life than met her eyes that she would see for herself soon enough. With the way things were going, it was hard telling what she would learn tomorrow. She soon drifted off to sleep. She had a dream about a very kind elderly man who wished to teach her many things. He sported a brown suit and a very proper watch chain.

*****

Castlethorn got to bed late and was very, very tired. He fell asleep immediately in his clothes. He had taken off his coveralls but slept, as was his custom, in his trousers, suspenders, and one boot. He got the first boot off and was ready for bed. He kept one boot on because if he was in a hurry when he woke up, it would take too long to get both boots on. This was just his way; it seemed reasonable to him, a semi-mad genius who was best friends with a ghost-and-magic-detecting lantern...named Lantern. His last thoughts were of Jimmy. Castlethorn's dreams were normally filled with green fog, that same fog that filled his head when he was awake and trying to remember things. No headache, just him running around in a green fog.

Tonight, he would dream and oddly still remember the dream in the morning. He never remembered his dreams, but this night, he would remember. He kept stock of this dream and even wrote parts of it down:

He was in a laboratory, working on things that seemed far beyond his current comprehension, but in this dream, he remembered being at ease with gadgets and gizmos. He had his slide rule and was doing all the functions on it! In this dream, he did things with it that he could not do in the waking world. He was interrupted in his work. A friend of his was sick! He ran and ran but could not find his friend. Then a familiar-looking man dressed in a brown suit with a proper watch chain appeared. He grabbed Castlethorn by the arm and gently pulled him to a big, big house.

Castlethorn knew this house but could not place it. He opened the door, but it slammed shut again. A window broke, and he tried to peek in from the front porch. People were crying. A man, he thought, lay sick in bed. He was not sure, but this seemed important! A tap on his shoulder. He turned around and was suddenly behind the house. The brown suit man pulled him again and led him around the spacious yard. He saw a funny-looking rock, and the man said, "I am here. She is not. Take care of her, please."

Castlethorn snapped awake, looked around with some confusion, and immediately went back to sleep.

Another dream started. Lantern was with him this time. He was spinning Lantern around and cackling at students. Only this time, Lantern fell out off of the pole and started bounding across the ground, and he chased it. Castlethorn was becoming angry at Lantern for running away like that. Then it stopped running. It jumped back onto its pole and spun itself. Lantern glowed red, a brighter red than Castlethorn had ever seen. Then he noticed that they were by the school field.

Lantern continued to glow redder and redder and projected the red light onto the field. The light took the shape of two people. Then a green light in the shape of a person joined the red ones. The green light shot white light from it, extinguishing the red lights. Suddenly, that dog who would not fetch leaped into the air and snapped like it found something. Then the dog was gone. Lantern had glowed for so long that it melted. Gone! Lantern was gone! Then the whole area started to glow green.

Castlethorn woke up again, and this time, it was because of his alarm. It was time to go to work. So he did, but only after writing a few things down.

*****

Simon I. Doesbad did not sleep. His night was filled with Patience Lovegood. His feelings for Coffenayle were still there, but there was something about Patience that overruled those feelings. With Patience, it felt...real. All night long he was like that, thinking of his friendship for Coffenayle's secretary and how that friendship was beginning to blossom.

His alarm went off. He got shaved and cleaned up. He had a bit of breakfast, grits and eggs, and he put on his poor man duds. He did have fun with the boys the night before; that was a great game of cards and home brew! Well, off to the office. He grabbed his broom and found his way to greener pastures. He looked back while waiting for the cab. He would miss this old neighborhood if he ever left it. Better things awaited, didn't they? He thought about that all the way to the office.

*****

Emily got herself ready for school, another day of "Miss Emily." In some ways, she dreaded having to play this role. If it were not for Mr. Mentor's kindness and teachings, she would be completely over-whelmed. She wondered what would have happened to her were it not for Mr. Mentor. She supposed that nothing would have changed, that she would still be there with her classmates being abused by Miss Whipshot. She wondered how Miss Whipshot was doing today.

She thought that it would be a good day to take the class out on a nature study. They would gather wildflowers, learn their names, put them in a nice jar, and take them to Miss Whipshot. She wanted to see Nurse Shadyknight too to give the students more confidence in their nurse and less confidence in the stupid rumors that were going around the school.

*****

Meanwhile, in the cafeteria, Miss Ladlepot, a super-early riser, was up to her usual escapades. The steam-filled kitchen was chugging and churning along, getting the gruel and sludge-like concoctions ready for the students. She loved her job, that was for certain.

Goliath was busy thudding away and chopping the meats and bones, getting them ready for the hopper to be chopped up into whatever version of foodstuff the cook was going to present to the school.

Ladlepot was running about, doing her thing, checking the gauges, sampling from the barrels of tea, hollering at her staff, and so on. Then she heard from out of nowhere, "Cassius. Remember Cassius." She stopped in her tracks, her sort-of-white cafeteria lady shoes sliding just a little on the wet greasy floor. She caught a countertop to balance herself, and a couple of cockroaches headed for cover. Green fog filled her head at the name of Cassius, and it caused her pain.

She had experiences like this before, but they were farther and farther apart. She found that as long as she kept her mind on "bidness" and conjured up swill for the "kidses," she did not feel the pain. Whenever she allowed herself to try to remember things from the past, from before a certain time, she would hurt. She did not like the pain.

Goliath stopped hacking and cleaving. He looked over at Ladlepot. He seemed concerned, worried. He laid his best friend down and walked over to her. He knew she was the mean boss, but something was different about her, something that the thick mist he lived in would not let him remember. He had never come this close to her before. She allowed him to this time. Her head swirled. In the mist, in the pain, a man kicked a ball toward a giant letter H.

She looked up at Goliath. He sort of cocked his head and looked at her like he was remembering something. Oddly, then, he did something that he never had done before. He grabbed a bucket off a shelf, dumped something out of it, and then kicked the bucket over the counter! He hollered for glee, and Ladlepot cheered too, but then they stopped. They looked at each other, wondering what had just happened here. Goliath said, "Cashus," and they just stood there, staring at each other.

After a moment, they sort of just went back to what they were doing but with less intensity. Their minds seemed to be on something else; they would glance at each other from time to time meaningfully. She stopped being so hard on Goliath, and he seemed to be a little quieter while he went about his butchering the furry things that lay on his many tables. This was a new day. Much to do.

It seemed that new understanding, though dim, had just dawned upon them. Breakfast was about to be served too. Good old gruel and muck. *Chop, chop. Hack, hack.* Grind, splash, serve. Ladlepot somehow wondered if there was more to this job than that. The headache reminded her to not think about that, though, so she did not. She went back to hollering at the staff, but not quite as loudly. Goliath too was less enthused about his chopping and hacking. It was as though he was mildly distracted by something. Maybe it was just an illusion of the mist, but it seemed that some of his moles were shrinking, and his teeth were a little straighter. If Ladlepot were paying attention, she would have realized that her hair was a little softer, and she had fewer varicose veins in her legs than she did even a moment ago.

28

The Class Mascot and New Discoveries

Nurse Shadyknight woke up and stretched. She was in the bed next to Miss Whipshot's bed. No need to sleep in her own room where she would have to go back and forth all night to perform patient care. She rolled Whipshot over and noticed that the teacher's face was not as bloated or wrinkled. It seemed like a wart or two was missing as well. One of the things that Shadyknight was certainly good at, and that was keeping track of a patient's details. She was always on the lookout for skin lesions, rashes, and so on. Coming or going, she would see such abnormalities.

It was important to keep abreast of any changes to report to the doctor, even if there was no doctor in this case. It was still important to know and understand what was happening with her patient. One thing that she did know, even if she did not understand it, was that her patient was definitely *changing*. She knew this to be a medical impossibility, but she also was wise enough to know that sometimes nature simply does its own thing, and that was all that there was to it.

She noticed in herself too that there were certain things changing. Her own clothing seemed to be getting, well, a little *bigger*. Not only that, but she realized that she was appearing a little younger too. The mirror cannot lie, and it was telling her that the lines on her face were not as deep, and her skin was softer. Very interesting, that, but how could that even be? People did not get younger with time. *Well*, thought the nurse, *no time to ponder over that. Not when there is a patient to take care of.* She looked on the new and improved Miss Whipshot, sleeping in unusual peace. Then she went off to shower and change uniforms. No use in her being all itchy and chafed after all!

Soon after she got herself in order, there was a knock at the door. She opened it, and there stood Miss Emily, the new teacher. *Well, surprise, surprise!*

"Good morning, Nurse Shadyknight," said the class in unison. Jimmy handed her a glass mason jar full of flowers. The jar had just minutes ago held some random nails and screws that Castlethorn evicted from it so that the students could present flowers to Miss Whipshot. Not bad for a man who scared them all half to death not so very long ago. As soon as the nurse took the flowers, a couple of boys from the classroom wandered over near the field where that odd crazy old dog was running about, having a wonderful time chasing nothing! They tried to call him over to fetch a stick, and he would run over toward the boys, then run back. Then run toward them, toss his head about, and spin in circles after his own tail, and he'd run back. They threw sticks and even an old rubber ball toward him, but he would not fetch.

"*Stupid dog!*" yelled one of the boys. The dog leaped happily in the air.

"Stupid dog!" yelled the second boy. The mutt leaped in the air again, yelping and spinning about.

"Ha! We thought about naming him…and I think we just did," said the first boy. "Stupid Dog is his new name!"

The second boy laughed and hollered at the dog "Stupid Dog! Stupid Dog!"

The dog yelped and leapt happily each time they yelled his name.

Soon they had the attention of most of the class. The students were all taking turns calling the dog by his new name and laughing happily, pointing their fingers every time the dog would leap and bark when they called it Stupid Dog. With his tongue lapping out, the dog seemed to never tire and appeared to have the time of his life entertaining the students. If one did not know better, they would say the dog was actually *smiling*.

Emily was talking to Shadyknight when the nurse pointed to the students. The rest of the class scattered to the fence to partake in the festivities. Miss Emily and the nurse joined them; the students were having a wonderful time.

They were not actually mocking the old dog out of meanness; they were just enjoying the spectacle of his dancing and strutting about. He was apparently having as much fun as they! The teacher and the nurse joined in the fun and were laughing alongside the students. After a few more minutes, the students had enough, and the dog departed to an area behind the big "H." He stood there, tongue hanging out and panting. The class turned away and went to see Miss Whipshot.

They all filed past their sleeping teacher and were amazed that she seemed to be, well...peaceful. Some of the students thought that she was even looking healthier than she did that day she crashed through the floorboards. They all thought that it was a strange thing, but they generally agreed that she looked better. Of course, anyone probably looks better when they are not screaming and beating on you. This, though, was something different than that. It was more like something they felt intuitively than it was something that they knew or overtly understood. This thing was more personal and deep.

The nurse did not share a lot about the condition of Miss Whipshot other than to tell them that she was resting very well. That much was apparent. She thanked the class for the flowers and lovely "vase." She would put them in a more suitable container later and return the mason jar to them. She would not embarrass them by doing so immediately. They were being so kind to their fallen teacher, and they were being so kind to her. No one whispered about "Nurse Nightshade" or any such thing. It was nice, so very nice to entertain an entire class of *healthy* students. Usually, she was meeting the kids at their worst when there was so little she could do for them. Yes, it was nice to meet real people in a real way, to have a human connection.

Time had passed, though, and they all had other things to do. The students had eaten breakfast, such as it was, so they turned down the idea of having breakfast with her. "A fried egg can do a body good," she had told them, but Miss Emily felt that it was time for them to go. Somehow, she knew that their purpose for being there was accomplished. What was it about that silly dog anyway? The class bade the nurse a good day and left. She smiled—yes, actually smiled *from her heart at their parting*. She told them to come back anytime they liked, and she actually meant it. They departed reluctantly, but Miss Emily not only knew it was time to go, but she also seemed to have a direction in which they should travel.

Nurse Shadyknight was suddenly glad to see them go without breakfast. It had just occurred to her: Where was she going find forty eggs to fry? Oh my! She smiled at her impulsive offer.

Miss Emily led the class through some of the usual buildings and so forth. They saw remnants of what seemed to be a very productive industrial area at one time. They saw cars in different stages of repair, they saw production lines for furniture; there was even an abandoned building that seemed to be filled with radio equipment that had fallen into disuse. One of the students found a large radio antenna that had fallen on the ground. It looked big enough to have once stood beside the building.

The boy who discovered it recognized it as a very powerful antenna; apparently, he knew enough about it to be truly impressed. He stated out loud that he wished this building was still operational. Several other students wished out loud the same thing for various buildings. There were places that looked like abandoned farmer's fields and a dairy. There was a building full of law books. On the outside, an old weatherworn sign read "Dozeman Building."

Miss Emily and her students discovered the contents of these places mostly by looking into the dusty widows or by actually peeking their heads into places where windows used to be. It seemed to Emily that many of these buildings would still have some good use in them if only they could be cleaned up a bit. She thought it a shame that some of the books in them were exposed to the elements. This really was quite the place at one time, she mused. She wondered what could have ever happened to cause all of this to shut down. There even seemed to be a place where people could learn science, mathematics, and medicine! All of these remarkable places were shut down and completely abandoned during their heyday, from all appearances.

Then Emily stopped in her tracks. She felt an urging for her to leave the buildings and turn toward what seemed to be residences. The class followed her as she asked them to, no one really asking where they were going. They were content just to follow Miss Emily. She had managed to show them many wonderful things so far; what could lay around the next corner, they just did not know! Emily recognized that they were working their way into an area very similar to the dormitories, but that was not what held her interest. What held her interest was this particularly rundown old mansion that seemed to simply reek of darkness. She felt that something there was dangerous, but it was being concealed. That feeling seemed to be the strongest coming from the house itself. She felt afraid of that place and sensed that it would be a grave mistake to go there. No, they were not "supposed" to go into the house, though she felt moved to wander the spacious yard around the house.

They approached the gate, and it had a big lock on it. Emily was curious and just reached out and touched the lock. Then she noticed a sound like the tumblers falling into place. The lock actually sprung open, with no effort on her part, in her hand! She looked at the students, but no one else seemed to notice. She pulled on the gate, and it squeaked open. That noise got the attention of already curious students. They all congregated around Miss Emily who walked onto the property cautiously but with the air of someone who had every right to be there. She knew that she should be there and was unafraid. She felt as though Mr. Mentor was guiding them on this journey.

Jimmy walked nearest to her of any of the students, not that Emily minded, and Margaret was not far behind. It just seemed natural, like the three were supposed to be together in this place, right now. All three of them knew it, and they did not have to say it to make it known.

Miss Emily instructed the students to just sort of look around but to stay away from the house. Everyone in the group was instinctively avoiding it anyway. Everyone was looking around and talking and pointing. They saw several old sagging fruit trees surrounded by their own rotten fruit as it lay on the ground. Apples and plums, it seemed they were, and it was a shame to see such waste. They all continued milling about when Jimmy sort of rushed around back of the house. Emily lost sight of him but was not too concerned; after all, he was Mr. Castlethorn's assistant and had proven capable of handling himself.

Jimmy was gone for a moment too long. Emily and Margaret looked at each other and nodded. They both carefully moved around the building and almost ran smack into Jimmy whose eyes were wide with either excitement or terror or maybe a bit of both. He said that they should follow him, so they did. He almost ran to this nearby patch of weeds and pointed to the ground. The spot where Jimmy was standing bordered on two white stones in the ground. Emily and Margaret looked at each other. "Are those gravestones?" asked Margaret.

"Yes," answered Emily quite simply. She just *knew.* Somehow, oddly, Emily was neither surprised nor afraid.

Jimmy was trembling, and Margaret was backing away out of sheer instinct. The names and dates were hard to make out under all the grime the dimming of time, but that was all right. Emily had seen all she needed to see.

"What does this mean?" asked Jimmy.

"Yes, Emily," quizzed Margaret. "You do not seem to be surprised."

"I am not," answered Emily, deep in thought. "Can I get a favor from *both* of you?"

"Sure," Jimmy answered with his head cocked in a questioning sort of way.

"I suppose," said Margaret, "depending on the favor."

"Naturally, Margaret, I would not endanger you or Jimmy."

Margaret felt relieved. "All right, then, if it is not dangerous, I will agree."

"All I need is for the two of you to not say anything about these grave markers to anyone. Please?"

Jimmy and Margaret both agreed to this because they were expecting something much harder to be asked of them. Keeping just one more secret among so many that they had stumbled across in just this one week alone was nothing. Emily was relieved and decided that they should go back to the other students before someone came looking for them. They came back around the house and encountered a group of students who had become curious and started to follow them.

Miss Emily told them that there was nothing back there that they needed to see. This was just a big old abandoned mansion, and they probably should leave the property because who knew if someone actually lived in this place? She explained that if someone did actually live there that they probably would not want to meet them anyway. She had no idea how right she was! Emily had no idea at all this was Miss Coffenayle's abode.

Emily led the students back to the classroom on the shortest route possible. They were gone for longer than normal, and she did not want to draw attention.

They arrived back at the classroom just in time. Miss Coffenayle came to visit just after the class settled in and were engrossed in their studies. She was pleased to see that Miss Emily ran such a tight ship. The principal did not remain long, and Emily was glad of it. It was just a surprise checkup. There were other things that Miss Coffenayle was doing this morning, but she thought that she would just swing by and see how things were. She left almost immediately, which was unusual.

The principal was actually on her way to a meeting with the school's general counsel. She had some annoying fool barge into the school to serve her yet *another* (yawn) subpoena. She needed to get Doesbad to appear in court and do his thing to make the judge either drop the case entirely or to get a continuance. Then they would keep continuing the case until the prosecutors ran out of money or time or just got sick of the judge agreeing to their every roadblock. She would burn them out like she always did. Then, if this was one of the rare cases that actually went to trial, well, InkRobe was on the job and held control over the presiding judge.

Coffenayle met her lawyer in the lobby of her office, and as she led the way with her usual jibes and insults, he paused ever so slightly to smile at Patience. She, much to his delight, smiled back at him. It gave him shivers to have so lovely a lady as that, and a true lady to boot, pay such attention to him. She was so kind and affectionate to him. He had never enjoyed attention as wonderfully unconditional as what she paid to him. She seemed to love to talk to him, no matter what the subject. Her eyes were as lovely as her attitude and her voice. There was no part of her personality that he found abrasive or disagreeable. Those eyes…reminded him of somebody, but his brain could not pick the memory out. That blasted foggy sensation that occurred when he tried to recollect certain things!

29

Operation: Coffin Nailed!

Once they were inside the office, lawyer and client both took their seats. She was seated behind her desk comfortably, and he took his place in a plain wooden chair. He could not help but to notice that the chair was lower than usual, causing him to look up at her and she to look down upon him. She stared at him for a good hard second that unnerved the attorney. There was something different about her.

Coffenayle opened the meeting with, "You worthless toad! *Another* subpoena? Do you think I have time or energy for this? Do you think that I *want* to deal with the authorities anymore? Hmmmm?"

He cringed. He could not believe this. Subpoenas were just part of this dirty business they were dealing in. She knew they were unavoidable, and she knew that he would deal with it. So why was she acting this way? He did not like what he was seeing.

Doesbad was accustomed to the fire in her eyes. He was used to that creepy feeling he got every time he was around her. This time, though, it was different. While she never lacked confidence before, this time, she was over-the-top *arrogant*. She was not only convinced of her own superiority; she was now very powerful in that belief. There was a spectacular type of fire about her this time. Something not just wicked but terribly *evil!* The light in her eyes that used to playfully tease him, keep him interested in her, was gone completely. It was as though he was seeing her true self for the first time, nothing hidden. She laid it all out on the table, all of her greed, her lust for power, her desire to force her will on the entire world literally—*it was all there, pure and unadulterated poison.*

This feeling just cut through him; it felt like a thousand pins prickling his soul all at once. He saw her sitting there, yes, but there was something that he saw in the back of his mind that was not mortally possible. He saw her being as this big fuzzy ball of energy that had no shape or form. It had her face, but it was a swirling mist of dark tendrils of energy that struggled to take a shape and keep it but somehow could not. This vision of his was dark and hopeless and terrible. Yet, this image had great power, power enough to kill thousands or even millions to satisfy a lust, a thirst for power that could never be slaked. There was a *hunger* there that could never be satisfied.

He knew now any overtures she made to him of friendship were faked. She had no regard for him any more than she would a common insect. He was there as a tool to be used, to be exploited for her own good and no one else's. There was no gratitude in her, no feelings of conscience or decency. Her idea of "good" was power. Money was love, dominance was friendship, absolute dominion of the world was her...*right.* Even then, taking over the world would not be enough to satisfy her. There was not enough power or money in this world or the universe to ever make her feel like she had enough. Her evil was beyond anything that he could comprehend.

Doesbad began to sweat and grow uncomfortable in his own skin. He could not comprehend what was happening to him just now. He was never much for religion, but he somehow understood that he was looking into the eyes of pure evil. He was fascinated and horrified at the same time, drawn to those terrible black flames in those terrible blue eyes, but he wanted nothing more than to run out of the office screaming at the same time. All of this was happening while she was berating him. The words were not any worse than before, but the spirit behind those words was...indescribably evil. Pure evil. She had achieved some mastery of herself, his gut somehow told him.

The word *master* kept playing over and over in his mind. He did not understand that he was being given a vision. He was achieving a true understanding for the first time of what he was doing at this school. Though he had never before considered the existence of such a being, he realized now that he was working for...*the devil himself.* The lawyer cringed and shuddered, much to the new master's delight, but not for the reasons she thought. He was not afraid of her power as much as *he was afraid for his own soul.*

If he could see what was truly going on, Doesbad would not have been quite as afraid. After all, an invisible Mr. Mentor was there with his hand on Doesbad's shoulder, strengthening him. Patience was in the other office, praying for him because at this moment, she somehow knew that something was going terribly, terribly wrong behind that closed door. Mentor was causing him to see the vision and giving him support at the same time, and the light from the prayer of Patience was giving him power to withstand the whole experience.

There were spiritual resources on the side of good pulling for him as well. Good has unlimited access to angels during times like this, particularly when a person was being honest with themselves for the very first time. This was his very first time. He was beginning to question the validity of his shiny car, his expensive suit; though they were fine things to have, they were just things and, well, his *friends in the poor neighborhood were real.* They were of real importance to him. Patience was talking to him about that during their office *dates*—he could admit now that he was dating her, wooing her, and he could admit that she was right. She not only was right; she was real. Coffenayle was not. Nothing about this...false "master" was real. *Nothing!*

He began to feel stronger in these thoughts of breaking free of her, and he began to feel better. He was feeling stronger the longer she went on about his ineptness and how he never got it right. She was telling him how lucky she was to have her in his life, to keep him set straight, to give him enough gold to afford his fine clothes and fancy car. Oh, yes, he was very fortunate to have her in his life or else what would he be without her? He could hear her words still, but now they were just a hollow echo. He was sort of drifting away from her in his mind now, calmly. Her words did not have any more power over him. The more she went on, the more he felt the help of Patience and others for his own good and truly his own good.

For the first time in his life, Doesbad believed that there just might be a God in heaven, and that thought gave him great comfort. He not only began to calm himself but actually smiled a little. Mr. Mentor and Patience began to smile a lot. Miss Emily, off in her classroom conducting her business and teaching geography, began to smile too, knowing that Mentor was nearby, doing some great thing!

Miss Coffenayle saw the renewed expression on the lawyer's face and *knew* that she had finally gotten through to him. She knew now that the spineless simpering imp of a man was seeing the light, seeing that she was his only way to have a life. Her way was the true way to wealth, power, honor, and glory untold. At last! This fool was beginning to take on her image, was beginning to understand that she was his master! Why, this was only the beginning, she thought to herself. He would be her right hand in creating her new global empire! She would be the true power running the world, even as a Coffenayle should be! He would be her understudy, her lackey, her servant, her student! Yes! He would be her student, and she would start to teach him the craft, the arcane arts that she had so fully embraced that made her powerful enough to cast magical spells without talismans or candles.

Of course, he would learn under her, the way she learned under Malovent. Doesbad would indeed learn to *do bad* under her tutelage! Yes! She would make him powerful as her apprentice, as her student. He would have to start with the books, then the candles and tricks with the mirrors, just as she did. He would progress faster than she did because she did not have a mortal master. He would. Doesbad would have the benefit of her teaching. He would become a master as she did. Then she would be become a master's master, progressing to the position of Malovent as she gained more and more masters such as this one. *Ahhh...yessss*, she thought to herself! The very power of the Underworld would be hers here on earth! *Yes!*

All of these thoughts were behind the very words that she was saying to her lawyer. So crystal clear, so very real to her were these ideas. Yes, she would let him go now to do his lawyer stuff, and she would call on Malovent to consult with her on how to make her dreams come true. She saw how confident Simon I. Doesbad was becoming in her presence. He was not even nervous or shaking anymore. This was because of her; because she was giving him confidence in evil. She had to break him first, to remove weakness, but that was just part of it. She could now fill in those gaps where weakness once dwelt with the power of she and Malovent. What a report she could give Malovent this time! She gave a broad smile. "Well, Mr. Doesbad, I believe that we have accomplished much during this meeting! You may go about your business now at the courts!"

"Indeed I shall, Miss Coffenayle...indeed I shall," he said with a smile as he rose from the uncomfortable wooden chair.

She had no idea what he was talking about. Neither did Patience as she saw him pass from that office with a very different kind of a smile at her. Not until he winked twice as he had promised. It was their special signal that he had actually accepted the plan Patience had outlined to him if he ever wanted to leave Miss Coffenayle's employ. She was overjoyed but did not dare to express it because Miss Coffenayle was near. But now it was time to get to work.

It was time to start *Operation: Coffin Nail!*

The principal followed her new apprentice out the door, overjoyed at what had just transpired between them...in *her* mind! She saw him to the door and told him that she had every confidence in his skills as her attorney, plus the "special assistance we get with the judge." Doesbad knew that Coffenayle had some influence over the judge, but he did not quite know how. He assumed it was a bribe but did not know about InkRobe. He turned and smiled at his client warmly. Soon, he would no longer be burdened by her filthy lucre in the form of gold bullion.

He drove away thoughtfully in his shiny fancy car. The car that was no longer as real to him as a bottle of illegal home brew and a game of cards with friends; and it certainly was not as real as Patience. His new girl said that she would one day talk to him about his home brews too, but that was another conversation for another day. He thought he knew what she meant and figured he better have some more brews while he still could!

Meanwhile, Mr. Mentor stood invisibly by in the office of Patience, the school's administrative assistant. She was busy gathering papers and records. Miss Coffenayle came back into the office, oblivious to Mentor. Indeed, she passed right through him. Mr. Mentor got a taste of her as she did so. The old educator winced a bit as he felt what she had become. He knew Patience was safe enough, so he needed to leave right away. He felt the absolute need to leave. He had to prepare the students, his three friends, one of whom was a teacher. Miss Emily, yes, truly was a teacher, Mentor realized. He would have to help do something about getting that girl a proper education.

Funny, though, he reflected, that even though he had been dead for several years, he still was so deeply concerned about the living. As a boy, he had read about hauntings and heard of the legends of the dead who would become banshees and poltergeists. He assumed, as many mortals did, that the affairs of the living were of no consequence to the dead, that they were two separate types of beings in completely different worlds. He thought that the dead could not any longer identify with the living. He made the false assumption that angels were winged harp-bearing creatures that could only offer sympathy but be of no use to mere mortals. He could not even imagine that the earth was covered by spirits of dead people such as himself who were actively involved with the living in the capacity of ministers. He was only one of an army of millions; and the Lord God attended to them all.

That's right! While they, the Soldiers of God, were necessarily commissioned to preach the Word of God, they were still involved with their families and people of interest. As angels, they would do many different things. They would help people fight off temptations to do evil, interfere with the actions of evil spirits, or even help recover very important lost objects. They could even become more involved with human affairs, working as Mentor was doing right now. This work is normally done invisibly. Mentor was given permission to interfere so openly because of the importance and urgency of the situation. True evil did not often find as willing a mortal as was Donatienne Coffenayle. Once Donatienne flipped to the darkness and became such a terrible threat, heaven responded with the greatest urgency!

Naturally, God knew about the world dominion plans of the Coffenayle line. He knew how they would eventually aid in fulfilling prophecies written in Revelation. Donatienne, though, was a different case. On top of all her wicked desires, her magics had become so powerful that she was beginning to bend the very laws of nature itself, turning humans into barely recognizable creatures, shadows of their former selves. Such abominations must not be allowed on the face of the earth. She must be stopped, and Mr. Charles Edward Mentor was the man…um…spirit to do it.

Mr. Mentor had the help of other angels, but he was not to introduce them to his student friends. They could not give too much knowledge of their existence to mortals because then they would become spoiled and expect their ministering spirits to solve all their problems. Plus, if they knew all of what the afterlife did for them, they would no longer have faith but sure knowledge. It is critical to exercise faith to gain sufficient strength enough to handle the sure knowledge. With that type of strength, the mortal would walk faithfully in the absolute knowing of the truth and not sin against it. To sin against the sure knowledge was to invite complete condemnation, the type of unholy curse that Coffenayle had intentionally invited, even demanded to come into her life. That would not do. No, Father had lost one-third of the hosts of heaven to the fallen Lucifer, and He would not allow anything like that to happen again.

So the pure knowledge was reserved for those who could handle knowing the absolute truth, knowing absolutely that there is a God, and to do so without blaspheming against Him. Faith and exercising faith by doing things to serve mankind were the keys to knowing completely the God of Creation. Some of the great prophets of Scripture and relatively few others learned to this level in this life. Keeping the vast majority of mortals ignorant until they *chose* to learn of God was to protect them from knowing too much, too soon. So it was not up to Mentor to teach these kids about God. It was up to them to learn according to the desires of their hearts. His mission was to save this school and all the lives in it. Then he would move onto other projects and missions. Now it was time for him to make a critical move. A move that would lead to open warfare right here at the school.

*****

The day went on in the classroom with Miss Emily berating her students often enough to not arouse suspicion. Mr. Mentor was there with her, moving and prompting her. She had released Jimmy to work with Mr. Castlethorn at the old genius-turned-janitor's request. They came and went. The students had eaten their—*ugh!*—cafeteria breakfast and lunch. Miss Emily had to start taking her breaks in the teacher's lounge so she would not arouse suspicion. She wanted to fit in, but she was failing to identify with her new professional peers very well. She sat uncomfortably alone while they held their coffee mugs and glanced over at her from time to time while in quiet conversation. She knew they were probably, undoubtedly, speaking about her. It was clear that they did not trust Miss Emily, the new kid on the block and Miss Coffenayle's newest favorite. Jealousy is a terrible thing among professionals.

She noticed that every one of them loved *that tea.* They drank it every day. It did not seem to be anything that special. The smell was sweet and was...tempting...but she noticed something very peculiar about it. Every time a teacher came in and took a cup, they seemed to become, well, *different.* They became cloudy or something in their eyes. Their conversation became a shade slower than it was in the hallway. Their language became slow, silly, and mildly crude. They were not drunk, but they were different than they were before they drank that tea. Some of them seemed to have problems with their limbs already, but they became more pronounced as they took the tea.

Whatever was in that pot, Miss Emily knew that she wanted nothing to do with it. She sensed that this was one of the big barriers between her and the other faculty members. She was the only one who was not twisted of body and mind. She was the only one who did not drink that tea. Once in a while, a teacher would fill their cup and look at Miss Emily, pointing to the tea, making a silent offer to bring her some. She consistently and flatly refused. The one making the offering would never push the issue or say much. They would simply return to the group of teachers all enjoying their tea.

They would look over their shoulder at her, pressuring her, but they would not say a word. Emily, though, would rather stay alone in the teacher's lounge than to become like one of them. She was grateful that breaks were short and that she could escape the awkwardness and return to her class where she had at least some kind of control. Little known to her, though, things were changing around the school.

In the cafeteria, things were becoming…better. The meals served up by the cafeteria these days to the students were a bit different. One would not call it quality food, as it was barely food at all, but it seemed have a little less water, and some of the goo actually tasted like something. It was hard to say what it actually tasted like, but there was some extra seasoning or something that made it little more palatable than it had ever been before. The students remarked on it in hushed tones, lest someone be alerted and they remove the "good stuff." It seemed to the student body in general that when they made compliments about some condition or another that they lost that thing. They learned that positivity in general was discouraged at Happy Valley Vocational School.

Back in the kitchen, the conditions remained unchanged, but if anyone were paying close enough attention, they would have noticed that Miss Ladlepot was in a better mood than usual. Not that her behavior changed much, but she did have a less sour expression, and some of her wrinkles seemed to be not as deep. She also did not have a cigarette dangling from her lower lip. That was certainly a change, but everyone was so self-absorbed with trying to stay out of trouble that they did not really look at her, much less pay attention to details of her appearance.

One such detail was a flower from the root ball she found on her desk. It now decorated her stained cafeteria uniform. Most unusual indeed. To put a cherry on top of the pile of evident changes, she had only hit two employees alongside the head with ladles today. There were several "warning shots" that came close to her workers, but they all knew how deadeye accurate she was with those ladles, and if she missed, it was because she *wanted* to miss you! The employees were just like the students in that they did not want to mention it where she could hear because they did not want it to change. They were perfectly happy to not experience the penetrating ring of a ladle bouncing off their heads.

Goliath was happy cleaving up the various unknown meats that were presented to him. He was laughing and cleaving, laughing and cleaving happily. There was a change in his routine, though: he would take the larger fractions of bone and drop-kick them into waste receptacles not in his area. The bones unerringly hit their target each and every time as though being punted by a professional, and he would yell, "Hoo-yay!" No one told him that this word was incorrect because incorrect language was naturally expected from one such as Goliath. They were just glad to see him enjoying himself.

Everyone failed to notice that he was losing some weight, and his shoulders seemed less bulky but more muscular at the same time. While he was violating a safety standard by kicking bones clear across the kitchen, no one cared what garbage went where, and the roaches never protested either. The fact that Ladlepot did not scream at him for "fooling around when there's work to be done, idiot" was different. This was certainly an indicator that things were changing on a personal level for the cafeteria staff. Again, those who did notice any of these little things, if anyone did, never breathed a word because they did not want to disrupt what was happening. Any change at all for the good, no matter how minute, was a welcome change.

After Miss Emily was done teaching for the day, and the students were properly dismissed, she checked the hallway and found Principal Coffenayle walking toward her. The woman was strutting smartly in her Napoleonic getup and looking even more arrogant than usual. That worried Emily to see her in such a state. She warmly approached Miss Emily and invited her to her office for a quick chat. She felt it was time to extend a special invitation. That was very worrisome because Emily was not sure what Coffenayle meant by "special." Such a person could apply any meaning at all to such a word.

Miss Emily dared not refuse because she could not think of a plausible excuse. She did not want to appear as though she distrusted her lead educator. She hoped Mr. Mentor was near. The pair reached the office entry, and Miss Coffenayle opened the door to the reception area and turned on the light. Miss Emily entered the lobby, and the principal gave a repeat performance, opening her personal office door for her, something that Miss Coffenayle never did for anybody.

Then a cold chill settled over Miss Emily. "Do not drink the tea," said Mentor's voice very distinctly. "Scratch the tip of your nose if you heard and understand me." Emily casually reached up and lightly scratched the end of her nose. "Good. Spill that tea into the wastebasket when she is not looking. Then pretend you drank it all. I will give you more instructions in a moment. Touch your nose again casually, just like you did if you understand me." She did.

Coffenayle was so busy being pleased with herself and making a show with her good manners and perfect tea service that she did not notice Miss Emily fiddle with her nose. She motioned to the young teacher to be seated in a chair. In front of it was a tea set on a silver tray. It appeared that the dainty cups and saucers were very old and high quality. The setup was on Miss Coffenayle's desk. She stood and poured the tea perfectly; there was only the one cup.

"One lump or two, dear?" Coffenayle asked so sweetly.

"Two," answered Emily with a smile. She noticed that a small waste receptacle was being carefully moved by unseen hands into a position where she could dump the tea without being noticed, if she was careful. Miss Coffenayle added the sugar and stirred the tea carefully as though she were handling a precious wine that she dared not bruise. When Miss Coffenayle laid down the napkin and set the cup and saucer upon it, she pulled her chair out from behind her desk and sat across from Emily. She looked so…dark…and yet happy. It was not a look Emily had seen before, and she was glad that Mr. Mentor was there supporting her efforts to not drink whatever was in this cup.

The steam wafted upward, and Emily recognized immediately that the aroma was precisely the same as that tea the faculty and staff were drinking in the breakroom. Mentor's voice chimed in again with "If you have a sip or two, don't worry. That is not enough to affect you. She will have to see you take that first sip, then I will distract her. Once she turns away, spill the tea into the waste basket, then bring the empty cup to your lips like you drank the whole thing. I will tell you what to do then." Emily made that same motion to her nose again. She understood. Good.

Coffenayle was settled in very well, and she put her elbows on her knees, interlocked her fingers, and rested her chin on them, smiling. "I hope you don't mind the informality, my dear teacher," she purred.

Emily wondered if Coffenayle thought that she was actually fooling anyone with this terrible performance. The "dear teacher" line was spreading it on a little *thick*. *Disgusting*, thought Emily through her own smile. Her own performance was flawless. Miss Coffenayle bought it hook, line, and sinker.

"No," said Emily, "I don't mind at all." She dared not say anything more because she could barely fake it any longer.

"Well, go ahead, dear, and have your tea."

"But what about you?"

"Oh, no, love. I've had my fill, and there was only enough left in the pot for your cup."

"Very well, then, it seems cool enough." She took the overly fancy dainty cup in both hands and touched her lips to it, hoping Mentor acted quickly. Suddenly, a bookshelf broke in half, and Miss Coffenayle leapt from her seat. With her full attention on the bookshelf, one that contained some of her favorite incantation books, she did not notice Emily deftly dump the tea into the trash can. The tea quickly disappeared, soaking into the papers. That same invisible hand turned the papers over with dry papers on top. Miss Coffenayle fussed with the shelf a moment and then turned back to Emily who was holding the cup up to her mouth with her head back as though she had quaffed the entire cup. The few drops that she tasted were very sweet and quite delicious. It tasted like the way a rose smelled in the early morning, and the aroma reflected freshly cut lawns and reminded her of her mother and father when they worked in the yard. She also knew that this stuff was bad news from the effects that she had seen it have on the staff. Despite that, she found herself wanting more because the taste was so attractive to her. She could see why her teachers and school staff drank it so much.

"Sorry about that, my dear Emily," said Coffenayle, apparently quite pleased with what she saw the girl doing. "Well! It seems that you really enjoyed your tea!"

"Yes, Miss Coffenayle. I did enjoy it!" she exclaimed, not lying. She just did not have the whole cup was all.

"What did it taste like?"

"Oddly, it tasted like the scent of beautiful roses on a summer's morning and smelled like freshly cut grass," replied Emily truthfully.

"Excellent! I take it that you *loved it*, then? Hmmm?" inquired Coffenayle, her eyes wide with anticipation and delight.

"Yes, oh yes. This smells like the same tea the school serves in the break room."

"How perceptive of you, my lovely new teacher. That is precisely what it is."

"I was hoping so. That means I can have all I like throughout—" She stopped talking.

"Emily," said Mentor's voice. "Stare. Stare into space for few seconds."

Emily stared blankly at nothing, eyes wide, and she followed the rest of Mentor's instructions by letting her hands fall into her lap, rocking back and forth just a bit, and then she started talking a little slower, like she was very sleepy.

"Throughout, um…the day…all I like…"

He told her to say something crude and then laugh about it.

"And I hope it makes my farts smell all rosy! Maybe my poop will be like chocolate bars!" she laughed out loud.

Miss Coffenayle laughed out loud too, very long and hard. The remark was not all that funny, but she loved it. What she actually loved was the fact that she had just inducted Emily into her army. Because the tea that tasted like roses to Emily, like honey to another, chocolate to another, she knew she had just made the poor girl the same as all the others. As long as she had that recipe and charm for Taste-all Tea (TAT for short), she could rule the school with an iron fist and all the teachers would follow her lead.

The effectiveness of the tea was due to it being a mind control potion. The taste of the tea was different for each person. The magic called for the fluid to taste like each person's favorite food, scent, or memory. The point was to cause the person to remember their favorite moments in life, and it would trigger a huge dump of chemical transmitters in the brain that would give them ultimate pleasure at the taste. That way, they would keep coming back for more, even as they were falling deeper and deeper under the spell of whomever made the tea. The staff who drank the tea were unwittingly keeping themselves all the more her slaves. An additional charm twisted their limbs, causing them to feel painful and grumpy all the time. Their negativity fed one another's bad feelings, and there was a synergistic effect of increasing evil upon evil, abuse upon abuse. Plus, it caused people to want to escape their condition by drinking more tea for its pleasures. Ah, the power of cyclical addiction!

Emily sat there, just smiling sleepily as Mentor told her to do. She needed to look completely entranced. She did so remarkably well. There was no way for Miss Coffenayle to know that she had just been conned.

"Well, my dear, dear teacher, you have had a wonderful day. Why don't you go home and get some rest?"

"Yes…is my house…all messy again?"

"Oh, no, no, no! I am pretty sure that will not happen ever again! You just need to go home and get some sleep. You have another day of teaching tomorrow, you know!"

"Yes…farting…roses…poo-poo like fudge," Emily slurred as she wandered out the door, slack-jawed and stupid-looking.

Coffenayle closed the door after her and laughed long and hard. She was always so happy to see someone get dosed with the tea for the very first time. Not only was it symbolic of her ultimate control over them, but it was so very *entertaining*. They all became stoned out of their mind on their first dose. She knew that Emily was still sensible enough to know her surroundings and to find her way home in spite of the tea's effects. The dopiness was not due to actual altering of perceptions, but it was due to the effect of the magic. She decided it was time to celebrate by firing off a few rounds from her miniature desk cannon. She had plenty of powder and fuses. She picked a wall and enjoyed about thirty minutes of shooting ball bearings into the plaster! This time, she was not mad at Doesbad and driving him off by shooting at the doorway as he ran!

Once the host got used to the effects of Taste-All Tea, and that took under an hour in most cases, no more than two in any case, they would walk around, perfectly perceptive. They seemed normal on the outside but were cloudy-brained on the inside and very easy to control because they all would soon forget the lives they had pre-TAT. Trying to recall their lives would bring terrible pain. Then other magic Miss Coffenayle practiced drained their natural energy and channeled it to her, keeping the principal spry and vigorous. Her magic also made all the tea drinkers become freakish-looking and strange, all the more to the evil witch's advantage. If the outside world rejected them, then they had to stay with her; not that they could actually leave anyway because of their addiction to the tea.

Mentor's invisible voice kept coaching Emily to act goofy, but not so much that she would accidentally trip and fall. She would giggle to herself, walk with a mild stagger, but keep her sense of direction. She kept the charade all the way to her front stoop where she fumbled with her key just a bit in case someone was watching. One never knew who could be monitoring her, even into the late hours. Once she got inside her house, she was allowed to become normal again. Mr. Mentor said he could come back when she had fully changed into some street clothes. She was not done yet. He told her to gently rap three times on her wall, and he would appear. She did so, and Mr. Mentor stood in her room at the foot of her bad where Emily was also standing, ready to go. "What now?" she asked curiously.

"You are going to Mr. Castlethorn's office. Stagger a little like you have been. No one will question your behavior because you are pulling off the first-time potion drinker bit with a stellar performance!"

"Castlethorn's office?" she asked.

"Yes. I will be there to give you further instructions. I must introduce myself to Castlethorn and Jimmy...*tonight.*"

"What?" exclaimed Emily. "Have you lost whatever ghosts have for brains?" Emily asked, very much in shock.

"I assure you, *young lady*, that my 'ghost brains' are very much intact. In fact, my intelligence has never been this sharp!" he spoke firmly.

"Sorry," Emily responded sheepishly. "But are you sure that they are ready?"

Mr. Mentor sighed. "No, I am not. But I have been informed that we must act now because Malovent and Coffenayle are getting ready to move forward with their plans to destroy the school."

"Destroy?" Emily stopped short. She would not let fear take hold because she knew that would play into Miss Coffenayle's hands. She took a deep breath and simply said, "Well...okay. I guess we have little choice."

"Indeed, Emily. I will go there ahead of you and try to prepare them."

"All right."

30

A Grave Desecrated

Mr. Mentor disappeared through the wall, and she went out through the door. She staggered a bit, as planned, and did not see Miss Coffenayle. She arrived at the office of Mr. Castlethorn, and Jimmy was there, as promised. They were both studying Lantern intently and were perplexed. Emily cleared her throat and made both of them jump.

"What are you doing here?" asked Jimmy, panting and holding his chest "You like to have scared us to death!"

"Yeses, Miz Emi-lee…what'cha duin hyar?" asked Castlethorn.

"What's up with the lantern, fellows?" she asked curiously.

"We see a green apparition, which is a good spirit," said Jimmy, "but it is moving around, knocking stuff off shelves and stuff. It's pretty bothersome."

"Maybe he's trying to get your attention," stated Emily matter-of-factly.

"Mebbe," said Mr. Castlethorn. "Wha'chu knows abboudit, anyway, Miz Emily?" He stared at her intensely for a moment. "My thinker seems ta thinkz youse knows more dan ye're tellin' us."

Emily stood silently for a moment and then asked, "What if the ghost wanted to talk to you? For real. Could you guys handle that?"

Castlethorn and Jimmy looked at each other.

"Fer seerious?" asked Castlethorn.

"For serious?" asked Jimmy.

"For serious," said Emily.

"I'm game!" said Jimmy.

"Hmm. Wahl, dat's gonna prove onced and fer all that Lantern duz what I sayees he duz. So, sure. If yese gots a ghost ta show me, den ah'm game too."

"All right then, gentlemen. Let's make a game of it. Use lantern to find the ghost."

"Ahl raht," said Castlethorn, "youse know dat Ah has a chant Ah sez wi'ff lantern some de times, raht?"

"Yes," said Jimmy. "Honestly, it is little unnerving."

"It's jest a fun thang dat keeps da stoodents off balance an' thinking I'm crazy! I am not crazy…mostly," he said, looking at his calloused hands and thick nails like there was something just not quite right about it all. "But I needs ta keeps da students outta muh office, an' youse two knows why. It's dangerous in there, and I can't remember wut I want to remember tuh make things better. Would you like to hear my rhyme? I wrotes it myself."

Jimmy and Miss Emily nodded.

"Okee…hyar it is:

I know I'm dead, not alive anymore,
I haunt here amongst my hosts;
I makes best friends with zombie and ghouls!
Wooooooooooo! I'm a ghoooost!"

Jimmy and Emily laughed out loud. They thought the poem was hilarious, mostly because it was a silly nursery rhyme and not something terribly sinister, like they always believed it was. Castlethorn looked at them for a moment and then joined in the laughter. He took notice of how close they were standing to each other, their hands on one another's shoulders. He smiled and chuckled too but with the knowingness of a wise old man in the presence of budding affections. They looked each other in the eye, noticed they were touching each other, and quickly removed their hands as though they had touched something hot. Indeed, perhaps they had? Something else, too, the old genius realized…that was some very clear speech he just delivered. *Mebbe he wuz gettin' betterz?*

Not wishing to embarrass his two young friends, the old genius janitor let this revelation slide; it did please him, though, and he resolved to not let on. He moved on and said, "Now, that's a funny pome. I knows more pomes, too, but they's in the back of my mind. How I loses them I dassn't knows. So…we dun had our fun, nows what ss-sayees yese dat we finds us a ghostee?"

The two youngsters composed themselves, glad to not address the elephant in the room, and paid close attention.

"Jimbo, Ah's gonna do somthin' ah never dun before. Ah's gonna lets a stoodint operates with muh best fren. Carefully, now…" He leaned the lantern toward the boy who stared at it, then at his new mentor in disbelief.

"Me?" asked Jimmy. "I…uh… I have no experience with this thing." He reached for the lantern reluctantly. He took the pole and used both hands to steady it. The lantern and pole were heavy, and Castlethorn helped him steady it. Lantern was tough, but the glass was fragile, and this was not the time to mess with cutting new panes to shape. When Jimmy had it steady enough, the old janitor let it go. Jimmy stood there, clumsily at first, then he braced himself and appeared ready.

"Now," said Castlethorn quietly, "all youse gotta do is to spin it. Start slow, then work up the speed. You don't have to say my poem or cluck lahk a chikin. Just spin it fast til he starts to glow. Once he glows, look in the window. You seen de colors a'fore. That's raht… spin it slow til you gets the knack of it. Okay, fasters, now, fasters… and—"

The lantern started to glow.

"That's right, Jimbo! Ye sees the glow? Now set the pole onto the ground. Stops yeses da lantern. Raht! Now we can sees."

The three of them gathered around the lantern with Jimmy out of breath for the effort of what he did. The lantern glowed a very pretty green hue and from the position in the glass window. "Whoa!" exclaimed Castlethorn. "He's raht on top of us!" Then, as if on cue, the three of them heard a voice.

"Hello, Mr. Castlethorn. And hello, Jimmy," said the man's voice.

Emily recognized her best friend right away but did not want to give it away. She would let Mr. Mentor handle his own introduction. This meeting was too important for her to say anything amiss.

The two men stared toward the sound of the voice, their mouths open, unable to believe their ears. "You have been chasing me for a long time, Cassius."

"But-but. I remember—aaaaagh! My head…all…foggy!" Castlethorn closed his eyes and covered his ears with his hands. He was that way for a moment, bent over and groaning.

Mr. Mentor was very sorry for all this, but he had to see how deep the curse was. It was worse than he thought.

"Don't worry, Mr. Castlethorn, you will be all right," said Mr. Mentor.

Emily felt warmth come from the old spirit's direction and knew that he was doing something for Mr. Castlethorn to make him feel better. The old janitor stood upright.

"Ghost…don'chu never do dat to me agin! Ya hurt me!" the old man hollered in pain rather than anger. "But ye's making me better, aint'cha?"

"Yes. I am sorry that I hurt you. I am making you better."

Emily noticed a trace of sadness in Mentor's voice. She had a good idea of what he was trying to do. She let things be, let the men worth things out.

"What's the matter, Mr. Castlethorn?" asked Jimmy.

"Is all right, boy. Ah'm fine, now. Jest the brain pains again with all dat green fog. Happens when I tries ta remember things that I shouldnts try tah remember."

"Shouldn't remember?" asked Jimmy. It did not make sense to him, but he took it in stride. Things had been very strange ever since that day Whipshot fell through the floor. He did not want to cause further pain, so he did not ask Castlethorn anything more. He was very intrigued by the voice. He decided to give it a try. "Um…ghost?"

"I have a name, young man," corrected Mr. Mentor with mild reproof.

"Your name is Youngman?" asked Jimmy naively.

Emily rolled her eyes and stifled a chuckle. She was experienced with this, and Jimmy was not. She remembered just days ago how hard it was for her too.

"No," said Mentor patiently. "My name is Mr. Mentor. You may call me that, if you please."

"Okay… Mr. Mentor," Jimmy responded. He was developing some confidence, already losing his initial fear. He somehow knew that this ghost was not going to hurt them.

Castlethorn was back to his old self. Jimmy noticed something though. He seemed to stand taller, and that rotten tooth was…nearly normal? How could that be? Jimmy just let slide. This was not the time for questions. He had so many, but he sensed that there was some urgency, somehow, and he just kept quiet. This was not the time to have a lengthy conversation. This was a time to listen…and learn.

"Mr. Castlethorn, do you have pain when I call you…that other name?"

"Yes!" answered Castlethorn with some hint of fear.

"Then I will only call you by your current name. I need you to do something for me."

"Wahl… I dassn't knows about dat! Ye're jest a voice in the ahr!"

"A voice in the air, you say? Well…then, what if I appeared to you? Would that convince you of something?"

"I s'pose it would," replied Castlethorn with great dignity, his chin up, being brave.

"Me too," said Jimmy but with a little quiver in his voice. "I want to see you too." he stood up tall and nearly defiant like Castlethorn, his friend. His voice no longer quivered. He was determined. He wondered what a ghost would look like. He saw some pictures drawn of haggard creatures in cowls, of banshees with straggly hair and mis-shapen forms. He wondered if Mentor would look like a half-eaten corpse with his eyes hanging out. Whatever the shape of the ghost or how he looked, Jimmy felt it deep inside that this man, this ghost, was not going to hurt him. He just somehow knew that this was a different spirit from that awful poltergeist.

He also knew now, courtesy of Miss Coffenayle, what evil power felt like. This Mr. Mentor did not have evil power because he did not make Lantern burn red. After befriending Mr. Castlethorn, Jimmy had learned that we should not judge people on their appearance. He was finding out that people may have a reason for looking the way that they do. Just because someone was smelly and had bad teeth, coupled with deep eccentricities, it did not mean that they deserved our scorn or shaming. It seemed that Jimmy had grown up an awful lot in the last week or so, and it did him good.

"All right, then, gentlemen. You found me with the lantern, so you deserve to see me. Get ready."

Castlethorn and Jimmy held their breaths. Slowly, a white outline appeared in the air and traveled to the ground in a kind of oval shape about the height of a man. Then the outline took on sort of a heat mirage appearance, like wavy lines of invisible energy in the air that gave form to the outline. They could make out a head, then shoulders and arms, then legs and feet. Slowly, the outline of a person became more distinct, and then they saw him. They saw the elusive Mr. Mentor! He was standing there just as Emily knew him—brown suit, cane, trim white hair and moustache, with the ever-present proper watch chain slung across his vest. His neatly tied bowtie was placed ever so smartly. He was in full color but sort of transparent.

The pair stared in awe of what they just witnessed. They were standing before a real live(?) ghost! What does one say? How does one behave? Neither man knew, so they just stood there, staring. It was getting late, and Emily grew tired of waiting for them to catch up.

"Snap out it, you two!" Emily snapped her fingers.

They shook off their trance and came fully aware of their situation. They had so many questions, but they did not know what to ask first.

"Um…what…what do you want? I guess…" Jimmy's voice trailed off. He was afraid he would somehow offend this spiritual visitor. He did not want for frighten Mr. Mentor off. Jimmy thought of a better question. "Are you the one that has been helping Miss Emily teach?"

Mr. Mentor smiled. "Jimmy," Mentor started. "You can address me like any normal person. I am, after all, a normal person. I just happen to be *dead*. It is all perfectly natural. All people die. Some sooner, some later."

"Why is yese be hangin' around de school an' not polishin' yer harp tuh play on the clouds?" asked Castlethorn. It was a perfectly honest and sincere question.

"Well," said Mentor, "I have some work to do. I want to do good things for this school. I have tried to do them, but there is someone here who keeps stopping me. I had to get special permission to actually appear to you three. We don't normally appear. We normally just encourage you to do good things for God by doing good for each other."

"Permission?" asked Jimmy. "You mean...we die and then have to get permission to do things?"

"Yes, Jimmy. We have rules to go by. You, Emily, Margaret, and Cassi—uh, Mr. Castlethorn have been chosen to help me set things straight. Let's just say for now that I have some unfinished business that I need to complete here at the school. Can you help me?"

"*Help you?*" Castlethorn and Jimmy asked in unison. "*You* need help from *us*?" asked Jimmy.

"Yes. I do. I have already helped *you* in some very important ways. Now it is time for you to help *me*. Emily will explain what she knows on your way to the task I have for you, but you have to agree to do the task."

Castlethorn chimed in with, "Ah unnerstans that you has beens helpin' Miz Emmily to teach the youn'guns, raht?"

"Yes. And that is only part of what I have done for all of you," responded Mr. Mentor. "I cannot explain everything now because there is not time. I can only promise that you will learn what I have done soon enough. But I need to know right now. Will you help me?"

"Mr. Mentor," started Jimmy, "if you just have been helping Miss Emily teach us, then that alone means you have earned my respect and my help. I will do what you ask."

"Mees too, Mr… Mental… Mr…uh…sir," said Castlethorn. "I will helps…wiff the expection of getting explanayshuns of jes wut is going on here."

"Yes," said Mr. Mentor. "You will get all of the explanations you will need. Now…time is of the essence. You cannot waste any more of it. The four of you will take shovels and go to that place where you, Jimmy, and Emily found those white rocks with Margaret. Then you will dig in the ground until you find two big boxes. Open them."

"Four of us?" asked Emily. "We have only three people."

"Get a fourth shovel. Margaret will meet you there. Trust me. I have to go now." With that, Mr. Mentor faded away with a smile.

Castlethorn and Jimmy looked at each other for a moment and then ran for the office to get to the shovels. They found the shovels and handed one to Emily. Castlethorn put Lantern away, grabbed two more shovels, and Jimmy found his own shovel. The three of them wordlessly left the school. Castlethorn followed Miss Emily and Jimmy because he had no idea where they had been to find the two white stones, whatever that meant. They walked through the dark and soon arrived at the big old house. The trio walked around back to the weed-covered yard, and Jimmy reached the stones first.

Castlethorn followed them and then was suddenly startled. "Ahhggh!" he shouted.

A figure was moving toward them out of the darkness. It was a small figure, about the size of Margaret.

"Margaret?" called Jimmy.

"Yes," called Margaret softly. "Are you Jimmy, Emily, and Mr. Castlethorn?"

"Yes," the three answered in unison.

"What are we doing here?" asked Margaret with a yawn. She approached the group, and they could see each other in the moonlight.

"We were sent here to do a job," answered Miss Emily.

"Was it by some bald on top old man in a brown suit?"

"Yes…but how did you know, Margaret?" asked Miss Emily.

"He came to me in a dream. At least I think it was a dream. He *insisted* that I sneak out. He said that he would make sure everyone stayed asleep so that I would not get caught. He said that if I did get caught, then I would know that it was just a silly dream and I could go back to bed. If I did not get caught, it would be a miracle, I would know it, and I would meet you here to dig some holes. On my way out, I knocked a tin water pitcher off a dresser. It should have awakened the entire house, but it was a *miracle* that it did not. So... I got here as fast as I could. With this strange several days we've been through, I decided to not ask questions."

"Well," asked Miss Emily, "did you think of any questions on your way here?"

"A couple dozen, but the old man said there was no time to waste."

"All rightees, then," said Mr. Castlethorn. "Wese best dig. Whar's de white rocks?"

"Over here," said Jimmy. He pointed to the spot in the weeds where the stones were. One stone read in the full moonlight "Ch___ Ment_r," and the other "Edna M__." The rest of the letters and numbering, possibly dates, were worn away. They had no time to decipher the stones; they sensed that time was passing quickly, and they had to get this *done.*

Jimmy and Castlethorn each took a stone. Intuitively, they decided to dig at the foot of the writing. No one wanted to say it, but it felt like they were about to rob a grave. They were able to move quickly because the earth was soft. They got down about four feet on both sides and hit something in both holes, one after the other, Castlethorn digging just a little faster than Jimmy. With an object in sight, both girls picked a hole and started digging. Somehow, Emily "managed" to dig with Jimmy. Margaret noticed this, and Emily noticed that Margaret noticed. They said nothing; there was work to do.

The four quickly cleared off the boxes, each about seven feet long and three feet wide and three feet deep. It did not take long for Castlethorn to realize that they were indeed correct about their suspicions. *These were coffins!* The four of them looked at each other immediately and jumped out of the graves they had just desecrated. Margaret made a remark about praying or something. Emily stood there, stunned and staring. Castlethorn leaned on his shovel in deep thought, but the fog and headache kept interfering, and he knew better than to try too hard to remember.

The fact that the fog came told him that this was important and something that he needed to look into. Since he had become involved with Lantern, Jimmy, Emily, and Margaret, he was able to discover a pattern that whenever the kids asked him about the past or other conditions around the school, he would become sick in the head with the "fogs and brain pain," as he called it. He somehow knew that he had to do something very unpleasant, perhaps even un-Christian, but it would not be a sin to do so. He had the kids stand back because he did not know what would come of this. He just knew that it could be pretty disgusting and smelly. He was used to disgusting and smelly, so he figured he was the best candidate to do this task.

Without a word, as soon as the kids were clear, he worked the tip of his shovel under the lid of the coffin below the stone marked "Edna." He pried at the seam of the coffin, jacking the shovel handle up and down, pulling it out, moving to another spot, and repeating this action until the lid pried loose. It took some effort and wood splinters flew, hitting the ground around the grave. He looked up at the teacher and her students. Both girls moved closer to Jimmy who puffed out his chest a bit and set his jaw. He was determined to be brave for them. With a faint smile at the boy's bravado, Castlethorn moved the lid. They all held their breaths and stared. They could not believe their eyes! The coffin...*was full of wooden planks!* There was no body, no evidence of a body. Just wood.

"Meses thinking dat someone dun faykeed a fooneral," stated Castlethorn matter-of-factly. "Maybees the other is faykee too!"

Jimmy helped pull him out of the hole, no longer a grave, and the old genius immediately dropped into the other grave. He was hoping to prove two fake funerals. But when he opened the second wooden box a crack, he gagged. The odor that spewed forth was horrible indeed, worse than anything he ever found in his shop. Pushing through the odor, the old man opened the box fully. The kids covered their mouths and noses, but the worst of it was over. The smell was gently carried away by natural air convection. The kids were feeling a little better and could pay closer attention. When the lid was open completely, and Castlethorn moved out of the way, the kids and he just stared.

They had a final evidence of truthfulness of everything they had passed through. They now knew that they were in a mortal battle for their immortal souls. The body in the coffin was that of an old man in a brown suit. He was shriveled, yes, and the suit hung loosely from the withered flesh, yes. Though the features of the face were ruined by the ravages of decomposition, beetles, and other grave-dwelling bugs and worms, the identity of the body was unmistakable! The particular piece of forensic evidence that clinched the case for this intrepid group was the tell-tale very proper gold watch chain carefully laid to rest across the vest of the brown suit. There was no doubt that this was the body of Mr. Charles Edward Mentor!

"Dis...bees yer friendlee ghost, Miz Emily?" Castlethorn asked rather reverently with a calm tone.

"Yes," Emily said with tears welling up in her eyes. The group followed suit and started to sniffle and tear up, including Castlethorn. He blew his nose on a greasy shop cloth and offered it to the kids. No takers, but they thanked him for the sincere if inappropriate offer. He put the cloth back in his back pocket.

"There will be none of that, my friends," came a voice as a faint glow illuminated the grave, beyond what the moon alone could do. The group looked toward the sound of the voice. It was Mr. Mentor, no doubt, but more glorious than before. His light was stronger, and he did not appear so transparent.

"Y-you woke me up," stammered Margaret. "You were the man in my dream, the one who put everyone to sleep so I would not get caught."

"Yes," replied Mentor to a stunned Margaret. "I woke you and I hated to do it, but you needed to be here. Your friends needed you. The three of you have been chosen for an important job."

"Well, um," said Margaret.

"It's okay, Miss Margaret, to not know what to say. Sometimes that is for the best," Mr. Mentor reassured her.

"Mr. Jimmy, Miss Emily, I must leave it to you to fill Miss Margaret in on the details. Mr. Castlethorn, will you please close that box? It is most unpleasant to see my body in that state," requested Mr. Mentor in a very calm manner. He needed to stay calm because these people relied on him to stay steady. The fact was that seeing his body like that, the first time he viewed himself since the funeral, was deeply disturbing. He was murdered by a trusted friend, a friend most beloved by he and his wife. Now he had to see to his beloved Edna, Mrs. Mentor, in a place of terrible torment, requiring rescue. No time to worry about that. He had to take care of business. Then Mrs. Mentor would be taken care of.

"All of you have just uncovered evidence of murder most foul. More on that later. For right now, you must cover these graves and speak of it to *no one*. Quickly! Cover them and then take your shovels off of the property! Move!" He was speaking most urgently with uncharacteristic desperation. Then he disappeared. He did not fade this time to allow his friends to see him go calmly. He just plain disappeared in an instant! Emily sensed that they needed to move *now*. *Right now*. And she quickly grabbed a shovel. The four covered the boxes and replaced the weeds as well as they could to cover the evidence of their being here. From Jimmy's recollection, the place was not visited regularly, and they could probably just lay the brush over the graves and cover their tracks. The holes were filled in, the brush was replaced, and the headstones were left undisturbed. If someone did visit here, they would surely see the evidence of the desecration, but from a distance, that would not be so evident.

The four grabbed their shovels and left the area carefully. They were all fairly shocked by the whole situation, so they said nothing. They worked their way toward the old house, and then...they *froze*. Was that a...a voice? Yes! It was someone coming toward the house! Castlethorn motioned for the group to follow him quietly, and they all hid in the shadow of a dead fallen tree. They hid behind it, lying on their bellies. They could not believe what they saw next! The new visitor was none other than Miss Coffenayle! And, boy, was she mad! She was hollering and cursing to the air with mud all over her Napoleon suit. It looked as though she had fallen head first into a large puddle of muck. From her tirade at the heavens, they determined it was very smelly too. Something about "How did a *cow* get *there*?" and she was going to fire that idiot who must have left the pasture gate open to turn that cow loose. She also could not believe that the cow was not only loose where it should not be, but the cow's *bowels were also loose*! Well, that cow would be on the menu after what her black magic did tonight! Yessir! That cow was roasted! The timing of it all… She had made it almost all the way home too.

"Home?" whispered Emily.

The others nodded, and Castlethorn put his finger to his lips. *Don't make a sound!* They watched their principal enter the house immediately, following her customary steps. The only thing that she did not do was to search the property with a perimeter walk. The small group of forensic detectives did not know that Coffenayle had a routine. They did not know that anyone lived in that old battered mansion. They could not see evidence of lights, really, other than a bit of light that would peek out here and there from around the shades. One would not notice it by casual observation. Even if you were looking, you would almost have to know where and what to look for to see the light.

The group was stupefied by these many discoveries. They waited a moment, and then once the coast seemed clear, they moved slowly as a group, giving the house a wide berth. As soon as they were clear, they ran for it to get all the further from the house. They stopped after they were down the road a bit to be sure.

When they stopped running, they caught their breaths while walking toward their home. On the way, they smelled something strange, like burned hair mixed with other foul odors. Then Jimmy noticed the source. "Look!" he exclaimed and pointed.

Everyone saw a partially fried corpse of a cow. It was quite pungent, and they moved away quickly.

"I'm glad she did not do that to *me*," said Jimmy.

Emily and Castlethorn agreed. When Margaret asked, they filled her in the best they could. Emily told her part, beginning with the pranks in the classroom and Miss Whipshot's "accident" that jammed her in the floorboards. She explained her promotion to teacher, and then Jimmy and Castlethorn told her what they knew. Margaret was very open to all of this and seemed to believe their stories immediately. Emily now understood why this girl was chosen. She was willing to accept so much on faith and was actually quite brave.

Jimmy was impressed too, Emily noted.

Castlethorn just smiled to himself and kept quiet until it was his turn to explain Lantern.

31

The Pieces Are in Place

When Margaret was all caught up on all past events, the discussion turned to the most recent events. The three of them concluded, after some deliberation, that they should have been caught digging up the graves. They would certainly have been had Coffenayle not been interrupted by what Jimmy called a "shower of liquid bovine sadness." The group had to laugh out loud at that, the tensions of the night's events finding their way out of four very humble brave people. They knew that Mr. Mentor was behind that cow's attack, somehow. They also knew more about just how powerful Miss Coffenayle was becoming. Jimmy tasted that power, and it was terrible, but he would have never suspected that she was capable of burning a whole cow! He determined that they might want to avoid any meat on the menu for the next day or two. Castlethorn silently vowed to himself that *steaks is steaks no matters for how deys gots cooked!*

*****

Meanwhile, back at the old mansion, a different conversation was taking place.

"Malovent!" shouted Miss Coffenayle. "Can you visit me?"

The evil spirit appeared instantly, bigger and stronger than ever! His belt of human heads became animated, mouthing the silent screams of the forever condemned. His cowl was darker than ever.

The black tendrils of energy moved around him, head to foot, faster and all the more powerful. The black fire burned colder and darker than ever before. Yes, he was growing stronger and stronger! "Here I am, Coffenayle! What need have you—oh!"

Malovent saw the filthy uniform on the floor. He looked at it and looked at her in the sunken tub of lavish soap bubbles. He seemed about to ask—

"Never mind that," Coffenayle said. "Unless you want to clean it all up."

He extended his arm, a ball of black fire energy forming on the end of his sleeve. Dark fire shot out of the sleeve and immediately destroyed the uniform, burning it into tiny black dust. He waved at the dust, and it blew out the front door that accommodatingly opened, then closed after the dust left.

"Well, that was surprising, Malovent. That saved me a great deal of trouble. I suppose I could have done that all for myself."

"You are still a new master testing your wings," responded the dark figure.

"Why could you not have warned me about the cow that did that?" asked the new master of black magic.

"I am not here to babysit you every moment of the day. I have other students to tutor," he responded with a hint of impatience. "I am not omniscient."

"Yes, yes. I understand your power of sight is not unlimited. Meanwhile, I am learning how to use my new power as a weapon. Since you did not know about the cow that soiled me, I suppose you did not know about my cooking it with a single blast of black fire!"

"You did that?" Malovent asked with mild surprise in his voice. "You must have been fairly angry. From the odor of your uniform, I am guessing that the cow showered you with—"

"Yes," replied Coffenayle abruptly, "she did. Now Miss Ladlepot will have Goliath retrieve the beast and serve it up to the students!" She laughed.

"How tasty black fire beef will be!" Malovent laughed as well.

Coffenayle had never heard him respond with humor before. She guessed that this must be how things were between masters. Then a wicked thought occurred to her. If masters could be friendly…just how far could that go?

"You know, Malovent. This bath is rather…pleasant," she cooed, blushing just a bit. "And there's room for two. Perhaps, um—"

Malovent's reaction was immediate. "*Sacrilege!*" he screamed. The foundation of the mansion shook! The lights flickered. Malovent howled in anger, almost as though he were in pain.

Coffenayle immediately knew she just made a mistake. She immediately recovered.

"I…regret saying that!" she shouted over the tumult. "While I am not actually 'sorry' for it nor do I regret desiring that pleasure from you, my former master, I will never suggest that ever again!"

He continued the rant for a few seconds longer, then dropped his arms, allowing the mansion to normalize. His cowl was turned in her direction. She was curious to see what was under there, but she had already made trouble with him by suggesting that. Malovent began to speak.

"You must remember," he said deeply and softly, "that love in all forms will destroy your progress. That includes ultimate physical pleasures. This is something you have never experienced and must never in your life if you are to be fully devoted to your throne in the Underworld."

"I understand, but I thought physical passion was a part of magic," she said, becoming again the student.

"It can be, yes, in lower forms of magic. You, though, have graduated beyond that. Your magic is higher and supersedes all forms of human connection. We may tempt mortals with lust, pornography, adultery, and all things akin to it, but that is to create negative energy and chaos for us to tap into. Proper love within marriage, the kind that creates blissfully wedded couples, is our worst enemy. This proper expression allows mortals the opportunity to have stable loving families, fidelity and loyalty. These are of our enemy. The strength of the family bond is the ultimate strength to mortals. We, the masters, must never allow our passions to create loving relationships."

Coffenayle nodded, accepting the correction. She wanted to become a tormenting queen more than anything. She knew that she was already condemned to the Underworld and that she belonged to them now. The only thing left for her now was to become a tormenter. It was either that or to become a tormented soul for eternity. Only becoming a queen would save her from forever torment. As she desired, so it should be done. She had complete control of herself now. All thoughts of passion or lust for Malovent were cast away from her mind. She was to become queen. This was all about her.

"So," started Malovent, "I suppose that you did not bring me here to do your laundry only?"

"Correct," said Coffenayle. "I wanted to give you a report… I have Doesbad, that fool of an attorney, fighting yet another subpoena. I think that InkRobe can keep the judge under control, but I believe that other legal avenues will soon allow the authorities onto the property. They will find all my records. They will see the conditions that the students are living under, and they will send me to prison."

"We knew that this school, as wonderful as it is, could not last forever," responded Malovent. "What do you want to do? I will help you carry out any evil you would wish to perform," he said with a slight bow, arms folded in front of him.

"I want to carry out the inferno we have before discussed. My new status of master and the destructive power I wield should be more than sufficient to burn this whole structure…and all the students. Imagine the negative emotions that will be generated! Imagine the terrorized souls of the dead, souls which will be too traumatized to move onto to their glory! Imagine the power we can draw from them as they remain frozen in time, haunting the living! Imagine the condemned souls, ones that are bound to the Underworld, that we will claim early in life into their torment! All of these, Malovent, all of these hundreds of souls will be ours to draw evil power from! We will capitalize on their misery, the horror of their deaths! Then, when *I* meet my own death, many, many years from now—"

"You may reign over your kingdom as tormentor," Malovent finished her sentence and laughed out loud his deep baritone throaty laughter, the kind of laugh that Coffenayle could fall in…well, you know, fall in love with if she were allowed to. She joined him in her best evil cackle. She could feel their power grow, and it was wonderful! She was becoming more deeply evil with time. With each passing moment, she was becoming more and more the master, closer to becoming queen. "I am ever so pleased with your progress, fellow master," he stated without adding "you fool." He could tell her the truth now as did some of his peers and leave her hopelessly dreading her fate to be forever tormented. Instead, he preferred to let the mortal languish in evil and possibly even convert more souls to their cause.

Then, upon their moment of death, he loved seeing their spirit diminish just at the moment they were expecting to become royalty in the Underworld. "Now, what is your plan? We need to have a fast way to burn the place. We cannot risk planting accelerants or bombs. It would be too easy to get caught. What do you suggest?" asked Malovent.

"Why, Malovent! I am surprised at you! You very well know that I can start fires now with my magic! Why would I do it any other way?" She smiled because she knew he was testing her, trying to see how comfortable she was with using magic. He was also testing her faith in her powers. So far, she was responding perfectly to every challenge he presented to her.

"Yes! That is what I hoped you would say. Magic is the only way that masters are permitted to kill. Since fire is your chosen way, then you need only to pick the place to start the fire."

"Oh, yes, Malovent! I have the perfect place! We are standing upon it! I will start the fires in all those weeds over Mentor's grave! The fire will naturally spread to quickly burn this mansion. This place is far enough from the school to not be noticed right away. By the time they see the flames, it will be too late. All of the grounds have a thick carpet of dry undergrowth due to my planned neglect. The fire will race from here throughout the whole campus! It will be glorious!"

"Glorious indeed!" said Malovent, relishing in the thought of all the pain and misery the new master was about to inflict upon oh so many souls! "When do you intend to carry this out?"

"I have all the plans in place. All I need to do is gather my gold out of the safe and leave. I only need to take a briefcase with me and do the deed. I can do it this morning after I get a little sleep. As a fellow master, I would like to invite you to my little party."

"Why, I would be honored! Shall your mother ring up my mother to confirm the invitation?"

They both laughed and cackled out loud at Malovent's little joke. After they finished laughing, Malovent said, "Summon me when you are ready. The sooner, the better. I will appear upon your summons."

"Very well then, Malovent, teacher of masters. I will summon you after I get some sleep."

Malovent bowed, turned away, and then disappeared into fire and a mist of wispy green smoke. Very dramatic, very fitting to disappear into smoke and fire when they were about to start an inferno. It was special to Coffenayle because he, a fellow master, was paying tribute to her plan. She left the tub, dried off, put on bed clothes, and dozed off, smiling. She dreamt of fires, thrones, and crowns of gold.

*****

The four investigators, meanwhile, had managed to get back to the school, undetected. They agreed to meet at the classroom in the morning, and Castlethorn would come in and ask for Jimmy. That would be the signal for them to meet and come up with some kind of plan. No one knew what to do now, not with what they had just learned. They were all reeling in their minds with shock over their discoveries and revelations. They found Mentor's grave. They knew that Coffenayle lived in his old house. They knew that she had something to do with the evil that was affecting everyone. The green fogginess of Castlethorn's brain confirmed to him that this was all very important. Mr. Mentor had told them that they were "chosen," and he obviously stopped Coffenayle from finding them. So they did not know what to do next, but they figured it would be smart to gather someplace.

They all went to their separate places to get some sleep. The morning was going to be very busy. They all went to sleep, hoping for a dreamless rest. Their wish was granted. They all slept well and managed to somehow arise at the same moment, surprisingly refreshed. It was odd because even Castlethorn slept well with both boots off and under a *blanket*. He had even removed his coveralls, and his back seemed to feel so much better. He was able to lay flat, something that he had not been able to do for years.

While speaking of sleep, it should be noted that Miss Whipshot and Nurse Shadyknight had a wonderful night's sleep too. If anyone was there to see them, they would have found two peacefully sleeping women. Miss Whipshot was even *smiling*, somehow seeming to be at peace. She had been asleep for many days and was expressionless. Now she was sleeping peacefully. In the dim light, both nurse and patient seemed to appear younger with the age lines disappearing from their faces.

The sun was rising in more ways than one.

Miss Emily woke up and got ready. She had to bathe to get the dirt off her. Then she had a cold breakfast and headed out the door with her supplies and teaching needs in her hands. Everything to the watching eye would appear completely normal. She arrived in the classroom without incident, and during a quick meeting, she found out that Jimmy and Margaret had also managed to get cleaned up without drawing any attention. Other than Jimmy and Margaret being there a little early, everything seemed nice and normal. Everything except, that is, for a desecrated grave, the team being coached by the spirit of a decomposing teacher, a cow killed by magical means, a principal empowered with dark magic living in an abandoned mansion, and a pile of boards buried in a false grave. Yes, other than that, it was just another day.

They were all grateful that they did not stink from the night before. Then a man appeared in the doorway. They did not recognize him, but he was holding Lantern. Oh, boy. Was that... Castlethorn? They did not expect him to look like...*that!* The man stood there for moment and smiled. "Gud morningz to yese, kiddeees! Is yese be hoomins?" the man said with a grin, a grin that was missing a black tooth! Mr. Castlethorn was in the doorway, *cleaned up,* and his hair was pulled back in a neat ponytail! He smelled...well, he didn't smell!

"Mr. Castlethorn!" exclaimed Jimmy first as he ran over to him. Miss Emily and Margaret followed him. They could not believe how good he looked! He was still his same old self but standing more upright, cleaner, and shaven! He talked funny still, but thank goodness because they would not have known him otherwise! They talked for a moment quietly and then turned back to go into the classroom. In Emily's teacher chair, there sat Mr. Mentor, looking perfectly human with his legs crossed and one hand on his cane. The group of four froze in their tracks, dead silent.

"How are you feeling today, Mr. Castlethorn?" he asked with a sly wink.

"Isee be feelin' betterz, Mr. Mentor. Do yese knows why? Cuz I shur dussn't."

"Never mind that. You four have work to do!" he exclaimed with a broad grin.

"What? After last night...you still want *more*?" asked Emily.

"Yes, Miss Emily, I am afraid so," said Mentor, perhaps a bit sadly. "I have no choice but to put you in action again. This was not how I planned it. I wanted to give all of you more time. I am afraid, though, that time has run out. Many lives depend on what you do next."

"No more graves?" asked Emily who was still terribly affected by digging up Mr. Mentor's body.

"No," said Mr. Mentor. "Today I need you to gather some warriors."

"Warriors?" asked Jimmy. "We have no soldiers near here!"

"Valiant warriors, young man, come in all forms. These warriors consist of a butcher, a nurse, a sick teacher, and a cafeteria cook."

"Yeses means da Ladlepot lady and that crazy Goliath? Yeses means Whipshot and Shadyknight?" asked Castlethorn.

"Yes," Mr. Mentor said simply. "Go and gather them right away this morning. Leave here now. Meet me by the football field as soon as possible." Then Mentor disappeared, fading slowly and smiling.

"Well, I guess we have our homework, don't we, Miss Emily?" asked Margaret with a sly grin.

"I guess we do at that!" replied Emily, highly anxious to get to whatever this was. "All right, how do we do this? Gather everyone? We can get Shadyknight, the nurse, and Whipshot, the sick teacher, to join us by the football field because the infirmary is right there. So that's handled. The other two…what do we about getting them out of the kitchen, especially during breakfast?"

"Hmm," said Castlethorn. "Leaves dat ta mese and Jimmy. Ah gots us a plans." He winked at Jimmy who had not a clue what he might be in for, but Jimmy smiled anyway. Whatever it was, it could not be worse than digging up a dead body. The class was beginning to file in, so they broke up their meeting. Margaret took her seat. Miss Emily assumed her teacher's role, and Mr. Castlethorn took Jimmy with him on a special project. It all appeared quite normal. After the classroom recited their anthem, Miss Emily suggested that they take a walk to see Miss Whipshot. The class agreed eagerly, and they all followed Miss Emily out the door. The only thing that was out of order was that Patience was not at her desk when they passed by the principal's office lobby. Miss Coffenayle was not present either, but that was not unusual.

32

A Merry Chase and a Marvelous Battle

At her mansion, Miss Coffenayle was executing her deadly plans this morning. She summoned Malovent, and he met her in her living room. "Malovent, how are you at being outdoors?" she asked.

"I am able to travel in daylight in full view. I just choose not do this very often because I don't like to have witnesses. However, in this case, any witnesses who see me will soon be dead anyway." They both laughed.

"Come outside with me then, if you please," said Coffenayle. "I want to show you something."

Malovent floated behind her to the outside, and she went around back to the graves. "This is where we buried that fool, Charles Mentor, and buried a ballast in place of his wife. A bunch of wood, I think. The undertaker arranged that part for a little bullion...and then suffered a terrible accident." She looked down. She could not believe it. The ground had been disturbed! Recently too. It looked like three or four people from the general appearance of the footprints. Seething with anger, she looked more closely. There were some large boot prints; that could only belong to one person: Castlethorn!

The once happy Coffenayle, in her very best Napoleonic uniform, jumped up and down, red-faced, and screamed in frustration! "That man is dead! I will kill him first! Him and whomever these people are! They can't be allowed to show the world what happened here! They have been in both graves! See the wood chips? I just know they opened the coffins! Aaaaaah!"

"*Master* Donatienne Coffenayle, calm yourself," said Malovent quietly. "Stop thinking like a mortal. *You are a master of witchcraft. Don't allow your rage to show.*" He floated calmly before her. His belt was teeming with tormented souls, more animated than Miss Coffenayle had before seen, animated in full color.

She immediately calmed down. He was right. She was a master and needed to act like it. "All right. Yes, Malovent. Of course, you are right. Here's what we need to do: we will not burn the school yet, as much fun as that will be. No, we need to discover who was digging in the graves and kill them immediately so we are sure they are dead."

"But why not kill them with the fire?"

"Because we don't know where they are for sure. We need to discover them first, then once they are silenced, we can start the fire. If we start the fire first, we won't know if they are dead because I will have to flee. I cannot leave any loose ends in this thing. If they are not present at the school, then we can still burn it but find them all later. For now, we simply *must* confirm their whereabouts!"

"Very wise, Friend Coffenayle. I am impressed," said Malovent as he floated beside her. "Very sound thinking. Your mind is worthy of a master of the dark arts."

The two of them headed into the school to find that old fool janitor and kill him. This should be a good one to warm her up for the day. Coffenayle was going to miss breakfast for certain, but where to have lunch after starting the fire?

*****

As Emily took the class to "visit" their sick teacher, Castlethorn and Jimmy were moving toward the cafeteria at a rapid pace. They both felt that they were on an urgent mission. They burst into the kitchen, unannounced, Castlethorn with Jimmy, "*a stoodint*" in tow just to provoke Ladlepot! Castlethorn yelled, "Hey! Lookit me, Ladlepot! I brung a student in here wiffout permission! Ha! And I dassn't cares, either! C'mon, boy, let's yu an me gets us some grub!"

Jimmy thought his friend and boss had lost his mind for real, this time. Goliath saw this and held his cleaver in the air in mid-chop of what appeared to be a partially burned cow. Jimmy thought of how efficient Goliath actually was because he was two-thirds of the way through the dead beast. Then he thought of the cleaver and suddenly remembered that he was trying, in the middle of a murder mystery, to not get himself *killed*.

"Hey! Ladlepot! You ugly cussed *cow!* How come Goliath ain't chopped yous up inta lunch meat, ya *dirty piglet?*" screamed Castlethorn.

Goliath lowered his cleaver and stared in disbelief, his mouth hanging open. In all the years that he could remember past the fog, he had never seen such boldness. Also, that guy *sounded like Castlethorn* but did not bear much resemblance. He smelled better than the old engineer too. Goliath stared, unsure of what to do.

Castlethorn grabbed a bunch of soup ladles and said, "Hey! I got'cher ladles!" and he started to run.

Goliath began to raise a cleaver to chop Castlethorn as he came out from behind his butcher's table, but Jimmy kicked him in both shins, one after the other…*hard!*

Ladlepot emerged from the kitchen's steamy innards and saw Goliath hopping back and forth from one foot to the other, trying to tend to both injuries at the same time. His cleaver had slipped from his hand. Then Miss Ladlepot saw a "stoodint" in *her* kitchen, and to boot, she also saw Castlethorn playing with an armload of her ladles! *Oh! Did he just lick one?* He sure did! And he started banging them on the counters and laughing at her!

"Ahhhhhh!" she screamed and ran at him.

Castlethorn took his cue and ran out of kitchen area, arms loaded with Ladlepot's most prized possessions, Jimmy close on his heels. They fled down the hall and hoped to not run out of energy before they reached the football field. Castlethorn was quite fleet of foot, Jimmy noticed.

They ran out the door, right past the principal, not even noticing Malovent who was fully apparent and floating in the air. The evil master hovered there, fully expecting to stop them in their tracks from fear at his very appearance. But they did not care *who* was there. There were being chased by an angry Miss Ladlepot! Malovent was stunned, his hood turning to follow them, raising his arm as though he would get their attention. He was speechless at not even being noticed. "Donatienne, what—" Malovent started to ask.

"That's them!" yelled Coffenayle. "After them!" Coffenayle and Malovent chased them with Coffenayle trying to conjure up some magical black fire on the run.

Ladlepot, along with a running and limping Goliath, were behind the principal and her evil partner. They noticed Malovent but did not care. What does a nine-foot-tall floating evil wizard matter when her ladles were being *abused*? King Kong himself would not have fazed her frenzy! This crowd ran across the schoolyard, Jimmy and his boss in the lead, Malovent and Coffenayle hurling black bolts of energy at them, barely missing them, Ladlepot growling about her ladles, and Goliath was already forgetting about his shins. He was also forgetting why he came outside to run around in the first place! He started laughing, having *fun!*

The chase continued with the poorly aimed energy bolts missing Jimmy and Castlethorn, but the small explosions were lending speed to their legs. Having dark energy explode all around you is quite the motivation for you to keep running! One might try to criticize the would-be assassins, but when you consider the reality of moving targets, moving arms, the natural instability of magic energy, and so on, it becomes clear that even with deadeye aim, it would be difficult to hit a moving target! This madcap group of runners and pursuers rounded the corner past the infirmary, right where Emily had led the classroom and the two groups nearly collided!

"Emily!" shouted Jimmy.

"Jimmy! Castlethorn!" shouted Emily.

"They're right on top of us! Run!"

Miss Emily saw Malovent first, and his appearance terrified her! "Run, class! Run!" Miss Emily shouted. She dropped the vase of wildflowers they had been gathering and took the lead. The class wondered what had gotten into Emily but then saw Malovent, Coffenayle, Ladlepot, and Goliath. They did not ask any questions.

They ran. The whole group of them ran the only direction they could go that would not trap them: to the open field! They ran into the weeds, and then Mr. Mentor's voice sounded in the teacher's ears. "Stop right here, Emily!"

She stopped, and the students followed her lead, stopping as well. Everyone was frightened. Their minds were in chaos because they saw pure evil chasing after them. Especially frightening was Malovent. This black-robed figure sped over the top of the weeds. He had no feet, the students noticed; he was a ghost! He was wearing a black cowl, just like the Grim Reaper himself. Many of the students guessed that there was a skull under that cowl and skeleton's hands hidden under that loosely flowing robe. Then there was that crazy Mr. Castlethorn! He was the one that could not speak proper English, looked terrible all the time, and smelled worse! But…he was *clean?* Why was he holding an armful of…*soup ladles?*

Now Ladlepot, the crazy cafeteria lady, was also there but wearing a pretty flower and gasping for air. She added to the chaos by catching her breath and finally yelling at Castlethorn about invading her kitchen.

The terrible-looking butcher, the one so handy at having fun with a meat cleaver, was also there. The students did not know who to fear first! They knew they were as good as dead; Death himself had come for them. The principal was there too, working alongside the Reaper. No one was terribly surprised at that! This whole group of five terrible people were going to kill everyone in the class. They all knew it. Some of the kids were crying; others were scared. Others still stood there in shock, not knowing what to do. There were some who were trying their best to pray, but "Now I lay me down to sleep" did not seem to be very workable.

"Now you'll pay with your *lives!*" shouted Coffenayle. "I will blow all of you to your doom! I am a master witch of the darkest order, and I shall smite you, one and all, with my terrible powers!" Then she screeched out a terrible cackle! Malovent hovered beside her and said nothing. His presence was fearful enough! Again, the students were not surprised at her announcement.

Then Ladlepot, somehow finding her voice in all of this after catching her breath, started shaking her fist at Castlethorn. Apparently, ladle-mania overrode her fear of being smitten by terrible powers. "You gimme back those ladles! Themses is mines!"

Castlethorn pulled back and clutched the ladles all the tighter. The message was clear: "*No, Ladlepot, theses is mines!*" Goliath was standing there beside Miss Ladlepot in his dirty pink-stained apron. He drew a meat cleaver from one of his pockets, looking toward Ladlepot for cues. Who should he start chopping up?

Then, receiving no specific instructions, Goliath began mimicking Ladlepot's every gesture and move to include mouthing her words silently. The pair looked completely ridiculous and distracted the students from their fear of Malovent and Coffenayle. They started to chuckle and giggle, pointing out the new show to each other. Though they believed they were about to die, they could not help themselves. Such as it is with the human mind; we can only concentrate on one thing at a time. We can feel only what we focus on. Not only that, but Stupid Dog decided to join the fun! He was out in the field, under his letter "H," romping around, leaping very high in the air, spinning and flailing about. He had found an old rag somewhere and was tossing it up in the air, barking happily, wagging his tail, and letting his tongue hang out. His show was stealing the day!

Miss Coffenayle looked around at the display. Between Stupid Dog and the Ladlepot Comedy Show, this was a circus! She was here to fight a war, not entertain at a freak show! She was infuriated! The angrier she became, the taller and bigger Malovent seemed to become. She noticed this and knew that his rage must be as great as hers! Why was he not saying anything? Had the daylight weakened him? She could not bear that thought and was surprised that with his vast experience and fearful abilities that he had not already taken control. He understood what was at stake here, and certainly, he must have understood that Donatienne had lost control!

This was not the dramatic fearful moment that she had played out in her mind over and over as she lulled herself to sleep last night. She had thought that she was going to deliver this wonderful speech, use her magical words to cause ultimate fear, and then suddenly, at the height of their terror, she would kill them all with the fire she had planned! Their souls would be so fearful that she and Malovent would siphon off the negativity and become all the more powerful!

Jimmy looked around for an escape and actually took a moment to sneer and shake his head when Stupid Dog started running around in circles and barking. What was he all excited about? Hopping about and jumping like an idiot! Why didn't the dog protect them? He thought that dogs were supposed save people, not run around stupidly. A couple of the students now joined Jimmy in watching the dog play with his rag. They started laughing and pointing. Soon, the whole class was chanting, "Stupid dog! Stupid dog! Got no sense! Brain like a frog!" They were laughing and pointing, and the dog was having fun! He had his rag in his mouth and was tossing it about, frolicking with his head weaving and turning in every direction. He was prancing all around, the perfect circus clown! All he needed was a frilly costume!

This was more than Coffenayle could take. She had Stupid Dog on one side making people laugh. She had Goliath and Ladlepot on the other side making people laugh. Everyone was laughing when they should be terrified for their very lives! This was not right! This was not fair! This was to be *her* moment of ultimate terrible revenge! Revenge on people who had never harmed her! Yet, here were the children pointing and slapping each other on the back, switching between amusements. Either the dog was doing something funnier or Ladlepot and Castlethorn were becoming more outrageous. She could not believe this! She was about murder them all, and here they all were…having *fun!* Well, that would come to an end right now!

"*Siiiiileeeence! All of you!*" Miss Coffenayle shouted with a shriek that seemed to shake the very earth.

The whole group of people stopped immediately. Their mouths were open as they turned back to stare at their principal, their most dreadful nemesis who was dressed in her finest Napoleonic uniform, complete with gold epaulets. Even the adults stopped their quibbling over ladles and such. Everyone was staring at her. Stupid Dog dropped his rag and just quietly watched; his tongue was no longer hanging out, and his eyes were narrow and keen. If a dog were to ever look serious, this was that moment. He emitted a soft growl deep in his throat.

Miss Coffenayle stood as tall as she could, a regal pose, even while she was red-faced and sweating, out of breath. She was imposing in that stance, in control, fearless. She had their full attention now. She looked up at a grandly magnificent Malovent who was taller and more imposing than she had ever known before. How remarkable! How wonderful. How...*divinely* evil he appeared. Oh, if only she were allowed to fall in...well...you know. No time for that, though.

The students were starting to tremble. Miss Emily stood in front of them, Jimmy on her right and Margaret on her left. She reached out for their hands, and the three of them stood there in front of the students. They were shaking but brave nonetheless...and blocking the evil pair from harming the students. If they got to the class, it would be over their *dead bodies!* Coffenayle looked at their pathetic display of defiance, even in the very presence of Malovent himself. She scoffed smugly and openly. She finally spoke after she was certain that she had their attention. After all, she was the master manipulator of minds! She would punish these kids first and then burn the mansion to start the whole grounds afire.

Perhaps they could spare Emily, make her the last to die so that she could watch her friends and students writhe in the flames! Her heart would shatter as she smelled their cooking flesh! Love was the greatest weakness of all, per Malovent, and Miss Emily would *know it with her last rattling breath!*

"Malovent here is my former master of the arcane arts," she began to lecture to the frightened crowd. "Would any of you care to meet him in person? Shake hands? Have a nice cold root beer with him? Hmmmmm?" she asked. Then she paused. There were no takers. Malovent hovered just a little higher to be certain that all of the children got a good look at him and the fact that he was not standing on the ground. He wanted them all to know that he was floating. Their fear was delicious to him, and it grew more powerful by the second. He had trained this disciple-turned-master very well. "He trained me," Coffenayle continued, "to cast magic without the use of talismans. Now, many of you don't even know what a 'talisman' is... and you won't live to find out. Are you ready, Malovent?"

Without a word, his arms down at his sides, the ends of his sleeves, where hands should be, began to *glow* black. It is a most strange thing to see dark power, blacker than night, actually *glow* with blackness. This made the crowd fall back in fear. It made Goliath drop his cleaver, and Ladlepot forgot all about her ladles that Castlethorn had dropped to the ground with a loud clatter. All of them were in deep foreboding fear.

Emily, Jimmy, and Margaret trembled but would not break their grip on one another's hands. The wind started to kick up, and the students huddled together behind their teacher and her two... no...*five* friends! Ladlepot had grabbed Margaret's hand, Goliath had Ladlepot's, and Castlethorn was on the other side of Jimmy, gripping his hand. He looked down at his young friend and winked!

Jimmy managed to smile. If they were going to die, at least it was good to die bravely with friends withstanding evil. Goliath stood tall, looking as brave as he could, and Ladlepot had her face set in grim determination. They were all determined to stand bravely and conquer...*or die trying.*

But how were they to conquer the very elements themselves? The wind began to churn around them as dark fire began to swirl in slow motion directly around the persons of Malovent and Coffenayle. The principal looked down at her feet, wondering at what was happening to her! Her magic was indeed powerful! She was truly a master. She raised her arms, and her hands began to crackle and glow with black fire! She was shouting unintelligible words and phrases and began to levitate, floating beside Malovent!

Donatienne was glowing black with the delicious taste of evil flowing over her whole body. She was covered with the dark flames from head to foot, swirling dark energy completely engulfing the woman...except for her *eyes*! Her eyes were a terrible sight to behold. They glowed white but with red retinas and black pupils. Those horrifying eyes would not blink but stared terribly. They actually seemed to radiate heat toward the students who were now completely frozen, unable to run. They were either fearful and awed or they were spell-bound. It did not matter which.

Emily could not believe what she was seeing. The winds grew stronger, the grass and sticks were blowing in circles, the sky began to darken with black and green swirling clouds, a column of dark fire rising from the two evil magicians! Miss Coffenayle laughed, and Malovent joined her, deeply and terribly, laughing that throaty baritone laugh of his. The six friends gripped all the tighter! Then, suddenly, there was a familiar voice!

"*That will be quite enough, Donatienne!*"

The chaos immediately stopped. The wind ceased, the fire instantly disappeared, and the clouds parted. All was suddenly quiet again, like a nice normal day! Coffenayle was standing on the ground again, having sustained a rough landing on both feet, nearly falling over. Her black fire was gone. Malovent continued to levitate, but he seemed smaller now. His black fire was gone too. The figures on his belt were no longer writhing. It seemed that they were suddenly overpowered.

Miss Coffenayle was now enraged and humiliated and screamed "Charles!" into the air. She could not see him.

Emily, Jimmy, Castlethorn, and Margaret smiled at each other with relief and delight. The air was warm and normal again; the chill of evil was dispersed.

"Charles! Come out from hiding! You coward! I buried you! How did you come back to life?"

"I didn't. I am quite dead to which fact my friends over there, those six people you've tormented for years, shall attest," stated Mr. Mentor in a matter-of-fact tone.

"You...you're the ones who trespassed on my property? Who dug up the ground?" shouted Coffenayle, looking right at Miss Emily and her new friends. She wanted to approach them but did not dare. She stayed right where she was, right next to Malovent, her protector. She killed Mentor once, and she could do it again! Malovent would show them all the power of evil!

"No, Donatienne. They were not trespassing. That land belongs to the school. So does the house."

"No! No! You old dead fool! That land is mine! That house is mine! Mine to *burn!*" She was turning red in the face now, like a spoiled child demanding candy at a supermarket. Malovent said nothing. He simply hovered with his sleeves joined at their openings, across his chest, head slightly bowed as though he were meditating or was just plain bored.

"There was a will, Miss Coffenayle. You were in it, but there were provisions. Those provisions, I am afraid, have not been met." The disembodied voice was soothing to the friends and to the whole class. Everyone was looking to the sky and smiling, looking around, trying to spy the man whose voice was so kind. The six friends were looking around too, smiling at each other and nodding. This just might be all right after all. They released their grip on each other and rubbed their hands. They had squeezed the blood out of them, their grips were so tight during the wind.

Even Goliath was quiet, waiting to see the outcome. He did his best to smile. Jimmy glanced over at Stupid Dog, who was just sitting now, quietly watching. He was perfectly still with his tongue in his mouth for once. His ever-wagging tail now still. His eyes seemed attentive. Cool. Intelligent.

"What? What? Are you suggesting that this school is not mine?" she screamed. "No, no, no! I killed you! Murdered you with poison! You are dead and *have no rights!*" confessed Miss Coffenayle.

"Haven't I?" Mr. Mentor faded into view and appeared fully human on the ground between the evil duo and the students in his customary brown suit and cane. He was facing Coffenayle and Malovent, but he took a quick second and turned his back to her, facing toward the class. He winked at his friends then smiled and waved at the class. He appeared as solid as flesh and blood. The class was stunned, to say the least. A few sat down on the ground right away, and the rest of their classmates followed. They were about to see something simply amazing, even more than they had so far seen. They just sort of *knew* it. They also all knew in the same moment that they needed to be more than quiet. They knew that they needed to be...*reverent.*

"Ha! You think I haven't seen a ghost before?" she spat. "Bah! I have cursed many of the dead, and I have seen their souls tormented! You don't frighten me! I may not have the power to fully destroy you yet, but Malovent does!" Coffenayle shouted spells and magical words of combat and approached Mentor. He stood there calmly, leaning with both hands on his cane with a half-smile on his face, completely unflappable, the picture of a perfectly tolerant gentleman, with his proper watch chain slung across his vest. She approached him, red with rage. Her cloaked companion was alongside her, growing taller and taller.

Malovent was becoming the center of the show now. He was getting bigger than before, and he suddenly ignited and glowed with even more black fire than ever! Miss Coffenayle was still approaching the old man who seemed so very unconcerned. Her curses and spells were coming out of her with greater force, and the sky started to darken once more. Then, just as the students and friends of Mentor started to worry again, Coffenayle was within reach of Mentor. He reached out and simply touched her on the throat with his cane. That was all!

She immediately stopped. She grabbed her throat and made odd croaking noises. A moth and some dust flew out of her mouth. She gagged and choked on her own efforts to speak, falling to her knees. She was holding her throat, breathing okay, but was completely mute and blowing more moths and dust out of her mouth. She choked and gagged, helpless to speak, much less to stand up and fight.

Malovent stopped in the air, and his cowl turned toward Miss Coffenayle. The he faced the students and shouted at them, "For your insolence, all of you will die by my power!" He reared back with one of his arms. The belt around his waist writhed with images of tormented souls, twisting about and screaming! They screamed out loud as Malovent conjured up even more power! He tried to attack the students, but Mentor stepped between Malovent and his targets. Mentor was leaning on his cane, and Malovent responded with a deep roaring laugh that made the ground shake! "Old man! Out of my way!"

Mentor held out his cane again in the direction of Malovent who shouted, "I don't fear a dead mortal's walking stick!"

Then something wonderful happened in an instant. There was a crackling of gold sparks, shining glittery sparks, and silver-white light that started at the tip of the cane and worked its way almost instantly up Mr. Mentor's arm. In its trail, the old olivewood cane became a shiny piece of steel in the shape of a blade! It *was* a blade, and the cane became a Samurai-style sword with a long white handle, properly called a *tsuka*. The sparks moved up Mentor's arm, and his brown suit sleeve became a white robe sleeve, loose, flowing, and glowing with the glory of heaven. The sleeve seemed to drift about with a power all its own. The sparks continued to move up his arm and over his head as his body began to shimmer with light. His whole person was now a glowing figure emanating white light! He was a beautiful man, clothed head to toe in a beautiful flowing white robe. He had a full head of white hair with full long-flowing beard and moustache. His eyeglasses disappeared. He was also barefoot now as he stood on the ground.

Malovent howled in rage, roared to shake the earth, and prepared to attack the *angel* named Mr. Mentor! The students and friends of Mr. Mentor screamed as Malovent took to the air to gain an advantage, retreated a bit to gain steam, then charged straight at the angel, his black cloak skimming the ground. The master of evil was glowing with black fire so powerful that he charred the green grass beneath him, leaving a trail of black fire behind him. His attack was so powerful that he roared like a hurricane as he charged forward.

Mr. Mentor set his chin, stopped smiling, and grabbed his sword with two hands and took one perfectly-timed step forward with a wide arching slash. The sword cut cleanly through Malovent's robe, slicing longways, cleanly down the middle. Malovent tumbled forward, leaving a trail of charred grass as he rolled head over heels several times. He ended up sitting on his rear end, wondering what just happened. He got his bearings, stood, ran toward the crowd, reared back with his arm, conjured a black fireball, and heaved it. Angel Mentor easily parried the fireball with his sword, completely neutralizing it. Malovent readied another fireball, and then...the evil being froze for a moment, standing up, hovering. The fireball waned. He dropped his arm as he looked down. He finally noticed the longways slash down his robe. He weaved and wobbled back and forth as though in shock at being wounded. There seemed to be absolutely nothing happening for a second, but then the slash began to glow with white light. Then the wound began to smoke, and actual black flames poured forth out of Malovent as lifeblood would from a warrior; Malovent, the Mighty Master of Mischief and Misdeed, screamed and howled, waving his arms about, staggering around aimlessly as the crowd backed out of his way.

Everyone was staring wide-eyed, mouths agape. Some started to cry out for fear. But Angel Mentor stood fast, pointing his glowing sword at Malovent, tracking the monster every direction he went. The students were all on their feet now, the better to get out of the path of wounded demon. All eyes were on him. It was unbelievable how frightening and deadly he seemed just an instant ago and now how vulnerable and weak he appeared!

The dark master continued screaming in agony and protest, the black flames burning and consuming him from the inside but leaving his robe intact. He quit wandering and began to wobble, his robe skirt now on the ground, supported by what seemed to be ever-weakening legs. He swayed to and fro, screaming and burning, holding his cowled head with handless robed arms. There was smoke, a white vapor as it were, issuing from his face, arm openings and from beneath the skirts of his robe. The vapor was slight at first, the black flames dominating the figure of Malovent; but then the white vapor was pouring out thicker and thicker.

The vapor turned to a green, then thick yellow smoke as the stench of sulfur had the crowd covering their faces however they could. Some were coughing. Then Malovent began to shrink. Slowly, he sank to the ground as the flames died down, but the white, yellow, and green smoke continued to pour out of the robe which was now settling on the ground. The once majestic Malovent was shriveling, his once proud gold belt, key, and chain were melted. The drops of gilded metal hissed when they touched the grass, disappearing but leaving no ash, mark, or evidence of their presence. The molten stuff simply vanished.

The robe finally wrinkled, shrank, and collapsed on itself, and Malovent's once-powerful baritone voice was now sounding like the air being released from a child's balloon with the nozzle being pinched for their amusement. He, the once-fearsome Master Malovent, now sounded ridiculous as his language was reduced to a slobbering, sucking gibberish. He was desperate and reached for Angel Mentor. He croaked the final words in his squealing new tone, "H-hab m-aawcy!" And the robe fell flat onto the ground. There was a lump, though, hiding inside the robe, not moving. The crowd began to advance on the robe, awed at the spectacle.

"*Back!*" shouted Angel Mentor, still pointing his sword at the fallen robe, never taking his eyes off it. "*There is still grave danger! Malovent is not finished!*"

Miss Emily was amazed at how…*regal* the normally reserved Mr. Mentor now looked! He was in complete command, in complete control, and he fully knew his place. He was truly a being of great power and authority!

The lump began to move under the robe. The crowd, now some distance from it, stared at the flattened black cloth. The lump trembled, creeped, and crawled about, aimlessly hoping to find its way out. The wiggling mass was alive, intelligent enough to seek an exit from the robe, but it was twittering and stuttering in a raspy screeching voice. Not a loud voice but a voice nonetheless. Back and forth, in circles, zigzagging like a fly in a jar, the mass struggled. It expanded in size now and seemed to grow arms and legs. Mentor kept the crowd at bay and his sword pointing at it.

"It's still dangerous, everyone, please stay back," said the angel. The mob did not need that prompting. Everyone was firmly rooted in place. No one moved.

A few students, who were knocked to the ground during the battle, shook off the stunned sensation of the moment, and stood up carefully. Coffenayle was red with rage but helpless. She could still not speak nor could she now stand. She was completely subdued. All she could do was kneel, hold her throat and watch helplessly as her mentor, her master, her friend, and her teacher of the dark arts was defeated by a glory she could hardly comprehend but one she feared terribly.

The students approached the robe but were careful to stay behind Angel Mentor and his mighty sword. They walked up slowly, all of them cautiously watching the wiggling figure within the robe. It appeared to be a person, and it was sliding its arms in the robe and standing up. Mentor brought his sword to a ready posture, and the students stepped back on cue. The figure wiggled its way into the cowl and stood up fully. It turned and faced the group, full-sized and apparently human. It just stood there, arms at its sides. Its head was hidden by the cowl, hands covered by the draped sleeves of the robe. The students and friends of Mentor held onto each other, not knowing what was to happen next.

33

The True Nature of Evil

"Show thyself!" called out Mentor, his sword still at ready.

The standing figure began to grow. The robe obscured the body that expanded inside of it. Angel Mentor was not at all shocked at this, but the students were. They backed away in fear. They had seen the awful things Malovent could do as he expanded his size. This, however, was something different. This was not a war anymore. The figure grew to only a certain height, a very familiar height and girth. It slowly turned toward Mentor, and it ever so gently and carefully reached up, exposing its human flesh-colored hands with beautiful nails, no less, apparently feminine, and then slowly, dramatically, drew back its cowl. It turned and faced the students. *It was Miss Coffenayle! Miss Donatienne Coffenayle was wearing the robe of Malovent.*

She smiled an evil smile, more wicked and dark than the principal had ever smiled before. She hissed at the students and Angel Mentor. She spoke loudly with her hands at her sides. "You have not defeated us, Mentor!" her voice sounded like Coffenayle's but was raspy, and it had the quality of being two voices at once.

The real Coffenayle was already rendered speechless, but even if she could have spoken, she would have remained completely wordless. Her eyes were wide with fear, awe, shock—give it a name; maybe it was all three. But she was face-to-face with *herself.*

The principal shook her head. She could not understand. Without taking his eyes or sword off of the creature, Mentor said, "Don't you see, Donatienne? The thing you revered, worshipped, and obeyed got his power from your adoration, your obedience. You followed his slightest suggestion, his every whim. Because of this, each time you met, he gained power. Then, when you sacrificed poor Mr. Angelton's mortal life to get gain, when you covenanted your body and spirit to evil on that day, your soul belonged to Malovent. He owns you now, Donatienne. I just want you to know that my family and friends, whom you betrayed for this...serpent...we all loved you."

Coffenayle knelt there, holding her throat, and tears filled her eyes. She did not know what else to do. She could not conjure. She was frozen. Her voice could not call out magic. Her master could not respond to her. Her master was not her master...she was *his* master that whole time. Now that she looked back on the events over her tenure in evil, she realized that each time she learned more magic, Malovent's costume changed. He became taller, more fearsome. She revered and feared him, this demon. She thought that he was giving her power, but the fact was that she was giving *him* more and more power the more she obeyed the devil's wishes. Oh, the woe in her heart. The misery and regret of suffering this humiliating defeat. She was not sorry for her sins, not in the least. She was not even sorry for murdering Mr. Angelton and Charles Edward Mentor. No, she was not. She would do it again a thousand times over.

She was sorry that she got caught. She was sorry that she could not burn the school. She was sorry that she was humiliated in front of everyone, that the once-fearful students were now staring at her with disdain, and some with *pity*. She did not want their pity! She did not want them to say how sorry they were. Better that they should beat her to death! *Kill me! All of you! Give into temptation! Take your revenge.* She could not speak, but that was what she was thinking. Even hell was better than the blows that she had just taken to her pride. But...what now? Was she a demon? Is that what this meant?

In a seeming answer to her unasked question, Mr. Mentor spoke to the robed Malovent-Coffenayle. "Demon, what is thy name?"

The robed Coffenayle began to tremble. "No," it croaked and shook its head. "Nooo!"

"Demon…what *be* thy *name?*"

The creature was trembling now, beginning to moan, swaying back and forth. It could not focus; it could not move. It began to slobber and drool, spinning in a bizarre circle. It was gagging and hissing. Mentor kept his sword pointed toward the devil's imp. Angel Mentor was not smiling or rejoicing; he was very somber.

"Demon, in the name of the Son of God, I command thee to speak thy name!"

It froze. It stopped dead in its tracks. Gone was the show of gagging and hissing. Gone was the foolish prancing about. The game was over. The devilish-thing-turned-human now knew it was all over.

For some reason, Jimmy glanced over toward the big metal H where Stupid Dog stood. The dog was deeply engrossed, intensely staring at the scene. Well, why not? This was quite the spectacle, Jimmy thought to himself. But was the dog…growing? No one else seemed to notice. Jimmy turned back toward to business at hand. No one dared breathe a word.

The demon was helpless, now compelled in the name of the Holy One to speak. It stopped; it bowed its head low. He spoke one single word, barely audible, *"Malovent."*

As soon as the Coffenayle doppelganger spoke his true name, he immediately shrank back into the robe. Yellow smoke issued from the cowl and sleeves of the black robe. The robe fell to the ground. The smoke stank of sulfur again. Hissing sounds issued forth. It seemed as if Malovent should be dead, but he was not. He was wiggling about, still in there, but significantly smaller. He shrank and shriveled, hollering in agony, his screeching balloon voice raging against heaven and earth, cursing all of creation in a language the students never heard before.

He struggled to get out of the robe, the students watching the wiry pitiful thing that Malovent had become…or more certainly, the thing that he always was. They stared in fascination as it moved about, trying to find its way out through the hood. It finally did. Mentor lowered his sword and quietly slid it into the scabbard suspended from the gold braided cord wrapped around his waist. No need for the sword now. They were all safe enough. The Malovent-thing began to emerge. The children all gasped and muttered. It was on two legs, hunched over, crippled, tiny, and sort of a pale sickly brown-gray color.

The face of the creature appeared to be mostly a big nose. Its eyeballs were too big for its head, and it had snaggle-teeth. It turned and stared at the crowd. This thing was wearing only rags of misery—filthy, full of holes, and threadbare. It was covered with bristly hair protruding from its wrinkled gray-brown form. The hair was especially thick on its head. It had large round ears that were pointed at the tips. The hide seemed almost scaly. The thing's vertebra jutted out, down its back, terminating in a stump of what may have been its tail at one time. Its ribs protruded under its scaly hide; the flesh collapsed over the bones as though it was starving to death. The belly, though, was inflated to twice the size it should have been. The arms were skinny again, to the bone, its legs short and stumpy with thick claws protruding from its to too-tiny hands and too-large feet. The fingers and toes were gnarled and nasty.

It shouted in a squeaky little helium-sounding voice, "Well! What are you waiting for? Pick up this robe! Do it! Do it now or I will slay all you! I will suck the marrow from your bones and eat your innards! I will murder your children if you don't obey! You will all be reduced to ashes, turned to green dust!" He gagged, coughed, and finally belched! A puff of smelly sulfurous smoke came out. The students held their noses. They were glad the gas did not come from *downstairs*. His belch was smelly enough. Oh…but then, yes… Malovent, the mighty mystic's eyes started to bulge out. Then its belly began to growl. No one really knew what to expect, and Angel Mentor brought his sword to bear again, quickly drawing it from its scabbard and pointing it at the creature.

Malovent seemed completely distracted now, though, not really wanting to fight. He sort of twitched and turned his head to one side. He grabbed his belly and began retching as though he was about to barf. Angel Mentor ordered everyone to get back, thinking that the demon was about to spit fire. He was not aware that Malovent had that power, but he was not privy to every secret and mystery of the Underworld either. The angel stood tall and straight, a grim look on his face, his eyes focused and drilling into the demon, daring him to try something else. Then Malovent suddenly stopped, closed one eye, stood on one leg, bent the other, grabbed his knee with both hands, and pulled upward toward his distended belly. He hopped up and down a couple of times, then leaned to one side and—*fraaaaa-aaaap-phoooo-ooooz-poot-pppooooooottttt-bbbbbbraaaaaaafffffffttttttt!*

The noise lasted for about twenty seconds. Probably some kind of school record set near a field of set and broken records!

Green smoke emitted from this thing's rear end with the most raunchy of stenches! When he was quite finished, Angel Mentor was appalled, and the crowd was in tears, coughing and gagging. The little horrible monster's belly was completely deflated, and now the loose flesh, complete with a navel, sagged to his knees. He looked around and then said, "Aaaahhh! What a relief!"

He looked so ridiculous that the students laughed at him. They were pointing and making rude razzberry noises to mock the creature. Angel Mentor shook his head with a quiet smile and put his sword away. Then he looked around and joined the laughter himself. "No! No! Fear me! Obey! Obey!" Malovent screamed in his helium voice. He covered his ears and demanded respect! He looked over at Coffenayle who was on her knees, stunned at what she was seeing.

Donatienne Coffenayle actually broke down and began bawling silently and held her throat while choking on her tears. There stood her "master," a ridiculous-looking creature whose stomach now sagged in front of him like a deflated balloon, the flesh actually dragging on the ground, getting dirty and full of dead weeds. Malovent began stomping on the dirt and kicking it harmlessly at the crowd like a spoiled child. He was drooling, spitting, tripping on his own stomach flesh, and blubbering in some unknown language.

Then he threw himself down on his evacuated belly and began kicking the ground and hammering with his fists in absolute frustration! He appeared completely absurd, this creature who only minutes ago appeared so powerful, exalted, frightful, and foreboding. His host, the former Miss Coffenayle, educator extraordinaire, just laid face down too, completely vanquished, covering her head with her arms. Her body was heaving with sobs. These two fearsome murderers were now helpless, slobbering, snot-faced nurslings.

Just then, Stupid Dog started running around, barking. Goliath looked up, and with his head no longer feeling foggy, his body no longer hurting so badly, his memories returning, he ran forward and grabbed the Malovent-thing. Goliath was suddenly remembering who he was and what he used to do, at least in part! Angel Mentor smiled and even laughed a little as Goliath picked up the horrible little creature and pressed it into a ball like a lump of clay.

"No!" the thing shouted. "No! No! No! You must ob—"

Right on cue, Goliath drop-kicked Malovent the Pale as hard has he could with the imp still shouting, "Eeeeey!" and the little monster passed directly through the middle of the goal post! Yet, that was not to be the final end of Malovent. With all the students' eyes on the feeble football, Stupid Dog suddenly leapt into the air and instantly transformed into a monstrous creature! He started out normally enough, but in the air, red sparks covered him, swept over him, transforming the dog in midair, gold light trailing behind him. The colors were reminiscent of a combination of bloodshed and justice.

Stupid Dog became a huge muscular hound, one with three heads! He was now a large brown furry musclebound beast! Snarling and barking from each head, his huge jowls opened up, and the center head was lucky enough to grab Malovent as he was shouting, "Noooo!" in that ridiculous voice. The other two heads slavered and smiled grimly at the center head, nodding their approval. Malovent writhed in agony and tried to twist free. The other two heads clamped down on Malovent's head and feet, and then the ground instantly opened up beneath the three-headed beast of legend!

Fire spewed forth from the pit in the earth, and a red-orange glow emitted from it. "Noooooo! Nooooo!" protested mini-Malovent as he was dragged to a pit of eternal fire where the worm dieth not.

Cerberus smiled from each of his three heads as he disappeared with his quarry into the pit with his eyes afire. The witnesses to this event would ever have in their minds the pitiful cry for mercy of "Noooo! Pleeeeease!" as the once-proud and terrible creature,

Malovent, met his fate, his scream echoing as it faded into nothingness. Such was his end; such was his new beginning.

The crowd was hushed with heavy silence. Even Angel Mentor stood in awe. "Cerberus," he said quietly. "I thought he was only a legend. Well, what do you *know?*"

Then the ground closed behind Cerberus, the stupid dog, leaving no evidence that anything had even occurred. At this very moment, some of the events this battle were beginning to fade from the conscious memories of the gathered crowd. Most of them would not be permitted to remember this day, not really, though it would appear to them in their dreams at times. They would all dismiss it as a mere nightmare, something odd that happened in the night, hardly worth mentioning. The only ones present who would remember with clarity were Mentor's warriors: Emily, Jimmy, Margaret, and Cassius, now fast friends. Now it was time to deal with vital matters newly at hand.

The group turned toward the former principal and terror monger. She did not seem so imposing now, on her knees again, gagging and hacking, tears slopping all over her face. Her master was not only gone, but he was never powerful! She was weeping but still unable to speak. Her uniform was a-shambles. She was a living wreck. No one there had ever seen such a broken being. A deformed broken body is one thing. In such a body, a person's spirit can still shine through.

However, when a *soul* is broken, when everything a person thought they were and thought they could become is suddenly taken from them, when all of their joy and reason for living is completely crushed, it is a terrible sight. In this case, it was not a natural painful humility that comes from being punished for known wrongs. No, this was completely different. This was a person's soul painfully uprooted and left hanging on a clothesline, glistening raw in the sun, skinned alive and salted! Death would have been a thousand times better!

Miss Coffenayle was a regular person now who had to come to grips with the reality that all she had based her very life on was a lie! Her sole reason for living, her whole human spirit, had just been torn away from her, her light extinguished for the darkness she embraced, and she knew that there was nothing left now but condemnation. She saw that the power of God was so great that the mere touch of an old man's cane rendered her completely helpless.

She witnessed today that the power of the mighty Malovent, self-proclaimed Destroyer of Nations, Crusher of Worlds, Ruler of All, was removed from the earth by the single swipe of an old man's sword in the jaws of a stupid dog. To top it all off, even death itself could not stop Mentor. Coffenayle realized now that even a stupid-looking stray cur playing in a field, mocked by everyone, disdained and rejected as useless could be a disguise for the ultimate power. Nothing was as it seemed to her! She was dealing with all this and could not even express a single thought of it because her voice was taken from her.

Not only was there all of that, but in her voiceless state, she was recalling all the pride with which she so gladly took on the name of Malovent. Oh, how she loved calling him "Master!" She loved evil and loved the idea of worldly power so much that she betrayed the very people who supported and loved her. She knew now that she sold her soul willingly for a shortcut to power that appeared so mighty, but was really just a pink, awful, pitiful little creature of no power at all. That *thing* was what she worshipped and adored because she thought that she could get something out of it. Oh, the terrible lies that he told her! Oh, the grand promises he made! Now…now it was all for naught. Now she was here to face up to it all, to face the people that she had cursed and affected so terribly.

No one had really taken notice, but Mr. Castlethorn, Ladlepot, and Goliath all were standing upright. Their bodies were no longer painfully deformed. Slowly, but as quickly as they could handle it, their minds and memories were returning. Mr. Mentor, of course, was fully aware but smiled to himself as he kept that little secret. Everyone would be so surprised when they finally noticed their return to normalcy. Everyone's attention, for now, was appropriately turned toward the former principal and would-be empress of the Underworld. What a pity! Everyone just quietly stared at this barely human blob of flesh and blood; she appeared perfectly normal on the outside, but she was completely broken on the inside. Her insides ached with the reality of being completely and helplessly humiliated in front of the ones over whom she had such great power! She looked up at them, not a bit sorry! Humiliated, yes, *but not sorry*. She would do it all over again, if she could. Well, she had an ace in the hole. She had the Clan to back her up! Then she would show them all!

Angel Mentor finally stepped forward. It was time to end this... now! He pulled his sword from his gold-braided waist as the class and school staff all watched, wide-eyed! Coffenayle defiantly bowed her head, knowing that she was about to be killed by beheading. Mentor raised his holy blade high over his head, gripped it both hands, set his teeth in a terrible grimace and, with a terrible shout, brought the blade down! The crowd gasped in wide-eyed horror, anticipating a bloody, morbid scene. Some people had their eyes closed. Others were riveted to the scene with a terrible fascination, unable to close their eyes. No one there wanted bloodshed; had they not seen enough?

But Angel Mentor did not finish the beheading stroke. No. He pulled the blade short, stopping an inch from the back of Coffenayle's neck. The he merely and gently tapped her on the back of her head with the flat of the blade. "Now you may speak," he said calmly.

Emily thought to herself that as an angel, the once mild-mannered Mr. Mentor had developed quite a flair for the theatrical. She smiled but so very reverently. She looked around herself and saw Jimmy smiling in the same spirit. Now what about... Mr. Castlethorn? Was he *taller* now? Was he somehow...healing? Looking better? Feeling better? Were his eyes clearing up? And was reason returning to his mind? Was his will now his own again? His spine was not as bent; his body was straight and strong. He was vibrant and brilliant once again; he was his old self! Yes! Yes! He was once again Cassius Lawrence Thorne, PhD. Yes, he was, and unbeknownst to Emily and the whole group assembled here, the *same thing was happening for all of the affected, afflicted people who were victims of the witch's curses and that magical tea!*

In classrooms all across the school, teachers were frozen in their tracks, dropping their chalk, stopping in mid-sentence, releasing their grip on some student they were punishing, suddenly puzzled and shocked at what they were doing. Inside the cafeteria, people leaned against counters and sat on the floor. Everyone was changing back to their normal healthy selves, restored to what they were before the evil of Coffenayle had afflicted them. They became what they were originally in their own lives. They lost their warts, their twisted limbs. They walked upright again. They stopped itching and clawing at their skin. Their natural good looks and strength returned. They could speak normally.

Crooked teeth were now straight. Tongues no longer felt thick. The green fog was gone from all of them; their minds were normal once more. The dreaded curse had ended! All was well again!

Students were stunned at the humanity they saw return to their teachers. Teachers were stunned at their pain going away and their minds clearing up. They remembered their own *true* names. Gone were Brewinghops, Nerdstink, Frankincenseless, Franmaldehyde, and a hundred other made-up stupid names. Gone was the desire to degrade students. The teachers were disoriented and shocked. So were the students, but there was an overwhelming sense of well-being that accompanied these sudden changes. All was well! All was well! Even as people wept for joy at the return of their lives, all was well!

Angel Mentor backed away from Coffenayle; his blade was in its scabbard. She could harm no one any longer, so there was no need to pose a threat. The kneeling mess of a woman stood now and straightened her back. She raised her chin in pride and looked down her nose at the entire gathering of people who were no longer under her curse. She was still determined to lord over them, and they knew it. They would not allow it, of course, but they also knew it. The students just looked at her in disbelief, shaking their heads.

After all that she had seen and had happen to her, she was still the proud haughty little Napoleonic woman! She cleared her throat and tested her voice. She was delighted that it had returned. She straightened her jacket the best she could and brushed off her pants. She was still alive. That fool, Charles, could not kill her! Even when he was sent by God himself to slay her, that coward could not destroy her greatness! He defied God to spare her life! That must mean she has some important purpose, that this world cannot get by without her.

She cleared her throat and began to speak. "All, right, everyone! We have all seen some very interesting things here today! But that does not mean *anything* is any *different!*" She eyed the crowd. She silently demanded their attention! She continued, "I am still the one in charge of this school! I believe that some of you are guilty of trespassing, a crime that I will fully punish when I find out who did it! I have a lead in the case because I found clues that cause me to believe that Mr. Castlethorn is one of guilty parties. Alongside of him, I suspect his little buddy in crime, Jimmy. Under my intense scrutiny, both of them will bend and break to tell me who the others are. I will show some mercy, but not much. Where is Castlethorn?"

She did not recognize him at first and had to identify him by his boots. He still needed a good scrubbing and a trip to the laundry…or perhaps to the incinerator to *burn* those clothes, but he was all there, tall and normal-looking. He did not avert his eyes to the ground. Not this time. She no longer ruled over him. She stared into his eyes for a moment, but the man did not budge. She knew that there was no getting anywhere with *him* right now, getting all cocky with her, like he was *somebody*. That's all right. She would get around to taking care of *him* later.

She looked around for Goliath the Butcher and for Ladlepot the Cafeteria Lady. She saw a tall, good-looking young man, athletic and broad-shouldered, clothes too big and a pink-stained white apron that hung loosely from his renewed trim frame. *Oh my*, Coffenayle thought to herself. *With Malovent out of the picture, maybe there was room for love!* Beside him was a lady that also stood tall and shapely, wearing an awful pink dress that also did not fit her. She still wore terrible cosmetics, but the cigarette was absent from her lips. She now answered to her proper name of Darla. She was a beautiful lady. Yes, they were Cassius, Steven, and Darla Thorne.

They were starting to remember! Coffenayle was simply amazed and very angry at the same time. They were all coming back to normal. Then she quickly recovered, not wasting time on anger. Well, of course, that was to be expected, what with her magic gone! That tea would still be pleasant-tasting enough, but it would not be addictive because the magic was all gone with Malovent dragged into the

Infernal Pit. Well, no matter. She was still in charge and quickly adjusted her tune to the conditions that now existed.

She changed colors to fit the current environment as easily as a chameleon changes colors with its current background. Yes, she was as cunning as a snake and as fast as a lizard! After all, she was Donatienne Coffenayle! She was born to *rule!*

34

Justice Is His Middle Name

"Now, friends. I understand that I have made some mistakes," she began speaking calmly and pleasantly, the consummate speech maker.

Angel Mentor watched her and shook his head ever so slightly. She still had no idea how badly she had just been beaten. His job was done, and he held his peace. He was still in his white robe, just in case something else happened. He was quite sure that the true danger had passed, but there was still one final loose end. He had to maintain his visage until she was finally under control.

She continued her speech. "I know that I have been hard on some of you. I have learned a great lesson today, and moving forward, I will be different. I will lead this school down a different path. We will be a different kind of team."

Keep talking, thought Angel Mentor as he saw what was coming up behind her. "I still own this school! I still own this property! Though I have had a change of heart, I will still crush anyone who does not do as I say!"

"By whut—" started Cassius Lawrence Thorne. "Ahem. By what right and authority do you say that?" His voice was no longer raspy. His English was perfect, and he sounded quite intelligent.

"As I said, you taller, better-looking, and more intelligent *toad*, for as long as I am in charge, you are my toady. I own this school and have every right—"

"To do nothing, witch!"

Coffenayle looked right at Angel Mentor. "You, sir, 'angel' or not," she said, making mockery quotation marks in the air, "are *dead* because I killed you and buried you in your own backyard, which, by the way, is now *my* backyard because *you gave it to me. Dead people,* angels or not, cannot own real estate in this world. It would be like a zombie back from the dead trying to a claim property deed. It just can't happen!" She boldly confessed to his murder, unafraid of the people around her. Who were they after all? They were just a big bunch of nobodies.

The officers of law and the state authorities who were now standing on the scene, but *behind* her, wondered what she was talking about. *An angel? A dead man? What…like a zombie?* This was all very puzzling to them. They looked at each other, shaking their heads and shrugging. They did just hear a confession to *murder* right in front of them…didn't they? As for the angel, all they saw was a pleasant old man leaning on his cane. There was no "angel" present, not in their eyes. *That is a nice watch chain, though. Very proper.*

Angel Mentor looked at her patronizingly. "I said nothing to you, Donatienne. Look behind you."

"Oh…that old trick. What are you going to do, stab me in the back with your little angel stick? You probably would. You want me to turn my back so you can murder me, don't you? Because you are a coward, you can only kill me without looking me in the eye! Well, you got rid of Malovent! You did your duty with him, but then you defied God's commandment by not killing me. So you are now a fallen angel and have no rights to be here! *I order you to leave the premises now! Off of my land, fallen angel!"* she screamed.

Some people in the crowd actually tittered a bit.

"Off of *whose* land?" the same voice said from behind her.

This time, Donatienne did look back and nearly jumped out of her skin! There stood Simon I. Doesbad, or more correctly, *a leaner, trimmer, and more confident Simon Justice Dozeman, Esquire.* He was a fine attorney, and beside him stood his new administrative assistant, Patience Lovegood. She had files of papers pulled in a wagon by one hand and was holding Simon's belted pants up from the back with the other. Even with the belt pulled completely tight, his very expensive slacks could not stay up without help. His entire suit sagged terribly; his fully buttoned collar that once barely contained his neck and four chins drooped and sagged a good four inches, silk tie and all. Though his very expensive clothing looked perfectly ridiculous, he was filled with a justified dignity and fierce righteous indignation. He was confident as stood up to Coffenayle, wondering how he could have ever been in love with such a horrific creature.

"You don't own this land… Donatienne Coffin-*nail!*"

She bristled at the intentional insult. She turned red in the face and started toward him…the toad! How *dare* he mock the great name of Coffenayle! In her rage, she did not even notice them at first…the dozen or so police officers and other agents of law. All of them were standing right behind her former attorney. One of them stepped past Simon and approached her, a man she had known for years as Jonathan Washington, a well-educated and poised man who had immigrated to the United States when he was a toddler, from Africa, and gained an education to work in education.

He was a man who had been a useful tool to her as she bilked the state government and school system. She had tricked him into approving some of her illegal equipment construction projects in the school's kitchen. His signatures helped push those projects and others through the courts. He was convinced at the time that she was a wonderful person. He wanted to help her in the light of the passing of Mr. Mentor whom he greatly respected. Oddly, he did not notice his old friend among the crowd. He was not allowed to because it would have caused him a great shock. It was not his time to die of that heart attack; not for a few more years.

Today, though, where Coffenayle and Mr. Washington were concerned, things were different. Mr. Washington was deeply saddened, and he was hurt by Coffenayle's betrayal. She had cast a shadow on his good name as a professional. She had betrayed him as person who broke the law, taking advantage of him and doing it in his own good name. There was no laughter today like there was in the old days as they would meet in his office. No. Today, he was solemn, angry, and hurt. He approached her with a sheaf of papers and handed it to her. The bundle was about an inch thick. His eyes smoldered, and his mouth was set firmly. No smiles for her today. All she would get out of him was a load of grief.

"Your summons to appear in court, courtesy of your many building code violations and other diverse encroachments of the law," he said simply. He stepped back.

Another agent approached. "I am from the Board of Education. I have another packet of summons for you. See you in court," he quietly stated as he loaded her up with more paperwork. He moved aside to let the others have their turn. They all approached her in like manner, patiently waiting for the others to finish. All of them had summons for her.

Coffenayle just stood there, mouth open, unsure of what to say. The papers were piled up in her arms. She could not believe this! Why, Simon must be there to defend her! Yes, that had to be the reason for his presence! To defend her and get her off, just like the old days. That was it; he was just being clever! He was pretending to be on the side of the agents so he could trick them into doing something he could use in court later. Yes, that had to be it! She had sent him to court to her special judge! There had to be a way out, and he was going to give it to her right now!

Things had not gone like she thought. In the courts, this very morning, there was an old judge, the Honorable David George Parcell who had a very interesting start to his day. He was in chambers first thing, long before his first case was to be heard, looking at the files from the Happy Valley Vocational School. He was in his usual cranky old mood, having a cup of his coveted tea which tasted like his wife's favorite perfume. He was all alone. He preferred it that way ever since that meeting he had with Miss Donatienne Coffenayle. That was the life-changing meeting, the one where took the bribe. He had his moments of regret over that, but that lovely tea seemed to make things better for him.

His morning was going normally when suddenly, he felt this burning sensation on his back. He pulled off his honorable robe and checked the mirror in his office. This *thing* that was attached to him was hissing and writhing about. The judge took the imp's appearance in stride; he had gotten used to its presence. Some days, he even liked the creature; it made some clever quips from time to time. It made the judge laugh once in a while, even as it made the public servant feel old and worn through.

But today, InkRobe was not doing so very well. The little imp gasped and gagged on the judge's shoulder, then rolled off, falling to the floor. Judge Parschall just stood over it, staring at the thing. Was it...sick? It lay on its black furry little back. It hissed and moaned. The thing twitched and convulsed, closed its eyes, and was suddenly still. The judge knelt down to examine his "friend" and gently nudged it with his finger. Strangely, he felt completely neutral about this whole situation. Curious, really, but with no emotion for the creature. Then it suddenly it opened its eyes, and with a maniacal grin said, "See ya in the funny papers!" and went suddenly limp, exhaling long and loud. Then InkRobe kicked once and died.

The judge then stood up, just staring. Was this possible, this *impossible* thing that just happened? As the judge was wondering what to do, the little corpse seemed to spontaneously catch fire and *poof!* It was simply gone in a cloud of gold glitter and black ashy dust. The judge retreated quickly from the dust, back to his desk, and fell into his chair. He reached for the pistol he kept in his drawer, and not knowing what else to do, pointed it and tracked the dust as it blew across the floor, into the air, and out a window his administrative assistant had opened to give him some fresh air.

Judge Parschall's body suddenly stopped hurting and his mind was clear. He shook his head. It took him a minute to understand what just happened. Even the terror of the moment, of seeing that little demon die, passed very quickly. He took a deep breath and felt like the man he once was! He felt wonderful! Then he felt a sudden urge to look at this case he was just reviewing. Something did not seem right. He turned his chair to face his desk. He could not have read that correctly. He blinked his eyes and shook his head.

He looked again at the papers before him. He started to remember some things and reviewed his work. Why, he was clearly in the wrong here! What was he thinking? These summons and subpoenas were perfectly legal! He called his paralegals and assistants into the room. One of them referred to him as Judge Parschall, and he thought it was a sick joke, somehow aimed at his being a "partial" judge! He did not understand and said so, but for some reason, everyone present thought that *he* preferred it that way, even insisted upon it. The clouds around his brain were departing. He requested files be brought to him *immediately* of anything related to the Happy Valley Vocational school. He needed them *now! Right now!* "And stop calling me 'Partial' or 'Parschall' or whatever that it is! My name is *Parcell*!"

His staff scattered, all of them mildly confused but relieved to see the venerated judge was back to his old self. He was not the same after learning of his wife's illness. She had gotten over it with some specialized and expensive treatment; but he himself had still had not recovered to his old self. They assumed that he was in shock from her being sick. Well, not anymore! They brought the papers to him, boxes of them, and he started shouting orders of various phone calls to be made and so on. The whole courthouse was a flurry of activity, and he even enlisted the help of other judges who were glad to see that Judge Parcell was back to his normal self, back in the business of dispensing justice. They had reluctantly begun to draft articles of impeachment against him, but maybe now they could cancel all of that. This flurry of activity and paperwork was interrupted by the appearance of the school's attorney whom the judge was expecting and who requested a private audience in chambers with his honor.

For some reason, though his first impulse was to boot the attorney out of his office, he did not do it. He really *felt* that he needed to hear the lawyer out. A lovely young lady was with him, burdened with boxes of papers on a cart, which was intriguing. *Was she holding up his pants? What an assistant to take such good care of a legal pro who could not even properly size his own clothes! The man needed another tailor! Look at that sagging shirt! Disgusting that he should come to court dressed this way.*

In spite of his misgivings, the judge heard Simon J. Dozeman, Esq., out completely, even on the condition of absolute immunity. Normally, such a demand would be rejected outright, but the old judge knew it was the right thing to allow it in this case. He heard the lawyer's story, and Dozeman told the judge that he brought these papers to prove all of it and would turn state's evidence. The lawyer made the plea that he did not fully understand why he was making the decisions necessary to hide all of the wrongdoings in the first place, but he wanted to come clean.

In consideration of what the judge had just seen happen with his very own body and mind, he had complete empathy! This was a strange morning indeed, and apparently, it was one for the books! After all, how often does one watch a devilish imp die? The judge had an agreement immediately drafted that the records of this conversation would be sealed by law, that the attorney would remain completely anonymous and that the state would act as the plaintiff for the case. That way, the accused could face the accuser, and the witness would remain hidden. Any attorney/client privilege between Dozeman and Coffenayle was suspended because it was a criminal conspiracy involving both the defendant and the attorney. The judge was very lenient, and in exchange for the information and documents, he would allow the attorney complete anonymity, and Dozeman could keep his law practice, which currently consisted of just one client. And that client was about to go to prison, so he would have to start over from scratch. This was not a perfect deal by the book, but it was the best thing they could do under the incredible circumstances in which they found themselves.

No one would ever know that Dozeman and the judge were at one time working together to keep the school immune from justice. Keeping their conspiracy secret was loathe to the good judge, but on the other hand, he felt it was somehow…forgiven. It was far more important to complete this prosecution than to dwell on the past mistakes of two men that were mutually compromised of mind and health. To try to prove in court that they were not responsible for their actions due to the outside influence of demons and witches would be a nightmare of massive proportions. It would land them both in the State Hospital for the Mentally Insane. Fortunately, both the judge and lawyer never changed their legal names. Though they insisted on being called "Parschall" and "Doesbad," their names on all documents remained true to their real names.

Because of this meeting, which took place immediately before their long drive back to the school, Patience and Dozeman were confronting Coffenayle with more than enough papers to lawfully secure her arrest. They handed her their paperwork after everyone else was finished. The former principal did not fully understand what was happening, even as uniformed police officers quietly stated, "You're under arrest" as they handcuffed her. Her! She could not believe that they were able to do so with her lawyer right there! This must be a ruse of some kind! Yes, a ruse!

"Doesbad! You worthless toad! Do something!" Coffenayle screamed.

"Yes. I will do something. Officers!"

The police stopped what they were doing. A lawyer was speaking. Coffenayle smiled. Now for the big finish. She knew he could come through. The ruse was over, and he would set her free. Her good friend, Simon I. Doesbad, Esq., was about to make a brilliant legal move and get her out of these dreadful unjustified handcuffs.

"I, Simon Justice Dozeman, Esquire, stand now as the legal representative of Mrs. Edna Mentor who has been discovered to be alive after many years. She was discovered recently at Happy Valley Vocational School, illegally incarcerated, with full knowledge and intent, by Donatienne Coffenayle. Said Coffenayle held Mrs. Mentor illegally captive under the name of 'Miss Whipshot,' disguised as an employee of the Happy Valley Vocational School. As Mrs. Mentor's attorney, acting on her behalf, I do press charges of kidnapping, assault, battery, conspiracy to commit murder, and the commission of the murder by poison of one Mr. Charles Edward Mentor, Edna Mentor's husband, and of conspiracy against one Mr. Angelton. Said Angelton was an employee of the school who was killed in a very unfortunate car accident. Nevertheless, there is sufficient evident to launch an investigation against Donatienne Coffenayle as the statute of limitations concerning conspiracy charges has not yet expired, per state and local statutes. These charges are among others pending in court.

"Judge Parcell has cleared his calendar, and a public defender has already been appointed to take the case as a *courtesy* to the accused in return for her years of service as an educator prior to these alleged criminal acts. As an additional courtesy to the accused, I advise the accused that she is under arrest that she has legal rights to have her public defender present during questioning and to remain silent until she can talk to her lawyer. She cannot afford a private attorney because all of her worldly goods, precious metals, and cash have been confiscated by local and state authorities as evidence in the cases being presented against her. Miss Coffenayle, *adieu*. Officers, take her away!" He removed his hat at his closing statement and placed it over his heart. Simon Justice just served service of justice…justly. Ha!

He waved goodbye as Coffenayle resisted and was forced to the ground. She hollered at the several police officers about how they ruined the polish on her combat boots by dragging her legs in the dirt. She should have a moment to say her piece! She should have her lawyer do something! Anything!

Yes, Dozeman did something all right. He did the right thing. Patience approached him and gently took his hand.

"I believed in you, Simon. The whole time," she said.

"Yes. I know you did, but—"

"What, Simon?"

"Do you believe in me enough to marry me?" he asked sincerely in front of the whole crowd.

Patience Lovegood looked around. The crowd was waiting.

"Yes," she said with a smile and a kiss. The crowd applauded and cheered.

"Well done," said a voice approaching from the infirmary. An elderly woman, modestly dressed in a bathrobe and proper pajamas, which she changed into after removing Whipshot's PJ's that were *much* too big was being followed by a lovely nurse who also had to change into a smaller uniform.

The crowd turned around. "Hello, everyone! Do any of you know me?"

The kids all looked at each other.

"Come, come, now…surely somebody here must know me."

Suddenly a voice shouted, "Mrs. Mentor! Mrs. Mentor! Edna! It's me! Cassius!" The tall-standing former Castlethorn ran toward her, smiling! They met away from the students; none of the kids were really paying attention. They were all gathered by the fence now, wondering about Stupid Dog and *just what happened here!* Their memories of the moment were rapidly fading.

"Cassius! My dear boy!" Edna Mentor lurched forward. She grabbed her old friend and gave him a long overdue squeeze. "It is lovely to see you...as you are, Cassius."

"Edna, where have you been?" he asked.

"Why, I have never left you. We could not remember each other before, but we never left one another."

"How do you mean?" he asked.

Just then the nurse walked up with *a pair of cat's-eye glasses with missing rhinestones.* Cassius knew in an instant! He was overjoyed at the healing Mrs. Edna Mentor had passed through.

"Oho! Wait... I have an idea," Cassius said with a mischievous grin. "Put the glasses on and shout at the students!"

Edna instantly loved the idea and immediately donned the glasses. "Stand at attention you miserable toads!" The class jumped, and a couple shrieked involuntarily at the lady's appearance. Then, after a second, they laughed! They did not quite understand yet, but this used to be Miss Whipshot! She was Mrs. Mentor, the lady teacher everyone thought was dead and buried. She was even rumored to have been buried somewhere on the school grounds! Yet, here she was, the former Miss Whipshot. Cassius looked around for the ghost of Mr. Mentor, currently Angel Mentor. He appeared to be nowhere in the crowd. However, Cassius did hear his distinct voice say, "You and Darla take good care of her. She has much left to do. Goodbye, old friend. I will always be near you."

Did Mr. Mentor say Darla? Was Darla around here? Cassius looked for a familiar face and in Ladlepot's clothing was...his wife! His darling Darla!

"Darla!" Cassius shouted. The woman in the cafeteria lady's stained pink dress looked around a bit and then finally saw him!

"Cassius!" she shouted back. The two excused their way through the crowd and embraced an embrace that was both long and overdue. They cried a little and then composed themselves. Already, the memories of the terrors were receding. In fact, a number of memories were receding. They kept hearing chatter about how greatly Steven had kicked that football. They looked at each other. Steven? Our Steven? "Cassius," Darla asked, hoping against hope "do you think, darling, that our Steven is here and normal like us again?" He took her hand. They started looking around the crowd. After a moment of intensive searching, Darla spotted him and pointed to him. They met him; he was dressed in Goliath's old clothes. It took him a moment, but he finally recognized them.

"Mom! Dad!" he shouted. He ran to them, and they embraced their son who was in smelly butcher's clothes, the father in greasy stinking coveralls and the mother in a horrible pink dress, wearing too much makeup and smelling of stale tobacco. None of them cared; not yet, though they would soon feel the need to change clothes! They were a family again. Genius father, compassionate loving mother, and football star son. A match made in heaven but restored by an angel. Steven's memories were fading, and he did not remember much about what had happened; not true facts, anyway. He was now the same athlete that he always was, the same kind and compassionate young man they raised him to be.

Emily stood back, just observing. She and Jimmy were holding hands, and Margaret was there too. She had determined to be a best friend to both of them; she had accepted Jimmy's choice with grace and aplomb far exceeding her age. Margaret knew that those two were a good match, and she would not spoil that. She wanted to be good friends with them still. The three of them listened to the conversations about what had happened on the football field. Steven kicked a field goal over the goal posts from a great distance to celebrate the principal's arrest. She was, according to the class, arrested after following some man in a black robe to the field. The robed man left the scene somehow, but an aggressive Coffenayle was subdued by an old man in a brown suit, who hit her with his cane. Then the cops took her after her own lawyer turned her in. The rest...well, it just did not matter. The kids did remember some of the ugliness with the teacher but would soon let those matters rest with the dead. They just simply did not have a desire to speak much of those times, which seemed more and more unreal with time. *What a morning!*

The only ones to retain accurate memories of the old times were Jimmy, Emily, Margaret, Cassius, Darla, and one who will not be named here. Steven's memories of those years were partial and spotty, but what he did remember was true. Cassius and Darla were content to leave it that way. Steven did not push either. He just wanted to live the rest of his life with his eye on a bright future. His memories were not complete enough to add to the process of writing the book.

Five of these six people, in years to come, would finally agree to collaborate and write the true story of the Happy Mentoring Vocational School the way they remembered and agreed upon. All of them made solemn promise to one other. They agreed to each keep a copy of the story safe and secret from the eyes of the world. They would show it to their children when they came of age and started asking questions. They would allow them to decide for themselves what they believed.

This story...this is that version. Decide for yourselves how it fell into the hands of the author!

EPILOGUE

Author's note

What follows from here is something that even the six mentioned above knew nothing about. The author, true to form, chooses to not disclose how he discovered this information.

The Patriarchal Meeting

The Coffenayle Family Patriarch, through whom all major decisions were made, stood behind his desk with his hands on the back of his very expensive, hand-tooled, Amish-made leather high-backed office chair on ivory wheels. The desk was made of the finest solid hardwoods, aged to perfection. One does not often get to see a hand-carved, hand-sanded, painstakingly tooled, and assembled desk. Each joint was held together with hardwood pegs and precision fitting, not a drop of glue or a single nail. The desk was as solid as its former owners, passed down from generation to generation of patriarchs. This was the office of ultimate power in the Coffenayle family.

The destinies of entire nations were decided in this room, walled with maps and globes. Images of many different businesses from across the world adorned the shelves and alcoves. There was a rumor that a Coffenayle may have discovered a concept design for a new type of engine called a "jet turbine" that could potentially change the world of travel...and warfare. The patriarch did not tolerate rumors. He had just dispatched some of his best men, investigators in the company of engineers, to find out about this "turbine" and to learn *all of the facts.*

With that done, his mind was on other highly critical business. In his 110 years, Patriarch Coffenayle had never seen anyone do what Donatienne had done. He had consulted with the family's finest sociologists, psychiatrists, and religious scholars. He had his accountants, logisticians, and advanced mathematicians crunch the numbers, the odds, the logistics with every possible computation known to man. He had long given up gambling because with his men working the odds for him, every roll of the dice or hand of cards came up a winner. His people had discovered too that even seemingly random games like roulette could be predicted. What, therefore, is the point of gambling if you know the outcome before they even spin the ball, deal the cards, or toss the dice?

Naturally, he and the Clan could get rich gambling at the casinos, but they preferred becoming rich by *purchasing* casinos—out of their checking accounts! Some of their minor casino operators who never knew they were working for the Coffenayle Clan made a pretty decent living, even after the Clan took their cut. Gambling laws varied from state to state, nation to nation. The Clan's speakeasy drinking establishments were *certainly* illegal.

That being said, the patriarch and his family leaders were far too well-insulated and powerful to ever face prosecution. Let the flunkies like Al Capone and Dutch Schultz duke it out in the streets and fight over territory; let *their* blood flow. The Coffenayle's made the same money, no matter who was running things! The true power behind the throne lay with them, the creators of nations and subjugators of all things worldly. Family blood would flow only across the generations of their progenitors to keep the Clan fully operational and growing. While the family name was passed down by the male descendants, the power with the name was also passed through the mothers. The power was the same. The gender of the individual did not matter when it came to passing family power and position through the generations.

Sometimes, a woman would rule as Matriarch. The Clan was pragmatic to the *extreme*. Logic and rationale ruled their decisions. At the death of the head of the family, normally about every one hundred and twenty-five years or so, they would gather in conclaves and choose their new leader purely based on the odds and numbers. They always maximized their chances of success by choosing who would be the best leader of all of them, no matter what they thought of the person. Once, a scientist was caught trying to doctor numbers to bring a favorite uncle to the ruler's throne. He was discovered, then was shot in the back of the head—twice—very *publicly* by mobsters who thought they were killing an embezzler of booze money as so ordered. The papers called it the "Senseless Gangland Slaying of a Brilliant Scientist." The Coffenayle Family called it "internal affairs." The boys who shot him thought they were killing a common stupid thug who happened to dress nicely. He could not be that smart if he got caught stealing. If only they knew…

Right before the shooting, the ruling council of the family had thrown a banquet in his honor for some wonderful discovery called "insulin," used to treat *diabetes mellitus*, which was a real achievement. The banquet, though, was in reality a disguised farewell. Such was the fate of cheaters within the family. Cheat anyone on the outside you wished, but if you seriously harmed, swindled, or cheated a fellow member of the Clan…well…they will always deeply regret your death and will cry at your funeral. Still, though, you knew better. You brought it on yourself. Even as you are fondly remembered and your accomplishments revered, you *did* know better!

It was not known to anyone outside of the family's ruling council who was being considered by the numbers and odds to be the best of the best to rule the family. The patriarch had their people run the numbers *three times* just to be sure. Each try at the numbers took twenty-one days, one hour, and seventeen minutes. This was a reflection of the precision with which the numbers were calculated! Each time, the results were exactly the same. There was no disputing it.

Donatienne Coffenayle had the best shot at ruling as Matriarch after the patriarch died. The problem was that she had chosen a strange path, one they were not resentful of, but her path was unknown to them. It was a wild card. They could not figure the odds on what her spiritual choices would do to her status. She literally had the world at her fingertips without even knowing it. She could have been the Matriarch ruler of an empire that had its finger in every pie, virtuous or criminal. At times, only pennies would flow in from some business interests, but when you get enough pennies flowing your way, a little bit becomes a whole lot. Any profit, no matter how small, was considered as important as any other. That was the way the big picture worked.

That aside, a decision had to be made. A very difficult one. The Clan had never faced a situation like this before. The one chosen as the best candidate to take the throne had refused to follow the Coffenayle tradition. This made her an anomaly. They had a difficult time predicting what she would do because she was very secretive. Her religion was not known to them. They had Buddhists, Catholics, Shamanists, Taoists, Baptists—you name it. However, witchcraft, though not offensive to them, had its own secretive laws that made it difficult to decide what to do with Donatienne. To further complicate things, she was in prison now, on death row.

Premeditated murder, they said. Guilty, they said. It was a capital offense because of the aggravating circumstances of the case. The number crunchers were able to cast their numbers with a few advanced mathematical models. They were able to discover that, yes, she was guilty of murder. They confirmed their numerical findings by behavioral analysis. There was no question at all; she had killed two very good men. An educator for one, the other a philanthropist, humanitarian, *and* educator no less. The other murders she likely committed, by magic and other means, including a cow(?) simply did not matter to them. The methods of the murders were slightly skewed because of the high likelihood of magic being used, at least in part. Thus, the imprecise understanding of the methods. Normally, they would be able to determine the type of weapon used, down to the brand name and model. This is what bothered them. They were not as precise in dealing with Donatienne as they were all others.

They were not disturbed by the murders, but the problem here was what they called an "X-Factor." The "X" was the unknown. There was some influence of force acting with her through her magical religion that they knew nothing about. They did know that they were dealing with demons, and frankly, they did not care, but they could not predict what that influence would cause Donatienne to do with the unlimited power of the family throne.

Devils, demons, imps, faeries, etc. were spiritual beings that were unpredictable. No data had been collected on them. If the egg-heads could run numbers on the demons to predict her behavior, Donatienne would have ruled the family if the results favored it. Since they did not know how to factor in the devils or their effects, this created an unforeseen and unknown problem. Thus, the meeting in the patriarch's office.

It was known by all that to be called into his office was a great honor but one that carried with it a terrible responsibility. They knew that they were up against some terrible assignment, though they dared not second-guess what it might be. The two men walked in without a trace of nervousness; they were supremely confident. They had flown all over the world and had committed all manner of insider trading, corporate espionage, assassinations, and the like for their family. Whatever the patriarch had in mind was fine with them, even murdering a cousin if it came to that. They knew of the research on Donatienne, having participated in it. They stood there patiently. "Davis" and "Smith" were their monikers. Their hands were folded in front of them, never reaching away to so much as to scratch an itch.

Though the patriarch was guarded by the honor of the Clan, one never knew what enemies might be about. That was the reason for the heavily armed masked men of secret identities who were standing in the corners of the room, ALL four corners, armed with the latest in military technology that the world did not even know existed. "Davis" and "Smith" knew they were dead men if they flinched the wrong way. It did not bother them; they had been in this office many times. They were used to the appearance of the Patriarchal Guard. Unbeknownst to "Smith," "Davis" was once one of them. Unbeknownst to "Davis," "Smith" was once one of them too. This is how well the Coffenayles kept their secrets.

"Men, please be seated," said the patriarch. He knew that he could trust these men with his life, but the guards did not care. The lobby guards frisked them very thoroughly at gunpoint before they let them enter the room where stood the other armed guards. It was purely ceremonial, symbolic to have all of that security. It tended to remind even the most trusted family members of the gravity of the business that was discussed within these walls. Though the corner guards were cleared and perfectly trusted, the patriarch dismissed them when the two were seated. The two men who flanked the patriarch remained in the room. They were the highest-ranking elite security personnel, known simply as "desk guards." Smith and Davis were direct relatives of the former school principal, Donatienne Coffenayle. The patriarch allowed them to settle into their leather chairs; he poured them each a mineral water with lemon. They needed clear heads for this meeting. It was not a reunion or celebration. It was purely business. Unprecedented business at that.

Today, this topic of discussion would never be spoken of outside of this room at the pains of *death*. There was no need to have these men swear an oath. They knew what they were bred to do; they knew what their loyalty meant. It was life itself. The patriarch did not need to remind them of that. This type of thing had never been considered before, much less been decided. This was definitely a patriarchal decision. The papers had been written, forms filed, numbers crunched, and results tabulated. All of that evidence was piled in neat stacks all over the desk. One piece of paper lay flat in the center of the desk. He slid it to the men. They did not flinch when the patriarch flipped it over. It was simply a picture of the *ace of spades*. They knew what that meant. One of them slid a large nonsmoker's ashtray over to himself and pulled an 18-Karat gold-plated cigarette lighter out of his pocket. It had been inspected outside and was deemed safe; the guards knew that such devices were sometimes used to destroy clues as to what the meeting had been about. The desk guards, two of them who were always present with the Patriarch, had been informed of which man would reach for a lighter. They knew he would reach into his right breast pocket of his jacket with his left hand. Any other move with his hands into a pocket would have brought him instant death.

The evidence burned nicely, fully consumed into a fine ash with no evidence of what it once read. Good quality paper, nothing but the best. The ashes would later be swept out of the ashtray and flushed down the toilet. No evidence was ever less than completely destroyed.

"Men, you know what you have been called to do. This has never, in the history of the Clan, ever been done before. I know that she is to you"—he nodded to the younger man—"a first cousin." He looked at the older man and stated, "To you, she is a niece. I know that both of you are naturally fond of her." The patriarch appeared stoic and firm. His eyes were resolute but...sad. Maybe just a bit of weariness in them too.

"That all has to be put aside for the benefit of our organization. All it would take is just one informed person to make our very existence known to the rest of the world. It would not take that much information, truly, to make someone just curious enough to do some checking. Know that this is being done without malice or anger. Know that we have the means to rescue her through the courts. We could have her set free by our lawyers. However, this cannot be done because she is a wildcard. We cannot predict what she would do if she were made the Matriarch after my death. Assigning her to a lesser position is forbidden by our laws. Either the chosen rules the family or the chosen must be neutralized. Those who are chosen are simply too brilliant, too dangerous to be left alive if they are unfit to sit in this chair. These laws and bylaws have existed since the beginning."

The men looked at each other and nodded. The younger one spoke first upon a gesture from the older one. "Father and I agree with you, Patriarch," he said firmly with a trace of a bow. "We are here to serve the order, to serve the family. We understand that sometimes familiar and even beloved blood must be spilled. We will carry out our duty. The two of us will meet here with you and the Clan after our work is done to drink to her memory, mourn, and reminisce."

"But until then," added the older man, "this is our task, our work. We will carry out our duty. What is the plan?"

The three men then discussed the whole plan: how to prime Donatienne, how to get into the prison, how to enter the death chamber and operate the electric chair. In, do the deed, out—a very clean operation. Even as they spoke, the plan was in motion. Three men were visiting the warden of Coffenayle's prison, explaining some things to him.

They held his undivided attention.

An offer he couldn't refuse

In her prison cell, Donatienne Coffenayle, dubbed the "Mentor Murderer" by the press, was pacing. She was to have a visitor. That could only mean one thing, and it was about time! Her date with Old Sparky was only days away. She was already hatching a scheme to expose the Patriarch, if she had to. She would not ride the lightning! Not her! Shave her head indeed! Who do they think they are? Now, if she spilled some of the smaller family activities that she knew about, that would buy her some time. Yes, she would talk and see to it that the Coffenayle family was exposed. She had to do *something* to save her own life. After that messy day with Malovent, she knew that he would not be coming back, and she needed *someone* to get her out of this. Her own power was ended by that cursed Mr. Mentor! Angel indeed! *Phah!* Finally, today, Judy "Jude" Ruth came to see her. A cousin! Family representation! Finally!

The guards arrived at the solitary holding cell to retrieve Coffenayle and take her to the visiting area. They chained her wrists behind her, hooking them to the leather belt around her waist. Another chain ran from the collar around her neck to the waist belt. Two more chains ran to the ankle shackles. She looked fine in prison stripes. Her once proud blonde hair was shaved close, like a boy's crew cut. Prison safety regulations called for it. "Don't worry," the barber told her, "it only gets much shorter after you get to buck the lightning!" He laughed at her.

The keepers of the condemned were especially careful with her because she was a media sensation. Besides…who knows what a prisoner with nothing to lose might be capable of doing? That is why there were four guards. Two in front, two in the back. They were none too gentle with her. They knew this one was charged with murder and child abuse, not to mention abuse of the elderly and the kidnapping of beloved Mrs. Mentor. To top it all off...*she was running a crooked orphanage!*

What made some of the guards mad at her on a personal level was that she ended the vocational school's football program when she corrupted the system. One of them had a talented son who never got to play ball because of her. He would be especially glad to see her take the big jolt! For that reason, he was denied his request to be part of the execution team. The warden would not have a man on the team who had a score to settle. He told that guard personally, in a closed-door one-on-one meeting, that the prison was there to dispense justice and not revenge. They did not need for the prisoner to be treated too roughly or verbally abused. There could be nothing for the press to use that would reflect poorly on the prison. The guard fully understood and spoke nothing further of it.

Secretly, the warden prayed for the guard. He hoped that this man would not rejoice in the death of the prisoner because that would be the same as entertaining murder in his heart. The warden needed good men on his staff, not preoccupied with dispensing justice. Justice was in the hands of the courts and the juries. Their job was simply to carry out the sentences, be they imprisonment or death.

They led her to a wooden table that was bolted to the floor, the same as the wooden chairs, one on either side of the table. The rest of the room had similar tables, but they were not occupied. Coffenayle and Judy had the room to themselves. Judy was already sitting down, waiting for her incarcerated cousin. She smiled when she looked up and saw Donatienne. She waved, so excited to see her!

Coffenayle waved by nodding her head. She smiled, and actual tears came to her eyes. No need to stab her own eyeballs this time. Cousin Judy was under very strict orders to not hug, shake hands, nor touch the prisoner in any way. To do so would result in both of them being strip-searched for needles, contraband, razor blades, piano wire, or anything at all that could be used to cause harm. Some death row prisoners would try to have relatives bring them items or poisons with which to commit suicide. The execution team and attendants really wanted that overtime pay! So they were especially careful with their searches.

The guards did move away to give them some privacy; what was the harm in that? Let them have their girl talk. Judy spoke quietly and quickly. Donatienne hung on every word. "We have a cousin and an uncle that will pose as prison guards. We have arranged for one of them to be the lead guard for your execution. Don't panic…shush… that's better. Now, the other will be in the room to throw the switches to the electric chair. We have our people who will work on the chair right before the appointed time, just when electricians always do the maintenance, so nothing will be suspicious. They have shaved your head. We allowed it for appearances, and they will lead you into the chamber just as they do for everyone because only our cousin and uncle will be in on this. Everyone else but the doctor is legitimate.

"Don't worry. The warden is in our pocket. This will go off without a hitch. We've been getting our people all over the world out of this kind of jam, and this is actually one of the easier ones we've done. Now, you will sit in the chair, the lead will set the head gear just right. There will be steam and sparks, but none of it will affect you. You will have to play along and *pretend* to be electrocuted. Our doctor will make like he is checking you over and will declare your time of death. You must stay really still as they place you on a gurney, and you will be wheeled out into a waiting van. Then you and I will be playing cards tonight, just like the old days!"

"So," replied Donatienne, "all I have to do is to play along and do some acting? Pretend to get the shock, play dead, and that is all?"

"Yes. Now my time is up. But keep in mind, we do this for you, and there is no leaving the family anymore. You have to change your name, take a new identity, and move to the Bahamas. We have a nice place and job all set up for you."

Coffenayle smiled. *The Bahamas!* She could live under the family rules very well in the Bahamas!

*****

Meanwhile, the patriarch's men were visiting the warden in his office. Three men in black coats, ties, and hats with dark glasses sat in his office like they owned it. The warden was shocked to see them there as he came in to sit down and look over Coffenayle's paperwork.

"What? How did you get in here? Guards!" he shouted.

"Don't bother," said the first man.

"They won't come," said the second man.

"Sit down," said the third.

They all three opened their jackets and showed firearms, movements perfectly synchronized. The warden was incensed. He grabbed his phone and tried to call out.

"Don't bother," said the first man.

"It doesn't work," said the second man.

"Sit *down*," said the third.

None of them smiled, though they wanted to. They all loved the "three-man" gig. They all three put their hands on their guns, perfectly timed and synchronized. They had rehearsed this move for hours; they needed to introduce ultimate fear into the warden. He needed to believe them. Make a man scared of you, and he will very likely believe whatever you suggest to him. That's just the way the mind works. At least it did in this case. The warden sat down. Naturally, they did not want to kill him. They needed him. But they would kill him if they had to. The warden sensed this as he sat down nervously. The men were supremely confident. They had a backup plan if necessary.

"Relax," said the first man, "we just wanna talk."

"S-so talk," stammered the warden.

"Coffenayle. She's gonna fry, right?" asked the second man.

"Y-yes, but that was not my deci—"

"Save it," said the third man. "We just need a favor. She'll die, all right, but we need to do it."

"What?" asked the warden, incredulous to what he was hearing.

"Yes," said the first man. "We need two uniforms. Here are the sizes. Badges and all. They need to look real. They need to be real. They need to fit and look very professional. Our guys have a cover story that you called them in from out of state and deputized them.

They are experts on executions. And yeah…they *really* are. We guarantee that this trip on the Edison medicine chair will go smoother than your *own* men could make it go."

"What makes you think I will agree to this madness? You can't come in here and—" stammered the warden.

"We made it this far," said the first man.

"And we have these," said the second man as he pulled three packages out of his pockets. He threw them on the desk in front of the warden who looked at him, unsure of what to do.

"Open them. Go on! Nothing there to hurt you. What? You think we're gonna blow you up and *us with you?*" asked the third man. All three men laughed like that was the biggest joke in the world.

The warden didn't laugh. He did reach for the packages, though, carefully untied the strings, and opened them. Inside the first was a diary that belonged to his daughter. Inside the second was a teddy bear that belonged to his youngest son. The third package contained a yo-yo with the name "Billy" inscribed on it that unmistakably belonged to his oldest child, just nine years old. The warden was stunned.

"That's right," said man number one. "Let that sink in really good."

"We've been to your house," said man number two.

The warden bristled with his every protective instinct and shouted, "Listen! If you've hurt my kids, I'll—"

"Do absolutely nothing because there is nothing you can do," interrupted man number three.

"Relax, Warden," began the first man. "The kids are fine. Keep their stuff. Take it home to them. They will be glad to find their things right where they left them before they went to school today. They don't even have to know their stuff was missing. We left absolutely no evidence of a break-in. And before you ask, your wife is fine. Nobody touched her. She did not even see us in the house. She was too busy ironing your cheap linen shirts," he said matter-of-factly. He smiled kindly but like a cobra who just killed a mongoose.

The warden was defeated. He had no choice. He would allow these insane people to execute Coffenayle. He did not know why and did not dare to ask why. That was clearly none of his business. He did not want to know their secrets, whoever they were. He just knew that they were bigger than him and could pretty well do whatever they liked. He knew that if he turned them in, the authorities would have either been bribed or intimidated ahead of time…perhaps both. It would be pointless in any case.

"Okay. Okay. Just leave them out of this. I will do whatever you want. I'll get the uniforms," conceded the warden.

"Great!" said the second man.

"Now for the best part," said the third man with a sincere smile. He was excited. All three of them were. He nodded to the first man.

"Here you go!" said the first man cheerfully as he threw a cloth bag on the warden's desk with a loud thump.

The warden jumped back in his chair. "What is that?" he exclaimed.

"Why, your payment, of course!" said the second man. All three of them were smiling now.

"Payment? But I did not ask—"

"That's right," said the third man, also smiling. "That is *one hundred thousand dollars.* We have an address that will turn that into clean cash for you. Cash that can't be traced. You will get 100 percent of the value dollar for dollar. The fee they usually charge has been paid ahead time. Don't ask."

"Take the money, Warden. Cash it in. Enjoy it," said the first man.

"What?" He shook his head; the warden was not impressed with the bribe, being a truly honest man.

"You see, *friend*, this money makes us *friends* now," the second man said with a smile.

The warden flinched at the thought of becoming part of a conspiring crime family for the rest of his life. They would own him… and now he was becoming even more frightened.

"Oh," started the third man, "you think that we're trying to *buy* you? Oh, no, no, no! Don't even think that. You don't have to worry about being inducted into a criminal enterprise. We are not *La Cosa Nostra!* Those guys are *small* potatoes. Too violent and too public. Those morons are too well-known! No, you get to keep the money with no special obligation other than to keep it. Try to *not* keep it, try to turn it and/or us into the authorities, and…well…just *don't.*" His smile disappeared, and he appeared to be quite grim. Man number three meant it. They all did.

"And," said the first man, "you won't ever see us again. We won't bother you or your lovely family, ever. We truly want you to be happy. This money will help. You can't turn it down, so you might as well spend it. Your accepting this payment for services rendered will make you a partner in this one thing *only.* You are not being asked to do anything other than to allow us to carry out an execution that will happen anyway. This way, none of your people get their hands dirty. All of the paperwork has been done to 'officially hire' our people into the Department of Corrections. They are on your payroll right now as we speak, and everything has been settled. All you're doing is changing the assignment from two of your employees to two of your *other* employees. It is all perfectly legal on paper."

The first man then passed him a large manila envelope with the assignment changes. The warden opened it. He examined the transfer orders. They were all in order, awaiting his signature. This was actually going to work! He did not know how they made these arrangements, but, well, things were complete and in order. He could not have done better *himself!*

"You are not doing anything wrong!" beamed the first man. "It's all set. All you need to do is sign."

"Then why the bribe if you have this all set up?" the warden asked. It was an intelligent pertinent question. He was calming down now and becoming morbidly curious.

"I was just getting to that," explained the warden's new partner number one with a patient and kind smile. "You turn us in, we ruin your career. You have an excellent admirable record, and all you have to do now is keep it admirable. Keep doing your excellent work at this fine establishment."

The warden looked reluctant still.

The three men looked at each other. They were actually impressed at how honest and brave the warden really was. This was the difference between the Coffenayles and the lesser, more public crime families. The Clan truly admired bravery.

In fact, several of the Clan were legitimately decorated veterans, up to and including the Medal of Honor, rightfully and justly earned. They would normally shield their people from going to war for their country, but if a family member insisted on serving, well... they would not stop them either. The family always made sure that their military vets received the best medical care and mental health treatment available. They were, after all, Coffenayles and deserved respect for what they did, even if they were fighting on a side the Clan did not agree with. They respected bravery, bottom line, even if it *was* misguided.

So now it was time to pull out the big guns. This was not a threat, actually, but more along the lines of a factual explanation. The first man was still smiling pleasantly as he continued with, "Warden... William. May I call you by your first name?" He waited for the warden to nod. "Please. I am asking you nicely." His smile disappeared slowly. "Take the cash or...and I will explain this clearly...we will kill you and ruin your name by framing you for crooked dealings. Your name will be publicly ruined. Your widow won't get your pension. She will be criminally investigated by the federal enforcement agencies who will also find evidence against her as your accomplice. All the evidence will be real, the investigation will be legit as far as the authorities know. She will go to prison, will never see your kids again, and...well, you get the picture." The first man let that sink in a moment.

The warden had become an excellent judge of character in dealing with men through his years in the prison system. He had guards whose jobs he saved simply because he believed in them. They turned out to be great employees. He fired men that he knew were corrupt. He advanced to Warden from the position of prison guard. He knew what he was doing. These men understood that he was a serious man or they would not have been so kind. So the warden had to gravely ponder everything that these three pleasant but armed and possibly insane men, with limitless influence, told him just now. His life had changed so much in just a few minutes. Ten minutes ago, and his biggest concern was his stomach ulcer flaring up at the thought of executing a prisoner.

He believed in capital punishment, but he would be less than human if he did not feel the responsibility. He knew that these men were very serious. He had no doubt that they could do everything that the first man had just explained. The three men sensed that it was time to close the deal. They all nodded at one another with a perfectly synchronized act in mind. *Lights! Camera! Action!*

"So," the first man continued, "either become a secretly enriched living man with a lot money in this current year of 1920 or become a publicly dead and crooked public official who was murdered inside his own prison in his very own office, surrounded by his own men. Imagine the scandal, the apparent lack of control, the apparent corruption! You don't have to *be* dirty to look dirty and become dirty in the public mind. You will become a man whose friends won't show up to his funeral, a man who will be publicly disavowed, and whose family ends up ashamed, shunned, and prosecuted. Then for no reason, they will wind up in the poorhouse forever. The choice is yours." All three of them stood up in the same instant and pulled their guns, pointed them in the air, and cocked them in perfect unison. They froze in time and just stared at the warden from behind their black sunglasses.

"All right! All right! You win! I don't know who you maniacs are, but I'll do as you say. Please—"

They all three de-cocked their guns and holstered them in perfect unison. An impressive display. They all three smiled warmly at the distraught prison boss. He was, after all, holding up well. Not even a sign of tear. They had to admire that.

After the orders were signed and put in the interoffice mail, they stood up. They shook hands with William, their new friend, and patted him on the back. They gave him the address to exchange the money. They treated him like they were old college buddies who just gave him a new life, which they did, even if they were not true friends in his mind. He shook their hands like someone who was stunned, suddenly rich, and unsure if he was doing the right thing; his head was reeling. He knew he just saved all of his family's lives. He was considering the consequences of this decision. How would he ever explain this to his wife?

He supposed, silently, that he would just keep his job for a few years and suddenly become very good at the stock market. His wife would believe that easier than she would believe this. The three men let the "maniacs" remark go. It was not personal, and they knew it. They were quite satisfied that the warden, a very good man, was finally convinced that they were who they actually were. They really did hope he enjoyed the money. The poor slob deserved it. They knew about his ulcer and knew his health would soon fail if he didn't retire. They sincerely hoped he would retire while he could still spend some time with his children. Family was very important to Coffenayles. Families made for stable societies. The three men left the office, and the heavy cloth bag was on the table.

William, in his mind, was no longer a warden once he completed this act. He opened the bag and looked in. He blinked and looked again. That *was* a lot of money! Somehow, he knew that every dime was there, and he did not have to count it. The next move was to conceal the bag in his secret locked safe, normally used for his firearm and sensitive communications. He could not let that cash be accidentally seen by anyone!

Next, he started making calls to let the execution team know about the changes. He reassured his men that the overtime was still in place for them; he knew they were counting on that money for their families. He just had them reassign the names of the lead and executioner. The former lead and executioner would simply be on hand as extra guards; William could pass this off easily as extra security because of the prisoner's high-profile case. No one would ever ask questions.

He silently resolved to use his good fortune to remember his men on the execution team at Christmas; they would each receive an anonymous Christmas card loaded with cash. Then he set about the business of typing up his resignation, postdated one day past the execution. He could not remain in his position; he was now dirty, choice or no choice. He would cite "unmanageable personal stresses and effects upon his health" as his reason. His assistant warden was a good man. He could leave the prison in his capable hands without reservation or hesitation. Unbeknownst to the warden, he just avoided a fatal gastric bleed that was coming in about six months.

His resignation was precisely as the Clan's number crunchers had predicted to a 96.90 percent certainty. The Coffenayle Clan even arranged for one of their own doctors to fix William's ulcer! They knew what medical clinic he would use. He was about to receive an "experimental medicine" from a doctor he would not know. His ulcer would be gone in a few days. The Clan did not bother to figure out where he would take his family to retire. They only knew that he would be gone within the next twenty-one days. "Good luck, William! Enjoy your new life! Take good care of your family with our blessings!" The three men would even convince the patriarch to protect the warden's wealth by putting people in William's path who would teach him how to invest properly. It would not cost the family anything to do that for him. The old warden would not even know it was them. The three really did admire William; that was why they went the extra mile.

The final hours

The days preceding the execution went like clockwork, and Donatienne Coffenayle was at ease. She did not seem as nervous as she should be, but the guards had seen it all before. Prisoners responded to their pending execution in all kinds of ways. Some went easy, some went hard. Some acted like they just did not care anymore and resigned to it completely. Others used it as an opportunity to show off for the press just one last time. One fellow actually dusted off the chair before he sat on it. His last words? "Can't go to the pearly gates with dust on my britches!" and so on.

Yes, they had seen it all, but none of them had ever thought they would see a woman ride the lightning. That was just a rare thing. Then again, women as hard as Coffenayle were pretty rare too. Because of her personality, no one thought anything of her behavior.

They just kept the normal extra eye out for suicide attempts. For some people, it just was not justice if there was a suicide, even if the prisoner was just as dead. Some folks needed to see that the state carried out the law and that the prisoner was "legally" dead versus... well, what would you call it? "Suicidally" dead? Is that a thing?

As zero hour approached, it was about ten at night, and the execution was slated for 12:01 in the morning. There were no appeals filed by the prisoner or by the condemned prisoner's family and no call from the governor; none was expected. The prisoner was still calm per reports from the attending officers. She did not request a last meal. She had little to say about the whole situation and did not appear even a little bit nervous.

She just sat in her cell, seeming content and nearly bored. She refused last rites or any other spiritual assistance. That was just as well. The prison chaplain did not particularly care for the way he felt around her. "Nauseated and nervous" was how she made him feel. The guards had never seen the chaplain grow pale before, and this was a man who ministered to hardcore felons and fiends on a regular basis.

The prison staff was surprised to see the warden bring two new guys into death row, particularly because one of them was going to take the lead in executing Coffenayle. She was a very high-profile convict. It did not take them long to convict her, and her crime was considered particularly heinous. The warden, though, did assure them that this boss was going to do fine, that he was shipped in particularly for this case, and would not be here after the execution. He and the trigger man who was pulling the switches had done this kind of thing before. They even had a letter from the governor of their great state certifying them as experts.

Apparently, the governor wanted this to go off without a hitch, not that their seasoned team had ever let them down. The regular men were assured that this was no reflection on them. It was simply something that the higher ups wanted. They were relieved, actually, because while good men will do their duty, executions were always tough for them. It was just as well in their eyes that someone else led, that someone else pulled the switch. They were still paid the same, no matter what.

Their guards for the event were all of the prison's regulars; only the execution's leader and the "lightning rod," as they called the man on the switch, had changed. So this time, all they had to do was lead the prisoner in, strap her down, and stand back. The lead and his lightning rod would do the rest. Fine by them. They just hoped it didn't smell too bad this time. The stench of cooked bowel had a way of spoiling one's dinner.

At eleven-thirty, post meridian, on the dot, with no visitors to see the prisoner, with her head fully shaved bald to prevent a fire, the guards brought her to the holding area. This is where she would breathe her last before being strapped in for the Big Ride into the Great Unknown. She was led, in shackles and chains, with a guard in front, one following up and the other two abreast, each with a hand on her arm in case she suddenly tried to bolt. This was typically the most dangerous time for the prison guards, and they knew it. Long and hard experience had taught them how to handle prisoners from the most terrified to the most passive, even if they went fully limp and had to be carried to the chair. The executions had always been carried out, no matter how much fuss the prisoner made. The end was always the same.

If the prisoner was going to fight, it was going to be either while they were being led into the final waiting room or on their way to the chair itself. Many of the condemned would finally realize that the whole thing was actually *real* when they said their last goodbyes to family and friends or when they had that last visit with the chaplain. Normally, the chaplain would follow the prisoner to the chair to provide final comforts, but Coffenayle had refused him entirely, and, man, was he *glad*. He had seen the worst of them: child murderers, mafia assassins, rapists, mass killers, serial poisoners, savage axe murderers—but not one of them had that same cold look in their eyes as she had. It was like that woman had *literally* sold herself to Satan himself and loved the very idea! He wondered silently if Hades was ready for what was coming.

The guards stood quietly while the prisoner sat silent and expressionless. It was creepy, but again, not unheard of. The guards just stood there, silently watching. She simply sat there, helpless in her chains, looking at nothing. Eleven forty-five finally arrived, and the prisoner was led on her last walk. They left the little room through a door with a smoked glass window. The chair was located in a surprisingly small room. There he sat: Old Sparky!

She looked at the chair with apprehension but *knew* she was not going to ride the lightning for real. All she had to do was act like she was taking the shock. Her body would have to tremble and tighten up, but there was no need to worry about the facial expressions. They were covering her face with a hood, and all she would have to do was groan a bit between clenched jaws. After the apparent shocks and the paid-off doctor declared she was pulseless, she would have to act like dead weight. She would have to do that all the way to the gurney.

Going entirely limp would be the hardest part, and then she would be covered with a sheet and would be wheeled into the hearse. After that, off to travel the world! She only hoped she didn't sneeze or do long rude razzing flatulence, like Malovent, while they were handling her. That would be tough to explain! She actually chuckled out loud at the thought. Her noise made the guards flinch a touch because she had been sitting so quietly, but they relaxed when she did not move, try to escape, nor make any other sort of trouble. She went back to being quiet and unconcerned, and so did they.

Her hands were being watched very closely by all involved in the execution. Everything now was all about time. The prisoner and clock were their only concerns; everyone's attention was on those two things. The guards motioned for her to stand and led her to the chair. They were ready to force her into it as most condemned people resisted at the last moment. Not this one; she sat down as easily as she would have sat in her own living room. The prison officials had no idea, but *she was going to the Bahamas!*

Coffenayle concentrated on her freedom that was surely coming. She was very cooperative with them taking control of her and strapping her down; they were not intentionally rough, but each man had his adrenaline pumping, and that caused them to move with less than gentle motions. After all, they were about to kill someone. The men were very precise about their methods in replacing metal cuffs, chains, and shackles with good strong leather straps. Coffenayle thought with some amusement about how weak these men were. They had good in them. To her, good was weakness. That was why they were upset at what they had to do. She could do their job all day long, every day, and relish in absorbing the evil of the souls that were being killed. She would enjoy it. She would be able to honestly say, "See you later!" to them. Yes, Donatienne would make a great executioner as she added names to the list of souls she would torment in the Underworld. Maybe the patriarch could get her a job like *that!* Oh boy!

Coffenayle felt the straps around her wrists and her ankles. They were hard but pliable. They tilted her head back against the chair. They strapped her torso with a wide belt, then buckled her chin and forehead tightly in place. The head had to be stable to take the extended shock without breaking the connection. Donatienne began feeling a little nervous about that; she also knew she would soon be free, and that knowledge calmed her. She could not see the next step but felt it as they tore the pants on her prison uniform to attach the electrode to her leg. The conductive brine-soaked sponge was wet and warm to her skin. The final step was to put the electrode on her head. They had soaked another sponge for that electrode.

She felt the warm salty water slop over her head and face. They wiped her eyes off with a towel as a courtesy and pulled a leather cap over top of the whole works and buckled it under her chin. That made her clench her teeth, but she would not give them the satisfaction of making a sound. The head electrode was firmly in place, and they screwed in the cables. She was now all wired up to be catapulted into the eternities. She sat still, perfectly still, and grimaced because of the chin strap. The boss stepped up, and she had to suppress a little smile. She actually wanted to laugh.

She immediately recognized the "boss" as her Uncle Frederick Coffenayle. She was one of his favorites at the family gatherings. He was practically inseparable from his son, her Cousin Herold, whom she figured was the man behind the wall with the smoked glass window. She believed Herold could probably see out into well-lit chamber better than she could see him in the semidarkness. She was correct.

Herold had a good view of his Cousin Donatienne Coffenayle, a woman over whom they had much debate through the years but little control. Now she had to pay the ultimate price for her rebellion and rejection of their oath. Rumor had it that she sold her soul to Satan, but really, had not they all? Well, it was better to reign in hell than to serve in heaven.

Donatienne thought the same thing until she learned at the football field and how weak evil was. She was the true strength of Malovent that whole time instead of the other way around. But Herold did not know that. Maybe, Coffenayle believed, she would explain it to them tonight over a mineral water with lime. Maybe they had strawberries?

Frederick stepped forward. The blind on the witness viewing window went up. Several people where there, all of them from the press, staring at her. Some them were swallowing hard. None of the people she had magically cursed showed up. She had hoped to see at least one of them one last time before she was sent to wherever the Patriarch wanted her to go. She wanted to mock them, to spite them. She wanted to give them a mocking last statement. They did not show, the cowards! They won this battle, and she had lost the school, yes. Even so, she was only getting started. As a true Coffenayle, she could hunt them down and gain her revenge by ruining each and every one of their lives! She would start with the employees of the Happy Mentoring Vocational School! Her attention shifted from her own fantasies to the grim reality surrounding her.

The witnesses were hanging on every precious second of this event. They were not permitted to bring cameras; the State considered that to be in poor taste. So they all wrote every detail they could capture of the end of a life, a person named Coffenayle, a headline-friendly name for a condemned prisoner!

One reporter quipped into the air about them pounding her, a Coffenayle, into her own coffin. Several stifled chuckles, and few coughs were heard around the room. The warden's frown and stern look silenced the crowd. He did allow himself a concealed smile at that remark when no one was looking. He could not let this turn into a circus, after all. A sketch artist was drawing pictures of her: The Evil Donatienne "Nightshade" Coffenayle. That was what the papers renamed her for the execution headlines. How droll! If only they understood how powerful she would be after she was "dead" in the eyes of the legal system and the world! Her revenge would be so sweet, she thought to herself.

Uncle Fred knew all too well that she would want revenge. He and Cousin Herold agreed with the patriarch that her vengeful feelings would be very bad for business. She would be far too hard to control. She would eventually expose them, according to the number-crunchers. They had finally been able to "estimate" the odds of her exposing the Coffenayle Clan to the world at 1004 to 1 *in favor* of her doing it. There was, in other words, only a .099601 percent chance that she would *not* expose them. Keeping her alive would endanger their entire operation all over the world. They still could not get accurate figures on the element of her strange religion. It was impossible to tell exactly how that would figure in to the whole picture. That is why the patriarch called on them to say they would "fake" the execution. They wanted her calm and wanted her to keep her mouth shut until she was dead. They would take no chances with her turning evidence over to the State as a bargaining chip to extend her life. This had to end *now!*

They knew that if she believed that the Clan would allow her to live a free woman, she would keep quiet. If they turned her over to the state legal system alive, she would sing like a canary, and their criminal enterprises all over the world could come crashing down. She did not know much, but if she exposed even what she did know, they could be easily infiltrated by undercover investigators, and that would damage them terribly. They could not allow that to happen. This, then, was the best plan, to keep her quiet by making her believe that she would live but then killing her in the ultimate double-cross.

They knew that their business would not be in immediate danger from what she could do. On the other hand, the destruction of their network would, with certainty, occur within the next hundred years. They could not allow that. That is how far in advance their thinking had become after generations of experience in global networking, stock markets, meticulously organized crimes, and highly advanced mathematics. Each generation stood on the shoulders of its preceding geniuses and with absolute cooperation toward the same cause. They all wanted to keep Coffenayle power alive; they all wanted to conquer the world. They knew that one day, The Clan would reign supreme. They figured it to be about 300 years in the future—a mere fraction of a tick in the cosmic clock.

The patriarch knew of the relationship between Fred, Herold, and Donatienne. He knew that they were her favorite relatives and that she would trust them the most. This was a tough thing to do; father and son killing a favored niece and cousin, but they could not let her expose them. They promised the patriarch that they would break his heart at 12:01 in the morning on the appointed day, and they would later cry the night away in their own rooms after the deed was done. Now, though, was the time for stoicism. Now was the time for courage. Now was the time to make Coffenayle history—to kill one of their own under the auspice of state law was new territory.

The clock struck 12:00, midnight. With unerring precision and in a very crisp, professional voice, the boss read the last formal statement Donatienne Coffenayle would hear on this mortal plane. He read her death warrant. He read it clearly and loudly for all to hear. There was not a hint of quiver or regret in his voice, despite his personal feelings. The sketch artist captured the moment. After Fred finished the legally required reading, he asked if the condemned had any last words. Without the school's people there, where would the fun be in that? She shook her head the best she could and remained silent. "Very well, then."

Next, the boss turned smartly toward the guard who was standing by the phone. He asked, "Any last-minute reprieve from the governor?"

The man picked the receiver up to check for dial tone, and the phone worked perfectly. He shook his head. The boss then turned smartly again, playing the part perfectly, just as they had rehearsed. "Place the hood," he said crisply. The guards put the hood over her face. It was heavier fabric than she thought, and it smelled all musty. Fred would hear about this tonight! She could not see him or anything else now. All was black.

Coffenayle waited for the signal to start the acting. She actually allowed herself a smile. No one could see it, so what was the harm? She knew that there were two switches and that the second one, when it was pulled, would start the crackling and humming sounds and the harmless smoke. That was when she was to start shaking, jumping, and twitching. "Pull on one!" shouted Fred.

Herold pulled the handle without hesitation. The chair started to warm up. That whirring, vibrating sensation made Coffenayle twitch with a start. Why, that did not seem right at all! They did not tell her to expect *that!* She still trusted them, but this did make her feel like peeing on herself. After the time for the chair to warm up had passed, Coffenayle's instincts kicked in. *This was real! They were actually doing this!*

She began to squirm again but for real! She fought against the chair, against the straps. She tried to kick the electrode off of her leg. She turned her head and tried to shake the leather cap off! She was pulling as hard as she could, but the guards had done their job too well. All she did was chaff her body parts against the straps. Though she thought she was moving quite a lot, there was very little struggle to be seen from the witness booth. The reporters hardly noticed any movement all. They would later report that the condemned calmly accepted her fate.

For Donatienne, nothing was further from the truth. She was terrified! Horrified! Ready to say anything that she had to say to escape this fate! She was not ready to accept her final judgment! She had things still that she wanted to do! She remembered Malovent, the magic, the candles! She remembered his lies and deceit, how he grew bigger, bolder, energized by her sins! She remembered the oath and how eager she was to accept it and to kill for gain! Yes! She remembered all that and how eager she was to become a queen in hell! She could not allow herself to feel regret! That was all! Get rid of all regret and feelings of guilt for sin and evil doings! That was all it would take!

Even though she recalled now, in her final moments of life, how Malovent was kicked through the goal posts and was fetched to Perdition by the three-headed hound, she still had hope. She could still become a queen! Yes, she could! Yes, to do so, she had to maintain her composure, and this thought calmed her. Focus on rage. This was going to happen, but the Underworld would receive her as a queen. Calm down. Let it happen. Then from the Underworld, she could exact her revenge on the school and the Coffenayle Family. She would do that. Yes. All she had to do was not feel regret. Then she would become queen. She heard the boss, her Uncle Fred, give the final words she would hear spoken in this life: "Pull on two." Her Uncle Fred! She loved him and her cousin, and now they had to do this to—

In that final thought, her brain was cut short. Every muscle fiber she had clenched all at once. The smoke out of the steel crown they put on her was not harmless. It smelled terrible and it hurt! Her body was burning, tingling, cramping, and clenched tight in like one giant charley horse! Burning, stinking, tingling torture from head to toe. Unable to reason any longer, unable to form words as her brain shut down, her last emotion was, *If only I had not—*

Then all went black for a moment as she died terribly, painfully, and in *regret!*

Not that this made any difference. As she was being electrocuted, she was still desperately fooling herself with that great lie Malovent told her, taught her, engrained into her psyche. The lie that she could circumvent justice by merely denying its presence; as though avoiding feelings of guilt and shame neutralized eternal law; as though she could actually choose the consequences of what she did to suit her own convenience.

Alas! There was no rescue from the natural results of her desires, thoughts, wishes, and actions, not even by removing all semblance of conscience. Regret or not, she willfully and willingly sold herself to the Underworld. The only significance that her feeling of regret had in this situation was that it destroyed all the false hopes she had, and that's all. That's the only difference her regret made in the big picture.

Her regrets had no power to condemn her; her will to entertain evil and carry out her evil desires set the wheels of justice in motion.

At the end of her life, she suffered the natural result of the sum total of her thoughts, actions, and desires. She never sought mercy, not until it was too late, and even then, she was not seeking forgiveness. She was looking to be set free to commit even more malicious actions against people. Even as she sat upon the only throne she would ever know, even when she wore the only crown her head would ever feel, there was not a speck of true contrition, only the regret of being caught. Had it been different, had she even the faintest spark of light inside of her, there could have been some kind of mercy, some kind of rescue.

Regrettably, there was not.

Dead, but…not?

As suddenly as it began, the pain was over. She found herself in the dark. Was it really over? How could it be? She did not feel that much, really…not like she thought she would. She thought a moment, and then…of course! This was all part of it! They had to rig the chair with that smell, and they had to shock her a little bit because they needed to get a response out of her! Of course! They needed to make sure that she had some kind of response so that the spectators would see it. They did not tell her what was going to happen so that she would respond naturally. Then, yes, they must have given her a sedative of some kind, or maybe the small electric shock knocked her out so that she would appear completely flaccid and would not sneeze or give any indication of life! Of course, yes, that was it. That had to be it!

She knew that she was not dead because she felt every bit alive! She felt wonderful! Yes, and now she could go and join her Coffenayle family members and discuss her future. She could now begin to plan her eventual takeover of the world! She could now get in on all the family secrets! She wondered when she would finally meet in the big office with the patriarch. Certainly, she would now since he took all this trouble, time, effort, and money to arrange one of the greatest scams ever perpetuated on the minds of the public! They fooled even the very authorities that condemned her, a *Coffenayle* to death. Ha!

She stood up, free of the chair or the gurney. Wherever she was, all was blackness. She went to pull the hood off of her head… but there was no hood? She clutched at her head a couple of times, unable to believe that her face was not covered with something. She could feel her hand to her face. She could feel her own person, but something was not quite right. She patted herself down, and it all seemed normal. She began to wonder if the electricity or sedative had caused temporary blindness. Oh, yes, that must be it. She figured that they did not tell her because to let her know that she would experience blindness would have clued her in that they were going to shock and drug her. They needed her to be ignorant so that she would respond and behave naturally. *That makes sense, of course.*

She called out, but somehow, her voice was different. Hollow, echoing, like there were no walls there. It was sort of like a cave but different. There was not only a wide cavern of space to echo her voice, but there was nothing…nothing indeed to echo off of. Her voice was simply lost to the eternities. But that would mean…she began to understand, finally. *No! No! It can't be! Nonononononono!*

Now she *felt* the darkness around her. It was cold and terrible, almost wet on her skin. She still could not see her hand in front of her face. She looked around, unable to determine where she was in space. Then she realized that she was not actually standing. She was not actually on a floor or standing on anything at all. She was drifting, but not really. Donatienne was simply suspended. No drifting or flying. She was just *there.*

There was no sense of up or down, no direction of left or right, no east, no west. No north or south. She was simply in…*space.* No gravity, no perspective. There was no gravity or forces acting on her substance any longer. She was no longer part of any creation or material essence. Even the sensation of being in an atmosphere with air pressure was simply gone. The only part of existence for her was her, was her being, but that being, the "she" that she knew herself to be was no longer attached to *anything.* There was no sensation anymore or any form of connection to anyone or anything. She was alone—

ultimately, finally, terribly alone. No more Uncle Fred or Cousin Herold. No more Miss Emily who still owed her one for that new life Donatienne gave her. No more Charles Mentor.

She somehow understood that there were to be no more club sodas with strawberry and lime. There would be no round table meetings with the Clan. In fact, there were no more tables or chairs. There were no more meals or celebrations. No more baths or furniture to sit on. Donatienne...poor, poor Donatienne was simply *nowhere.*

She was in complete darkness, in a kingdom of no stars to give light, no moon to stand on, no earth to be drawn toward. She was simply in plain, dark, cold, airless, no-pressure, vacuous *space.* To label what she sensed as "loneliness" is a gross understatement. It was not loneliness or hopelessness. It was utter *aloneness.* She now was utterly with no hope of ever having hope again. No more sensations ever again. What was this place?

A voice came out of the darkness. "Remember me?" She knew it was Malovent, that squeaky terrible voice that came out of him when he was diminished after speaking his own name. "Someone came to see you." She heard a growl. She remembered the hellhound. She knew what Malovent meant. The beings that were coming to see her were not real, not even Malovent, her old master. She was alone now, living with herself and all of her evil desires and their fruit. It was her own memories and good desires unfulfilled that punished her. She remembered that her last mortal thought was regret! Her inner memory of Malovent suddenly screamed in her own mind! Sudden torment twisted the long, terrible, howling scream out of her, vocally! Then the next scream and the next and the next! There were no kings here! There were no queens! There was only torment. Torment and regret for not being able to walk in light, in love, in friendship.

There was not even an Underworld, she now knew. A world of any kind would have organization. She was in a place that could not become organized, for there was *nothing upon which to organize things.* All of the preaching of hellfire and brimstone were merely symbols that people would understand. Who has not before smelled sulfur? Who before has not been burned? Even the vision of Cerberus taking Malovent were symbols for the people to witness so that they would understand eternal punishment in hell was a serious matter.

Speaking of "matter," organization required matter and order. There was no matter in this vacuum of vacuums. There was no matter here; there was no order. There was no law. There was only… nothing. The lawless desires of her heart were now known to her. She was so foul and evil that she would not even be permitted to haunt anyone, like a banshee, like a poltergeist. Her mind was so disarrayed and unkempt that she could not tolerate any rules at all, not even the rules that kept her mind together. Oh, the agony of disorder! The horror of disarray! The angst of not having even any material to her being to become disorganized or to place in disarray! Oh, to have even a molecule or just an atom to call her own! Feeling a drop of water even for a second would deliver her from this nothingness, this burning disorder! All was taken from her now. Even the very matter that was her spirit was being pulled from her intelligence!

She had seen souls in torment! Malovent showed her these shapeless creatures forever tortured, forever torn from creation. In those selfsame visions, she saw herself, though sitting on a throne and controlling the torment of those souls. She saw herself with her golden scepter or trident or whatever she wished in her hand. She saw herself drinking fine wine as she turned up the heat on the tormented. That, though, was the great lie. She knew now that there was no throne to sit on or wine to drink! There was no gold or fine robes. There were no queens or kings in this place that was not a place. There was only nothing. There was only her intelligence and nothing to contain it. And this—this *prison* was a place she could never leave.

The moaning, the screaming, the terror all came at her, then in and out of her in waves. She thought it was not possible to feel such fear…and yet there it was! Fear that burned her intelligence that could never die! She burned as a wave of blackened evil intelligences of endless darkness washed over her. They too were just like her! They could not emerge from the endless darkness to grab her; they could only draw her in. There was a magnetism of empathy, a power drawing her to those like her of a similar character to hers. She could not resist! Coffenayle loathed these evil dead, even as she loathed herself. She loathed the very life force that God used to create her. The thought of God loving her only burned her more.

As she writhed in agony, she was among the newest of the condemned. She also sensed that there were many condemned who were old. They had been there for a very long time! They had no relief, not even after thousands of years, as if time even existed anymore for them. They were simply timeless now. Her torment was only beginning. She felt that many, many intelligences were being added to the terror each second. Each intelligence added to the moaning and the misery. The screams that came from them—that came from *her*— were terrible! All of the screams grew louder and more horrific, and she screamed and moaned along with them. She could not help it; the misery was so great that she could not prevent the horrific noises from being pulled out of her.

The other tormented intelligences were more than willing to share their pain! They floated and flew about, surrounding one another. Often, they darted through each other, feeling the pain of the intelligence they just invaded. At the same time, they shared their own pain and horror with that individual. The suffering was exponential, never decreasing, growing worse and worse without relief. They were injecting one another with the punishment for their sins; sins that they so willing took into themselves while on earth.

Some burned not only in their intentional sins but also in the pains of addictions which accompanied their wretched, selfish, murderous souls. Addictions that would never be slaked—the hunger for drugs, tobacco, the thirst for alcohol, and pleasures of the body or even masochistic pains of tortured flesh! They hungered terribly, never to be satisfied again. The desire to kill, to have gold, to hold power over other people; none of their desires, lust, or greed would be satisfied. Even the desire for food, for water, for clothes or some shelter haunted them! These were normal sinless desires that could never be satisfied either! The desire for basic life sustenance was now a frustration that only added to their suffering. Oh, for that drop of water!

Each one them existed now only to bring their rage for others to feel. Each of them that passed through the others added exponentially to the misery all of them felt. Their only existence now was to make others suffer as much as they. So, yes, Donatienne Coffenayle was now a tormentor. She was now a queen, but only as much as all of the others were queens and kings in their own misery. She was also as tormented as they.

She joined the orgy of pain, horror, and misery because there was no choice, not anymore. They had all made their choices, bad ones, over and over again. Now they reaped the rewards of their selfishness, their lack of compassion. There was no buying their way out. Many of them had murdered and caused misery and were "innocent" by mortal laws because they paid bribe money. Others were professional murderers, for pay, and were never caught. They had their reward, but they could not benefit from it any longer. Gold or currency were of no use here. There was no currency and no hope. There was only judgment. God was not even there to judge them. They passed judgment on each other and upon themselves. They all knew that they were too filthy to return to God. The very thought of light in any form only tormented them more.

There was no joy in the suffering or in making the others to suffer. There was no revenge. There was no hierarchy or people in charge. All were equal here. There was nothing now but pain. Pain and blackness! Just when Donatienne thought it could not get worse, she felt herself diminish and shrink! Her being was no longer able to hold a human's shape because she had no shape! She was no longer able to even *imagine* herself as human. The only thing she could now imagine for herself was chaos and pain. Now her limbs were twisting, shriveling, as were her head, her face, her whole body—all of it was shriveling and twisting.

She was burning with cold and blackness! She now knew the stink of sulfur far worse than that stench of the steel headpiece! That body she once inhabited was just now being pulled off the chair by prison authorities! On earth, she would have determined that her already endless suffering was so far less than five earthly minutes. Quantum exponentials were something she had never learned about during her education; nevertheless, the effects were now quite *real*. Einstein was right. Time was relative—relative to one's perception and dimensional conditions. Coffenayle's dimension and perceptions were stretching time into ages per each second that passed.

She was dead, that was true, but now she was more conscious than ever and more capable of feeling this torment! Suffering was multiplied infinitely in this kingdom because of its very nature. She demanded of life an existence without love, without God, and she was so rewarded. Her desire was fulfilled, and even she knew that if she were to be rescued from this fate, that the light would only give her more pain than the darkness where she now dwelt. There was no escape for her now. She felt her voice become higher and squeaky, just like Malovent. She knew she would soon lose the intelligence and identity that she had as a living person, giving all that up to simply suffer. Knowing this, she used the last of her cognizant thoughts to summon up one final human thought: *Abandon all hope ye who enter here.*

ABOUT THE AUTHOR

George E. Kellogg was born in Ohio. He was the oldest of five children, and his father was a South Dakota native and a Vietnam veteran. His mother was born to a migrant steel worker's family in Pittsburgh, Pennsylvania. When George was fifteen, his family moved west to Arizona.

George started his college education late in life, graduating from Mesa Community College in Arizona as a member of Phi Theta Kappa. He holds an associate of the arts degree in general education and finally earned a master's degree in the science of security management from Bellevue University in Nebraska.

George also spent some time in Colorado and lived in Washington state where he served a two-year-long mission for his church. Today, George and his wife, Valerie, who encouraged him to publish this book, along with his adult son, Steven, reside in South Salt Lake City, Utah.

CPSIA information can be obtained
at www.ICGtesting.com
Printed in the USA
BVHW030458240222
629775BV00014B/5

9 781638 145042